Love

is

Love

Love

is

Love

Ricardo Sinclair

MONSTAR, INC.

GEORGIA

Copyright © 2009 by Ricardo Sinclair
Conyers, GA
All Rights Reserved

Printed and Bound in the United States of America
Published and Distributed by:
Milligan Books

Cover Design: Kevin Allen
Formatting: Milligan Books

First Printing, January 2010

10 9 8 7 6 5 4 3 2 1

ISBN# 978-0-9820249-0-4

Library of Congress Cataloging-in-Publication Data

Love is Love, Sinclair, Ricardo

Monstar, Inc.
2600 B Fieldstone View Lane, S.E.
Conyers, GA 30013-2180
Phone 770-366-2009
Website www.diradiocast.com
Email monstar.biz@gmail.com

prologue

Ricky Jones

W hen I was 12 years old, my younger brother and I watched our mother die at the hands of our father, who injected a syringe in her vein and shot her up with some step-on, poisonous heroin that killed her instantly. In turn, my father, not being able to cope with the guilt of killing the mother of his two little boys, put a .45 Magnum to his head and blew it clean off. Sadly, not only did we see our mother die at his hands, but we both witnessed Dad commit suicide, too.

At the time, my little brother Dwayne was only eight years old and both of us were too distraught and in disbelief to even shed a tear. Later, we stood alone with a social worker and watched as people lowered the casket containing the remains of our mother, Pamela Jones, who was only 30 at the time of her death. We were old enough to understand death, but still too young to grasp the cruel finality of it.

With each thud of dirt falling on her casket, I heard the sound of our childhood being buried. May she rest in peace. Nearby stood a closed casket for my father, Andrew Jones. May he burn for eternity in hell.

After the funeral, we were escorted away by the social worker named Amy Taylor. Ms. Taylor took us to a treatment center for mentally traumatized dependent children. At this time, Dwayne and I made a pact that no matter what happened, as soon as I turned 18 years old, I would find him and take responsibility for him. Ms.

Taylor took our information and soon after, we were admitted to the clinic for psychiatric therapy. Two months later, Dwayne was placed with a foster family who eventually adopted him.

As for me, Ricky Jones, I was placed in a group home until I was 16. During that time, I was in and out of trouble until I finally landed in a juvenile detention center in Panthersville. I was convicted of armed robbery—caught on camera robbing the pizza place on W. Mountain Street. The group home was on 2nd Street, less than a block away. The judge gave me two years to serve and one year on probation.

Once incarcerated, I began exercising fanatically, and, as a result, I developed an exceptionally muscular body compared to the other inmates. I also excelled in learning the finer details of an advanced education in criminal knowledge and developed the art of getting along exceptionally well with other criminals. I learned most criminals just want to be respected. They love being around those who make them feel proud to be evil, and most of all, they want to feel better than the rest—especially being richer, stronger, braver, smarter, and more devious and treacherous.

I left juvenile when I was 17 years old and made up my mind that no matter what it took, I was going to get rich real quick.

Chapter 1 — *Ricky Jones*

It was 6:00 a.m. and my cell phone was already ringing. I reached over and grabbed the phone in aggravation. Absently, I looked at the caller ID. It was a number I'd never seen before.

"Yeah," I answered.

"Good morning, Mr. Jones," a woman's voice said on the other end.

"Yeah," I replied, still not fully awake mentally.

"Mr. Jones, this is Stephanie on behalf of People Finders, and I'm calling to tell you I have located a Dwayne Jones."

Suddenly I bolted upright, fully awake now.

"Where is he?" I said.

"You can find Dwayne Jones at Sparford State Juvenile Prison in New York," she replied. "The address is ..." she began calling off the numbers.

"Hold on a minute. Let me get a pen and piece of paper," I interrupted her.

I got up naked and hurried to retrieve a pen and a piece of paper from a portfolio on the desk in the other room. I then wrote down the address, thanked her, and hung up. I made my way to the refrigerator, which, as usual, was stacked with food. I moved food out of the way until I found the orange juice, poured me a glass, and headed back to the bedroom. I pondered what could have happened to send my brother to the penitentiary, but then I remembered how we were scarred by witnessing our parents' murder/suicide and thought, "There but for the grace of God go I."

I strolled back to my bedroom where my girlfriend, Lisa, was still asleep, lying on her stomach, stretched out naked across the bed. Standing there, I took a moment to admire her beauty. Lisa was from a well-to-do interracial family. Her black father and white mother had given her a magnificent butterscotch complexion.

Making my way over to the other side of the king-sized bed, I sat down on it and took out a cigar from my pants pocket that was still lying on the floor next to me, along with a quarter ounce of hydro, purple Kush marijuana, East Side Bubba Kush. Then I emptied the 'dro out of the sandwich bag on the nightstand and began to split the cigar down the middle with my fingertips.

After I completed splitting the cigar, I emptied the tobacco into the sandwich bag, licked the cigar paper to keep it together, then laid the paper in the middle of my palm and begin to crush the soft purple Kush into tiny buds into the cigar paper. Then I rolled up the cigar paper as if one would roll a joint. As I placed the blunt in my mouth and grabbed the lighter out of my pants pocket, I felt a slight movement behind me.

Staying focused, I retrieved my lighter and lit the blunt. As I inhaled, I felt the tinkling sensation of the Kush in my mouth. I took a deep breath, then released the smoke from my nostrils. As I took another drag, I could feel Lisa's nails working up my back, to my neck, and through my dreadlocks. She parted my hair with her hand and placed her soft plump lips on my neck.

"Good morning, birthday boy," she said.

I turned my head to the side as she reached over my shoulders and kissed me passionately on my mouth. Then I drew my head back. She was still in the groove with her eyes closed. As I lay back and puffed on my blunt, she asked, "What you want for breakfast?"

I gazed in her eyes. "You."

"Seriously, anything you want."

"You. Seriously."

Lisa's smile lit up the room as she admired my 6-foot-3, 195-pound physique. I was built like an Olympic gymnast.

Lisa then asked me to move over to the center of the bed. I did. She got on all fours and crawled in a slow, seductive, catlike motion between my legs. Lisa looked like Vanessa Williams with voluptuous buttocks and soft, firm, 36 C cup breasts that sat high and full on her chest. Like a temptress, she began to slowly lick around my nipples with her intoxicating tongue. I watched and relaxed as she gently moved down and placed my aching manhood in her mouth.

Once the head of my penis was in her mouth, she started going around the head with her tongue in a circular rubbing motion. Next, she inserted as much of my penis as possible down in her mouth without gagging and went back up to the head. She continued this method repeatedly until she felt my manhood throbbing in her throat. Then she expertly placed one of her hands on her vagina, inserting two fingers in herself and her thumb on her clitoris, moving her thumb in a circular motion.

I took a long drag off my blunt and closed my eyes. "I'm about to cum."

"Mmmhmm, mmmhm," Lisa groaned sensuously.

Going up and down on my meat rapidly, she felt my hot semen shooting down her throat. She still did not stop; she just increased with the suction pull of a vacuum.

"Oh, my God! Oh my God!" she finally bellowed out.

I moaned, quivering in enjoyment. Lisa leaned her upper body weight on her elbow, while using her hand to gently massage my testicles.

She continued this until my manhood was hard and throbbing again. Then she grabbed hold of my penis with two hands, squatted over me, and smoothly inserted my throbbing manhood inside of her hot, wet vagina. The look on her face was one of pure pleasure as she bobbed up and down vigorously with delight. Lisa leaned back on one hand as she used the other to massage her clitoris. I started squeezing her breast with my left hand as I pumped upward with intensity.

"Oh, oh, oh, ah, oh, yeeess, ooh," Lisa yelled.

She began to shiver in ecstasy and goose bumps rose on her arms as she climaxed.

Now exhausted, Lisa lay on my chest as I pumped my manhood inside of her with Olympic thrusts. The Olympic gods would have been pleased to see the vigor which I put into each thrust. The great impact made her respond, chanting, "Oh, oh, ah, ah, ah, I, I, I lu-lug-you."

Her soft voice in my ear sent an immediate chill to my spine and hardened my penis to the max. I began breathing like a woman in labor and ended off with a "Wow!" as my sperm was released into Lisa's throbbing, all-consuming vagina. We then looked into each other's eyes, laughed simultaneously, and kissed briefly. She lay her head on my chest and went back to sleep. I took another drag on my blunt, placed it on the night table, and then fell asleep again.

Mark Cooper (Cat)

M ark Cooper, also known as Cat, was up earlier than usual. Normally, he stayed up all night and slept all day until evening time. However, he had an important business arrangement planned with a person name Steven from North Carolina. Steven said he would be in Atlanta, Georgia, before noon to do the usual pickup.

Now Cat had been up since 7:00 a.m., pacing his hotel room, anxiously awaiting Steven's phone call. Cat grew more and more impatient the longer he waited. He grabbed the remote on the bed and turned on the TV. Mindlessly he flipped through a few channels, stopping on BET's Rap City and turned the volume up before he ambled over to the nightstand, opened the top drawer, and took out a gram of cocaine from a clear jewelry bag and he picked up a straw.

Cat placed the bag of coke on top of the nightstand, took a quarter out his pocket, and then began to crush down the solid cocaine into a powder form, then he smoothed over the bag with the quarter until he was sure the powder was fine enough for nasal consumption.

Satisfied with his inspection, he picked up the bag and opened it, and stuck the straw in the sack, carefully placing a finger over the top of the straw to prevent the powdered cocaine trapped in the tip of his straw from falling back into the bag. Carefully, he inserted the straw into his nostril and sniffed all the coke from it. He did this same procedure for his other nostril. He did this twice, and then went to the cooler and got a 22-ounce Bud Ice, twisted it open, and guzzled it like cold water.

Feeling a hot rush, he walked over to the air conditioner and turned it up on high. After that, he turned off every light and made sure the hotel room was as dark as possible, turned up his music to the highest level, and start bouncing fanatically to Triple Six's "I Gotta Stay Fly."

After the song was finished, Cat turned off the TV, finished snorting the last half gram of cocaine he had left, and drank the rest of his beer. He went to the bed and sat in the middle of it with his arms folded across his chest and his back against the headboard. His teeth were clinched tight, and his facial expression was beyond serious. Sitting there, with his 5-foot-5, 135-pound frame, his eyes had expanded to the size of half-dollar coins. He looked like a fruit bat in the dark.

Suddenly his cell phone started ringing. He calmly took it out of his pocket and gazed at the time. It was now 11:45 in the morning. Hours had passed with him still sitting there on the bed, and he hadn't even realized it. It was a 706 number. Just what he was waiting for.

He picked up the phone. "What's happenin'?"

Steve, on the other end, replied, "You know what it is. Hey, Cat, I want a little more than the last time."

"What you need? You know all I got to do is to make a couple quick calls."

"Yeah, I'm going to need three of them things," meaning three keys of cocaine, Steve replied.

"Mane, that ain't nothing, mane, not here in the 'A.' I'll have my folks ready with it by the time you get here," Cat told him.

"Well, I'm coming off I-85 N, heading east on 285 now. Where you at?"

"I'm at the La Quinta Inn on Stone Mountain Industrial Road. Just come 285 until you get to Hwy 78 East, get off at Stone Mountain Industrial. The road sign is going to point you to the direction it's in. I'm in room 313. You got me?"

"No, man, repeat that one more time."

Cat, in a slow, patient fashion, made sure that Steve understood fully where he was going. Cat also told him if he had any other problem finding his location to call him back. Steve was originally from New York and still spoke with a heavy northern accent. Because of that, mostly all his comrades called him New York.

By noon, Cat's cell phone rang again. It was Steve.

"Yeah, New York," Cat answered. "I just got off the phone with my connection. He said that ain't nothing to do, but he doesn't want to meet nobody he ain't known. You dig?"

"I'm outside your hotel pulling in right now," Steve said.

"Okay. I'm coming outside now so you can see me."

Cat saw a blue 2005 Mercedes-Benz approaching with 22 Lionhart rims. The car's tinted windows were so dark that Cat could not see inside, but he calmly approached it anyway. The Benz had a Hummer behind it with a female driving it.

Suddenly the windows were lowered enough for Cat to see New York. Cat opened the passenger door and sat down silently. His baggy Dickie outfit and his Atlanta Braves hat made him look like a 12-year-old boy, but, he was, in fact, 20 years old and knew a thing or two. Cat placed his Air Jordan sneakers on the paper foot mat and tried his best not to soil Steve's new car. Looking over at Steve's 6-foot, 245-pound strapping body made Cat feel inferior and he hated that.

Cat noticed Steve had on a new Jacob watch filled with pink and blue diamonds. His blue 4X T-shirt fit him exactly right. He had on a necklace embedded with blue diamonds and his Jesus pendent was clustered with blue diamonds as well. As Cat looked down, he noticed the semiautomatic Mack-11 on Steve's lap, resting on his Yushua jeans. His shoes were Babe and Apes, and he smelled like Issey Miyaki.

Cat looked forward, put his game face on, and said, "We going to Clarkston, right up the street."

"My comrade want fifteen stacks ($15,000) apiece for a bird (key of cocaine)."

"It's the same old thing," Cat said. "I'll go buy it for you, and you give me a stack. So you have the 45 stacks ready."

"Look in the glove compartment," Steve replied.

As Cat opened the glove compartment, Steve clutched his gun. Cat took out the money that was in a pouch and started counting all hundred-dollar bills until he reached $46,000.

Cat took his phone slowly out of his pocket, telling Steve his every move. He then made a phone call, had a brief conversation, and then hung up.

"Okay. Everything's ready," Cat told him.

Steve called the female driver in the white Hummer and told her to park in the lot and wait until he got back.

Cat overheard his conversation and gave some advice. "Let her take my hotel key and wait in the room. It's a lot less suspicious looking."

Steve called the driver again. "Chyna, come get the key and wait in room 313 until we got back."

Cat looked on as Chyna approached the car. She was the most beautiful woman he'd ever seen. She was 36-20-42. Her pretty face was almond-colored graced with thick lips and sexy, slanted eyes. She sashayed over to the car in a two-piece Louis Vuitton dress suit, looking sexy and trés sophisticated.

Cat rolled down the window and handed her the key. "I'll be back to talk to you in ten minutes." He instantly rolled the window back up. It was too hot to permit the blistering May Southern heat flow inside.

"All right, New York, just pull out of here and get on the highway going 78 West," Cat said.

They got off at the next exit and made a left, went down to a stoplight at Ponce de Leon and made a right, then drove straight down two miles until they reached Highland Apartments and went to building M.

Cat then took the pouch filled with money and told New York, "I'll be right back in five minutes."

Cat put the stack with money in his pocket, exited the car, and marched inside M building. After he knocked on the door, it was opened by a teenager smoking a blunt. His cigar filled with marijuana left a pungent smell in the air.

"What's happenin', shawty?" the teenager greeted him. His pronunciation added the Southern twang version for shorty, that is, homeboy; friend.

"What's happenin, Lil' Pee?" Cat said as he grasped his hand and gave him dap, bumping chests.

Cat stepped in as Lil' Pee closed the door.

Lil' Pee immediately went back to playing his Play Station game "John Madden" football. Cat went over, took the blunt that Lil' Pee was smoking, and took a deep drag. He then looked out the window while speaking on the phone. "Yes, the guy is in a blue Benz in front of building M." He hung up after calling the local police department.

Cat then went to the back door, opened it, and before Lil' Pee could say something to him about his blunt, he and the blunt were gone.

Cat ran down the stairs, opened the back door, and looked out to make sure no one saw him. He then ran 12 feet, jumped the 3-foot fence, and ran through the neighboring houses' backyard and ended up on Northern Avenue. Next, he ran up to an '86 Buick Regal, jumped into the passenger seat, and reclined the seat all the way back.

He turned to Keisha, the driver, and said, "Drive!"

STEVE HAD HIS car seat reclined waiting on Cat, and he was wondering what was taking Cat so long. When he looked up in his rear-view mirror, he saw a Dekalb County police car pulling up directly behind him.

Steve pondered his options for a moment. What should he do? He couldn't afford to be interrogated by the police. Steve was wanted for questioning on a string of murders in New York City.

However, he had long since moved to North Carolina and changed his life from a murderous extortionist to a successful businessman. As long as the cop just wanted his license and registration, everything would be fine. Steve already did 10 years of his life behind bars and at 36 years old, he did not intend to do anymore.

Meantime, the police officer was supposed to wait on backup; however, he decided he could handle this one himself. Office Malone took his .40-caliber Smith & Wesson from his holster and approached the driver's side. He then went to the windshield to see the suspect and touched the roof of the car. The suspect had a pleasant smile on his face.

Officer Malone stated, "I'm here on an anonymous caller complaint about this vehicle selling drugs from the parking lot. I just want to see some ID."

Steve knew better than to trust a cop. He slowly reached over and tapped the unlock button three times so the officer could hear the door being unlocked. The officer quickly opened the door, reached in, and grabbed Steve by his shirt collar with one hand while he held his gun outside the car in his other hand. Steve grabbed him under his armpit, pushed him forward while he simultaneously retrieved his gun from behind his reclined seat and pressed the trigger. Before Officer Malone knew what hit him, he was shot three times, twice in his face and once in his neck.

KEISHA SNAPPED AT Cat with her usual attitude. "Where we going, nigga?"

Cat did not respond to her. He just reached over and turned down the volume on the Eight Ball and MJG CD, "Coming Out Hard" in the CD player. He took his lighter and a black pouch out of his pocket, then lit the blunt that was already in his mouth, took a deep pull, then released all the tension of his ordeal with a slow, heavy exhale. After a few more hits, he placed it in the ashtray.

More relaxed now, he opened the money bag and dumped the bills into his lap. He knew how much was there. He just wanted the pleasure of counting $46,000 again. Keisha's eyes shot open when she saw Cat empty the cash on his lap. She then became nervous and started speeding on the expressway.

"Be cool and drive," Cat said with his newfound confidence about his position in life.

Cat and Keisha were high-school sweethearts. They met in the ninth-grade at Shamrock High School and had been together ever since. Keisha was 19 years old, a year younger than Cat, but she'd always been the breadwinner. Cat influenced her to start using drugs and alcohol when she was 17. He also encouraged her to become an exotic dancer after she graduated from high school. Keisha was drop-dead gorgeous, but she had been shy and reserved, not like a ghetto girl from Scottsdale.

Keisha and Cat became friends first, then lovers. They struggled through enough hardships to create a strong bond between them. No matter what Keisha told herself, she would always be there for Cat. Over the years, she outgrew him by 2 inches, and her 5-foot-7, 130-pound frame was sexy and athletically defined. She had cocoa-brown skin and a beautiful, pearly white smile. Her shoulder-length hair was permed maroon red with bright red highlights on the tips.

Keisha would do anything for Cat, but she felt she didn't owe him any respect due to the fact that since they had known each other, she'd been paying for everything. Cat would be in their hotel room getting high all day while she was selling herself to strange men to pay their bills.

Over the years, Keisha moved from a shy sweetheart to a conniving, money-hungry woman. She would do just about anything for money, degrading or not. She didn't care. As a matter of fact, now she enjoyed it. As Keisha looked over, Cat reclined all the way back in his seat, counting his money. He didn't look so much like a loser anymore.

In fact, he looked damn good. He looked like a real man, someone she could be proud of. Keisha became overly turned on as she approached Ponce de Leon to make a right turn. She put on her turn indicator, then placed her hand through her Daisy Dukes and felt her vagina. She had quickly become incredibly moist and hot. Using her right hand, she took the blunt that was still burning in the ashtray and started smoking it.

11

Keisha took a long drag and blew out the smoke quickly as she saw a Clarkston police car coming in her direction. Panicking, she started to throw the blunt out the window, but the police car made a rapid left turn into the Highland Apartments. Keisha looked around, made sure no cars were behind her, and continued smoking.

STEVE PUSHED OFFICER Malone out of the car. His body was still twitching when he hit the ground. Taking the handkerchief he had in his car, he wiped off the blood which had sprayed on his face. The corpse had fallen on the ground with eyes open and gun still in hand. Steve started his car, put it in reverse, and backed up until his car bumped the police car behind him. Then he turned the steering wheel all the way right and stepped on the gas, speeding off to exit the complex.

While Steve was coming up to the entrance of the complex, he noticed a Clarkston police car coming inside the complex. He took a deep breath and rolled down the front and back passenger windows. Steve slowed the Benz down to a crawl while approaching a speed bump on the road.

Officer Williams of the Clarkston Police Department was hurrying to get to the scene to back up Officer Malone. He entered the complex at a high speed, and then slowed down when he saw the car that was identified in the 911 call. His first intuition was that the matter had been resolved.

Steve grabbed his .40-caliber weapon. As Williams' car reached the speed bump, the officer looked over to the right of his vehicle to see who the driver of the Mercedes was. It was the last sight he ever saw. He was greeted with a swarm of bullets. One hit him directly in the center of his forehead and exited the back of his skull. Blood and brain fragments splattered against the driver-side window of his squad car.

Officer Williams' head fell forward on the steering wheel, which sounded the horn. His lifeless foot hit the gas pedal and sent the car launching forward. The out-of-control police car ran right into a parked '96 red Toyota Camry with a tremendous impact that turned the parked car vertically and brought the police cruiser to a sudden stop, its horn blaring out like a siren.

IN HER REAR-view mirror, Keisha noticed a car coming up behind her. She put the small blunt back in the ashtray as she was traveling on Ponce de Leon Blvd. Then she saw a Mercedes-Benz 500 on 22s that was approaching her.

STEVE STEPPED ON the gas and in a matter of seconds was at the exit of the complex. He was about to go back in the direction that he came from when he noticed a beautiful redhead passing him in a white Buick Regal with no passenger seat. He quickly turned right and got behind her.

ONCE KEISHA DROVE past the Highland Apartments billboard that was posted up high, Cat started smiling. But suddenly, he looked in the rear-view mirror and his heart almost jumped out of his chest, racing so fast. He broke out in a cold sweat and stooped lower in his seat.

"Keisha, where's your gun at?"

"It's under my seat," she replied.

He reached behind her seat and pulled out a black pearl handle .38 Special. He placed the gun in his lap and lay as low as he possibly could.

STEVE PRESSED THE accelerator, and his Benz shot forward. He passed the Regal on the left-hand side, ignoring the no passing lane.

In a second, he was right on the Regal with his hand gripping his Mack-11. He was trying his best to see who, or if, someone was in the passenger seat. As soon as Steve believed he recognized someone on the passenger side, the woman driving gazed over at him, gave him a mesmerizing smile, and turned immediately right onto the expressway. Steve braked and stopped suddenly, only to have cars behind him blocking his entrance to the highway, irately blowing their horns at him.

ONCE CAT SAW that New York was no longer in pursuit, he raised up his seat, still clutching his gun, constantly looking behind him. All this excitement had Keisha's hormones going crazy. She wanted Cat more than she ever did in her life. She was thirsting for him so badly, she could taste him. Unconsciously, she started to slowly lick her lips and touch her privates with her left hand. Cat looked over at her. She was giving him a look he had never seen before.

"Hey, Keisha."

"Yes, Cat Daddy," she said in a sweet, seductive voice. He was not use to that type of tone, but he thought he could damn sure get use to it.

He turned to the side facing Keisha and looked to the back of him at the same time. Then he continued, "I want you to get off at the next exit up and get us a suite at the Marriott Hotel. Then I want you to take the Regal and go rent a car. Leave the Regal there at the rent-a-car place and come back and meet me."

She nodded her head yes like an obedient little girl.

Steve hit the steering wheel in frustration, said a few choice words in French, then proceeded on. He ran straight through the red light and turned right on Indian Creek Court. He drove down, and then took a left on McLeaden. He was driving down the street at the 30 mph speed limit, saw a white woman in her late 40s leaving her house, locking her front door. He pulled up at the side of the curb, making sure not to block the driveway, and stopped.

Steve turned off his car, placed his keys in his pocket, and then opened his door. He got out without closing it. He crept in a low squatting position and caught Mary-Ann by surprise as she was turning around to come down her steps. Her house was built in a design that made it impossible to view the driveway from the front door of the house.

By the time the lady saw Steve, it was already too late. Before the startled woman could say anything, Steve placed one of his monstrous hands over her mouth and the other behind the back of her head and twisted her head so hard and fast, it almost decapitated her. There was a brief, "Whaaa," then an evil-sounding snap. Mary-Ann's eyes rolled back as the extreme pain knocked her unconscious.

In one swift motion, Steve bent down, picked her up, and threw her limp body over his shoulders like a 10-pound sack of potatoes. He then hurried over to his car and threw her in the backseat. All this happened within minutes.

KEISHA GOT OFF of Hwy 285 and exited off Lavista Road. She made a right off the expressway and searched until she found an available room at the Holiday Inn where she made a deposit and got a suite for one week. She went back, got in the car, and gave Cat one of the keys. "We'll be staying in room B635."

He took the key from her. Cat already had a thousand dollars ready for Keisha. He handed her the money and told her to go rent a car for a week.

Keisha took the money, then jumped over on the passenger's seat on top of him and started kissing him deeply. She stuck her tongue in his mouth and sucked his tongue out of his mouth, kissing him passionately. Her engine was on fire, red-hot. She placed her hand down on his cock and started massaging his manhood up and down. Then her hands traveled up on his flat chest, and she warned him he better be ready when she got back. After that, Keisha got back over in the driver's seat, put both hands on the steering wheel, and looked focused with her full luscious lips poking out.

Cat placed the .38 revolver in his waistline, put the money he had been counting in both pockets, and exited the car.

STEVE SEARCHED HIS Benz well to make sure he did not leave behind anything he needed. He lifted the armrest of the middle consol and retrieved a stainless steel .44 Magnum revolver. He also grabbed his cell phone and its charger off the floor on the driver's side, placing them in his pocket.

Mary Ann's body began going into convulsions. She started shaking violently, as if she stuck her hand in a live electrical socket. It was a grand mal on the grandest scale. Meanwhile, Steve placed the .44 Magnum that was already in a clip on a holster in his waistline. He held the Mack-11 in his right hand while placing the cell phone and charger in his pocket. He retrieved the Benz keys out of his pocket. Hurriedly, he closed the door and pressed the keyless entry device to lock the doors.

He ran back to where he'd assaulted his victim and picked up the keys to her gray Volvo S40. Steve used the keyless entry device to open the doors, quickly climbed in, and adjusted the seat. He started the car and turned the radio off, then put the car in drive, made a left out of the driveway, passed by his abandoned car, and proceeded down McLeaden until he reached Valley Brook Road. There, he made a right on Valley Brook and drove until he reached Hwy 78, where he then made a right turn, going west. At that point, he took his phone out of his pocket and called Chyna.

She answered. "Hello."

"Chyna, this is Steve. I want you to leave the Inn and meet me at the next exit going west on Highway 78, at the Waffle House on Brocket Road."

"Okay, I'm on my way."

Chapter

3

Lil'
Pee

L il' Pee was rolling up another blunt when he heard the gunshots. Curious but not disturbed, he got up to look through his second-story window, where he saw a Benz on 22s speeding towards the exit of his complex. Then he looked down and saw a cop car with the driver's door open. Close to the building, he saw a cop sprawled out on the pavement. *This can't be good*, he thought.

The next thing he heard was about 17 shots in rapid succession, followed by a massive boom, and a car horn blasting nonstop. Lil' Pee who was 15 years old and expelled from school for numerous suspensions knew better then to get involved in this type of incident. He finished rolling his blunt, turned off the Play Station 3 and the TV, took the ashtray to his room, but was too nervous to smoke so he put the ashtray under his bed and decided to go to sleep until his mother came home with some food from her job at McDonald's.

A while later Lil' Pee woke up to a knocking on his bedroom door. It was his mother, Angela. She opened the door to discover her son lying around, doing nothing.

Angela snapped, "Why don't you get up and clean up around here? When I'm at work, all you do is play video games and sleep."

Lil' Pee got up and yawned as if this was just a usual routine.

Angela continued, "You need to get a job and go get your GED. Stop wasting time, Peter. All that hanging out with your so-called boys is not going to get you nowhere in life but dead or in prison."

She paused suddenly, then sighed, knowing all she was saying was going in one ear and out the other. "Your food is on the kitchen counter," she said. With that, she left the room.

Angela worked about 80 hours a week to make ends meet. She knew she never had time for Peter, and the boy practically raised himself. So now that he had become a man without a father figure in his life, Angela just let him do what he wanted, because he was going to do it anyway, and prayed that somehow God would guide him through it. Lil' Pee was young and without direction. As usual, Angela was exhausted from her job. She went to her room, closed the door, and locked it.

Lil' Pee took the blunt from underneath his bed and lit it. He began recalling the incident and went back to look through the window to see what was going on. As he peeked through the blinds, he could see residents standing outside, talking to the detectives. He went to the back window. The police were there, too.

Lil' Pee decided to go to the bathroom, smoke his marijuana, and blow the smoke in the suction vent like what he used to do before his mother found out he smoked. He made sure he locked the door. After lifting the toilet seat, he stood on the commode and lit his blunt. He started blowing the smoke out into the vent.

When the blunt was halfway finished, he jumped down and put the blunt in the sink, washed his hands with soap, and sprayed the air freshener.

Suddenly, he heard a loud knock at the door. Not expecting anybody, Lil' Pee ignored the knock and went over to play his video games. As soon as Pee turned on the Play Station and the television, he then lay back on the couch and put his legs up and crossed them in a comfortable position.

Another knock sounded at the door. Angela stormed out of her room with her hair in a stocking cap and her robe hastily thrown on. She motioned to the door in aggravation as she stormed by the couch. Angela opened the door to see a man in a Polo dress shirt and tie with a notepad in his hand. A uniformed police officer stood directly behind him.

"Good day, ma'am. I'm Detective Turner on behalf of the Capital Homicide Division of Dekalb County, and this is Officer

Parker of Dekalb County Police Department. I would like to have a word with you."

"I already told you I was at work all day and I can't help you," Angela snapped.

Turner noticed Angela's tired face still held a hint of beauty. However, years of hard living and stress had hardened her facial features. He could also tell by her standing there with her robe slightly open that she still had a lovely body and was a free spirit.

Turner looked over her shoulder while she was talking and observed a shabbily furnished apartment. He also noticed a teenager with his hair braided in cornrows. The boy had a joy stick in his hand, glued to the TV set. Detective Turner didn't recall seeing him come from school with the rest of the children earlier. That's all the view he got before he heard ...

"Please don't knock on my door again." Angela slammed the door shut and stormed back to her room. Without paying Peter any attention, she locked her door. Once inside her room, she disrobed. She wore only her panties. Her breasts sagged, and her stomach and legs showed a bit of cellulite. Even so, she was still in decent shape for a lady 39 years old. She dropped down on the bed, pulled the sheet over her, lay on her belly, and fluffed up her pillow. After sinking her head into the pillow, she promptly fell asleep.

After three hours passed, Pee looked through the window and saw that all the commotion had died down. Then he went to his room, walked into his closet and took a 4X black T-shirt off the shelf that made his 5-foot-9, 145-pound body look even smaller. He reached on the floor of the closet and picked up his black Dickie pants.

He put the baggy 36-inch waist pants on over his blue gym shorts, took a black bandanna out of his back pocket, and pushed the bandanna through the two front belt loops, then tied the bandanna in a knot. This fastened the pants to his butt without them sagging to his knees. He then took some socks out of a bag in his closet, slipped them on, and put on his Air Jordan black sneakers.

Lil' Pee then went to the corner of the closet and lifted up the carpet. Three hundred fifty dollars and seven grams of crack cocaine were hidden there. He pulled out the crack that was in a small clear bag and placed it in his sock, then he went to the bathroom, turned on the lights, and stood in front of the mirror, admiring himself. He noticed a little peach fuzz on his face and plucked it off. He smiled in the mirror, revealing perfectly straight, white aligned teeth.

Lil' Pee had light-brown skin and puppy-dog eyes, which made girls think he was cute. He opened the medicine cabinet mirror, took out his toothbrush, and squeezed Colgate toothpaste on it. While he brushed his teeth, he leaned forward over the sink to make sure toothpaste didn't soil his T-shirt. Wrapping up his dental duties, he spit, rinsed, and placed the toothbrush and toothpaste back in the medicine cabinet.

Lil' Pee then retrieved his half blunt he was smoking earlier and placed it in his mouth. He went back in his room briefly to get a lighter and his keys, which were next to the bed on the floor, left the apartment, and locked the door behind him. Running down the stairs two at a time, he stopped short when he came to the entrance of the building. There he saw yellow police tape sectioning off the area where the shooting took place. As he got closer, he could see the chalk outline on the pavement where the cop's body had been.

Lil' Pee wanted to get away from the area as soon as possible. A group of teenage boys lingered on the porch of a nearby apartment with the door wide open. Two girls stood in the doorway. They probably were talking about the incident that happened earlier, he thought.

"What's happenin', Lil' Pee?" someone yelled from the crowd.

Lil' Pee threw up a peace sign while keeping his head high, looking straight forward with his chest poked out. He continued his walk with a small bop while dragging his left leg slightly. He thought this walk made him look like an ice skater gliding gracefully on ice.

Once he reached the front of the apartment, he crossed over Ponce de Leon, and then crossed the railroad tracks. Soon, he came up on North Avenue. After passing the Chevron gas station, he lit up his blunt and smoked as he walked until he reached Post Oak Apartments. Post Oak used to be Forest Cambridge. However, the new owners decided to change the name to stop the bad reputation of drug trafficking it had developed over the years. Well, the name changed, but the traffic stayed the same.

As soon as Lil' Pee entered the entrance of the apartment complex, a white pickup truck pulled up alongside of him.

"Hey," a white man said, rolling down his passenger-side window. "Hey, man, you got some hard?"

Pee knew he was talking about crack cocaine. He jumped inside the truck on the passenger side and asked the man who looked like he had a starring role in *Tales from the Crypt,* "What you want?"

The man said "I need a *fifty.*" He held two twenties and one ten-dollar bill in his hand.

Pee made haste and took the dope out of his sock and broke a piece off and gave it to the J (junkie).

"Come on, man, give me a little more than this! Man, I'm spending the whole fifty with you."

Pee broke off a tiny piece more and gave it to the J, who handed him the fifty dollars, anxious to leave.

Lil' Pee told the man to drop him off at the next building down. The junkie did it and burned rubber as soon as Pee hopped out and closed the passenger door. Lil' Pee sauntered over to Building K, walked up to apartment 10, then turned the doorknob, but the door was locked. He then went to the back window, raised it up, and climbed in. Once inside the apartment, he did a walk-through to make sure nobody was there. When he approached the second bedroom of the abandoned three-bedroom apartment, he discovered his comrade, Shawn, better known as Blue, standing rigid and alert, with his legs spread wide apart.

Blue had one hand on the wall and the other hand lifting up his blue T-shirt, which revealed his chrome 9mm pistol. His long, hard, erected penis stuffed the mouth of a woman who was on her knees with her hands wrapped around Blue's legs. Blue was already 6-foot-2 at 14 years of age.

He was turning 15 on August 13 and was already well respected amongst his peers. However, at 150 pounds, he looked like a stick man in his current position. Blue suddenly realized there was a shadow coming from the doorway in the dark moonlit room. He swiftly drew his 9mm and pointed it in the direction where the shadow was coming from. He was about to pull the trigger when he heard a voice.

"Blue, don't shoot. It's Lil' Pee."

Blue still had his gun pointing in his direction until he saw Lil' Pee enter the doorway, unarmed. Peaches was a real trooper. She didn't allow the drama going on to interfere with her performing oral sex on Blue. She stopped only briefly to see who it was, then went right back to giving Blue a superblow job. She was extremely comfortable doing this task. It appeared to Lil' Pee that she would be comfortable performing oral sex in front of a audience of 20,000 on stage at the Civic Center.

Blue lowered his gun to his side and ask Lil' Pee, "What you doing sneaking up in this trap?"

Lil' Pee didn't answer. He just left Blue to continue doing what he was doing. Lil' Pee went and hid his dope under the hot-water heater. He closed the boiler-room door lightly and left the apartment through the front door. He stepped outside and sat on the stairs until he spotted some crackheads. He wanted to make a few more sales. However, they were either looking for someone else, or they didn't have any money.

Inside the apartment, Blue started smiling, exposing eight gold teeth, four at the top and four at the bottom. "Yeah, suck this bigass dick," he repeated. "Suck it! Suck it!" He grabbed Peaches by her shabby, short, permed hair, pulled her head back, and ejaculated hot semen all over her face.

Blue came out of the apartment smiling as he approached Lil' Pee, who was sitting on the stairs. He gave Pee some dap.

Lil' Pee looked at him and smiled. "What's the business?"

He smiled back. "Mane, a player got to get his, know what I mean?"

He gave Pee more dap as they both laughed.

Blue continued, "Shawty got some damn good fire ass head! Look, my nigga, we about to get paid," Blue said with a serious expression on his face. "Trust me, my nigga, this lick is going to set us straight. I always get the better end of deal."

"Nigga, you know I'm down," Lil' Pee replied.

"For sure, my nigga. Wait right here. I gotta run to the crib and get some shit," Blue said then walked towards his apartment complex.

He crossed the street from Post Oak. Lil' Pee watched as Blue swaggered away, his chest poking out and his back in an erect posture. He walked like he was the colonel of somebody's army. Lil' Pee began to wonder what lick Blue was talking about and what he'd gotten himself into.

Chapter 4
Peaches

After sleeping all day, Peaches woke up at 9:00 p.m. She'd been up for 2 days the last previous nights and needed the rest. She got up as hungry as a bear that just woke up from a looong hibernation. The house was empty. She remembered her mother told her she and Peaches' children were suppose to go on some special fundraiser trip in Alabama for the weekend to raise money for the church's new gymnasium.

Still sleepy, she made her way to the kitchen and opened the refrigerator and took out some leftover baked chicken and rice that her mother, Mrs. Brown, had cooked for the children yesterday. Peaches mixed the rice and chicken, placed it inside a Tupperware dish, covered it, and put it in the microwave. She then went to the bathroom, took a quick shower, and brushed her teeth.

Wrapped in a towel, Peaches strolled into her 3-year-old daughter's room, where she slept on the floor next to her daughter's bed, opened a traveling bag, and pulled out a short blue jean miniskirt with no panties which she put on along with a small white T-shirt.

Hearing the microwave beep that had been set on 10 minutes, she rushed back to the kitchen, grabbed the hot dish, uncovered it, and began to ravenously devour the food. But before she finished her meal, she started feeling agitated. She felt turned off by the food and threw the rest of it in the garbage disposal, then rinsed off her dish and put it in the dishwasher. She turned around, opened the fridge, and took out a jug of cherry Kool-Aid. Sweet as usual. She drank two glasses.

But she still didn't feel well, so she headed back to her daughter's room, feeling weak and a great emptiness inside her stomach. Slipping on her shoes, Peaches left the apartment and locked the door behind her.

The cool mist of the night's summer breeze felt good on her face. Although she was 25, Peaches was still good-looking and was healthy. She was high yellow, weighed 137 pounds, and was 5-foot-8. Her butt was big and wide, and she had thick, firm legs. Even though she had had three kids, her abdomen was still in great condition. Her size D breasts were no longer firm. They sagged, and her big nipples poked out in her tight T-shirt.

Peaches had been a beautiful, young, church-going lady until she met Big Ron. Big Ron, a crack-smoking ex-con, met Peaches when she was 17 years old. He was just coming home after doing seven years for armed robbery. He studied the Bible a lot while incarcerated. With his knowledge of the Bible and his powerful physique, he impressed Peaches. After Big Ron charmed her, he enticed Peaches to smoke crack. She already smoked weed and cigarettes and saw nothing wrong with smoking as long as she stayed focus on her schoolwork.

Unfortunately, Peaches was soon enslaved by crack cocaine and was under the control of Big Ron, who then introduced Peaches to the streets as a prostitute so she could support their drug habit.

In spite of Peaches' drug abuse, she managed to give birth to three normal children, each one a year apart. Shortly thereafter, Big Ron was convicted of his second armed robbery. This time, he had the bad luck of getting caught while murdering the victim during a local convenient store holdup. When Peaches was 22 years old, her baby daddy got sentenced to life plus 20, with no possibility of parole. Afterwards, Peaches' mother took the children and has been caring for them ever since.

Peaches made haste to leave the complex to see which trick she could turn. After all, she was a lady of the night. While walking, she heard someone calling her. She turned around and walked in his direction, her breasts swinging loosely and her blonde-dyed hair fuzzy like Albert Einstein's. She approached Blue.

"What's up?"

"I got some hard," he replied.

Peaches wanted some of that coke. "Let me get a wake-up." She needed some to get going.

Blue smiled. "What you gonna give me?"

"I'll suck your dick," Peaches offered.

"Shit, that's a bet." Blue beckoned to Peaches. "Come on, shawty."

She followed him into an abandoned apartment.

"Damn, you don't have no light in here?" she asked.

"Nope," Blue answered.

They made their way through the moon-lighted apartment and stopped in a room in the center of it. Blue walked over close to the wall and stood like a soldier at ease. She told him to let her get a hit before she started.

"Shit, the last bitch I gave my dope to before she started didn't even let a nigga bust a nut."

"I swear I'll let you cum. Just give me one hit," Peaches pleaded.

Blue lifted up his shirt, brandishing his gun. Peaches didn't say another word. She got right in front of him and looked up to admire his best mobster facial expression. He looked cute to her with his slim, stone-hard face and Snoop Dogg cornrows that came down in two braids.

She got down on her knees and managed to pull out his enormous penis from his boxers. His pants were already sagging low enough for her to do this. She grabbed a handful of his already fully erect wood, started licking on the head, then placed it in her mouth.

Peaches began to jerk his penis softly as she bopped her head forward and backwards, rapidly consuming as much of his penis in her mouth as possible, while her lips pressed tightly around his cock. Fifteen minutes into her blow job session, she felt his manhood beginning to throb in her mouth. She placed both her hands on his skinny legs for better balance, then started thrusting forward to send his penis down her throat with every insertion. She was in deep concentration when she was interrupted by a boy standing in the doorway.

Peaches stopped to look at him, then went right back to what she was doing. Shortly after, Peaches felt her head being snatched back and sperm being ejaculated in her face. She leaned her head back to take the pressure off her hair and embrace the semen shower. In ecstasy, she grabbed his penis and sucked the last bit of juices he had left in it while locking eyes with him.

Finished, he tucked his shriveling penis back in his boxers. Peaches was still reaching for his manhood while he was stepping back, putting it in his drawers. Her hands and her head dropped to the floor simultaneously like a spoiled brat when she doesn't get what she wants.

Blue reached down his side Dickie pocket and pulled out a small Ziploc bag with 17 grams of crack cocaine. He broke off a small piece about five dollars worth and handed it to her. She stared at the dope disappointedly.

"Come on. You can do me better than this."

"Shit, this dope cost money. When you bring me some money, I'll take care of you." Blue walked out, leaving her staring at his back.

Peaches remained on her knees, staring at Blue with disgust until he exited the room and disappeared. She then looked at the piece of crack rock in her hand with pure hatred. Now, she felt like throwing the drug away, but could not command herself to do it. She then pulled out a napkin that was in her jean skirt pocket. She unraveled the napkin to reveal a burned-out small, narrow, hollow glass tube with a small piece of hanger and a new glass tube with a miniature plastic rose in it, and two wooden corks at both ends.

She took her little short hanger and pushed the slightly burnt Brillo pad out of the burnt-out tube and went to the bathroom to wash it off. She came back and knelt in front of her napkin with her instruments of self-destruction and picked up the new tube. Peaches placed the crack cocaine on the end of the shooter and placed the tube in her mouth. She put fire to the end where the crack was, her eyes steady, staring at the crack and the flames.

Inhaling with all her might, she heard the sizzling of the dope stop. She held her breath and released as little smoke as possible. Instantly she felt rejuvenated, her eyes widened. Suddenly she wanted to see some excitement. Her hormones were racing. All of a sudden, she felt good and carefree.

Peaches placed the glass pipe back in her mouth and lit the end again, trying to get some more out of the residue. *Damn,* she thought, *I got to get some more of this. I can't afford to lose this feeling.* She felt more of a woman, like she could take on any man, anything, and the world. *Bring them on,* she thought, *I'll conquer them all.*

Then, Peaches gathered her things and fled from the apartment. She was eager to get to the track where the other hoes hung out and the pickin's were good.

Once she was out of the breezeway, she stopped to admire how peaceful the night was. Everything seemed wonderfully enhanced to her, like she was now entering a different dimension. But she was frightened by an unexpected voice behind her.

"Shit, shawty, what's up?" Lil' Pee asked.

"You," Peaches said, turning around.

He was sitting with his back to the corner of the stair, his shoulder leaning on the wall.

"Ah, you got a cigarette?" she asked.

"Nope," he answered.

"What you doin' sittin' out here?" Peaches lifted her eyebrow.

"Trapping."

"Shit, you got some dope?"

"For sure."

"Shit, give a hoe a dime until I turn some tricks. You know I'm good for $10," she said.

"I can't even do it," he said.

"Let a bitch suck your dick or something," she replied.

"I'm straight," he said.

She analyzed him with an awkward look. "What? Are you gay or something?"

"Fuck no, shawty," he snapped.

Feeling that refusing a sexual favor might be a dent in his manhood and knowing how fast a rumor could travel through the hood, Lil' Pee said, "Shit, I'll let you suck my dick for a nick."

"Shit, nigga, a nickel? *Five dollars?*" she protested. "Come on, nigga, but only for you." She led him into the apartment.

Once they were inside, Lil' Pee locked the door behind him, retrieving his dope, and followed Peaches to the back room. This was the master bedroom, and it was connected to a bathroom. Peaches took out her napkin, placed her shooter in her mouth, stretched out her hand, and looked Lil' Pee in his eyes with a serious stare.

"I need mine before I start," she said, holding the crack pipe firmly between her teeth.

He complied and broke her off a piece of dope he took from his sock and handed it to her. It was a decent dime, but she still asked for more. He refused. She started feeling irritated and in a few minutes, if she didn't take a smoke of crack, she was going to fall in a severe state of depression along with irritation. She made haste to the window to use the lunar lamp to see.

Peaches placed half of what she received from Lil' Pee in the pipe and placed the other half on the windowsill. She smoked that piece, felt well, and smoked the other piece and felt greatly enhanced. She turned to Lil' Pee and asked him if he was ready.

He entered the master room bathroom, leaned in a sitting position on the bathroom sink, and whipped out his nervous penis. Peaches came in right behind him and got down on her knees on the hard, cold bathroom floor. She inserted Pee's manhood into her mouth and attempted to swallow his limp penis down her esophagus with her lips at the base of his penis.

She clenched her lips as tight as possible and squeezed his penis with her lips going up to his head. She then suckled on the head like a pacifier, then inserted his whole penis in her mouth swiftly and held her lips at the base of it. She could feel his penis fully erect and throbbing in her throat. Peaches' hormones started going crazy. She lifted her skirt under her big, juicy breasts. Then, she placed one hand behind her and pushed her middle finger in her anus.

Her other hand was in front of her, with her two center fingers inside her vagina and her lower palm rubbing her clitoris. She worked both hands in and out her anus and vagina simultaneously.

Lil' Pee couldn't believe he was feeling so good. He looked down on the person helping to transport his physical body to paradise, only to see a beautiful, wide, spread ass with her hand in the middle. He closed his eyes and felt every inch of his body tingling with ecstasy.

Peaches felt his penis get even harder and start to throb with greater force. Without hesitation, she inserted all of his penis into her mouth until her lips touched his pubic hairs at his penis' base. She stuck her tongue out and began licking her breasts, curling her tongue underneath them, sucking them in her mouth as well.

Lil' Pee's body started jerking like he was being hit with a 10,000 volt Taser. He could not restrain from moaning. As he released a loud moan, tears begin to roll down his face.

As Peaches felt the hot sensation spraying down her throat, burning its way down, she sensed what she was doing and peered up at him through the darkness with a confident smile. *I got you,* she thought to herself.

Their moment of ecstasy was rudely interrupted by a banging at the window. Lil' Pee hurried up and pulled his penis away. He peeped through the dark bathroom to see Blue banging on the window again. Lil' Pee came out where Blue could see him clearly. Blue gave him a wide smile and started "bouncing," his shoulders moving up and down simultaneously in rhythm. "Come on, my nigga," he said.

Lil' Pee was making his way to the door. When he heard a hiss, "Hey, come here," he turned back in Peaches' direction to see her observing him. She looked demonic, like a witch or a wild creature of the night. She was motioning for him to come to her with her index finger. She stared at him, wide-eyed, with a smile plastered on her face. She leaned against the bathroom sink countertop with her legs wide open. Her pubic hair was clean shaven and her plump, pink-lipped vagina was clearly visible and definitely inviting.

Lil' Pee stepped over to her and looked deeply into her eyes.

"Let me get a little more. You know I'm good for it," she wheedled, putting emphasis on the *"You know."* He took out the dope he had and gave it to her. He then left her and headed through the front door.

Peaches went to the back window, broke off about a dime from the less than one-half gram, put it in her shooter, and smoked it. Now she felt totally energized. She placed her glass pipe in her napkin and back in her pocket. The crack sack she put in her smaller pocket. She was ready for some excitement. Most of all, she needed some money for liquor and cigarettes.

Peaches exited the complex and made her way down Northern Avenue. She was walking with a seductive swivel of her hips. A couple of passersby blew their horns, however, nothing serious. Before Peaches could reach the bottom of the hill at Northern Avenue, she saw a Chevy Astor van with a work ladder on top of the minivan. The van turned at the street directly in front of her and waited for her to approach.

When Peaches arrived at the van, a Hispanic man started speaking to her. *"Hola,"* he said.

She approached the car while running her hands down on her hair, putting it down. This made her facial appearance looked more presentable. The driver of the vehicle was short and chubby, with low-cut, porcupine-like hair.

"I no speak good English," he said nervously. "I need good sex with you."

She looked over to see his friend smiling in the passenger seat. Peaches motioned her head, nodding yes. He pointed over to the man in the passenger seat that was slim with the same hair style as he had and said, "This is Juan, *mi* brother." He turned and pointed to the rear of the vehicle to a very short, pot-bellied, Hispanic guy wearing a ponytail. "And this is Ricardo. I'm Raul," he pointed to himself.

He turned and gave his attention to Peaches' nipples. "I have $200 for all." He showed her the money with his hand on his crotch. Peaches went over to the rear sliding door and got in next to Ricardo. Once she was in and the vehicle took off, she told the driver she wanted some Newport cigarettes too. He said no problem and stopped at the local package store on N. Decatur Road.

He came back to the minivan with a 24-pack of Budweiser and handed her a pack of Newport 100s and a bottle of Night Train. She thanked him for his kind consideration. Raul made his way up N. Decatur and made a right in the second entrance of N. Decatur Manor. He drove to Building 18 and parked in front.

They got out of the van and entered their apartment. Raul opened the door for everybody to swiftly enter the apartment, and Juan turned on the lights. Peaches observed the one-bedroom apartment that had one sofa bed, with the bed already pulled out, and a TV on a stand with a VCR at the bottom of the TV stand. She noticed everything was fairly clean, except for all the Budweiser cans laying everywhere.

She asked to use the restroom and Juan motioned her in the direction of it. As Peaches sashayed to the restroom, which was adjacent to the bedroom, she looked back in the bedroom and noticed a neatly made bed with box springs and the mattress was covered with brown sheets. She entered the bathroom, turned on the water faucet, and let it run. Then she fastidiously checked her private area to see if she was clean. To make sure, she tore a thick roll of toilet paper, dampened it a bit, and wiped her private area clean. She sat on the toilet with water still running and took out her napkin.

Next, she took out her shooter and the sack of crack from her small pocket and broke off a little more than a dime, smoked it, but didn't get the feeling she wanted so she broke down two more small pebbles and smoked them one at a time. Now she felt high. It was a good feeling. She stepped in front of the mirror and stared in her eyes, then dampened her hand and patted down her hair. Satisfied with what she saw, she stripped naked, dampened her hand with more water once more and massaged her breast toward the tip of her nipple in a circular squeezing motion.

She repeated the procedure on the other breast until the nipples stood erect, then slapped and rubbed her heavy buttocks until they started jiggling. Peaches was primed and ready to rock. She looked in the mirror once more, gave a mirthless smile, and turned off the water.

Opening the bathroom door wide, Peaches stood in a seductive pose until she had the Mexicans' full attention. Slowly she switched off the lights next to the bathroom door and made her way to the sofa bed like Jessica Rabbit in *Who Framed Roger Rabbit?* Her walk was so seductive the Mexicans seem to be stuck in time watching her. Their eyes were wide and unblinking, and they seemed to forget to breathe. When she reached the sofa bed, she crawled to the rear center of it.

Next, she leaned back with her arms stretched out, resting on the upper sofa, then slowly spread her legs wide open. Play time.

The three amigos were sitting in front of her. They had been watching a porno flick on television. Raul had a bag of cocaine in his hand that he was snorting and Ricardo and Juan had cans of Budweiser in their hands. Raul took a couple more sniffs and passed the bag and a pen top to Peaches. She took the bag and started snorting.

Raul then went to the kitchen and came back with a Budweiser and a small sandwich bag filled with some blue pills with a square in the middle. He took one of the pills and washed it down with beer, then passed it to his comrades and they did the same. Juan passed the bag back to Raul.

Raul's eyes were glued on Peaches's privates. "You take Ecstasy?"

She stretched her open hand forward, and Raul handed her the bag of pills. She took three out of the bag and handed it back to Raul. As he took the bag, he motioned with his hands like a crossing guard recommending a stop. "Easy, easy," he warned.

Peaches shot him a sarcastic expression, got up, clutched her bottle of Night Train and her cigarettes, then returned to the center rear of the sofa bed and spread her legs once more. She then placed an ecstasy pill in her anus and used her middle finger to push the pill all the way up. Once it was in place, she then inserted another pill in her vagina and pushed it inside of her.

The three Mexicans stared in disbelief and amazement. She had them lusting with great anticipation. Peaches then popped a pill in her mouth and swallowed it down with two big swigs of her Night Train. She took one more chug of her alcohol and sealed the half-empty bottle and laid it beside her. She finished by lighting a cigarette out of her pack and took a long drag.

Usually Peaches would've been in a haste to turn a trick, however, she was enjoying herself. Plus, the Hispanic males were cool, and she loved being around cool people. They were all standing in their boxers and briefs, which, by then, were fitting waaay too snug to hold in their thoroughly aroused manhood by the time Peaches finished her cigarette.

As if she were a martial arts pro, Peaches placed her open hand in front of her with her fingers together and beckoned the tres amigos on. They stared at her nervously while hastily taking off their underwear, then looked at each other briefly, probably wondering who was going to do what and when.

Peaches, meanwhile, watched them standing there, then her eyes dropped down to their penises which consumed her full attention. The lady had no shame. She then took out another cigarette and started smoking. She was feeling good and enjoying all that man-meat in front of her eyes, and the amigos uttered a few words, mostly in Spanish. That didn't phase Peaches, because she wasn't paying any attention to anything above their hips. Raul was filled with lust as he admired her fabulous body and suddenly jerked off as the other two followed suit.

As Peaches was smoking her cigarette, she felt the pill inside of her making a tingling sensation that worked its way up to her spine and electrified her entire body. This enhanced the enjoyment of her cigarette. She was ten times as horny as a bitch in heat. She put out the cigarette on the Night Train bottle and flicked it away, then hastily crawled over and engulfed Raul's swollen penis in her hungry mouth. This caused the other two to jerk off more intensely as they enjoyed their private show. The macho that he was, Raul started laughing, holding her head in his hands.

"*Es muy bueno,*" he exclaimed, then sipped his beer.

Peaches moved her head away from his penis, then started jerking it with her left hand as she turned her attention to Juan's penis and started devouring it, her hunger no less abated by the hors d'oeuvre she had just sampled. Juan was amazed how talented Peaches was.

Not to leave anyone unattended, the lady of the night then reached her right hand over and massaged Ricardo's huge testicles and gave him a hand job. Her mouth had engulfed Juan's penis, which was definitely the biggest of the three, then she paused and motioned for Juan to lie down in the center of the bed. By virtue of his size, he was to have the position of honor. She then kissed his penis with much love, then grabbed it and inserted it inside of her.

Like a master choreographer, Peaches then pointed to Raul and commanded him to come over and lie beside Juan, who was moaning by now. She then put his penis in her mouth and started pleasing him orally in slow motion.

Ricardo was still standing there, masturbating with a lusty smile spread across his face, guzzling his beer. Peaches would have made a damn fine Marine. She firmly believed in leaving no man behind. She then motioned towards him and used her index finger to direct him behind her. He instantly finished his beer and jumped in place. He knew how to obey promptly. Peaches spread her butt cheeks wide by opening them with her two hands, and then tapped at her anus with her middle finger.

Ricardo laughed merrily, every ounce of his body intent on obeying the command just issued to him like a good soldier. He inserted his stiff penis inside her anus and sank in as far as possible. She then pumped until she had Ricardo's and Juan's penis going in and out with perfect rhythm. She was in bliss and felt herself gyrating. Still hungry, she gobbled up Raul's penis with fresh vigor, which only intensified until she shivered and dropped herself on Juan.

The three amigos laughed wildly and conversed rapidly in Spanish until Juan interrupted with a howl as he ejaculated in Peaches. He then grabbed her legs and squeezed her firm, tight cheeks, praying she would have mercy on him. However, she didn't. She just became more intense.

Shortly after that, Ricardo pulled out of Peaches, stroked his penis twice, and ejaculated on her back. She felt the hot, trickling sensation on her skin and prayed he'd rub it in.

She was disappointed when he didn't. Peaches slowed down on the rhythm of her oral sex so Raul wouldn't climax in her, but it was too late. He'd already start ejaculating. She opened her mouth to allow Raul's fluids to ooze down on him while staring at the porn flick, wishing she was the woman in the movie having that massive manhood pounding in and out of her.

5 *Keisha*

Keisha drove into the West Mountain Shopping Plaza and parked in front of Enterprise Car Rental. She surveyed the plaza and thought how convenient it was for her that the shopping center had a Chinese restaurant and a Pro Hair beauty salon in it. When she entered Enterprise Rental, a flirtatious male sales representative greeted her.

After filling out her personal information on a form, the sales representative inquired how she would be paying.

"Cash."

"That will be a $250 deposit since you're not using a credit card. What size car?" the sales rep asked.

"An SUV."

"That will be $75 a day, plus insurance."

Keisha decided to get the car for one week, with an option for her to rent the vehicle another week. He told her she was eligible for the weekly special of $495 plus tax and her deposit and she agreed. Next, the sales rep asked her what type of insurance she would like, either liability, which was seven dollars per day, or full coverage at $23 per day. Keisha requested the full coverage. With all the extra money Cat had given her, she felt like money was no problem.

"By the way, we do not take cash or checks. You'll have to go across the street to Chevron to get a money order for $764.05."

He assured her that her paperwork would be processed by the time she got back.

Within twenty minutes, Keisha drove across the street and purchased the money order for $1,000. When she returned to the rental car office with her money order, the sales rep processed her paperwork. She noticed the look of respect the man held for her when he saw she'd returned with the money order. *Yeah, that's my man, Cat, looking out for me,* she thought smugly.

"You're a woman of your word," the young man said. "Step this way."

As she followed him, he pushed the door, holding it open for her.

Keisha watched him out of the corner of her eye as he admired her well-rounded rear end as she passed by him. She knew she was looking good. Out of habit, she wore her clothes in a seductive manner. The end of her butt cheeks hung out of the bottom of her shorts like two, sweet, ripe cantaloupes.

He then passed alongside her and led her to two mid-size SUVs, a platinum-gray Cherokee and a midnight-blue Dodge Durango. Without deliberating, she confidently chose the bigger Dodge Durango.

"Good choice," the sales rep said with a charming smile. "Now, all we have to do is a thorough inspection of the vehicle to make sure there is no damage and if there is, please point it out."

Keisha inspected the outside and inside. She pointed out a few small scratches on the passenger-side bumper, which he circled on a drawing of the vehicle on his form. "Okay, the gas tank is full. Let's get your keys and you're finished."

When they went inside, he handed her a copy of her paperwork and the pink copy as well. "You have to have the car back by June 6," he informed her politely, handing her the keys.

Keisha nodded her head. She walked over to the Regal and retrieved everything she thought she was going to need, or that someone might steal. She decided to leave her car in the parking lot.

Then she walked over to the Durango, pressed the keyless entry, and climbed in. Once inside, she plopped into the driver's seat and placed her CD holder in the middle console.

Next, she reached over, placed her detachable CD face in the glove compartment, and laid her purse next to her. After she started the vehicle, she took out a CD labeled "Juvenile 400 Degreez" and put it in the CD player.

When the music came on, she turned the volume on high and flipped on and maxed out the air conditioner. Adjusting the steering wheel so she could see properly, Keisha put the truck in drive and drove over to the Chinese food restaurant. Once inside, she was greeted by an Asian lady who handed her a menu.

"Smoking or nonsmoking?"

"Takeout, please."

The lady took out a pad. "What would you like?"

Keisha took a moment to look over the menu. The restaurant was very quiet; apart from the two people in the back, it was empty. But the restaurant was elegant. The interior design was decorated with gold and red Chinese embroidered walls. Keisha strolled her finger down the menu and ordered chicken wings with pork fried rice.

"I would like some beef and broccoli with white rice," she added. "Also, please give me your seafood combo and some large french fries." Keisha knew how much Cat loved french fries. She also ordered eight snow crabs and some sweet and spicy shrimp that she loved so much, then paid the lady $52.

She stepped next door to the Pro Hair Beauty Salon and Training School for Beauticians, entered the salon, and approached the receptionist at the front desk. The lady smiled.

"Welcome to Pros. I'm Susan. How may I help you today, ma'am?"

Keisha replied that she wanted a manicure and pedicure, as well as a perm and a touch-up on her split ends. She also wanted her hair dyed black, accented by blue highlights on the tips. Lastly, she also requested a facial.

Keisha glanced around and noticed that the salon was fairly empty. A group of stylishly dressed women stood around chitchatting. Only three clients in the spacious salon made the place appear deserted. The hair styling section alone had 27 empty chairs. The ten spas for the manicure and pedicure were completely unoccupied.

The desk clerk called over three beauticians and introduced them to Keisha. "This is Diane, Carla, and Stacey. They will be your stylists for today. Your cost will be $275. Please return to the front desk when you finish with your treatment. Thank you."

After the treatment, Keisha gazed in the mirror in front of her. The stylist held up a mirror behind her for her to see the back. As she studied herself in the mirror, Keisha marveled at how beautiful she looked.

"How do you like it?" Carla asked.

"A'ight."

Enjoying her new look, Keisha stood up, strolled confidently to the front desk, and paid her bill. At the front desk, Susan complimented her, "You look so beautiful."

Susan took the $300, gave the change to Keisha, and handed her a card saying in a voice dripping with sex appeal, "Thank you. You have a great day and please come back soon."

Keisha lowered her eyelids, then returned Susan's stare. She sighed a little, then left.

She went back next door, picked up her order of Chinese food, then climbed into the truck, where she placed the take-out bag on the passenger seat, being as gentle as possible not to damage her freshly done acrylic nails. As she started the ignition, the loud music came on, so she turned it down, ejected the CD, and replaced it with Mary J. Blige's *My Life*. She turned the volume to a low frequency and began her journey.

Keisha waited at the red light, vibing to the music playing on the surround sound. She thought to herself that Cat more than likely was going to need some beverages and cigars, so after the light turned green, she drove to a package store that she knew would not ID her. She pulled up at Bib's Packaging right next to the Chevron and parked.

When she climbed down, Keisha was greeted with howls and whistles of appreciation from the males hanging out in the parking lot. One man approached her, but she made haste and entered the store before he got to her. He was persistent, however, and entered the store behind her in hot pursuit, asking her many questions, but she paid him no attention as she walked over and picked up a bottle of Hennessey, a liter of cranberry juice, and a liter of Coca-Cola. She handed those items to the man who was pestering her with questions, who she had been ignoring, and flashed a magnificent smile.

The stranger gladly helped her and smiled back, revealing four sparkling upper gold teeth. By then, she had made her way to the counter and asked the clerk for a box of Dutch Masters cigars. The clerk added up the price, totaling $22.20. She took the money out of her small Daisy Duke's pants pocket and handed him $25.

"I need to see some ID," the clerk told her.

"Mine's in the truck," Keisha sighed. Suddenly she looked over to the man standing beside her. She gazed longingly in his eyes and smiled.

He graciously obliged, retrieved his wallet from his back pocket, and handed his ID to the package store clerk. "It's for me," he lied.

The clerk viewed the man's ID and quickly glanced at his manager who was watching them. The clerk paused, but handed the ID back to its owner, handed the stranger the bottles, and gave him two dollars and fifty cents in change.

Like a gentleman, the stranger carried her bag back to her vehicle. Keisha pushed the keyless entry and climbed in, switching on the air. For a moment, she sat with the driver door open. The man then handed her the bag and asked for her number.

"I don't even have a phone," she lied.

"How you going to be looking that good and don't have a phone?"

"I'm living with my mom, and she's very strict."

"Well, here's my number. Call me sometime. I can take you out or something." He handed her a piece of paper.

"I will." She grabbed the number, slammed her door, and drove off.

Once out of the parking lot, she uttered to herself, "That bastard kept my change!" She crumbled up the paper and tossed his number out the window.

Next, she accelerated, sending the engine into overdrive. The Durango rocketed forward with a minute whistling of the engine, launching her chariot straight forward to Highway 78.

By the time Keisha arrived back at the room, it was already nightfall. The hotel parking lot was packed with cars and all the rooms where now filled with occupants getting their weekend groove on. When she reached the room with the two bags in her hand, she could hear loud music floating from her room so she kicked the door repeatedly so that Cat could hear her knocking.

STARTLED, CAT WAS frightened by the loud knock at the door. He placed the large Ziploc bag of cocaine in the nightstand drawer and left it open. Next, he picked up his pistol that he kept beside him, turned off the TV, and with revolver in hand, he cautiously crept to the door. Peering through the peephole, he was quite surprised to see a stunning-looking Keisha smiling like he had never seen before.

She was about to put the bags down and use the room key when the door flew open. Cat stood in front of her with a pistol in his hand. Right away, she recognized how much he looked like a zombie. His eyes had a vacant look, like a deer's eyes would reflecting a speeding motorist's headlight just before it got struck by 4,000 pounds of metal at a velocity of 60 miles per hour.

She stepped in front of him, planted a kiss on his numb face, and walked right past him. He stood there, robotlike, before he placed the "Do not disturb" sign on the outside of the door and closed it behind Keisha. Making his way back to the spot on the bed where he had been sitting, he reached down, took out a beautiful bud of marijuana, and began to crush it up on top of the nightstand.

Keisha placed the cigars and the bottle of liquor right next to where he was crushing his herbs. As she looked down in the drawer, she noticed a large Ziploc bag of marijuana and a large Ziploc bag filled with cocaine, next to a very large sum of cash. Her eyes opened in amazement at the sight.

Slowly, she stripped naked in front of Cat, exposing a flat abdomen and a nice, athletic, sleek body. Her full breasts were perky and her nipples stood straight forward at attention. Seductively, she turned around to sashay over to the Chinese food. As she glanced in the mirror, she saw Cat admiring her round, firm, cantaloupe rear. She bent over and took out the food, scanning through the box until she found the beef with broccoli and white rice, pausing long enough to allow Cat to focus on her hot, plump vagina. Then she sat on the bed and began to eat out of the boxes with a plastic white fork.

After a few bites, Keisha went to the bathroom for a couple of paper cups. The bathroom mirror captivated her as she admired her naked figure. She bent her wrist forward to examine her nails, then gently ran her hands over her hair that framed her pretty face. Satisfied with what she saw, Keisha turned the lights off and went to the small fridge next to the dresser in front of the bed with a microwave on top of it. She opened the refrigerator door, reached in the small freezer compartment, and retrieved an ice tray. Luckily, the tray had some ice cubes in it.

She put ice in both cups, brought them over to the nightstand, and poured some Hennessey over the ice and left them on the table. She then went over to the bags, took out the beverages, and opened up the cranberry juice. After pouring some in her cup, she placed the Coca-Cola in the miniature fridge, returned to the bed, and sat down. More relaxed now, she took a sip and gazed over at Cat, who was lighting up his blunt. He blew out a heavy cloud of smoke in her direction.

"Two niggas called for you today." He threw the cell phone beside her.

Ordinarily, Keisha ignored her phone. She proved that again by tossing it aside, ate a little bit more, then placed the remainder of her uneaten food in the refrigerator. But she gulped all her drink, then fixed herself another glass. After drinking about half of it, she decided to take a shower. She picked up a towel, wrapped it around her head, then walked over to Cat, took the blunt, and walked into the bathroom.

The blunt was between her lips as she fastened the tip of the towel under the wrap around her head. Then she then stood in front of the mirror, smoking it in an elegant fashion, like a seductress in a Humphrey Bogart film. Keisha liked what she saw as she admired her sleek body. It was a body to make a man die for. After a couple of more hits, she took the blunt back to Cat, walking like a queen. She handed him the blunt and disappeared back to the bathroom, picked up the complimentary bar of Dial soap, and stepped in the steaming shower.

Because she didn't want to ruin her makeup, she stood in the rear of the shower stall. Using her hands, she lathered up the bar of soap as the water beat off her firm, erect nipples and cascaded down her ebony body.

By now, she had the bar of soap quite foamy and placed it between her legs. Slowly, totally enjoying the sensations, she gently caressed her vagina, her clitoris, back from her vagina lips up to her anus. Wonderful, exotic thoughts burned in her mind as she focused on the pleasure of her tingling clitoris. Yeaaa, she was digging this. Turning around, she spread her butt cheeks wide, allowing the water to flow freely down the crevice of her rear.

Now, Keisha leaned forward and let the warm water rinse off the suds on her vagina. Her abdomen was next to receive a lathered massage with soap foam, then she worked her way up to her cleavage. As she thought about her man in the next room waiting for her, she lathered her erect breasts in a circular motion, paused to enjoy the sensation from her self-stimulation, then continued working her soapy hands up her neck, down her shoulders, and over her arms.

Not forgetting her back and hips, she then worked her way down those ballerina legs, hard calves, dainty feet, and between those slender toes. Finished, she placed the soap in the built-in soap slot on the wall, stepped forward enough to allow the water to drizzle on her neck, and rinsed her body.

Wanting to make sure that every inch of her was totally rinsed, she lifted one of her feet and placed it on the protruding ledge of the shower wall so her legs would be spread wide open and her vaginal area was projected frontward. Again, she experienced erotic tingling sensations as the water pounded against her clitoris and ran down the curvets of her legs.

Then cupping her palms, she used her hands to finish rinsing her vagina and anus thoroughly. Now fully rinsed, she stepped out of the rear of the shower, turned the faucet off, and was ready for whatever came next.

She dried herself and picked up the complementary bottle of baby oil, opened it, and squeezed, but nothing came out. So she removed the top and used her teeth to pull off the seal of the miniature bottle. As though performing a ritual, Keisha slowly poured some oil into her palm and gently caressed it into her soft moist skin, feeling her open pores absorbing every delicious, scented drop. Not only did she want to feel good, she also wanted her man to enjoy and be aroused with every place his hands would touch on her body.

Once her body was marinating in the perfumed oil, she placed the tip of her finger onto her lips, then rubbed her lips together, transforming them into a glossy, thick softness that would invite Cat's lips to greet them with wild abandon. Keisha was ready to rock and roll.

Cat sat with his back against the wall, pistol beside him, and a large bag of cocaine in his lap. He rolled a hundred-dollar bill into a shovel with the end of the bill twisted to hold its formation in place. It seemed as if he were in deep meditation, staring into the future.

Then he snapped back and took another snort of the white powder through his right nostril. He felt the numbing sensation crawling down his throat and snorted twice again, even more deeply. Not satisfied, he reached for the Hennessey and took a big swig. Wanting to bring his high down a notch or two, he picked up the blunt in the ashtray next to him and lit it. With hungry, twinkling eyes, he stared through the hazy smoke at Keisha, still nude, standing in front of the mirror, playing with her hair. Her body fascinated and turned him on.

"Hey, baby, comes take a bump of this cocaine."

His eyes roamed and locked onto her swollen vagina. He could feel his manhood becoming hard. Lusty thoughts began to fill his head. Even from a backside view when her legs were spread apart, her vagina was magnificent. It reminded him of a ripe cherry from the back, plump and ready to eat. He was getting hungrier by the moment.

Keisha sensed his desire. She turned around and slowly walked towards him, almost seeming to float on air. His erection was getting harder. She climbed on the bed and rested her head on his shoulder. Getting turned on herself, she placed a hand on his sweating stomach and massaged his sweat around his chest and stomach region.

Cat put the scooper back in the bag, then held it to her nostril so she could sniff the small hill into her nose, which she did with the skilled suction force of a tornado.

Then she took the scooper from him, knelt down by his side over the bag of drugs, dipped in, and took a snort in each nostril. Her eyes opened wide and rolled to the back of her head as the cocaine hit her brain. Numbness crept down her throat. She scooped another portion of the coke, extended her tongue forward, and sprinkled the snowy powder on it. Then she glided her tongue over her teeth and sucked down like the reaction you get after eating a grapefruit. Yummy.

Cat picked up the remote from beside him and pressed power. When the TV came on playing a Young Jeezy tune, he began slightly bouncing his shoulders and bopping his head, similar to the bobble head car ornaments that people put on their dashboard.

Keisha gazed at him, feeling happy because her man was feeling happy and feeling good because he was feeling good. She picked up the bag of coke from off his lap and placed it on the night table next to him, along with the shoveling utensil. Crouching down, she rested her head on Cat's firm stomach with her buttocks up in the air. She was feeling it.

In one fluid motion, she had unbuttoned his pants, zipped them open, and pushed them down almost to his knees. Then she pulled down his boxers, releasing his swollen dick looking like a rocket ready to launch and his plum-size cojones. She gently played with them as she then lay on her side with her head on his stomach. Like a serpent, her tongue shot out and she began licking the tiny hole on his dick where urine comes from, rubbing it with the back of her tongue. Like a pro, she curled her tongue backwards around his penis head and squeezed it. Keisha had nice moves.

She kept a nice rhythm going while watching a music video. Cat held his blunt over the ashtray. He was having difficulty taking a pull on it because all his attention was drawn to the center of his body. He thought he knew all the tricks of the trade, but Keisha definitely had taught him a few pointers and he wanted to experience more under her expert tutelage.

He slid his hand between her warm legs and inserted his fingers in her hot, moist vagina. Cat probed deep. He was feeling it. He tried to relax, but the sexual tension was rapidly building into a crescendo. He leaned his head back, faced the ceiling, and sighed. That released all the tension of his soul. *Bliss.*

"Don't stop, babe."

Keisha nodded. She had no intention of doing so.

Chapter 6

Ricky

I woke up to my cell phone ringing again, and the screen indicated I'd missed 23 calls. The screen proclaimed it was Keisha.

"Yeah," I answered.

"What's happenin', mane?" the male voice responded.

It was Mark, a comrade I knew from Shamrock High School.

"Yeah," I said with fatigue punctuating my words.

"Mane, you still asleep? It's almost two p.m. I need some work—pronto."

"What you need?"

"A bird (kilo of cocaine)."

Now *this* revived me. "A whole chicken, huh?"

"Yeah, shawty, I'm trying to get this for my homeboy."

"Let me come and talk to you in person because we over the wire."

"I'm at the Holiday Inn, off Lavista, Room B635," Mark said.

"'Ight. Let me take a shower. I'll be there in an hour."

Looking around, I realized Lisa wasn't in bed. I heard the shower running and figured she must be in there. I picked up my blunt, put it in my mouth, and sparked it up. That was followed by a deep inhale on my first drag and a slow, prolonged exhale. Finding the remote, I turned on the television. Fox 5 News had a breaking news report about some police officers named Malone and Williams being gunned down in Highland Apartments on Ponce de Leon. *Daayum. That's up the street from where I live. As if things aren't bad enough around here as it is.* The news broadcast went back to daytime TV, and I changed the channel to CNN Headline News. The gas prices were going up as usual and another soldier was blown up by a suicide bomber.

I could not understand why someone would risk his life meaninglessly for a piece of foreign soil. *Patriotic idiots.* Then a speech came on by the commander in chief, informing the American people that we're making great progress and we will win the war against terrorism. That canned speech we've heard hundreds of times.

Now I'm sitting here, thinking the president illegally cheated his way into office. Created a diversion to stop the investigation of his ill-gotten victory with the orchestrated plot of flying American Airlines jets into the monument that symbolized worldwide democratic unity, a landmark of the world—the World Trade Center. Next, he pointed a finger at a guy his family had a relationship with and rivalry against.

People are so occupied with their own selfish, capitalistic mentality that they don't even realize we are all about to be eliminated to start a new world order. Now, I thought, this guy has the whole world about to erupt in war and never even threw a punch in his life. I smoked a little more, finished watching the president's speech, then turned off the TV. Enough.

Stretching and standing, I walked into the bathroom and slid the shower door open. Lisa looked at me, smiling gently. Taking that as an invitation, I stepped in behind her and admired her big round ass. She turned around and started lathering my body with lilac-scented body wash. She started with my behind cheeks, then swiftly moved down to my penis. She lathered me up well, and the sensation gave me an erection. Her face lightened up and her lower body began wiggling like a belly dancer side to side in slow motion. I rotated with her and positioned her facing the wall as I bent her in a ninety degree angle, with the shower water beating off my back and sprinkling on her rear end. I bent down and pushed my dick in her pussy. It sank deep inside her tight vagina, and she turned to look at me in the face.

She flashed me an "I can't believe you feel so good inside of me" expression on her face. I was feeling such intense satisfaction that I went into a trance with both hands stretched flat on the wall. I pumped fast—hard—feeling her tight pussy squeezing on my dick.

I could feel the bottom of her pussy walls every time I pushed my dick deep inside of her. She looked back at me and fell into a sexual trance and started pumping back fiercely. I increased the tempo as she opened her mouth wide and started panting like she was on the brink of dying from dehydration in the midst of a waterfall.

My tempo increased more, sending my dick launching deeper inside of her. By now, Lisa quivered hard, her knees buckled, her legs were about to give way. So I took my hands off the sides of her ass and positioned one hand under her pelvis with my fingers rubbing her clit, raising her hips up, keeping her in position. I then grabbed hold of her long, curly, Indian hair, and thrust my dick into her with all my might.

She was screaming, quivering, and panting. French words came from her mouth. I was on the verge of cumming. Then it blew. I nutted inside of her, then continued to slowly stroke in her a few more times as she kept on repeating, "Thank you, thank you."

She turned around, sighed deeply, and yelled, "Thank you, God." Looking well pleased, she gave me a kiss and disappeared out of the shower. After she left out, I lathered my body up once again and could hear Lisa yell, "What you want to eat?"

"Two turkey sandwiches," I yelled back. "I'm in a rush."

Stepping out of the shower, I turned off the water, grabbed a towel, and dried off. In the bedroom, I put on the same clothes I had on the day before. Yushua boxers, Yushua pants, and a Yushua tank top.

Using one of my locks, I tied my dreadlocks into a ponytail, stepped over to the dresser, and devoured my two turkey sandwiches. Nothing like a morning workout to make a man hungry. Lisa had been staring at me ever since I left the restroom and now she made her way to bed, still staring. I think she was still hungry. The girl had a healthy appetite. She could keep a man busy.

I went to the night table and picked up my 28-inch, white gold, double Cuban link chain with the Warner Brothers brain pendant and put it on over my head, grabbed my Presidential Sinclair watch, and put it on. While Lisa was kneeling erect on the side of the bed, I bent over and gave her a kiss. Like a shameless nympho, she began unzipping my pants, but I hopped back.

"I have to go."

Reluctantly, she got up, went to her pocketbook, and took out her car keys. "Your car burns too much gas," she said, handing me the keys. She was right. I took her keys, kissed her again, then left, placing my blunt in my mouth.

I stepped outside into a magnificent sunny day, the sky saturated with color. Catlike, I stretched and pulled in the warmth of the summer air, then stepped over to my ride, a black Pontiac Catalina 455 convertible with a creamy white top and matching interior. It was sitting on some 22-inch deep dish gold Sprewells that were gleaming in the sun.

I used the keyless entry to open the door and took out my CD case and my P 89 automatic, 9mm, 17-round handgun. It tucked nicely in my waist under my tank top. I pressed the start button. My baby cranked up instantly. Then I then hit the button again and went over to Lisa's BMW x5 4.8, hit the keyless entry, and hopped in.

I started the Beemer and ejected the Jill Scott CD out of the CD player, then popped in "Project Pat Ghetty Green." My cell phone went into Lisa's charger since she'd bought two cell phones for the price of one and gave me one. Driving out of Cinnamon Ridge Apartments, I took a right on Franklin Road. A Marietta police officer sped up behind me, ran my tag, saw it was clear, and drove off. When I got to 285, I got on heading eastbound.

It took me 20 minutes to get back to the Eastside, then I exited on Memorial Drive, took a right, made a quick left on Northern, took another left on North Decatur, and then pulled into my apartment. Brookside.

The drug traffic was busy as usual, and young girls were out whoring right alongside crackheads, who were willing to do anything, no matter how degrading, for money. I think of Mahatma

Gandhi who said, "Poverty is the worst type of violence to place on a man," and he was surely right.

No one recognized me until it was too late, so I made it through without the usual flock rushing my car. These were the boys who were desperate to make a sale of crack, then go snort it right back up with coke. Many sell the high to get a high; a lot of them were selling narcotics, robbing, killing, pimping, and taking penitentiary chances for fun. These people had a negative impact on the environment. Absconding the law has become a lifestyle and the national pastime. You're a pimp, a player, or a thug; if not, on the contrary, you're lame and just not cool.

I pulled up in front of my apartment in Building G, hearing loud music. It was 2Pac Shakur's, "Shorty Wanna be a Thug." The tune was ending, then was replaced by 2Pac Shakur's, "No More Pain."

As I opened the door, I saw my roommate and longtime comrade on the couch with a little young girl under him, her legs spread wide apart. She looked at me in discomfort. However, my comrade looked at me with contentment. He held the stereo remote in his hand, while at the same time, he held her legs spread wide apart. He was fucking the dog shit out of her. I ran upstairs to my room. Only two rooms in the three-bedroom apartment were occupied, mine and Lucky's.

Lucky and I went way back from my group home years. No matter what, he always had my back. Even though he was 6 foot 5 and weighed in at 235 pounds, he was a decent, sociable, charismatic character. We were totally opposites—except for the fact we were both hustlers. He was careless and unambiguous. He spent all his money on enjoyment. However, he had never been a traitor or disobeyed me. He was loyal and trustworthy—except when it came to women. He had to fuck them all.

I unlocked my bedroom door. There were so many whores in and out of here, I had to put a master lock on my bedroom door. The entire hood knew I was doing good. I made sure of this.

First checking to see that everything was the way I left it, I entered my room and closed the door. My closet was filled with brand-new clothes from Akademiks to Yushua. Shoes and sneakers were scattered all over my room, and boxes of footwear were stacked on my closet floor and shelf. I located one of the center boxes, took it off the shelf, and placed it on the bed, the only furniture in my room. My TV I got from a crackhead for a quarter ounce of crack. It was a Phillips flat screen TV mounted on the wall. My other TV I gave to Lucky to put in his bedroom.

I opened the shoebox and took out a quarter key of coke, closed the box up, left it on the bed, and left the room, locking the door behind me.

When I returned to the front room, Lucky was fully dressed from the waist down and the lady was still lying in the same position, with one leg draped on the upper part of the couch and her other, on the ottoman. Her knee was bent.

She was smoking a Newport and looking at me with admiration. Lucky was using his fingers, playing around with her pussy and talking to her. There was still a hole shaped like a donut in her pussy. She was petite and cute with a nice brown body and wore long, braided extensions. Unfortunately, her lips were way too big for her face, but her Siamese cat eyes were really sexy. If she wasn't so young, I would date her. She looked 16, but I know she's only 13 by the look in her eyes.

I was on my way out the door when Lucky holla'd at me. "Hey, cuz, I need some more work."

"Do you have any money?" I asked.

He reached in his pocket and gave me $600. That was all I charged him for an ounce. I took the money and told him he'd have to wait until I came back. The lady looked at me with even greater admiration. I just shook my head and walked out, put the dope in the brown paper bag under my passenger seat, and started the car up. The engine purred, I reversed, and pulled off.

When I reached room B635, I knocked. Cat opened the door and gave me some dap. I dapped him back, reluctantly. He turned and walked back inside, so I followed him in and closed the door. Cat sat on the bed, but I sat on the front of the dresser, next to the TV, with my feet firm on the floor.

"Yeah, I have a nigga that wants me to get him a whole key of coke," Cat said. "Yeah, yeah, and a pound of that LA confident Kush.

"I could have used my money, bought the dope, and brought it to him, but why risk the chance at my expense?"

"Yeah," Ricky nodded.

"How much that's going to run your boy?"

"Just give me twenty-five stacks. I'll have it for you in half an hour."

Cat took thirty stacks out his pocket, counted off five, and put those back in his pocket. I went over and checked the one-hundred dollar bills to see if they were real. *Damn, they were real.* Then I lifted up my shirt and pulled out the brown paper bag from my trousers, revealing my 9mm. When Cat saw my gun, he hesitated, then looked as if he was going to grab his .38 lying beside him.

"Be cool, baby, it's all love," I told him to ease his tension.

I pulled out the powder from the brown paper bag and handed it to him. "Now, look," I began, "that's nine ounces. I'll be back with 27 ounces and your pound of Kush in half an hour."

I gathered the money and counted it. I could tell Cat was trying to read me for deceit. However, I was used to people fearing me for my size and demeanor.

I stood, straight-faced, with a confident expression, put the money in my pocket, and exited the room. On my way to the car, I began to ponder what would make Cat trust me with $25,000 of someone else's money. Either he figured I could rob him and take it, or he just don't give a fuck.

Either way, I respect it. I have a motto: never betray trust and never underestimate the little guy.

Soon, I arrived at Stone Mountain's Vineyard subdivision and entered Vineyard Circle, pulled up to 994, and parked in the driveway. I swiftly went through the side gate and made my way to the back. When I reached the side door of the cabin, I knocked.

Popi was sitting on his fluffy cushion watching old reruns of *The Three Stooges.* My knocking interrupted him. He peeked, saw it was me, then opened up his door and let me in.

"How you doing, partner?" was how he always greeted me. I nodded and placed $20,000 on the table.

I told him what I needed. Popi took the money and entered the house via the connecting passageway. After a few minutes, he came back to the cabin and handed me a grocery bag. I checked it. Everything was good, so I left.

"Be easy, partner," he said, as I went through the door. I entered the car and put my package under the passenger seat.

Then I drove north on Memorial Drive until I saw the Starship, an adult entertainment and tobacco accessory and novelty shop. The parking lot was near-empty. I parked and entered the shop where I was briefly identified and permitted to look around. I knew exactly what I came for. I went to the counter and ordered a large bottle of isotope and paid the clerk $35. With no time to waste, I left, jumped in my vehicle, and headed to my apartment only three minutes up the street.

I arrived at my location, jumped out with my bag, and scanned the area to make sure no one was around or close enough to ambush me. You can't trust nobody nowadays. I opened the door, walked in, locked it behind me, ran up the stairs, unlocked my door, and entered. Then I took my trusty scale out of my shoebox and put it on top of the box. After turning it on, I reached under my bed and pulled out a Timberland box with no top on it. It was filled with bags.

Quickly I pulled out a Ziploc sandwich bag and opened the bag with the block in it, broke off a chuck, and placed it in another Ziploc sandwich bag. Next, I put it on the scale. It weighed 7.7 ounces. I broke a piece more off the large block and put it into the sandwich bag. 9.5 ounces. I threw the 9.5 ounces in the shoebox, readjusted the scale, and put the 'Dro on the scale in measures of 16.8.

I took out six grams and left 16.2, give or take two grams for the bag. Then I took three sandwich bags and weighed out an ounce for each bag and tied a knot at the end of the sandwich bags. After that, I put the block on the scale. It weighed 24.8. I opened the bottle of isotope and poured some in the Ziploc with the three-fourths of a block until the scale read 27.8. I shook and broke up some cocaine into large, still-solid fragments, then put it in the grocery bag with the pound of hydro.

Finally, I put the three ounces in my pocket with the half ounce of Kush. After putting everything back in place, I left my room and as I locked the door, I yelled out, "Lucky, where are you?"

He hollered, "I'm in the guest room."

I went there and opened the door, only to see him fucking a fat woman with an Afro. She still wore her T-shirt, and her huge silhouette ass with her thick elephant legs and matching calves were visible. He had her standing up, but bent over, touching the ground, and her face looked like she was about to cry.

Lucky was behind her fucking her from the back. He looked over at me with his thumb and his index finger squeezing his nose shut, while his other hand fanned her ass in a slow side to side motion.

Barely able to contain my laughter, I took an ounce out my pocket and tossed it to him. That's when a skunk odor floated my way and savaged my nostrils. Without a word, I ran downstairs, looked through my window to make sure the course was clear, exited the building, locked the door, and entered the car. I put the bag behind the passenger seat on the floor and looked down at my cell phone. Thirteen missed calls. Three customers and ten calls from Keisha's number.

I called back.

Cat answered. "Waddup?"

"Yeah, kinfolk," I said. "I'm on my way."

Chapter 7

Agent Peter Lynch

Detective Turner arrived on the scene as soon as possible in his gray 2003 Crown Victoria. He parked alongside the other law enforcement vehicles that were already on the scene of the bank robbery. The suspects had murdered a young, 24-year-old bank clerk while committing a robbery in Chamblee Tucker. They'd escaped with $75,000 from a Nation's bank inside of Kroger.

The suspects, Jerome Piece and Paul Goodman, also forced the Kroger general manager to open the store vault. After the manager handed them $23,000 in cash, they shot him with a .357 Magnum they'd stolen off the security guard at the back entrance. The two madmen continued their robbing spree at a McDonald's drive-through window. There, they robbed the clerk for $115 out of her register and stole a carry-out bag of french fries and all the burgers she could throw in it.

Jerome Piece, 23 years old, had been discharged from the United States Marine Corps for experimenting with delusional psychotropic drugs. He came back to his native home of Atlanta and teamed up with Paul Goodman, a 17-year-old gang-involved high-school dropout. Paul had been in and out of trouble with the law since he was nine years old, when he committed arson by setting his elementary school on fire. The two Atlanta natives were said to be armed and extremely dangerous.

Law enforcement had a lead that the two bank robbers were hiding out on Hillandale Drive in Lithonia, Georgia, at Jerome

Piece's, a.k.a. K-9's, baby mama's house with Paul Goodman, a.k.a. Mack 10.

Detective Turner parked, got out of his car, and motioned towards where the other law enforcement officers were standing in a circle, strategizing their arrest tactic. He unbuttoned and removed his dress shirt. A police officer ran up to him with a Federal-issued, bulletproof vest and handed it to him. Once he reached the group of officers, the other enforcement officers started formally introducing themselves.

"Detective Turner, I'm glad you could make it. I'm FBI Special Agent Peter Lynch, and this is FBI Special Agent Sam Roberts. We have had this house under surveillance for 2 days, and we believe that the suspects are hiding out at this location." He pointed at a one-level, two-bedroom house half a mile down the hill from where they were congregated in a circle.

"We'll move in 10 minutes," Lynch said, looking at his Seiko kinetic watch.

Detective Turner walked quickly to his Crown Victoria, opened the driver-side door, made sure his bulletproof vest was secure, and retrieved his Smith & Wesson 9mm automatic handgun that was in a clip on a holster, and fixed it on the center of his lower back. He then reached in again and popped open the trunk of his car. He made his way to the back and retrieved a brown Mossberg pump-action shotgun.

Next to his car was Officer Parker, who was holding a paper in his hand. Detective Turner looked over his shoulder with his hand resting on the top of the open trunk to acknowledge Officer Parker's briefing.

"Sir, we have got a response from our people in North Carolina. It seems the Mercedes-Benz, license plate number AMG 356, was registered to a Marvin Brown of 358 Lyon St. Charlotte, North Carolina. However, our investigation found out no one lived there by that name." Parker handed Detective Turner a sheet of paper with a colored photocopy of the suspect's North Carolina driver's license.

Detective Turner slammed the trunk shut and took a moment to scan over the bald-headed individual on the photocopy. Then he looked up to see the Channel 5 News van park at the end of the barricaded street.

"Parker, what the hell are they doing here? Stop them from going any further."

"Yes sir," Officer Parker responded and rapidly complied. Accom-panied by three U.S. marshals, Detective Turner and the two FBI agents made their way on foot to the suspect's house.

The marshals were also making their way up the opposite side of the street on foot to surround the suspect's location. All officials had their weapons drawn by the time Detective Turner reached the house. Squad cars raced up and parked several cars in front of the suspect's location. After parking, they stormed out of the vehicles and took their positions behind them.

K-9 and Mack 10 were in K-9's baby mama's house. Kim had K-9's baby and usually stayed inside her bedroom with the 3-month-old newborn.

Meantime, K-9 and Mack 10 were sitting on the couch in front of the TV, watching the DVD movie *Belly*, by Hype Williams. Mack 10 took a razor blade and sectioned off a narrow line of cocaine from an ounce piled up like a small hill on a plate mirror. He sectioned the coke into a straight line, then placed one hand over his nostril and faced the plate and sniffed the entire line. After that, he passed the plate over to K-9, who did the same. Mack 10 relaxed and lit up a cigarette. The two had been doing the same routine since they'd become two of America's most wanted.

They holed up in Kim's house and sent Kim and her sister Tasha on errands, but they were back now. America's most wanted spent their money on drugs, DVDs, and guns. The majority of their ill-gotten gain went to their numerous female companions in some way, shape, or form, and these two sisters were lavish spenders. The women had accumulated large quantities of material possessions over the past year and a half, including Kim's small house and her Honda Accord parked in the driveway.

The two comrades were suddenly interrupted when Tasha ran out of the opposite room, stark-naked, and into the living room, directly in front of K-9 and Mack 10. She was jumping up and down. "Police outside! Their comin'! Their comin'!" she shouted hysterically.

K-9 and Mack 10 jumped up from the couch and tossed off the sofa cushions to reveal an AK-47, M-16, a Mossberg pump, and a sawed-off shotgun. K-9 set the plate of powder on the TV, grabbed the AK-47 with its 100-round clip and extra ammunition, along with the sawed-off shotgun.

Mack 10 grabbed the M-16 aligned with his belt and the black Mossberg shotgun. As if to build up his courage, he then placed his entire face in the plate with his nose in the hill of powder and snorted like a charging bull inhaling deeply before he attacked a matador waving a red cape. Then Mack 10 just stood there, as if hypnotized, shook his plaited braids, and ran into the bedroom that Tasha had run from. Meanwhile, K-9 leaned over the plate and tried his best to vacuum every bit of cocaine that remained with his nose.

Detective Turner made his way around the rear of the house with his shotgun hoisted in the air in front of him. He moved in a military-like fashion and kept his back to the wall. The U.S. marshals hit the door with a battering ram and stormed in with Sam Roberts behind them, waving a search warrant in one hand and gun aimed forward in the other hand. Automatic gunfire erupted.

K-9 spun around to the sound of the door crashing open. The marshals had stormed in, firing AR-15s. However, K-9 stood firm, firing a steady flow of bullets on them. He looked like the image from *Scarface*, when Sosa's hit men bombarded Tony Montana's mansion to kill him.

Upon entry, the U.S. marshals were drenched in a hail of bullets that made them immediately retreat. Two of the three marshals sustained gunshot wounds to their arms and legs. In their hasty retreat, they stumbled over Special Agent Roberts, who had been hit by a hail of bullets and shot in his Adam's apple with the round exiting the back of his neck. He had the unfortunate luck to be behind the marshals and became a standing target when they rapidly sidestepped to the walls.

The marshals grabbed Roberts and pulled him out of the house by his vest and dragged him around the corner for safety. Other enforcement agents rushed to Agent Roberts' aid, only to become sitting ducks themselves. They ran back to take position behind their vehicles.

K-9 ran to the door, closed the steel frame door shut, then ran and pushed the couch in front of the door, all done with the swiftness of military precision. With his trim, 215-pound frame, he looked like an Army Ranger.

Mack 10 stood staring out the window in the Malcolm X, "any-means-necessary" famous stance. He had a devil-may-care attitude. Mack 10 saw an enforcement officer shoot at the front of the house. In retaliation, he dropped the Mossberg, smashed the window with the back of his M-16, and open fired.

The law enforcers retreated, ducking low and zigzagging to get the shooter off target. One of them was struck in his hind leg. Mack 10 continued his assault on the agents, moving the target of his rage to the destruction of the squad cars, riddling them with bullet holes and busting their windshields. He punctured a couple of car tires, and then he struck pay dirt. When he hit the gas tank, the squad car violently exploded, sending flames raining down on the frantic, screaming agents. By now, Mack 10 ran out of rounds, so he grabbed his Mossberg.

As agents recklessly scattered to escape the carnage of this gruesome attack, Mack 10 cocked his Mossberg and started picking off visible targets, most of whom were fortunate enough to survive because they were wearing their protective armor. However, Officer Smith was not so fortunate. His head was blasted clean off his body. Officer Brown was hit in his lower torso, which severed his legs from his body.

The law enforcement officers aimed their AR-15s and shotguns on the suspects' location and began firing nonstop rounds into the house. All this gunfire sounded like World War III had just begun.

"Hold your fire! They have hostages," yelled Lynch, using his hand as an amplifier. Detective Turner, leading Special Agent Lynch, made his way from the rear of the house, which had no windows or entrance, to the side, where they could see the suspect squatting and aiming a black Mossberg pump-action shotgun.

Kim ran out of the bedroom with her baby in her arms and got behind K-9. "Honey, stop! They're going to kill our baby," she said, crying.

Gunshots began to engulf the house once again.

"Lay the fuck down!" K-9 shouted.

Tasha was already lying down on the kitchen floor with her hands over her ears and head, still naked. K-9 rose up off the floor and cleared out the glass with the muzzle of his rifle. He fired a few rounds, then reached down beside him and grabbed another hundred-round clip, reloaded, and continued his assault.

All of a sudden, Mack 10 was pricked an instinctive vibe that he was being watched and was in danger. He gazed over to see a baldheaded, stocky man observing him. K-9 whirled around rapidly, aiming his gun, and shots erupted from the Mossberg. Without warning, Mack 10 was hit in his stomach by something that had the impact of a cannon ball. It curved him into the capital letter "C," then laid him out into a lower case "l." By the time it was over, he lay dead with his hands straight over his head.

Hearing gunshots close-by, K-9 stood up and began walking backwards, stepping over his baby mama. While firing rounds in the direction of the police with the sawed-off shotgun in his hand, he ran to the kitchen and snatched Tasha up by her frail neck like a cheetah toppling its prey. He then fastened the sawed-off gun under her chin and motioned to the door.

Tasha and Kim were screaming and crying, "Jerome, please don't!"

K-9 shouted, "Shut up, bitch, or I'll blow your head clean off." He quickly pulled the couch from the door and made an exit. He stepped out with his naked hostage and started making demands, this time standing directly behind Tasha with his hand gripping the side of her neck and the weapon at her temple.

Detective Turner noticed that the assailant had spotted him. Mack 10 lowered his weapon and fired two rounds, then cocked his Mossberg again, discharging a shell.

Detective Turner began to hear the hostage negotiator. Remembering a technique used by a law enforcement agent to apprehend a suspect, he handed Agent Lynch his shotgun. "Give me a boost," he told Agent Lynch.

Holding the shotgun straight across in a dumbbell-curling type manner and in a slight squat, Agent Lynch used the shotgun as a lifting device to elevate Detective Turner onto the roof of the house. Turner slowly and stealthily made his way across the roof. The hostage negotiator, who was already trying to de-escalate the situation, became more reluctant when he noticed Detective Turner closing in on the suspect.

"Please, be calm. We'll give you whatever you want. Just please don't hurt her," the negotiator pleaded.

Tasha stood there shivering, naked, crying silent tears that ran down her cheeks like raindrops. Her limp hands were glued to her wide hips.

"I want for y'all to start that squad car you are standing behind and get the fuck out of here. And if I see one of y'all within a mile of me, I'm gonna kill this bitch."

By now, Turner was close enough to see the suspect's gigantic wild Afro and took aim, making sure he only hit his target and cost no further lives.

"Okay, whatever you want," the negotiating officer said, reaching behind the steering wheel of the open car door, which he was standing in front of. He started the car and began backing up slowly, with his hand in the air. Turner was on the verge of pulling the trigger when the assailant swiftly turned around and fired a round, hitting him under his abdomen area. The sudden impact sent him stumbling off the roof like an electrocuted squirrel on a telephone pole.

The gunshots sent Tasha running away, screaming, "Oh, Lord! Oh, Lord!" her hands shaking wildly in the air like someone possessed by the Holy Spirit in a Pentecostal tent revival while walking barefoot on some hot coals. As soon as she broke free from her captor, the snipers in place immediately start firing upon K-9. Round after round hit K-9. He looked like he was doing a combination of the Harlem Shake and the Electric Slide before his collapse.

The incident that cost four government agents their lives and wounded 13 others was suddenly in the history books. Paramedics rushed Special Agent Roberts into their truck. He later would become paralyzed from the neck down.

Special Agent Lynch ran from the side of the house were he was stooped down holding Detective Turner's rifle and ran to his aid. He knelt down over Detective Turner and encouraged him to hold on; the paramedics were running over.

However, it was too late. The shotgun impact had hit Turner directly under his vest and ruptured his lower intestines.

Special Agent Lynch entered the house to see Kim holding her baby in her arms, kneeling down on the floor. He retrieved a paper from his pocket and handed it to her. "You can place your claim for the $100,000 reward at the agency." He then turned his back on her and walked away.

Blue

8

Blue opened the door to his apartment and walked in to see his brother John sitting on his leather couch, watching the nightly news. Blue marched right by him and headed to his room. He wondered why John wasn't at work.

John, a deliveryman for UPS during the day, usually spent his nights delivering pizza. He worked hard to support him and his little brother, Blue, after their mother died of breast cancer two years earlier.

John was aware of Blue's unlawful activities, but he figured he couldn't stop Blue from what he was doing. He decided he would just give his brother time to mature. After all, John had been a delinquent teen until he was arrested. Following an 8-month sentence, he changed his attitude towards life. He'd been released with a second chance.

In his bedroom, Blue bent down and pulled out his dresser drawer on the bottom right, and scattered his hands through the drawer until he found his screwdriver.

He then went to his closet and grabbed his baseball glove and a black bandanna. Walking to his bed, he lifted up the mattress to reveal a 9mm handgun and $750 in cash. He grabbed the clip and placed it in his back pocket. Blue then quietly made his way to the door, trying not to be noticed by his brother. He crept behind the couch John was sitting on and opened the front door, hoping his older brother would not hear any noise.

"Be careful," John said as Blue opened the door.

Blue acknowledged his brother with a nod of his head downward and continued on his way. He jogged down the hill and out of the entrance of his apartment complex as he wrapped his screwdriver into the bandanna, placed it in his back pocket, and then hurried over to be reunited with his longtime comrade and colleague, Lil' Pee. The two friends met at McLeaden Elementary and had been comrades ever since. Blue had been defending Lil' Pee since he could remember.

Lil' Pee was such a mama's boy back then—that is, before Blue taught him the way of the streets. Blue was the one who enticed Lil' Pee into selling crack. The two began selling dope because everybody around their environment was doing it. So the two adapted to this way of making money because it was profitable. Blue and Lil' Pee first started hustling illegally to support their marijuana habit, but, as time passed, they started getting a better understanding of the business. They began accumulating clothes, sneakers, jewels, weapons, and other things money can buy.

Blue reached the steps where he'd left Lil' Pee. To his surprise, he was not there. *He must be in our trap house,* he thought to himself. Blue went over and tried to open the door.

Yeah, he's in there, Blue was thinking. He ran around to the rear window and began pounding on it like a hammer with his lower fist.

Blue didn't stop until he saw Lil' Pee appear from the bathroom. *Must have been taking a shit,* he thought. Blue motioned in a hand gesture, "It's time to get hyped," with an energetic little dance, then ran to the front door. He waited eagerly until Lil' Pee opened the door.

"What took you so long? Are you crying?"

"Sinus," Lil' Pee replied.

"Come on, shawty," Blue said as he briefed Lil' Pee on his mission.

"Mane, I've got a gravy (good) lick. My J told me Big Mo just got locked up today, so I went up the hill, snuck through the neighbor's yard, and began watching his house all day. I saw his bitches leaving in a car.

"Now I was in this nigga house yesterday re-in-up on some dope. This bitch nigga started showing me stacks. I peeped where the nigga went back to stash the cheese (money). I already know where he hides the dope. All you have to do is sneak through the window and open the front door and we got it made."

Lil' Pee was as nervous as a seven-time convicted felon in front the same judge for the same crime. He looked up at Blue. "Let's get it," he finally said.

"My nigga," Blue replied, giving him a pound (fist-to-fist handshake like boxers do before they are about to box).

Blue and Lil' Pee reached their destination in about five minutes flat. The three-bedroom brick house was pitch-dark, with houses on both sides.

"It's on and cracking," Lil' Pee said, laughing.

"Lil' Pee, be quiet. We don't want the neighbors to call the police," Blue warned him.

The two jogged in a low squat over to the bushes and waited five minutes to make sure the coast was clear. Blue then led Lil' Pee to the window at the rear of the house. The window was high enough for Blue to stand up and try to open it with his gloved hands giving him grip on the windows. Unfortunately, the windows were locked.

Blue took out his bandanna and screwdriver. He then placed the open bandanna on the crevice of the window, jammed the screwdriver in the corner crevice, and pushed it while rocking the tool up and down. The window silently cracked at the corner.

Lil' Pee looked on silently with fascination. However, his heart was pounding fast and heavy. Under the cover of pitch darkness, Blue then returned the screwdriver to his back pocket, balled up the bandanna, and pressed the condensed cloth against the crack in the crevice until the crack ran silently up the window. He then used his gloved hand to push the cracked window apart and remove the top piece of the broken glass first.

After removing the bottom piece, he paused for a minute. As if he had rehearsed this job many times, Blue reached in easily, opened the window, and raised it all the way up like a weightlifter effortlessly lifting 50 pounds over his head.

He then grabbed Lil' Pee closer to him and boosted him up through the window with his hands clasped together as he squatted down. Lil' Pee put one foot into Blue's clasped hands and was elevated through the window.

He entered Big Mo's house successfully, stood up, and took a deep breath. Then slowly, he made his way through the dark house into the front room; he crept through the hallway like a cat with his back and fingertips touching the walls. His heart was racing, and his adrenaline was pumping with anticipation.

Not knowing what danger lurked behind the next door, Lil' Pee reached the front door and opened it. Blue came in with his gun drawn and swiftly closed the door. Blue then turned on the living-room light that was right at the entrance door. He saw a burgundy Italian leather sofa furnished the living room.

Blue quickly led Lil' Pee to the lounge-chair cushion and picked up the couch cushion, zipped it open, and removed the sponge from within. When he emptied the cushion cover, a key of cocaine dropped out. Lil' Pee's eyes popped open in surprise.

Now his adrenaline pumped off the chart, and his body broke out in a cold sweat. Blue commanded Lil' Pee to check the whole couch and all the cushions thoroughly. Blue then went to the bedrooms and switched on the lights and discovered an unmade bed. He ran over and lifted the mattress completely off to discover a large quantity of U.S. currency.

Without missing a beat, he hastily grabbed the money that was rubber banded in sections of $1,000 stacks and filled his pockets with it, his pistol in his hand the whole time. He picked up all the money and every piece of jewelry he could find. He started towards the closet, but felt he was spending too much time there and did not want to risk the heist, so he ran for the exit. He found Lil' Pee with two cushion covers filled with spoil. He was also stealing Big Mo's Play Station and video games.

"Come on, Lil' Pee, let's go, let's go," Blue barked, heading for the door.

Once outside, Blue grabbed one of the cushion covers and both of them trotted over to the La Carr Apartments, where Blue's apartment was, five minutes up the street.

Once they reached Blue's apartment, Blue hand signaled for Lil' Pee to keep the noise down.

Before he opened his apartment door, he noticed all the lights were off. He then motioned silently for Lil' Pee to head to his room. Blue respected his workaholic brother and was cognizant that he needed his valuable sleep whenever he got a chance.

Blue and Lil' Pee silently made their way to the bedroom. They emptied out half a key of cocaine, four pounds of Northern Lights marijuana, a tech-9 semiautomatic, a .38 Special, and a .32 automatic handgun on the bed.

Blue then divided the spoils and gave Lil' Pee two pounds of marijuana and the .32 automatic handgun. He reached in his pocket and carefully pulled out two stacks and handed Lil' Pee $2,000. Lil' Pee ecstatically took his share, then went and sat on a small sofa Blue had in his room. Blue informed Lil' Pee that they would ration the cocaine tomorrow.

"Let's just chill now," Blue said, reaching in his nightstand drawer. He pulled out two cigars and tossed one to Lil' Pee. Blue rolled his blunt filled with marijuana and started smoking a godfather-like cigar. Lil' Pee observed Blue and did the same. Lil' Pee took his first few pulls, then lay back to let the high marinate.

I am rich; hood rich anyway, Pee thought.

Blue patted his hand on the fifteen stacks left in his cargo pants pocket and looked at the TV with his eyes slanted and definitely bloodshot red. His brother would have a fit about him smoking in the apartment. *But who gives a fuck?* he thought to himself. "I don't give a fuck," he said out loud to no one in particular.

Chapter

9 *Mark*

After getting some sleep, Mark Cooper, a.k.a. Cat, woke up at 12:08 p.m. He'd been up for the last two nights, getting high, drinking, and smoking, until he finally fell asleep. With Keisha's help, he'd ejaculated three times before dozing off. He really felt drained now. He was tired of lying around getting high, so he revived himself and fully awakened his senses.

He looked over and observed Keisha. She was naked and sleeping peacefully like a newborn baby. Even though she had a contented expression on her face, she still looked worn-out from the past few nights. Mark sat up and yawned, then stretched his body, fully extended. He could feel his body again, and it felt good. He reached out and gently rolled Keisha over on her back. Keisha, extremely tired and exhausted, slumped over on her back with an arm extended to the side.

Mark glanced at her magnificent body and found himself becoming aroused again. He swiftly moved and positioned his head under her lower torso and used both hands to spread her legs wide apart. He then moved his head over her vagina and zeroed in on her clitoris. Building up a hunger, he began to lick her clitoris in the same manner a cat drinks its milk, with thirst and focus. Mark continued this until he got a response. Keisha became aroused and began wiggling in her sleep. She woke up with an "Oh, baby," then lay back and spread her legs wider, bent at the knees.

She was his lollipop. Mark was licking gently around her clitoris with his tongue, then he spread her vaginal lips with his tongue, slid his tongue up in her vagina, and sucked on her clitoris. He drank of her juices, then his tongue rapidly tickled the tip of her clitoris. By now, Keisha's hormones shot into overdrive. Her hips began to gyrate, and she was moaning.

Now Mark became more intense with his tongue wash. His tongue began to dance and swirl on her clit in a circular motion until Keisha screamed, climaxing. She was panting heavily.

Mark wasn't finished. He pushed the tip of his middle finger in her anus, and used the tip of his thumb and index finger to spread her vagina open with his other hand. That way he could lick up and down the inner lips of her vagina. Quickly, like a man driven, which he was, he licked his way up to her clitoris and sucked on her cherry. Now, he was gasping for air like a fish out of water. This morning, Keisha was Mark's breath of fresh air.

All of a sudden, Keisha exploded with sexual excitement. She moved like the little girl in the *Exorcist* who was possessed. Grabbing his head with two hands, she pulled him up with all her might and kissed him passionately while she hugged and squeezed him tightly.

In response, Mark raised his body up just enough to place a firm erection into Keisha's vagina.

Now, *really* like a woman possessed, Keisha pumped on his penis, thrusting her lower torso up and down with vigor and force. Mark rose out of her hug and looked in her eyes. For a second, she looked like a madwoman in rage. He squeezed one of her firm breasts and sucked on her nipples while maintaining a rhythm with her. Their tempo increased until the headboard began knocking against the wall.

Keisha's vagina was well lubricated with a heavy burst of cum, which made Mark slide in and out of her with ease and great pleasure. He grabbed her and ejected himself into her with enough force to break his spine. Now *he* started panting like a thirsty dog. His eyes were closed as he released himself inside of her. Then Mark gently kissed her. After a few moments, he went to the bathroom to urinate, brush his teeth, and take a shower.

Keisha came in behind him and used the second complimentary toothbrush to brush her teeth. A huge smile lit up her face. When

Mark came out of the shower, he playfully slapped Keisha on her rear, causing her to jump to the side with toothpaste coming out her mouth, even though she was trying her best to keep the foam in her mouth.

"You better stop, boy."

Mark grabbed the towel, twirled it in two hands, lashed her on her cute buns, then ran off, wrapping the towel around him. Keisha was enjoying his playful mood. She wrapped her head with a towel, then stepped into the steaming shower.

Afterwards, the couple got dressed in the same clothes that they wore to the hotel. Keisha mentioned to Mark that they needed to go to the other hotel and get their clothes.

"Shawty, don't worry about those old clothes. We about to get fresh ones."

That is *exactly* what Keisha wanted to hear. She went over and kissed him. Mark placed the drugs in a pillowcase and put all the money in his pocket. They then exited the hotel room and left the "do not disturb" sign on the door. After Keisha started the car, they exited the hotel grounds and Mark put in Young Jeezy's CD, "Trap or Die."

He lay back in his seat, took out a cigar, and rolled up a blunt. Once he lit his blunt, he told Keisha to drive to Ricky's apartment and asked her to hand him her cell phone. He called Ricky, who was already up.

"Hey, kinfolk, I need you to cook something for me."

"Hey, Cat, come holla at me at my crib."

"'Ight. I'm on my way," then Mark hung up.

Next, Mark called Lil' Pee's house phone. Lil' Pee picked up.

"Hello," Lil' Pee said.

"Hey, Lil' Pee, what's happenin'? I need you to help me get off some work."

"Cat, first you run off with my blunt. Now you want me to help you get off work. If you weren't my cousin, I'd whip your ass," Lil' Pee laughed.

"You going to move this for me or not?"

"Shit, how much?"

"How much you can handle?"

"Nigga, anything you bring me I could handle."

"'Ight, Lil' Pee. I'll be there in an hour." Mark hung up.

By now, Keisha had pulled up in front of Ricky's house and parked.

"Wait here. I'll be right back," Mark said.

He went and knocked on the door. Lucky was in the living room playing Master P's, No Limit Record's "TRU." He was sprawled out, relaxing on the couch, enjoying his addicted customer pleasing him orally. He stopped the addict for a moment. "Hold up," he said.

Lucky made his way to the door, looked through the window to see Keisha in a car and Cat at the door, so he opened up and gave Cat some dap. "Where you been, homie?" Lucky inquired.

"Shit, stayin' low, man. I don't want no trouble." Mark stepped in to see a teenage Caucasian girl in her panties sitting on the couch, twirling her blond hair with one index finger.

"I see you still you," Mark said as Lucky closed the door. "Hey, where's Ricky at?"

"He upstairs, mane. Go ahead. He told me you were coming over."

Mark ran upstairs to Ricky's bedroom. The door was wide open, and he was watching the CNN news channel.

"What's happenin', Cat?" Ricky asked, sitting at the head of his bed. He turned from the TV, giving Mark his full attention.

"I need you to cook up a quarter bird for me real quick, mane," Mark said.

"All right. Where is it? It's going to take me fifteen minutes," Ricky replied.

"I left it in the car."

Mark went back to the car, grabbed the pillowcase, and ran back upstairs. He passed Lucky with his girlfriend sucking on his manhood. When he returned to Ricky's bedroom, Ricky was sitting next to a shoebox. Mark pulled out the bag of cocaine and told Ricky to cook half of it for him.

Ricky opened his shoebox, took out a scale and two Ziploc bags from under his bed, all the time watching Mark carefully.

Ricky placed the bag of cocaine on his scale to see that it was only half an ounce different from what he gave Mark a couple of days earlier. He weighed out two separate nine ounces into the Ziploc bag. Mark put the bag back in the pillowcase, but then thought to himself for a second, *Lucky is a good person*, so he asked Ricky to weigh out two and a baby for him.

Ricky took the bag back from Mark and told Mark to reach under his bed and grab a sandwich bag. Mark complied. Ricky weighed out 63 grams, tied the sandwich bag, and gave it to Mark with the 15 ounces back. Mark put the 15 ounces back in his pillowcase and told Ricky he was going to get something to eat and would come back shortly. Ricky assured him everything would be ready by the time he returned.

Mark went back downstairs and saw Lucky lying back in a trance. "Lucky," Mark called out.

"I need some help getting rid of some work. You wanna help?"

"Cat, that's how I survive, kinfolk."

Mark tossed Lucky the two and a quarter ounce. Lucky grabbed it. Meantime, the girl who was doing Lucky widened her eyes as she paid attention to all of this. She accelerated her oral performance while looking at Mark. She acted as if she wanted to show off her oral skills to Mark. Mark watched the action for a brief second as Lucky smiled a wide-mouthed grin. Without further delay, Mark left the apartment and jumped in the vehicle.

"Let's go to the Waffle House," he told Keisha.

Keisha gladly obliged. "Good, baby, I'm starving."

She drove to the Waffle House that was closer on Memorial Drive and Park. After she parked and they entered the restaurant, they took a seat in the rear next to the window. When the server came over with the menu, Keisha instantly ordered for the two of them.

"I'd like your strawberry waffles, a patty melt with double cheese, and hash browns. He's having a chicken patty with extra cheese, french fries, and a milk shake."

The waitress scribbled her order down on her pad and asked about something to drink.

"Yeah, I'd like two apple-cranberry juices."

Mark sat slumped in his seat, waiting for their food and looking at Keisha. Suddenly, the dishes and windows started to vibrate. They looked around to spot an '86 Box Chevy on 24-inch gold rims come up the street with its music thundering Mike Jones' Who Is Mike Jones? The blaring music reverberated for miles, pounding eardrums of anyone within that distance. Mark observed Keisha watching the car until it disappeared into the horizon.

The server came back with their meals, and Keisha asked for a third apple-cranberry juice. They ate in silence. Mark was the first one finished and waited for Keisha to take her last bites. When she finished eating, she felt satisfied and excused herself to go to the bathroom.

Mark didn't have anything less than a hundred-dollar bill on him, so he placed it on the table and walked out. Keisha came out of the bathroom, saw the hundred-dollar bill on the table, picked up the money and the check, then walked over to the cash register. The clerk charged $12.50 for the meal and gave her the change. Generously, she tipped the server five dollars and pocketed the rest. Mark was waiting at the passenger door.

Keisha came out and opened the door with the keyless entry. She started the car and waited for him to say something. He lit the blunt, took a deep drag, then told her to go back to Ricky's apartment. So, like a faithful pilot, she headed in that direction.

When they arrived at Ricky's apartment, Mark knocked on the door. Lucky's female companion opened the door.

"Hey, I'm Kerry," she said in a cheerful tone.

Mark walked right by her like she didn't exist.

"Where's Ricky?" Mark asked Lucky, who was sitting on the couch speaking on his cell phone.

"In the kitchen," Lucky said, pointing his index finger.

Mark then walked right past Lucky, took a left, marched past the guest bathroom and into the kitchen. Ricky was still cooking over the stove, sweating, with a bandanna tied around his face like a desperado about to commit a bank robbery. He looked at Mark and told him his crack was in the freezer.

Mark picked up the four, large, cookielike dishes and dropped them in a large Ziploc bag that Ricky had on the kitchen counter.

Next, he placed the dope on the scale: 18.8 ounces. He gave Ricky, who was wearing latex gloves, a pound and left rapidly. Ricky was still cooking up four ounces he got earlier from the half key of cocaine from Mark.

"Hey, Mark, how am I supposed to reach you when I'm done?" Lucky inquired.

"I'll call you from my cell phone number later on, mane."

He walked out through the kitchen door, hopped in the truck, and told Keisha to take him to his cousin's house. Shortly, she pulled up in front of Lil' Pee's apartment. Before he exited the truck, Mark looked around carefully, grabbed Keisha's .38 revolver, and tucked it on his waist clip. Then he made a dash for Lil' Pee's house, with the crack buried safely in his underwear.

Seconds later, he reached Lil' Pee's apartment and banged on the door. Lil' Pee answered with a big blunt in one hand, and a .32 automatic in his other. Mark told him to get his scale, which he did while Mark pulled out his bag of crack from its hiding place. Lil' Pee placed the scale on his mother's center table and asked where he got the dope.

Mark lied and told him, "Someone gave me a few birds to move for him." He then weighed out nine ounces and told Pee he needed back $750 apiece from the deal.

"Seven hundred fifty?" Lil' Pee snapped.

"Shawty, I need your help. I'm getting it for $700. I need to make at least $50 off every ounce."

"All right, man," Pee said.

"I also have some hydro green. Call me if you need some," Mark said.

"Cuz, I need some right now," Lil' Pee replied.

"Well, you got the money?"

"How much you charging?"

"Seven hundred an ounce."

"All right. How much you charge me for a quarter pound?"

"Twenty-five hundred."

"Okay. I'll want a quarter pound then."

"Where your money, shawty?"

"Go get the 'dro, man," Lil' Pee said.

Lil' Pee went to his room, closed the door, then came back with $2,000. Mark counted the money. He now had more confidence in Lil' Pee's hustling ability and trusted him with his dope. Mark ran downstairs and came back with his pillowcase. He took out the Hydro Kush and told Lil' Pee to weigh out a quarter pound. Lil' Pee looked at the pound of Kush with astonishment. He then ran to the kitchen, got two sandwich bags, and went back to the living room, where he weighed four ounces and handed the bag back to Mark.

"Cuz, keep this shit. Everybody be wanting the good shit these days," Lil' Pee told Mark.

They gave each other dap with a one-hand hug at the end. They were both proud to see each other escalating financially in life. Mark exited the apartment with his gun drawn until he made it back in the car.

"Let's head back to the hotel to drop this shit off and go do some shopping."

Keisha said, "Yeees sir" with a happy smile stretched across her face.

On their way to Lennox Mall, Keisha asked Mark if they were going to rent an apartment or a house. Mark answered by telling her to start looking for a two or three-bedroom house to rent right away.

"I'm tired of spending all my money on hotels," he said.

Keisha was more than excited. She made a stop at the nearest convenience store and bought a newspaper, then asked Mark to drive while she browsed through the newspaper and began calling the available houses for rent. She circled a few houses she was interested in, then folded the newspaper and put it aside on the seat beside her.

"Honey, I just called about this one house on West Mountain Street, and the landlord only wants a $1,500 deposit and we can move in immediately. I think it'll be perfect. It's on top of a hill, secluded, and has one acre in the backyard."

"You still got the number?" Mark asked.

"Yeah, I got it programmed in my phone."

"Well, call back and tell the landlord you'll be moving in today then."

Keisha called Mr. Lee and reserved the house, assuring him that she'd pay him his deposit and the first month's rent if they could move in today. Mr. Lee sealed their agreement. He took all her info over the phone. He told her to meet him at the West Mountain location at 7:00 p.m. with a money order for $2,200 and a valid picture ID, and the house would be hers. Keisha said a joyful, "Thank you, Mr. Lee," and hung up.

The pair arrived at Lennox Mall at 3:00 p.m., just beating the rush-hour traffic. They agreed to spend two hours shopping, and then they would head back east to meet Mr. Lee. The atrocious Atlanta traffic would crawl for the next two hours.

Inside the mall, they immediately entered the Foot Locker. Mark purchased two of the latest Air Jordan shoes and a pair of Timberlands. Keisha had Mark purchase her two women's Reeboks classics, white and black. Mark also got 10, 3X T-shirts, two Atlanta Braves baseball jerseys, and three pair of socks. When Mark went into the dressing room, Keisha followed him and asked him for some money to go to the JCPenney's to buy herself some clothes.

He reached down in his pocket, took out $10,000 and gave her $2,000. Her eyes lit up like a Christmas tree before she kissed him. Then he handed her an extra $200 and told her to get him two Yushua pants, black and blue jeans. Keisha left him with her bags and quickly vanished.

Mark then made his way to Prize Jewelers. He glanced at the dazzling diamond jewelry for a moment then decided to try on a Benny and Company watch with a big round face with full Belgian-cut diamonds, including diamonds that float inside the glass around the dial. The watch was priced at $5,500.

Fred, the salesclerk, introduced himself to Mark. "I could negotiate a lower price if you buy this watch today," he said with a strong Middle Eastern accent, taking out his calculator. "I'll give it to you for only ..." He then showed Mark a figure for $3,500 on his large calculator.

Mark said, "Give me my watch," as he handed him the cash.

Fred became even more hospitable than his previously overly polite demeanor.

"Sir," Fred said, then paused for a response.

"Call me Cat," Mark said.

"Cat? Meow? Cat, I like that. Thank you very much, Mr. Cat. Your Benny and Company comes with interchangeable bands. Which would you like, sir?"

"Give me red, blue, and black."

Cat already had on the white gold band, studded with small carat diamonds.

"Great choice, sir. Would you like insurance in case your watch is damaged?"

"What if my watch is stolen?"

"Sorry, sir, but we don't cover theft. You have to go through a private insurance company for that."

"How much is the insurance?"

"It's just $350 more, sir!"

"Okay, let me get it."

"Smart move, sir. This way, if anything ever happens to your watch, you just bring it here with your receipt and we'll fix it for free."

The clerk placed his box in a jewelry bag and thanked him gratefully. As he was turning, Mark was captivated when he saw a 24-inch chain with a cross studded with diamonds. He pointed and asked Fred to let him try it on.

"Marvelous choice, sir. This is an exquisite piece."

Cat put it on over his neck, and the two became inseparable. Fred took out his big calculator again. "While it's priced at $5,000," he said and pushed a few more buttons, "I can give it to you for only $2,500."

Cat said, "Throw in those diamond earrings too."

"For you, sir, I will."

Mark put on his jewelry, looked in the mirror, and felt like a made man. He picked up his boxes and exited. Three women were paying close attention to Mark's generous spending. They began walking behind him, being conspicuous, hoping to get his attention.

However, Mark now felt nervous and paranoid. He wondered why everybody was watching him. He went to JCPenney's and met Keisha at the cash register.

"Hey, Big Baller, where's my jewelry?"

"I'll get you some later. Let's get the fuck out of here and go get something to eat."

Keisha pulled up at a McDonald's drive-thru. Not wanting to miss her appointment with Mr. Lee, they ordered two Big Mac value meals and continued their journey on to the east side. Mark counted his money; he still had $10,000 left, a car full of expensive attire, and he was about to live in a decent location. He had money being made in the streets, and he was coming up in the world. Feeling contented, he gazed over at a happy Keisha, reclined his seat, and lit his blunt.

They reached the West Mountain location at 6:30 p.m. and waited for Mr. Lee. Mark surveyed the house and its surroundings, and he loved it. The two-bedroom brick house was hidden by trees and bushes and was sitting on a secluded hill on two acres of land. They decided not to smoke so that they wouldn't give the property owner the wrong impression. Mr. Lee arrived at exactly 7:00 p.m. in a Lexus 300.

He met with Keisha briefly for the money order and a copy of her driver's license. He then showed her around the house to assure her the house was in excellent condition. Keisha signed the rental contract agreement. Mr. Lee handed her the keys and left in a flash. Keisha exited the house, smiling, and went to greet Mark, who was asleep in the passenger seat.

"Cat, we got it. We got it."

"Good. Let's move this shit outta the car so we can go get me a cell phone before the cell phone place closes," he said.

Chapter 10 *Blue*

Blue woke up that morning feeling exceptionally drained of energy. He had been quite busy for the last few weeks. He sold off what he'd stolen from his heist in a matter of days. He was known to supply his comrades, who, in turn, were supplying the users. His sudden success came surprisingly quick. Blue had never imagined that what he was doing could amount to so much collateral. He woke up, staring at his mother's picture, and figured it must be her essence watching over him that was creating these financial miracles in his life.

He finally climbed out of bed and rolled up a Kush blunt in a Hugh El Producto, smoked, then took off his boxers and dragged himself to the bathroom. After urinating, he placed the blunt on the toilet next to the shower, and stepped in the shower stall. In less than two minutes, he had lathered, rinsed, and was out, just long enough to catch his blunt before it went out. He smoked a little more and began to feel revived after his shower. Blue experienced a vibrant mood.

He stood naked in front of the bathroom mirror, admiring himself. Before he picked up his toothbrush and toothpaste, he gave the mirror a million-dollar gold-toothed smile, then began brushing with the blunt firmly fixed between his fingers of his opposite hand. After a quick brush, rinse, and spit, Blue walked to the window and looked outside. He was startled to realize he hadn't seen sunlight in a longtime. He then walked back to his bedroom and put on some clothes.

Considering himself a soldier, he put on his usual black army cargo pants and a 5X T-shirt and some Babe and Apes he'd recently purchased. Now his blunt fixed between his lips, Blue lifted up his mattress and pulled out a brown paper bag filled with money, which he emptied on his bed and began counting. He marveled at the point when he reached $25,000, but he became *really* ecstatic when he counted almost $39,000. He grabbed his house phone and called his main supplier.

"What's the business?" he said.

"Whatever you want," Ricky answered.

"Hey, shawty, you still gonna sell me the car, man?" Blue asked. Although he was young, Blue looked older than his true age. He felt that driving a car would fit his new baller image.

"You got the $6,000?"

"Just have the title ready when I get there," Blue said, hanging up. He called a cab and lay on the bed with his back against the wall as he counted out $15,000 and placed it into his cargo pants pocket. Hungry and thirsty, he went to the fridge, drank some Kool-Aid, and ate two slices of cold, leftover pizza. Usually, he would nuke it in the microwave, however, this time, he couldn't wait. Grabbing a bag of barbecue potatoes chips from the counter, he sat in front of the living-room TV.

A cab blew its horn as he was watching music videos. He put down the bag, left, and locked the door behind him. Once he settled himself in the cab, he told the driver to take him to Brookside Apartments on Northern. Blue reached down and adjusted his pistol more comfortably in his waistband.

"Young man, that address is so close you could walk," the cabdriver said in a thick Arabian accent.

"Then you would make no money," Blue replied.

"That's true, my friend. Thank you for your laziness."

His comment made Blue want to laugh. He was tickled even more when he thought how funny it would be if he pulled out his 9mm and splattered the cabbie's brains all over the windshield.

They reached Blue's destination in three minutes. He looked at the odometer and saw a charge of five dollars. He gave the cab driver a twenty. The driver insisted he take his card.

"My friend, I'm Abeeb. Call me anytime you need a ride. I'll come quickly for you, my friend."

"Thank you, most kind sir." Blue took the card, jumped out, and slammed the door.

He walked up to see Ricky removing his belongings from the car, obviously cherishing his last few moments with his prized possession. Blue entered the passenger side of the Catalina and caught Ricky gliding his hands gently over the steering wheel. This made Blue feel even more eager to buy the car, knowing that he would possess something loved and appreciated.

Smiling, he immediately threw $6,000 bound in a rubber band in Ricky's lap. He just sat and stared intensely at Ricky. Ricky had bought the car for $2,000 and put $500 into the automatic starter and a CD audio.

Ricky looked Blue in his eyes. "Well, you got her. Let's go inside and fill out the paperwork."

"Don't worry, man. I'll take good care of her," Blue promised with a wide smile and devious eyes.

The two made their way upstairs to Ricky's bedroom. From a shelf in the closet, Ricky retrieved the Pontiac's title, along with a bill of sales. He filled out the paperwork, they both signed it, and Ricky kept a copy of the bill of sales for himself. Blue then asked Ricky if he could have some more work.

"I wanna get a half of bird from you, too."

"Blue, I only have a quarter left. I'll give you that for $5,000 and give you the other half for $4,000 when you get back."

"Okay, that's a bet," said Blue.

"Yeah, just wait for me downstairs in the living room for a second."

Ricky came downstairs with the four ounces in a clear bag and a scale. He called Blue over to his stereo wall unit, where he weighed the dope in front of Blue and handed it to him. Blue stuffed the bag of coke in his cargo pants pocket and headed for the door.

"Blue, you forgettin' something."

Blue looked dumfounded, then Ricky tossed him the keys to his car. He smiled and exited the apartment, walked over to his car, which was immaculate, jumped in, and started it up. He enjoyed the fact it started instantly and ran smoothly. Lil' Jon and the Eastside Boyz, "Put Yo Hood Up," came on, thundering through his audio system. Blue start bobbing to the music, put his car in reverse, and exited.

He entered the La Carr and parked in front of his apartment, ran in to drop off his dope, grabbed another $3,000 and his Heckler & Koch RP90 from under his bed, then rushed out of the apartment and back to his already-running motor.

He jumped in the car and punched the gas pedal, which gave him a whiplash and sent his engine roaring up the street. He quickly calmed down, realizing he was fully armed and didn't have a license.

Reaching Interstate 285, he jumped on it, gunned the car two exits up, and got off at Covington and Memorial, his destination Godfather Custom and Accessory. Blue went inside and looked around until he discovered what he wanted—24-inch deep dish spinners on sale for $3,000. He called for assistance and the salesclerk immediately came over and stood next to him.

"That's what I want mounted on my ride." Blue's voice was decisive.

"Okay, dude. They're $4,500 mounted on rims and tires."

"Bet."

"Excuse me, dude?"

"I'll take it."

"Okay, right this way."

The salesclerk led Blue to the front desk. Blue was counting out his money on the counter when he spotted a Pioneer CD/DVD player on sale for $1,000. He told the clerk to get him one of the Pioneer's audio DVD systems. He also pointed out a pair of 15-inch kicker and a JVC 2000 watt amplifier. In all, he paid $6,700 for his merchandise.

The clerk counted out the money and gave Blue his receipt. He advised Blue he had a 1-year warranty on everything and that he'd have to wait patiently for two hours before his vehicle would be ready for him with everything installed. Blue handed him the key and led him outside to his car, where he opened the car door, grabbed his Tech-9 from under his seat, and walked it back to the trunk, unconcealed. He gave the clerk the notion he was legitimately carrying arms.

Alarmed, the clerk still smiled at Blue and drove his car to the garage. Blue ran across the street to a cell phone connection and distribution shop and picked up two camera phones. He stepped to the counter and gave the clerk two different sets of false information to hook up the Metro PCS phone services. Blue's attention swayed when two attractive young women entered the store.

"Hey," he said in a loud, confident, authoritative manner. This brought the girls' attention immediately over to him. He gave a broad gold-toothed smile, strolled over to them with his arms wide apart, like how a dad greets his daughters when coming home from work. Oddly, they were magnetized by his arrogant, friendly demeanor.

"Today must be y'all lucky day because I was just looking for two sexy-looking women that I could take home and fuck."

The two girls looked at him incredulously, like "Is this person for real???" One of them had short brown hair with a slim figure and nice, voluptuous breasts and hips like Halle Berry, and her friend looked like a shorter resemblance of Naomi Campbell, with full lips and a seductive, very well-sculpted body. The two just squeezed past him, indifferently. He came up behind them while they were paying their phone bill, took out a bundle of cash, and paid for his two cell phones and his connection fee.

"Oh, yeah. I'm paying for their bill, too."

He did this in a manner that made him look larger-than-life. Cool, calm, assertive. Oh, yea. The ladies began to feel like they may have missed a chance at a cool person. They stood back and observed Blue. He had become a focused, nonchalant businessman and no longer paid them any attention. He then grabbed his bags and made his way to the door in his usual, on-top-of-the-world swagger.

The Halle Berry look-alike said, "Hey!" as Blue was walking through the door.

"What'd you said your name was?" she continued.

"Blue, my name is Blue," he said with one hand holding the door open and his head turned, giving them a confident smile.

It happened that the two were sisters, Kim and Stacey. They lived with their mother across the street. Kim, the oldest, was 18 years old, and Stacey, the youngest, 17 years old. In the spirit of the spider extending an invitation to the fly, Blue asked if they would like to have a meal with him while he waited for his car to be customized. They saw no harm in it.

Blue was entertaining them equally, making neither one feel left out. He knew he was a big-enough man for the task. They walked to Mama Eats, ordered some soul food, and sat in the rear of the restaurant and conversed. Blue informed the women he was an up-and-coming rapper that just signed a million-dollar record deal with Universal Records. After this disclosure, the ladies became even more excited to be in his presence and got into the grove, feeling more comfortable to speak about themselves. They were Miami natives who came to Georgia to get a new start in life. Blue found out that they both loved to smoke, drink, and party. They were not working, and money was tight in their household. Blue assured them that he would put them in his music video next week.

"Yeah, I'd love to have y'all in my music video. I just need to see how y'all look in y'all swimming suit," he said flashing an anaconda smile. "We doin' a big shoot at Savannah Beach, and I need some beautiful, firm bitches around me."

That clinched it. They started to feel smaller and smaller in his presence, looking up at him with more and more admiration.

"Hey, there go my baby. She's ready. I need y'all ladies to be riding with me tonight and fuck with this real Atlanta baller. You feel me?"

Since he had already taken the initiative to step in, take control, and be their boss, the two sisters felt enslaved by his charm. They complied with a nod of their heads. Blue then marched across the street with Kim and Stacey walking behind him in hypnotic trances.

Waiting for him beside the vehicle was the blond-headed sales rep, who handed him his keys and the remote control for his audio DVD system. "We left a Southern crunk music video DVD in the DVD player for you—compliments of Godfather Customs."

Before the clerk could finish speaking, Blue's attention focused on the ladies, who were awed and impressed to see how cool his ride was. Nonchalantly, he pressed his automatic start and the CD audio on the Lil Jon CD that was in the CD player. The whole earth started quaking. His body began dancing while standing still, and his smile was so wide that all thirty-two of his pearly whites were sparkling.

He looked at the girls standing beside his car. "Y'all fucking with me or what?" he asked.

In reply, they looked at him, smiled, and slithered inside the car without a word. Without delay, Blue opened the trunk, grabbed his Tech-9, hopped in his car, and put the convertible top down. The westering sun would soon be giving way to the lunar light, and the romance of the cool summer night's breeze was beginning to spin a web of enchantment.

Blue cruised out of the lot, pulled up to the light, then started bobbing and bouncing frantically and ecstatically. The girls were looking at him like he was a madman doing his best Mr. Freely impression when he thought Jack Tripper was making a homosexual pass at him.

Everybody in the nearby cars were totally focused on Blue, and he was soaking it up—until a group of men with faces made for police mug books pulled up alongside of him. Reaching down, he picked up his Heckler and Koch RP90, put it on his lap, and got extremely serious.

The light turned green, and Blue floored the gas pedal. The monstrous engine growled and projected them forward, as if they were being teleported to Mars.

Blue made it back to his apartment, and when he opened the door and turned on the lights, he was pleased when he saw that his brother was not home. That meant at this time he was probably at work or out doing who-knows-what. Most likely, wherever he was, he would be away for a while. Blue would not see him for the next two days.

The sisters looked around to see a well-furnished apartment. Like a man on a mission, Blue then led them to his bedroom, opened the door, and let them enter first—not to be a gentleman, but to let them see all the money and coke he left on the bed. Duly impressed, the girls went and sat on his bedroom couch.

He turned on the TV to music videos, took two cigars out of his drawer, and handed the hydro to Stacey and Kim. They were captivated by the beautiful buds and took out a portion to roll up. Blue was rolling up his blunt when they asked him for a little cocaine. He broke off a bit and handed them two grams.

Stacey took out a dollar bill, placed the cocaine in it, and crushed it with her hand by folding the dollar and applying pressure to it. Blue watched keenly while rolling his cigar up. The two took a sniff in both nostrils using their fingernails before sprinkling the rest of the coke into the cigar. They rolled the coke on top of the marijuana.

Blue lit up his blunt, watching them, as if he were a lion eyeing his prey. He began smoking, waiting on the sisters to finish rolling their blunt. Once they did, they lit it and started smoking. As they got high, the two sisters became more relaxed and open.

Blue started gathering up his money in one pile where they could see the large quantity of bills. "Yeah, I'm a give y'all a thousand each to be in my video shoot. Why don't y'all stand up and let me see how y'all look in y'all bathing suits?"

"We don't have on a bathing suit," Kim said.

"Okay then. Let me see an image of y'all naked. It would be good to tell the director how beautiful y'all body parts look." They looked at each other, smiled, then stood up and started slowly stripping. They knew what Blue was doing. They just thought it was fun playing along. Catching the rhythm of the music, they both began dancing suggestively.

Kim's watermelon, light-brown buttocks were looking sweet and voluptuous. Her big round soft breasts had nipples centered right in the middle.

"Kim, you have a nice ass. Perfect for a thong."

Stacey's breasts were medium-sized with erect, pointy nipples. However, her huge, apple-shaped buttocks looked extraordinary in contrast with her tiny waist. In addition, her vanilla-cream skin made her sensitive areas look red and lustrous. The ladies were already high and craving excitement. This added seduction and flair to their erotic performance.

"Okay, you two are the next hottest things to hit the video scene. Come lay beside the next multimillion-dollar rap star to hit mainstream."

They crawled on the bed gleefully. Blue motioned them, one to each side.

"I want some more powder, Blue," Stacey cooed.

Blue opened his bag of coke, and the two girls practically panted, wide-eyed with anticipation. He broke off another two grams and put it in a twenty-dollar bill. Carefully, he sealed the big bag and placed it in the night table drawer. Then he gathered his money, placed it in his cargo pants pocket, and handed Stacey the twenty-dollar bill with the two grams of cocaine on it.

He stuck his blunt between his lips and started to finger both Kim and Stacey with his middle fingers. Both sisters snorted and passed the coke back and forth. Kim was dripping in moisture and stuck her tongue in Blue's ears. The tingling sensation sent the blunt rolling down his shirt. But he remained cool, reached down, and picked the blunt up, placed it between his fingertips, and rested his hand on Kim's buttocks.

"Damn, you have a nice soft ass," he said.

Kim headed down for his midsection, where she unbuttoned his pants and pulled down his boxers to reveal a huge-sized penis, fully erect. She started jerking it up and down with two hands as she looked up at Blue, who wore a wide grin, nodding his head slowly up and down like a master negotiator using psychology to close a deal. Kim placed his head in her moist mouth and started sucking on his forefront with passion.

Stacey stared at Blue's enormous manhood. She was now extremely high and excited and placed the drugs on top of the night table. Nudging her sister over, she joined Kim and chowed down on Blue's erection to pacify him. Blue just lay back, smoked some more, and gave himself over to pure enjoyment.

"Yeah, I'm taking y'all straight to the top. Yeah, yeah, yeah. Straight to the top," Blue said, placing his blunt on the night table. The two paused and got on their knees, admiring Blue's package.

Blue sprang off the bed and undressed rapidly. Marveling at the precious, beautiful, soft creatures awaiting him, he tossed his pants in the closet, placed his 9mm on safety, and pranced back in bed. Blue opened Kim's legs and sunk his head in her soft tenderness. He consumed her sweet flow of juices. With every suckle, he masturbated and appreciated her sensitivity. With every lick and suck to her vagina, she opened herself and let her love flow freely.

As Blue lay on his side and Kim lay on her back, Stacey grabbed ahold of his manhood, inserted his dick in her mouth, and rained saliva down his love muscle like a waterfall. She consumed him down her throat. Her saliva rained on his love muscle repeatedly.

Blue turned Kim on her side facing him and he lay on his back. He was savagely battering her clitoris with his tongue while breathing in her love like a choking man desperate for a breath of much-needed fresh air.

Meantime, Stacey climbed over Blue, inserted his penis in her, and squatted repeatedly up and down on his erection. Her movements relaxed her tension, converting her high energy into a liquefied pool of lust and passion, which transformed her into a wildly erotic, carefree spirit knowing no bounds. She reached her climax with loud moans and groans.

Blue rested for a minute, recouping, then moved over to Kim and inserted himself into her warm cushion of comfort. She exploded with fluids like a pregnant mother's amniotic sac before childbirth. Kim railed and gyrated, as if a demon were erupting from her soul. Meantime, Stacey lay with her eyes wide open, watching in pleasure. She had her legs wide open, her hand massaging her privates. To her surprise, she was satisfied and lay in tranquility.

Blue looked over at Stacey's vanilla-cream skin. It was so creamy looking that it resembled café-au-lait. It was a stark contrast to her flaming red, open organ of pleasure. He positioned himself and his captive sex slave closer. Then he sunk his tongue in Stacey's passage of ecstasy.

The two women joined hands and squeezed tightly. They were excited to share such an erotic fantasy. They orgasmed simultaneously and moaned and quivered until their bodies were drained of all energy. This had the tendency to elevate them to a higher level of experience where their bodies were no more and their minds were trapped in frozen time.

The ladies looked up at their young god; he had reigned his dominance over them for eternity. They admired his love muscle of pleasure. Their hearts throbbed for Blue, and they were elated as they positioned themselves in front of his cannon in order to be showered with his rain of life.

Chapter 11

Chyna Lu
Atlanta, Georgia

Chyna Lu pulled her Chrysler Firepower into her Defoors Court condominium garage. Chyna is the daughter of a Chinese father, who had a successful construction empire in Jamaica, West Indies, where she was born. Her mother is a Nubian black, well-mannered, educated Jamaican woman.

Mr. Chin Lu and Dr. Audrey Lu raised their daughter in the lavish upbringing of Uptown Kingston. However, their daughter had a lust for negative company, especially her significant other. Mr. Chin thought it was best if he isolated his daughter from the readily overwhelming influence of Jamaica. Consequently, she was sent from Jamaica to China, then to England to be educated and raised by her boarding parents.

Eventually Chyna graduated from Oxford and received her bachelor's degree in political science and psychology. She then returned to her native homeland to reunite with a childhood lover, the notorious Spraggs Banton.

Spraggs had committed his first murder at the tender age of 8. He'd borrowed his comrade's gun and shot a uniformed Jamaican police officer in the back of his head in an outdoor market in order to take his handgun. After that, the young man grew from a ruthless murderer and climbed up through the ranks to second-in-command of the Jamaican crime underworld. Dullas and Blacka Brown, the sons of the legendary Jim Brown, oversaw Spraggs' training.

In fact, Dullas and Blacka Brown were the brothers responsible for all Kingston's crime du jour. That is, until Blacka was gunned down by his opposition because he was showing off carelessly in their territory. This left Dullas the sole heir of his father's criminal, multibillion-dollar empire. The young 24-year old was responsible for 80 percent of the cocaine trafficking on the island and over 50 percent of Jamaica's murders. He also developed an international reputation for dealing in death.

In fact, the young man had killed more people in America than deaths totaling from the gas chamber or the electric chair. The young warlord had the most determined, lethal army of hit men and criminally organized henchmen in the world. And he had the backing of the world's richest political figure behind him—the Jamaican prime minister.

Spraggs Banton was respected in his ranks as second-in-command—until he started becoming more respected than his master. Mr. Dullas Brown, feeling threatened by Spraggs' growing influence and perceived ability to commit murderous treason against him, ordered Spraggs' assassination. Spraggs, informed of Brown's hit on his life, went into hiding in their enemies' territory. He exiled himself from his beloved island. The only person who he felt loved him and who could help him, was Chyna, and she was thousands of miles away.

"Yes, baby, yes, baby, you know I love you," Chyna said as she exited her car, speaking on her cell phone. "Of course there is no other man in my life. Everyone knows my heart belongs to you." She spoke in a light, compassionate, English accent.

"Baby, I have my people in London working on your paperwork right now," Chyna said as she was unpacking groceries from her car trunk. "All you have to do is travel by boat to Barbados and contact the connection that I was telling you about, at the location I was telling you about. Once you're in London, you will be escorted to Liverpool to meet your man with the other identification that will get you into Canada successfully. Once in Canada, my people could smuggle you into the U.S. easily. Baby, just listen to your guide's instructions. I'm counting desperately on your safe arrival."

She made her way to the door of the basement. When she reached the door, she kicked it repeatedly.

"Yes, dear, I hear. I'm coming," Steven said.

"I'm just unpacking the groceries from the car," Chyna said.

Steve opened the door in his Yushua pajamas. He took the bags from Chyna and made his way upstairs to the kitchen and placed the bags on her kitchenette counter.

"Baby, baby, I love you," Chyna said as she entered her small office in the basement to check her answering machine. She saw one new message and pressed play.

"Chyna, this is Daddy. I sent off your money. I would be happy to hear from you. Bye, sweetheart," her father's voice said from the answering machine.

"Baby," Chyna said into her cell phone, "I promise everything is arranged perfectly. I'll be seeing you in a couple of days." She kissed the phone and hung up.

"See who?" Steve asked, as if *he* was still the boss when *he* was the one who had been hiding in *her* residence for the past six months.

She wanted to say, "None of your business," but instead, responded, "It's my good friend. He's coming in from Jamaica. Probably you two can get acquainted." She typed some information into her IBM computer. "It looks like the shipment coming in by UPS will be here shortly." She looked at Steve with devious eyes. "You look quite ready to go back out into society."

Chyna studied Steven with approval. He now had a full beard that was neatly groomed to cover his once-clean-shaven face. He also let his hair grow longer, though he kept it styled fashionably.

Chyna handed him an envelope with some Canadian IDs and credentials, along with a North Carolina temporary driver's license. Steve gazed down at the fraudulent material which read, "Robert James." He, too, approved of his new bearded photograph.

"Or would you still rather be Steve McScott?" She barged past him with her sarcastic remark.

Steve, knowing that he needed Chyna more than she needed him, didn't respond. He just stepped aside with gratitude. Without a word, he returned to his guest bedroom and went back under the cover, watching crime TV.

Chyna made her way upstairs and started unpacking groceries. But first, she opened the patio door which overlooked a beautiful landscape of majestic Flame of the Forest trees and fan palms and Royal Poincianas and a cobblestone path that meandered lazily through beds of flowers bursting with the colors of the rainbow.

She observed the neighbors and their guest enjoying the swimming pool and Jacuzzi. It inspired her to go upstairs and marinate in the Jacuzzi in her bathroom and then take a leisure bubble bath. Instead, she finished putting away the groceries and left out some unshelled shrimp and vegetables. Dinner tonight was going to be something simple and quick.

She took a medium pot from off a hook and a frying pan, placed the stainless steel frying pan on the stove, and turned the burner on low. The Kitchen Aid stove heated instantly. After filling the other pot half full of water, she placed it on a burner and brought it to a boil.

Next, she cut half a stick of butter and combined it with a spoonful of olive oil in the pan, cut up some fresh green peppers, scotch bonnet peppers with all the seeds, an onion, garlic, and small pieces of potatoes and let it all simmer while she put the rest of margarine in the medium pot, threw in some salt and two cups of rice. She washed and fried the shell-less shrimp in the frying pan with black pepper, paprika, garlic powder, and curry while the rice boiled. Once everything was cooked, she combined it all, stirred it together, and covered the pot. Like a good cook, she then washed her hands and headed upstairs.

In her room, Chyna slipped off her Prada blouse and skirt, eased out of her Prada shoes, and headed to her Cherry Oak dresser wearing only her Versace underwear. The mirror reflected her superb body. The Creator could not have sculpted a lovelier vision. Her voluptuous breasts were size 36 C, she had a mere wisp of a waist, and her hips measured a magnificent 42 inches. She was a fabulous work of art on a canvas of almond-colored skin.

Opening the dresser drawer, Chyna pulled out her thick, knitted, Fendi sweater and slipped on a baggy pair of Gucci sweat pants to wear around the house. Slipping on her Prada slippers, she padded into the bathroom and turned on the Jacuzzi, filling it with boiling water, to which she added a packet of scented bubble bath.

She stood in front of the wide mirror and put her long black hair into a ponytail and with a quick reach, grabbed a face cleanser pad and massaged her face in a circular motion using only her index and middle fingers.

After masking her face in Noxzema, she jogged back to the kitchen. Her fifteen-minute meal of curry shrimp and white rice was now ready. Opening her Kitchen-Aid refrigerator, she took out a bag of ready-made salad, put it in a china bowl, sprinkled honey vinegar on it, and began eating her first course. Then she went back to soak in the Jacuzzi while the entrée cooled off.

Chyna loved music, so she turned on her Infinity Stereo system. The music filled the bedroom and the bathroom with the ceiling-embedded speakers. It was evening now and she wanted to bask in the starlight, so she opened her Levolor blinds and pulled her Versace curtains aside. She vibed to her Sizzla "Black Woman and Child" CD, singing words she knew by heart.

"Only for you I have so much love o-o-love."

The Jacuzzi was ready and waiting for her. The bubbles were well formed and inviting. She walked over to the stereo and put the song on repeat mode, then walked to her dresser and took out her favorite silk Armani robe. She hung it on a rack next to the Jacuzzi.

Chyna unbuttoned her bra to reveal her small strawberry nipples. She squeezed out of her size 6 panties to expose her small, clean-shaven vagina, which had the plump tenderness of a baby girl's.

She gently inserted her foot, one at a time, into the hot water, then slowly lowered her body in the water in a squatting position. The sensation called for a deep breath. Chyna lay back and let the water caress her breasts and her neck. She relaxed, closed her eyes, and repeated, "Only for you I have so much love."

12 Agent Robert Lynch

Robert Lynch was in his office, putting in some overtime in order to investigate the Malone and Williams murder case. He shook his head in disgust. Seven months and no trace of the killer, in spite of a $250,000-dollar reward for information leading to the arrest. This person could not be your average, street-level criminal, Agent Lynch deduced. He wondered how many more lives this maniac was going to take and destroy before he was apprehended.

A female agent walked past and threw some folders on his desk. "Here's the nationwide photo match-up you requested, Robert." She walked off. Robert sipped his coffee with his face glued to the paper in his hand.

He opened the file to see a list of identities. What interested him was the birth name Steve McScott. Arrested on numerous charges for murder, attempted murder, kidnapping, assault, robbery, and aggravated battery, this suspect had been arrested all these times and finally served a 10-year sentence for a murder charge in the New York State penal system. Now here was a person with his mother and father deceased and no listed brothers or sisters or no significant other through which to trace him.

Besides his birth name, documented dental information and fingerprints, this bastard was untraceable, Roberts thought, removing his pencil from his mouth and tapping the open file with the eraser. As he sipped his black coffee, the 42-year-old seasoned vet dropped the pencil, leaned back in his office chair, and placed his thumb through his suspenders. He stared at the suspect's photo, looking into his eyes as if to generate some kind of telepathic intuition about this psychopathic monster.

Robert studied the photograph, thinking Steve McScott looked as if he would have made a great running back or a law enforcement officer. Absentmindedly, he breathed in his Starbuck's Sumatra dark roasted coffee aroma. *Yep*, he thought, *a cop has to be as ruthless and as devious as a criminal in order to apprehend one.* Ironically, to prevent apprehension, the criminal has to think like a cop.

Criminal or law enforcer—what's the difference? One was working for the ultimate criminal organization—the U.S. government—and the other was a renegade, thinking he was governed by his own institution.

Well, I don't know where to start, he thought. *All I can do is call up my friend John Walsh and view this bastard on America's most wanted.* Somebody greedy was bound to imprison this idiot for the rest of his stinking, worthless life, Robert reasoned.

Suddenly he had what he knew was a politically incorrect thought that he would never admit out loud. *It beats my understanding why we ever let them niggas free in the first place. Now we have to waste our time and taxpayers' money locking them ingrates back up, anyhow,* he thought. He broke his concentration with a devilish grimace that made him look satanic with his receding blond hair. *Yes, we're going to lock you all up,* he thought. Putting his coffee aside and picking up his pencil in both hands, he twirled it around with his index finger and thumb.

He focused his eyes on the photo like a cobra locks eyes with its prey, preparing himself for the thrill of the chase and the anticipation of a satisfying kill.

13 Officer
Paul Parker

It was nightfall when Officer Parker arrived at his Lithonia Estates location. He pushed his genie to open his front gate from half a mile away, drove up the 40-yard driveway around back, and parked his black Cadillac in the center of the four-car garage, next to his roommate's black 750 BMW with tinted glass. With a quick click of the garage genie, he closed the garage door. When he exited the car, he saw his reflection in his 5-percent tinted windows.

He used the keyless entry to open his trunk, took out a large gym bag, and carried it to the basement level. He wanted to prepare himself for his date with Marsha, a stunning, exciting, aerobics instructor he'd met at LA Fitness in midtown. She was just his type—big breasts, energetic, athletic, and white. He was supposed to meet her at her house tonight for a candlelight dinner and an evening of star-gazing.

Inside the basement, he stripped down to his Calvin Klein's boxer briefs and went to his Gold Gym bench press machine. Generally, he worked out three times a week to keep his 6-foot-3, 247-pound figure well muscled and toned. He did ten sets of ten with his 265-pound weight bar. Next, he moved over to his squat machine and did ten sets of twenty with his 405-pound weight bar. Jumping jacks were next. He went to the center of the room's loft-style designed basement and turned on the hot water and set the spa on medium. He wanted to relax in the Jacuzzi to loosen up.

He left the water running, went upstairs, and placed a packet of Mega-Man protein shake on the marble countertop that matched his midnight-black Travertine marble tile floors imported from Tivoli, Italy, opened the frig, and took out the milk carton and a banana. He placed them all in the Kitchen-Aid metallic-red blender, mixed it, then drank the whole thing straight from the blender. When he finished, he placed it into the Whirlpool dishwasher and turned it on. Now that the edge was taken off his appetite, he went downstairs and climbed in the Jacuzzi. With his massive chest above water, he laid back and relaxed.

With his low fade and clean-shaven face, the 34-year-old looked very young for his age, partly because he had no children, and partly because he was in exceptionally good shape.

Officer Parker sat thinking about all the positions and slips that Marsha could maneuver into. He wondered if she could deep throat or if she was the one that he would marry. *Naw. Forget about marriage—that gives women the right to possess all your belongings and run your life.*

I'd have to be a fool to get married and be dedicated to one woman my entire life, he thought. *Now, Jen Jamison, I would most definitely marry her.* His thoughts were interrupted when his roommate, John Pines, walked in, still dressed in his Dekalb County uniform.

"You're home early," John said.

"I got a date," Paul replied.

"Who?"

"Marsha Beckford."

"Marsha Beckford? The work-out-all-day-long aerobic instructor Marsha Beckford?" John sounded incredulous.

"That's her."

"Dude, she's hot," John said.

John exited the basement and went upstairs. Paul sat there, trying to grasp a scene of peace. However, it seemed like the trauma of his occupation and his affair had his mind always wandering with some deep down internal issues that soon would cause him to go crawling and whimpering to a psychiatrist's couch—or probably he needed one right now.

John was back downstairs, standing in front of Paul with a towel wrapped around his waist. He lay it aside and entered the Jacuzzi.

Paul first met John when they were enlisted in the U.S. Marine

Corps. The two cadets were stationed in North Carolina before Paul was transferred overseas to Japan. They quickly became friends and used to leave the base to go scavenging some Okinawa Japanese whores.

Both were natives of Georgia and had a love for law enforcement. However, it was John who first received his job as a Dekalb police officer. However, Paul, being more tenacious, moved up in the ranks to make sergeant faster. John, now a lieutenant, could have moved to the station of detectives long ago when he received his degree in criminal law. Nevertheless, he was comfortable in the position that he was in and did not want to be bombarded with the hassle and the paperwork of being a detective.

Now the two colleagues sat in the Jacuzzi and marinated for a few minutes. Then Paul rose up and headed for the steps. He was at the top of the steps when he felt a slow crawl up his leg. With a bewildered expression on his face, he looked back at John. John closed in on his prey until he reached Paul's waistline and engulfed him into his warm sea of seduction.

Paul stood there like the statue of Alexander the Great while John licked and sucked his sexual organ like a 2 year old would lustily consume a lollipop. Every taste brought him satisfaction. Finally, Paul broke the tantalizing grip of John's clutches and walked upstairs with a throbbing erection.

John exited the spa anticipating a torrid affair and followed behind Paul like an enchanted—and very horny—teenage girl following a rap star to his private dressing room. John made his way upstairs in the six-bedroom house to find Paul in his bedroom, masturbating and waiting, like a black widow spider once her web is woven, knowing her prey will eventually come along.

John flamboyantly jumped on his bed, which set the satin sheet waving like a mystical light wind hovering over a black moonlit ocean. He lay on his side in a suggestive pose until Paul overshadowed him and placed him on his stomach. Paul used his legs to keep John's legs apart as he inserted himself in his anus. He sent John into an emotional and sexual high that surely reached another galaxy. Moaning, John hugged his pillow, bit down into it, and closed his eyes tightly to keep them from exploding out of their sockets.

Paul thrust himself aggressively inside of John until the constant friction created an explosion. Once Paul withdrew, moaning, John flipped over and attacked his target with the swiftness and precision of a venomous cobra. He consumed every drop of semen that erupted. John more than loved his fellow man. He envied him to the point of consumption.

14 *Ricky*

I gazed down at my Swiss watch to see the time. I'd been hustling for the past 10 months and finally had the time to take care of my personal business. "Baby, slow down," I told Lisa, who was driving. "We ain't in no rush. I have no time to be wasting on no police harassing us."

Lisa had rented a Cadillac CTS-V for the long journey to New York City. She figured the ride was going to be long, so it might as well be comfortable. We rode, listening to the sounds of Outkast's "ATLiens" CD.

I had just entered South Carolina, and the freedom of not having to answer my phone to negotiate or supply someone else's wants lifted a burden off my shoulders. My clients had held me captive to their needs and demands, but now I had a chance to get a breather. I knew it wasn't going to be for too long because as soon as I started getting too relaxed, I became too comfortable. I guess I'd been running these streets for so long that it has become a part of my nature.

My adaptation to my fast-moving, decisive environment now had me feeling uncomfortable. I needed to hassle or deal. It's sad to say, but I'm just as addicted to my lifestyle as addicts are addicted to the drugs I supply. I adjusted my Cartier sunglasses to a more comfortable position on my face, reclined my seat, and relaxed.

Lisa was driving because I really loved sightseeing when traveling. If I didn't have to oversee everything all the time, I would travel more often. The fresh air—every state, every area—had a different feeling, a different aspect of culture and lifestyle. It comforted me and gave me peace to just ride the open road and be a part of it all.

Meeting and interacting with new people that did not even know or care about my background made those lifestyles more intriguing. They're just comfortable with what they know—their upbringing and environment. That is what I love the most—the reality of it. To me, there is nothing as exciting as traveling the great highways of the United States of America.

I looked over at Lisa's hands firmly gripping the steering wheel, flashing the diamond ring I'd bought for her. She adored it, and I loved the fact that she loved it. We'd made reservations at the Hilton Hotel and Resort in Manhattan with a great view of the city's nightlife. I planned to do a little catching up on my shopping while I was there. I would probably venture in Canal Street and get some cheap, fashionable, brand-name attire and bring them back with me to sell to my homies or something.

However, my main objective was to contact and visit my little brother, Dwayne. I'd spoken to Ms. Taylor, and she said he became involved with a vicious, notorious street gang, the Bloods, who were responsible for 90 percent of the violence since 1998, after the major influx of gang activity in New York City. Ms. Taylor told me that my brother's adopted parents had moved to New York City for better opportunities.

Unfortunately, while my brother was there, he got in with the wrong crowd. Because of his ignorance and brutality, Dwayne quickly elevated himself amongst his peers, earning him the rank of general.

One day Dwayne was supervising his soldiers when a large ex-con took a dime of crack from one of his smaller members and refused to pay. Someone informed Dwayne, who, in turn, decided to enforce order by attacking the massive man—and stabbing him seventeen times. Somehow, the man survived.

From the social worker, I learned that Dwayne had played linebacker since Peewee League football, which was sponsored by some drug dealer wanting to give back to the community, so he'd always been athletic. Dwayne also had a love for lifting heavy weights, which increased his bulk tremendously.

Although I had not seen him in years, Dwayne was the only family that I have knowledge of. Me, being who I am, loved the feeling of genuine love. I've noticed that nobody will love you unconditionally like your children. Next was your family, because no matter what the feelings may be between them, when times get rough, family always stick together.

My brother was the only person I genuinely loved, I guess because we came from the same exact beginnings. I'm in love with my woman, but if I couldn't do what I do for her, would she still be there for me? In addition, if I could not be the man I'm supposed to be, would she help guide me? Or was she manipulating me for her own selfish needs? I wondered.

Lisa pulled over in Virginia. She said she was tired and needed some rest. We decided to fill the gas tank, go have a decent meal, and book a hotel for the night so she could get some rest, and we'd be back on the road in the morning. We found a great Jamaican restaurant to eat where the food was terrific. I ordered stew fish and rice and peas, with a side order of sweet plantains, and a fresh salad with Italian dressing. Lisa ordered her usual curry chicken and white rice with sweet plantains and a Jamaican beef pattie. We sat and ate while listening to a live band and even danced to a rendition of "Red Wine." It was a pleasant dinner arrangement.

After we left that location, we entered a close-by, upscale lounge and ordered a couple of drinks. I had a double shot of Chivas Regal Gold whisky and ordered my woman a double shot of Grand Marnier Cuvée du Cent Cinquantenaire, which I was surprised they had. A friend of mind introduced me to it, and I figured Lisa would love it.

The surroundings were elegant, and the people wore casual dress. We had no problem fitting in. Lisa had on her H. Stern black dress, and I had on my black Gucci slacks and Truzzi Milano shirt, halfway unbuttoned, with my black Versace tank top and Gucci shoes. My face was spotless from a recent, clean trim. Lisa had her black shiny hair hot pressed and flowing lustrously down her back and shoulders.

We sat at the bar and gazed into each other's eyes, as people in love do. Then I realized that I had not taken the time to look in her eyes for months. I guess it was from putting up my armor of defense that I needed for my occupation. Doing what I do, you have to be militant, faced with the hurt and suffering one faces every day in illicit hustling. My self-defense mechanism was due to the fact that any and everybody around me had the intention to replace or end my existence, so there was no room for me showing weakness, like the sensitive sensation that I get when I gaze in Lisa's eyes.

Instantly, my armor was demolished and I was exposed in my nakedness. For the moment, I had no worries; I was in a zone of extreme comfort, which I did not dare be in when I was around everyday mobsters.

We finished our drinks and then exited the lounge, feeling fantastic. We made our way back to the car and drove to our other destination and pulled in at the Comfort Inn, where we got a room for the night.

After signing in, we entered the hotel room, took a shower, then had sex from the bathroom to the bed. I fell asleep with my dick in her pussy and with her grasped tightly in my arms.

We woke up, took a shower, and at 6:00 a.m., we checked out and ate the hotel's complimentary breakfast before continuing our journey to New York City. That morning, we were dressed a little more formal. Lisa had on some tight brown pants and a brown and black tight Polo button shirt. I was dressed in a Guess jeans outfit she had bought me. Afterwards, we made a stop at a store and purchased some junk food for the road, you know, sodas, potato chips, honey buns, and all that kind of stuff.

Lisa got us in the city by evening. We maneuvered our way through the hazardous New York traffic. By the time we reached the hotel, she was exhausted, but, on the contrary, I was ready to be a part of the nightlife. We checked in and made our way to the room. I generously tipped the bellhop who carried our bags to the room.

I told him any special accommodations or events going on in the hotel I wanted to know about. He assured me that anything he could do for me, he would. We entered our spacious suite with a spa in the middle of it. I promised myself I was going to lay out one of my bedrooms just like this one.

Lisa crashed on the bed with her shoes on. I took off her Elizabeth Claiborne sandals and placed them on the floor, ran my hand through her hair, brushed her hair away from her face, and gave her a kiss. She looked just like my little baby, lying on the huge king-sized bed.

I took the car keys out of her hand, took $1,000 of my money that I had given to Lisa for safe keeping, and left her with $4,000. Next, I went in the Luis Vuitton traveling pack, retrieved my Degree antiperspirant, rubbed some on, sprayed on my Eternity cologne, and left. On my way downstairs, some old Caucasian people clutched their pocketbooks. This action insulted me.

Anyway, I did not pay the bigots any mind. I was feeling good, and I was not going to let them spoil it. I entered my car, put on the navigation system, and inserted my CD, "All on Me" Volume 2. As I rode off into the night, the city was illuminated in light coming from everywhere. It was almost hypnotizing. I could tell by the horns sounding and the hostile shouts that the natives weren't used to my laid-back, calm, Southern driving.

Man, there were people everywhere on the streets. I see why they call it the City that Never Sleeps. I saw a group of dreads from the islands, so I parked my car and approached them. They looked at me with suspicion. However, they paid attention to the out-of-town license plate and saw me as an opportunity. I approached their group, and a Rasta man strolled up to me with a serious expression on his face.

"Greeting in the name of the Most High, Haile Selassie." He gave me a pound. I knew more than likely they would be cool. From what I knew of dreads, it seemed most of them fashioned their lives being cool.

I asked the Rasta man, "Where I can get some green from?"

"You want green?" he repeated. "You sure you no police?"

"I'm sure I ain't no police," I told him. He gave me another pound, this time with a smile.

"Irie, mon," he said with a huge smile, swaying back and forth, swinging his long, thick dreadlocks side to side. I finally realized this man was high and out of his mind.

"Come, man, come," he commanded me, swinging his dreads around with him. When he quickly turned around, his locks almost slapped me in the face. I followed him as he walked through his parting comrades like Moses going through the Red Sea, but they were observing me like a pack of hungry wolves. Rasta Man was walking with his legs high in step and his right hand swinging as if he was chopping a pathway through a jungle terrain. He led me to a minivan and opened the sliding door. I was immediately engulfed in a delightful and highly intoxicating cloud of smoke.

"Cool, my youth, everything cool," Rasta said, motioning me inside the van. He took a big joint from his little Rasta woman companion.

"What you want?" he asked me.

I gave him $500, and he tossed me a half pound of ganja. I could not believe I was getting a chance to smoke exotic ganja in the States.

I concealed my package under my jeans outfit, got Rasta Man's phone number, gave him another fist pound, and left. Walking to my car, I placed the half pound in the trunk and drove off, went to the liquor store, and picked up some cigars and some X-rated liquor for Lisa. Once I placed the programming in the navigation system, it guided me on my route back to the hotel. After I put the ganja down in my pants, I rushed upstairs using the stairwell, pushed my card in the door, and entered. Lisa was lounging in the Jacuzzi.

"You had fun?" she asked.

"It was 'ight."

"Where you been?"

"Don't question me."

Once you make a woman feel comfortable asking you personal questions, they feel no limit on how personal they can get, which was all right—sometimes. However, I did not like it. Her interrogation made me feel like the police grilling me. Anyway, I retrieved some ice and glasses and set them by the Jacuzzi next to her. Then I took off my clothes and got in the water. It was lukewarm and the built-in massage was on low. I had a blunt in my hand, so I began rolling.

"Ricky, you know you can't keep doing what you do forever. Why don't you invest your money and start a business or do something that's going to benefit you in the long run?"

I took out a bud, crushed it in my blunt, and kept rolling. "Huh, huh," I replied.

"Baby, it's just that what you're doing is dangerous, and I would love for you to branch off and do something more productive and less risky," Lisa said.

I took a cigar, slid over close to her, and gave her a kiss on her sweet, juicy-red lips. I loved her always caring for me. Even before I understood how to make money from my criminal activity, Lisa was supportive of me. I sat a level above her in the spa, placed her between my legs, and hugged her back up against my chest with my hands under her breasts.

"Baby, I know you be worrying about me, but I have things under control. I've even been inquiring into a car dealership business. They told me all I need was a business establishment and a surety bond and I could get my dealership license."

Lisa reached over, got the bottle of X-Rated, and handed it to me to open for her. I did, and she poured herself a glass and took a sip.

"Damn, baby, this is real good," she said and filled the glass up.

"We're going to go ahead and fill out the SS-4 form. I'll send it in once when we get back, since you're so concerned about what I need to establish."

Lisa was a computer analyst for Hewlett-Packard in Marietta, Georgia, making $60,000 annually.

"Baby, it's just a start until I can fully invest my time into something else. Therefore, I'm going to give you $20,000 to get the surety bond, and then we're gonna start going to auctions and buying and selling cars."

Lisa switched the topic. "So how you like the city, baby?"

"Baby, this shit is spectacular," I responded. "Apart from all the police they have constantly surrounding the place, I love it."

See how women always find a way to get what they want from a man? They are a lot better manipulators. For instance, women like to fuck way more then we do—right?

Part of their womanly existence depends on sex. A heterosexual woman requires sex for assurance, completion, and making babies. We men just love to dominate and bust a nut. However, the female species manipulates the male species by pretending that they're not as subject to sexual desires as we are. Many women will be very attracted to a man, and if he does not approach her on that intimate level, he may never know that. I'm sure every woman is programmed to be sexually strong and make the man put forth energy into charming them for his sexual desire.

I know a man and a woman are definitely different creatures. However, I also know we have the same wants and desires. Damn, I was in a total higher zone. *Damn, this weed is good as hell,* I thought. It seemed like my mind was traveling light years ahead of me. I had to put this shit down before I started hallucinating.

I got up out of the spa, dried off with a towel, and went to bed. By then, I was exhausted and needed some rest. Lisa stayed in the spa and started reading a book, Solace, by Ricardo Sinclair. I guess she knew I was very tired, or she was just enjoying her quiet time.

WHEN I WOKE up in the morning, Lisa was already up. She was sitting on the sofa watching TV, dressed, and ready to go. I had told her we came up here to catch up on shopping, and she didn't waste anytime waiting.

"Baby, I see you up. Let's go. I want to hit all the stores on my list."

I rolled over and pretended I was still asleep.

"Okay, I guess I'll get a head start, then come back and get you," she said aloud and started walking to the door.

"Okay, I'm up, I'm up," I said.

She didn't enjoy anything without my company, so I got up, took a shower, and brushed my teeth. I hurried, put on my Calvin

Klein pants and my Yushua V-neck sleeveless shirt and my Wallabee Clarks, and then I was good to go. Last came a splash of some Kenneth Cole. Me and my woman put the "do not disturb" sign on the outside of the door and left.

Lisa wanted to go to Saks Fifth Avenue, so she programmed her destination and the navigation system did the rest.

After arriving at 703 Fifth Avenue at 55th by 11:00 a.m., we entered De Beers. Lisa got herself a platinum snowflake necklace and matching ring. I got a 24-inch opera necklace and a Sinclair timepiece. I bought this watch because of the legacy it has. I like watches, and this watch was like the mother of all watches. It was endowed with a lavishly decorated three-quarter plate made of untreated German silver, gold clusters, and a precious screw balance and unique whiplash percussion in the adjuster. I got in platinum.

After we finished jewelry shopping, Lisa and I went to Dennis Basso, where she got two dress ensembles. I hated watching Lisa shop, but I loved to see her change into her outfits. Lisa was paying for everything on her American Express card, so I had to tag along with her. After making our purchases, we placed the merchandise in the car trunk.

I had never seen people marching like ants until I reached New York City. Everybody seemed so busy, so preoccupied, so obsessed with their own affairs and business. Finally, we took a break to get something to eat. We decided to eat like a native New Yorker, with two slices of a big New York pizza. I had straight cheese, which was the best pizza I ever ate.

This guy Tony made a hell of a pizza. Lisa ate two pepperoni pizza slices, then we left Tony's and continued our shopping spree. Next, we went to Neiman Marcus, and I got a black Stefano Ricci suit and some Gianluca slacks. Lisa picked up five more outfits, and then we left. We cruised around sightseeing for an hour or two before we ended up in the Bronx, at Dr. Jay's on Third Avenue. Finally, we wrapped up our shopping with $15,000 worth of Phat Farm, Sean John, and Rocawear fashions.

We also bought Babe and Apes footwear, then headed back to our hotel. By the time we arrived there, it started raining. I let Lisa go on ahead and run out of the rain while the bellhop and I carried our bags upstairs. After tipping the bellhop in the room, I ordered a steak with baked potatoes, a lobster and shrimp combination, and a bottle of wine.

Lisa opened the window shades, which showed a magnificent view of the city skyscrapers in the dim light. The rainfall set a soothing, romantic mood. The thunder and lightning created an enchanting, almost mystical atmosphere that drew us into each other's arms. The server arrived with our meal an hour later.

The hotel staff set our table while we relaxed and waited. Finally, we sat at the table and poured two glasses of 7777 vineyard-reserved wine and Lisa made a toast, to love, peace, and prosperity. We ate and drank.

Lisa had on a sexy, formal dress she'd bought at Neiman Marcus. I had on an Oxford blazer and slacks, along with a red Versace button-up shirt. The candlelight dinner had me feeling more romantic than usual. I stood up and reached one of my hands over the table for Lisa to put her hands in mine.

She did, and I sidestepped from behind the table and gently brought her closer to me. I hugged her, did a little close bumping and grinding dance, then gave her a passionate kiss. I inhaled her lobster breath. Next, I kissed her on her cheeks, her forehead, then began kissing on her neck. I gently kissed my way down to her knees. I elevated Lisa while undressing her at the same time, pulling her dress over her head to reveal her beautiful body.

In turn, she started undressing me. While doing her seductive wiggle, she unbuttoned my shirt and slid it off me. She stood back and admired me for a moment, holding my hands. At the same time, I was admiring how delicious and alluring she was in her bra and panties. I kissed her gently on her lips again, swept her off her feet and into my arms against my chest like a newborn baby. After walking over to the bed, I laid her in the very center of it. Arching her back, she took off her bra. Then I slowly slid her panties down her thick, track-starlike thighs and took them off.

Grasping her ankles, I spread her legs wide apart, elevated her left leg straight up, and then moved my tongue down her leg, gliding my tongue over her calves, stopped behind her knee, and licked around that particular area. Next, I moved my tongue down to her center thigh and quickly moved on to her clitoris. Grabbing the back of her other leg, I positioned both of them straight up in the air while I was sucking her pussy lips gently. I licked up her pussy with a flat tongue, which gave her a thrilling sensation. Her back arched and her nipples hardened. As they called to me, I placed my hands on her breasts and started caressing them.

By now, Lisa was shaking her elevated legs and moaned while I was sucking energetically in the midst of her essence. When I felt her about to climax, I began flicking her clitoris with my tongue gently to sooth the tension off my passionate vacuuming of her pussy. Her juices began flowing on me like a raging river of lust. I continued to pleasure her with my tongue until I was exhausted and passed out.

I woke up the next morning tired, not tired from physical fatigue, but psychologically tired. I wanted to go home. All this vacation had me feeling homesick. However, I had to finish my main objective. So I dragged myself out of bed and took a nice, hot shower. After brushing my teeth, I got dressed and put on my regular street attire: a large T-shirt and a pair of Guess jeans. I put on my new opera diamond necklace and my Jacob and Co. Tourneau watch.

With a little spray of some Vera Wang cologne and a quick good-bye kiss to Lisa, I left, went to the parking lot, and retrieved my car. Sparford Juvenile Prison was my destination. I programmed it into the navigation system, and the satellite guide did the rest.

I arrived at Sparford Juvenile holding facility at 10:00 a.m. and gave the front desk officer my out-of-state ID, went to the visiting area, had a seat, and waited. When Dwayne arrived and sat in front of me, I didn't even recognize him. If he hadn't sat in front of me, I would not have known he was my baby brother.

The boy was 6-foot-1, 240 pounds, with muscle busting out of his uniform. I tried to display some type of enthusiasm, however, he looked void of all emotions. He wore thin-framed glasses, and if one didn't know him, one might think he's a devoted college football player.

I mostly did all the talking. I really missed the little guy. I hadn't seen any family since we were separated and I was feeling a sense of union, not that phony love that can die anytime with the comrades I have in the streets. For the most part, he was happy to see me and he missed me, too. He'd just forgotten who I was. I understood.

Dwayne told me he wanted to turn his life around and start doing something positive. I told him I was about to start a business and he was welcome to assist me. As a matter of fact, I told him if he felt like coming and living in Atlanta, I would give him his own place to live and a car as soon as he got his license.

However, he took my promises reluctantly. I knew exactly how he was feeling. Growing up without your biological family is hard because people tend to make an adopted family member feel like an outcast. Therefore, more than likely, Dwayne was going to spend his whole life trying to impress the people around him so that he would feel accepted. However, it backfired because people were more afraid and intimidated by overachievers. He informed me that he already did two years of his three-year sentence and should be out early next year.

I told him to call me as soon as he got out, and I would arrange for him to come back home. His demeanor was one of a terminator-like android. But I cracked his armor when I mentioned I'd just placed a dozen roses on our mother's grave, prayed, and asked her to watch over us.

"Mama," he said softly and lowered his head in sorrow.

Dwayne was Mama's baby boy and was always close under her wings. Mention of her brought back memories. Memories of Mama were always good because no matter what, even through her addiction and hard times, Mama was always there to make sure we were unharmed, and she treated us with the utmost love and care.

Dwayne moved close to stare into my eyes. He could see the pain and the loneliness there. Then he began to realize we came from the same place and went through similar trials and tribulations. First we reminisced on a few childhood memories, mostly about hard times and growing up in the struggle. Then he paused and looked me over from my head to my watch.

"I can see you ain't done too badly," he said, admiring my watch.

"Yeah. You like it? I'll give you one as a welcome home gift," I told him.

"Hell, yeah, that's what I'm talking about, man. You better believe I have your back to the fullest when I come home. Just hold down the fort until I'm released. I'm glad you came and saw me before I had to come see you."

That was the last that he said before he was ushered away by the correctional officer. I left that visit with a sense of peace, feeling that things happen after all for a reason. I had learned that if a person goes through great suffering and keeps persevering, it will positively affect his health and wealth, as well as his mental and physical development. In fact, that individual will excel and surpass the average person in these areas.

Once I hit the Lincoln tunnel, I programmed the navigation system for the quickest route to Atlanta.

Chapter

15 *Spraggs Banton*

Spraggs Banton made a successful journey across the Canadian boarder and used his fraudulent government-issued North Carolina driver's license to catch a first-class American Airlines flight from JFK to Hartford International airport in Atlanta. Exhausted from his constant traveling, ducking, and hiding, Spraggs lay back the leather reclining chair, relaxed, and dozed off.

When the airplane landed at LaGuardia Airport at 2:00 p.m., the airplane stewardess gently tapped Mr. Banton on his shoulder, trying to awaken him for his deplaning. Even though he was in a sleep-induced stupor, Spraggs caught her hand with the reflexes of a striking cobra. He reached for his gun, but suddenly realized there was no gun on his waistband.

Wide awake now, he remembered the reality of it all, looked at the stewardess, and apologized. "Pardon me. I was frightened out of a bad dream."

With an alarmed, but still charming look on her face, the flight attendant apologized and proceeded to escort the rest of the passengers off the plane.

Spraggs stood up, grabbed his travel carry-on luggage, and exited the plane. Walking in the terminal, he felt relieved of half his burdens. He marched through the airport with the swagger of a movie star and the confidence and posture of a CIA agent.

He wore a pair of black frame Gucci sunglasses. His silk shirt flowed off his body as if a gigantic fan was blowing in his direction. He wore tightly fitted Iceberg pants with a shiny pair of black, all patent leather Prada shoes.

Chyna waited, anxiously anticipating her beloved's arrival. Once she saw him, she was once again transformed, like the moon under a sunray of light. She began to glow. She instantly became more assured of herself. She could feel his power already captivating her. Relieved, she took a deep breath, happy that her man made it through all right and that they would once again be reunited.

Spraggs took his first two steps out of the airport's entrance and motioned his head from left to right like the terminator looking for Sarah O'Connor.

Chyna hopped up and down and flagged a cheerful one-hand wave. "Sweetheart, sweetheart, over here," she yelled with an alluring smile on her face. Spraggs walked over to her as she rushed towards him and gave him a great hug. She kissed him on his stone-faced expression and hugged him again quickly.

"Come on, rude boy, come on," she said as she led him to her Firepower.

He threw his one bag in the backseat and sat quietly in the passenger seat. She was playing a Buju Banton CD, "Shilo," which she turned down low. "So, how was your flight, rude boy?"

Nobody called him rude boy since he was a kid. However, that was his nickname, and Spraggs wasn't concerned about what people called him. Besides, he had been called a lot worse things. He did not respond to her. Chyna's heart started racing. Once again she was around a man that was not intimidated by her extraordinary beauty, her intellectual ingenuity, and her powerful connections all around the world.

She loved the fact Spraggs dominated every person and situation he was confronted with. Ever since Chyna knew the man, he had never shown fear. His only pressure point was the instinct and wisdom he had for his own survival.

Chyna drove down Highway 85 North from the airport to Interstate 75 North. Spraggs kept his head looking straight ahead of him, and then he grabbed ahold of Chyna tightly and squeezed her soft flesh. Chyna sat erect but opened her legs in comfort. Spraggs' hand moved instantly up her Burberry tennis skirt and reached her lace panties. He pushed her panties to the side and tried to insert his index and middle finger in her vagina. When he saw that both fingers would not work, he just inserted one finger. This excited him a bit because she was as tight as a virgin.

Chyna glanced over at Spraggs' hard face and fresh Caesar haircut framing his face. He was even more handsome than she could remember. His narrow nose resembling an arrow, his sexy thick lips, and his perfectly arched eyebrows made her orgasm instantly. The tip of her tongue licked her lips as she moved his hand from inside of her to down her thighs.

With some of her sexual tension released, Chyna relaxed more in her seat. Her head was held high. She felt more enhanced, thinking she could do whatever she endeavored and desired. It had been years since she felt this way, and she missed it immensely. Chyna knew she definitely loved this man. When they were younger, she saw his potential, and his ruthless ego. She nourished his ego and gave him a lust for financial rewards and social refinement. Now she felt like a proud mother, seeing her prince had graduated to the top of the ranks, graduating class valedictorian.

They made their way to her house. Once there, she pressed the genie to enter their garage and parked next to her black Jaguar XK-Series and the 21-inch deep dish Giovanni rims caught Spraggs' eyes.

Exiting the car, they entered the condominium through the basement garage door. The basement had an expensive home theater that consisted of a 63-inch Phillips television and entertainment system. Spraggs observed the room with his eyes only, always keeping his head straight in front of him. He moved like a politician, never displaying too much emotion for anyone to act on or figure him out.

Steve was sitting on the Armani leather couch, but Spraggs paid him no attention whatsoever. He just kept his head fixed in front of him and walked behind Chyna. Her short tennis skirt showing her Versace thong strap underneath gave Spraggs an immediate erection. Chyna was definitely one of the most beautiful women Spraggs had ever seen. She caused his heartbeat to increase with every step, and his hormones were pumping wildly. The sexual tension was so great that even his hands balled up in a fist, and his facial muscles tensed up to the point that they started twitching.

Chyna was not making it any easier for him, walking slowly, flaunting her beauty in his face. She weaved her way through the Avery Boardman-designed living room and elegant Elizabeth Taylor-designed dining room, then glided up some stairs, past some pricey Henry Moret and Hans Brendekilde paintings on the wall. A moment later, they reached the bedroom that was lavishly furnished in Cherry Oak and a super ultra king-sized bed. The 27-inch HP computer and TV and futuristic electronics made the household looked state-of-the-art.

However, it was not nearly as lavish as Spraggs' living conditions in his native land. He dropped his bag at the door and walked up behind Chyna, grabbed her around the waist with one hand, and quickly placed himself inside her wet midsection. She placed her hands on her thighs for balance. She then pumped back on him with intensity. His pythonlike tactic frightened her and thrilled her at the same time. His sexual introduction made her climax with ease from the excitement and longing for his touch. Her pumping and heavy breathing turned to wiggling and moaning.

She sent a gush of liquid love down his erection. Spraggs positioned her over at the cobalt-blue Ultrasuede settee, then she stepped out of her panties. He motioned for her to place one leg on the settee while standing up and leaning over with one hand resting on the arm of the settee. Highly aroused, Spraggs began to pump himself inside of her as if he had a hula-hoop around him and he was trying to keep from losing momentum.

His long slow strokes kept Chyna exploding with pleasure. She was sweating profusely. He worked her until her legs were quaking. Then he commanded her to strip and get in the bed. She quickly undressed and crawled into bed and he walked over and closed the door. Turning around, he undressed completely.

Chyna was mesmerized by Spraggs' 6½-foot, 186-pound, Bruce Lee-type frame. Likewise, he was motivated by her sexy, remarkable beauty. She lay on her side with her plump, hairless vagina poking out between her closed legs that were bent at the knees. He walked over with his horse-size penis and placed one hand on her breast and the other hand on her butt cheeks and inserted himself slowly and gently. He began pumping himself into her in a hula-hoop fashion, never inserting his entire self in her in order not to cause her any pain, and just enough to feel her soothing warm tenderness.

Spraggs enjoyed Chyna for hours. They were both drenched in perspiration. Suddenly Chyna started having an orgasm that would have hit the Richter scale at 8.3. She began going insane under his sexual prowess, pumping on him passionately as she longed to feel all his love muscle expand and fill the inside of her.

In response to Spraggs' thrusts, Chyna hugged her pillow and started crying tears of pleasure. Spraggs tried to ease up on her, but she would not allow it. She kept grabbing his hips and thrusting her vagina upon his penis with aggression. At last, Spraggs began to climax. The two caught each other's eye as they kissed, and she captured his tongue. When he began to ejaculate inside of her, she intensified the wonderful feeling by rotating and gyrating her hips in a circular motion.

He finally rolled off her, gazing at the ceiling with his hands and legs extended and his penis still erected. Looking upon him, Chyna was still quivering and trembling. She shook like a wet cat before she fell asleep.

Chyna woke up to see Spraggs standing, looking out the window, his hands together behind his back in an at-ease military position. His bare back was rippled with muscles, defined with a gigantic marijuana plant tattoo covering his entire back. In addition, two .45 automatic handguns were tattooed on his lower back, running down his thighs. He wore fitted Armani pants, and had on a fresh pair of Armani underwear. Spraggs had been up and out of bed for hours. He had taken his shower, brushed his teeth, and found his way to the kitchen, where he drank a cup of coffee and ate two boiled eggs.

"Good morning, sweetheart," Chyna said, getting out of bed and heading to the shower.

She entered the bathroom, put her hair in a ponytail, washed her face with Neutrogena, turned the shower on, brushed her teeth, then entered the steaming water. When Chyna came back into the room, Spraggs was still in the same military position, looking through the upper balcony window. She went behind him, kissed his upper back, and placed her hands around his waist.

"Baby, things would have been better if the hired help didn't cause us to lose half a million dollars of merchandise recently," Chyna informed him. "We have another package coming in from England, and we need a good distributor to supply it to. Once we find a trustworthy distributor, we're guaranteed a two million dollar a month deal from my Nigerian connection by the way of London."

"Where's my guns?" Spraggs asked.

Chyna kept her composure to keep from shivering from excitement at the sound of Spraggs' voice. She slowly backed away from him, all the while observing him and pondering over what his thoughts were. She knew whatever it was, his reputation for handling business and getting the impossible done were flawless.

After she slipped on her Versace robe, she led him to the basement into the billiard room. In the center of the room stood a fine, contemporary pool table, and the couple stood on opposite sides of it. Chyna reached down under the table, pressed a fixture, and the center board of the pool table revolved completely around, revealing two black Calicos with several extra one hundred-round clips, two black .45 automatics, a pair of AK rifles, a pair of black 16mm rifles, an ARP 90 black, and a 50-caliber sniper rifle, along with seven grenades.

Spraggs lit up with contentment when he saw the artillery he had to work with. He grabbed the .45 Heckler and Koch semiautomatic and tucked it in his waistline. He then asked Chyna to give him the car keys to the Jaguar.

Spraggs glided his hands over a few weapons of choice, then began to cock and load them. Next, he commanded her to get the help ready immediately. She closed her robe more conservatively, looped her robe straps tightly and proceeded.

"Very well, sweetheart," she said, gracefully.

Spraggs put on his Prada shirt and Yushua sunglasses. He then loaded an M16, AK-47, and a Calico with a hundred round clips.

During this time, Marvin arrived in a grey Sean John suit and Babe and Apes footwear. Spraggs handed Marvin two M16s and an AK-47 without looking at him and led him to the car, with his Calico in his hand.

Spraggs opened the passenger door and sat down while Marvin got in the driver seat. Then Spraggs handed him his car keys and said, "Take me to the people that owe me."

Marvin looked over at his stone-faced, emotionless colleague, placed the keys in the ignition, and pressed the genie to open the garage door. The Jaguar purred to life, and he backed out of the garage. They rode in silence until they reached Ashley Street.

Spraggs told Marvin to stop at a local gas station, where he purchased a 5-gallon gas container and filled it with gasoline. He also bought two bottles of lighter fluid. Spraggs sealed the gas container and placed it in the trunk. They continued their journey until they reached a shabby little house in the center of the street.

Marvin was about to pull in front of the house when Spraggs stopped him and told him to park half a mile away. The windows were ultra-dark tinted and the two men were hidden in plain view. Meantime, they kept the house under surveillance for hours.

The traffic going in and out was constant. At least one thousand people had entered and exited it during the four hours they had been observing. They noticed that two men were stationed at the opposite ends of the street on walkie-talkies and that men guarded the front door of the location.

Finally the two men drove off and parked at an abandoned parking lot ten miles away. "Tell me what you know about the inside of the location," Spraggs demanded.

"They have two guards at the door that pat you down on entry," Marvin informed him. "They usually stay there, and the boss has an escort that covers and guards him with a Mac 11 and shotguns. Some armed gang members hang around the house, fucking junkie whores, and people are working side deals. The majority of the heroin is kept in the freezer. They have a chemist preparing the heroin with Quinine and there're two baggers, bagging the supply in $50 and up pockets."

The blazing sun finally set. The sky was saturated with color before a wine-dark evening sky settled and coated the horizon. Then, as if to indicate a brooding change, the night was preternaturally silent.

Spraggs kept his comrade hungry all day for a reason. He knew Marvin would become more agitated on an empty stomach.

"I want you to go inside and have a meeting with Rico," Spraggs told him. "Tell him we are willing to forgive his ignorance and supply him with a greater amount of supplies if he complies and give you the $200,000 he owes you."

They drove back to the location and parked in front of the door. Spraggs had his seat reclined all the way back and took off his sunglasses. Marvin exited the car. He turned the car off but left the keys in the ignition. Spraggs watched keenly from his low position as Marvin was patted down and escorted through the one-way-in and one-way-out entrance.

Spraggs swiftly opened the trunk and grabbed the gas container and the lighter fluid. He threw one container of lighter fluid in the car and jogged to the side of the house, holding the Calico around his neck by the shoulder strap, his finger on the trigger. He was certain no one saw him. He opened the gas container and poured it at the base of the house, while running and spraying the lighter fluid on the sides of the wooden stucco. Moments later, the can was empty. He ducked low and ran back to the car.

He took the top off the lighter fluid he'd left in the car, tore off a few sheets of paper from the car's manual book, and rolled it up in a cylinder. After inserting the paper in the neck of the container, he turned the container upside down until the entire paper was saturated by lighter fluid. He then plugged in the car lighter.

Marvin now reappeared with some hostile escorts trailing him. Again, Spraggs quickly lowered back in his reclining seat. Marvin climbed in the car with an aggravated look on his face.

"Well?" Spraggs said.

"He told me my people and I could fuck off and stick our shipment up our ass."

Before he finished talking, Spraggs took the heated cigarette lighter and lit the paper in the lighter fluid bottle.

"He said if I come around asking for any more money, I'll be dead," Marvin said.

I figured he would say that, Spraggs thought as he flung the lit container to the side of the house. Crashing against the wall, it left a trail of fire as it raced its way around the house.

"Drive up the street and kill the guard on that corner," Spraggs ordered Marvin while handing him the .45-caliber handgun. Then he popped open the trunk, turned around completely in his seat, and aimed his Calico, giving him a clear shot at the guard at the opposite side of the street.

Marvin rolled up on the guard with his window a quarter way down.

"Hey," Marvin yelled.

The guard looked around and received a bullet in his face at close range. As soon as Spraggs heard the gunshot, he released an assault of bullets on the other guard, who was riddled with lead before he fell and died.

"Reverse back to the house quickly," Spraggs ordered. Marvin put the car in reverse and pressed down on the gas. The 32 valve dual overhead Cam all aluminum 4.2-liter V8 accelerated backwards in seconds.

The house burst into red-hot flames. Spraggs reached in the trunk and grabbed the larger artillery. He then held his body position with his legs fastened between the crevices of the car seat. By now, everybody was fleeing the house and looked in the direction of the Jaguar, a look of surprise on their face, only to be riddled with a swarm of bullets like African killer bees. Spraggs was firing ecstatically through the back trunk. He hit the two security guards that held a shotgun in one position and an AR-15 in another. They were down and coughing terribly from smoke inhalation.

Spraggs handed Marvin the M-16. "Cover me. I'm going inside," he said in a calm, composed voice.

Spraggs grabbed his AK-47 and cocked it. Marvin was already out of the car, standing behind it with his weapon on top of the car, assaulting anybody who was unfortunate enough to be near the facility. Marvin was firing all around him; it seemed like people were appearing from everywhere with guns. He gunned down another two males and a female.

Meantime, Spraggs made his way to the entrance, gunning down four men who came out of the facility holding their noses and faces. They looked astonished as they gasped for air before dying.

Spraggs ran through the flames at top speed, bending low and making his way through the dense smoke. He saw a man loading up a traveling bag, and hammered him with seven rounds from his Calico. He swooped up the bag, quickly looked in it and saw that it was stuffed with money. He zipped it, placed it over his back, and then shot as many assailants as possible as he tried to escape in the confusion.

Spraggs made his way to the kitchen and open fired on the three men loading the brown-mud substance from the freezer. They were dead before they had a chance to reach for their guns. Spraggs rapidly threw the last two blocks in the bag. He was about to run off when, intrigued, he decided to search and opened the refrigerator. It was filled with cold hard cash, literally. He loaded as much of the money in the two big traveling bags as possible before the smoke engulfed him and he could no longer see.

Holding his breath, he closed his eyes and made his way out of the house the same way a blind man remembers his steps and feel his way around. Once he saw some light, he ran for it. He escaped the engulfing flames with the two big traveling bags under his shoulder and the AK-47 in his clutches. By now, his eyes were blurry and he could not see anything but a miragelike image of his car as he stumbled towards it.

Without warning, a gunman in the area had Spraggs in his sights, however Marvin gunned him down just in time. Spraggs stumbled to the car.

"Drive! Drive!" Spraggs commanded. Marvin slammed the trunk shut, jumped in, put the Jaguar in gear, and sped off. A 2002 Chevy Suburban had almost blocked them off with their assailants hanging out the windows with a Mack 11 and an Uzi. However, the Jaguar squeezed through in a split second.

Undeterred, the assailants in the Suburban let out a vicious hail of bullets on the Jaguar. Fortunately, the Jag's speed was too much for the Chevy to pursue. It blasted forward with the speed of sound. In a minute, the Jaguar was miles ahead of the Suburban and out of the assailants' shooting range. The Jaguar screamed and whistled its way onto Interstate 20.

Once they entered Highway 75, the car slowed down to a normal speed. Spraggs closed his eyes tightly until they teared enough to wash away some of the smoke and enable him to see. His skin was covered with the residue of dirty-grey smoke. He suffered a few second-degree burns, and he looked through smoke-stung eyes still hurting and filled with tears. However, if you looked at how calm he was sitting there, no one would have ever known.

The men returned to the house, hungry, exhausted, and slightly burned, after having taken out their revenge laced with arson and murder. Spraggs entered the house with the traveling bags over his back and his AK still fastened to his hand. They made their way into the kitchen, drawn by the delicious aroma of Cajun rice, peas, and sweet stew chicken. Marvin went straight to the stove and started dishing himself some food to eat. Spraggs went upstairs where Chyna was working on her big screen computer.

He tossed the bags on the bed.

"Good heavens!" Chyna exclaimed, standing up. "What in the world were you doing? Playing bloody Saint Nicholas, sliding down the chimney all bloody day?" She approached Spraggs and led him by one hand to the bathroom, where she started cleaning him up with a rag while she ran the shower water. Although his weapon was still in his hand, she undressed him. "You burned yourself horribly, sweetheart," Chyna said as she took out some cocoa butter.

Then she gently led him to the shower by his penis.

"Come now. Get nice and clean. I'll have your robe waiting for you."

Spraggs soaped himself thoroughly, then stepped out to a large Yushua beach towel and dried off while Chyna held his Versace robe open for him. She followed behind with the cocoa butter in her hand to massage and coat it into the burned areas. Oblivious to his pain, Spraggs tied the strap on his robe, made his way to the bags, and emptied them out on the bed.

An enormous amount of U.S. currency and 13 kilos of pure heroin spilled out. Quickly Chyna closed her bedroom door, brought over the AK-47, and placed it beside Spraggs. Then she walked into her closet and got the currency counting machine. She plugged it in and started helping Spraggs arrange the money according to denominations. There were piles of hundreds, fifties, twenties, tens, fives, and ones. They placed the currency in the money machine, and it counted off $3,305,096. The heroin was worth 13½ million dollars.

The two seemed to be energized by the counting of money. They were so focused they were not aware that hours passed before they sorted and counted everything and then put the money and heroin away.

"Sweetheart, our distributor in North Carolina said he's up to his neck in demands, and he needs more quality cocaine like what we've been giving him or he's not going to give us what he owes for the shipment. I've tried to reason with him, but he has been so disrespectful. He wants us to bring him 100 keys or more; if not, he said to leave him alone," Chyna said, giving Spraggs a back massage.

"Call him and tell that pussy that his hundred kilos is on the way. Just make sure he has my money," Spraggs said, while dozing off.

"Well, sweetheart, straightening Rico was the easy part. Now we have to find a source to trust. We were $3,000,000 off, and now we'll have 20 kilos of heroin every month."

16 *Peaches*

Lucky was interrupted by a constant loud knock at the door. The past week had been very busy. He looked through the window and opened the door.

"Hello," Peaches said with ebullience.

Lucky stepped aside to let her in. With unfailing enthusiasm, she glided over to the couch and plopped down.

Lucky, on the other hand, trudged over with fatigue. "Come on," he said. "I'm tired. I'm going to bed."

Peaches immediately jumped up and ran in front of him, sashaying up the stairs to his bedroom. She was wearing a black Polo miniskirt and a red halter top. With her hair freshly permed and fashionably cut, and, as usual, bare bottom, Lucky felt himself starting to get aroused. His senses were captivated by the alluring fragrance of Elizabeth Taylor's White Diamonds. It almost seemed as if Peaches pranced with every step she took in her Liz Claiborne high heel sandals.

Lucky observed Peaches with compassion because she was such a lovely woman; however, he knew she was self-destructing with her abusive addiction lifestyle. At the same time, he admired her because Peaches was the only woman that could satisfy the cravings of a sex addict.

She went to his room, opened the door, and walked in. The room looked as if a tornado had swept through it.

Lucky ambled over to the bed and dropped on it, then turned on his TV. On the left side of the bed were two Rubbermaid storage containers he used to store his clothing. But his clothes weren't there; they were all over his room.

Peaches began cleaning up. She placed his dirty clothes into a big Hefty bag, putting everything in his room in an orderly fashion. Then she went downstairs to the laundry room, threw some Cheer detergent into the washer, and turned it on. After a moment, she bounded back upstairs to find Lucky asleep, lying on his bed. Steve Harvey's *Kings of Comedy* was on the TV. She figured he must have intended for them to watch it.

Lucky knew she loved comedy and was trying to accommodate her. These were the things Peaches loved about him. Apart from him always badgering her to stay off drugs and stay focused on the right things, he was the only man Peaches adored for more reasons than just sex or anything else. She honestly respected Lucky.

Peaches had had a busy week and was counting the money she'd accumulated when she said, "Lucky, wake up."

She pushed on his shoulders until she got a response. "Lucky, wake up. Look what I got for you." She handed the stack of money to him.

"How much is this?" Lucky asked.

"Count it while I go make you some coffee. I miss you. I need you up now," she said, walking to the kitchen.

Lucky woke up cranky, but he managed to start counting the large quantity of bills before him. He really did not like to take Peaches' money. However, he figured if he did not, she would eventually waste it on foolishness. Lucky counted $1,733 and put it in his pocket. He was amazed by how much money a prostitute could make running the streets.

Peaches returned to the room with a cup of coffee and two ham sandwiches. He sat up, started eating his sandwiches, and drinking the coffee.

Peaches lay on the bed on her side, watching *Kings of Comedy*. She began to laugh at Cedric the entertainer. She was feeling great. She knew that Lucky was not the type to be a pimp, but like most powerful women, she found a way to mold the man in her life to whomever she want him to be. Peaches loved the fact that she knew somebody that cared about her, but did not get emotionally involved enough where he would want to change her lifestyle. She had a desire to please Lucky in every way and fashion, apart from just sexually. She also loved the fact that he attracted so many women.

"Damn, this's some strong-ass coffee; you must want me to be up until next year," Lucky snapped with a broad smile.

Love was truly the most powerful of all emotions, and Peaches was a living example of this theory. When she was around Lucky, she refrained from her lusting desire for crack cocaine because she knew he didn't want her high.

"Daddy, come lay down beside me," Peaches said with the cuddliness of a furry kitten. Lucky went and lay next to her. He held her in his arms as she lay on his chest. The two were laughing hysterically at Cedric's black man in space routine.

When the telephone rang, Lucky answered. "Hey." He paused for a second, then moved away from Peaches to the other side of the bed and listened.

"Okay, here I come," he said as he hopped up, went to his closet, retrieved his stack, and headed downstairs. He opened the door, and there was Cat sitting on 26-inch rims on his candy-painted '86 Regal. The music was turned down low, and the ground was still vibrating. Lucky climbed in and sat down. Cat sat facing forward.

"Here you go," Lucky said, handing Cat the money.

Cat counted it. "Fifty-five hundred. Right-on." With a serious facial expression, Cat asked, "You want another one, 'folk?"

"Nigga, you know better than to ask me that," Lucky said with a sarcastic grin on his face.

Cat reached under his seat where he kept his gun, pulled out a quarter key of cocaine, and handed it to Lucky. Lucky took the dope, placed it under his shirt tucked in his waistline, and exited the car. He watched the Tropicana-tangerine painted vehicle on the 26-inch rims sparkle as Cat rode off.

Once inside his apartment, he closed the door silently and listened to the sounds of laughter and applause echoing throughout the whole apartment. He took quick, light steps upstairs and entered his room, catching Peaches smoking crack in her glass pipe.

He scared the bejesus out of her, coming back so soon. She sat on the bed, looking at him with embarrassment.

Lucky went and put his dope up in the closet, then walked over to Peaches and slapped her with aggravation. The pipe flew in the air, and she hit the floor with a thunderous thud. She looked up at him in shock. She'd never seen him like this. He had never laid a hand on her before.

"Is this what you want? I told you never let me catch you smoking that shit," he snapped, then began stomping her. "You want to die, huh? You want to die, bitch? I'll fucking kill you myself."

"Please, Daddy, don't hurt me," Peaches screamed and pleaded, holding out her hands.

He stopped. Enraged, he began huffing and puffing. "Get your worthless ass up and get out," he shouted.

"I'm sorry, Daddy. I'm sorry, please doesn't be mad at me," she said, crying on her knees in a pitiful plea. "Please, don't kick me out. I'll do anything to be with you."

Peaches crawled over, trying to rip his penis out his pants and stuff it in her mouth. He opened his hand and smacked her again with a thousand pounds of pressure. She collapsed backwards. Her surroundings started spinning, and she felt the start of an excruciating headache.

Lucky held his composure. He hated to see such a lovely woman do herself the way she did, and he had genuine love for Peaches. There is a thin line between love and hate, but there is a thinner line between genius and insanity. His extremely high IQ, combined with his love for Peaches, had become a hateful act of insanity. Now Lucky was bewildered. The more he looked down on her, the calmer he became. He felt himself descending out of his state of rage, but sadly, he became depressed.

He went over to the bed and lay on his back with his arm folded, facing the ceiling. He had an icy demeanor from extreme anger, not at Peaches, at himself for his lack of self-control.

Peaches staggered to her feet, holding her stinging face with one hand. She grabbed and held on to the bed to brace her standing. She wanted to take a good look at the man who made her, for the first time in her life, want to truly leave the addictive substance alone. Peaches looked at the man whom she only wanted to make happy in every way possible. All he wanted was for her to be self-righteous, and that, she could not do.

Now all that was running through her head—besides a migraine—were the words, "Get your worthless ass out." Peaches stood there realizing there was no higher stimulation than the one she got from being with Lucky, and the fact of the matter was she didn't want to leave on bad terms where she could never see him ever again. She realized there was no other place that she would rather be, and no other person she'd rather be with, than with Lucky. Traumatized, she broke down and started crying.

"Daddy, please, I love you. I swear I will never do it again. Please give me another chance. I promise I'll make it up to you, Daddy, please," Peaches pleaded through her sniffs and tears.

Lucky, feeling ashamed of his outburst and actions, was afraid that he was becoming too emotionally involved and caring too much. He looked Peaches in the eye and began speaking from his soul. "Peaches, I care about you and really like kicking it with you, but, shorty, I cannot trust you. I really do not want to hurt you, so I got to ask you to leave me alone."

Peaches' crying became even more intense. "Daddy, no," she said, falling to her knees. She was thunderstruck with disbelief. Here she might be losing the only essence that gave her hope and a sense of tranquility. She grabbed his feet. "Daddy, I'll never make you mad at me again, I promise. I know I did wrong. Please, please, please, give me another chance to do right."

Lucky could not bear seeing her look so pitiful so he allowed her to hug his bottom torso as she sobbed. Suddenly the telephone started ringing and Lucky answered,

"Hey, what's happenin', man? Yeah, I'm glad you're on your way back. What you left is finished and things are busy as hell … that's just Peaches … all right. I'll see you in a minute," Lucky said, hanging up.

The phone rang again. "Hey, yeah, here I come," he said, then hung up again.

"Get off me, Peaches," he said coldly as he scurried to the closet to get a package.

Lucky went outside, went around the building, and walked through a gate to an adjacent apartment complex. A Ford Taurus was waiting for him. He climbed in and met a slim Caucasian lawyer who wore an Armani business suit. Lucky handed the man half an ounce of cocaine, and the man handed Lucky $450. Finished with the transaction, Lucky climbed out of the car and waited for the man to exit the complex before he made his way back to his apartment. Once he stepped in, he noticed Peaches at the washing machine, placing clothes in the washer.

"What you want to eat, Daddy?" she said in an upbeat tone. "I want some fried chicken wings with french fries."

Lucky went upstairs and made sure things were straight. Everything was in the same order he left them in. Peaches had developed great trust in him, but he didn't trust her. However, in the five years he'd known Peaches, she'd never betrayed him by stealing from him. The only thing he held against her was her addiction, which he hated, because it changed the most decent people into deceitful and deceiving demons. This type of behavior could not be tolerated, especially in his type of business.

The telephone rang again. "Hey, what's happening, man? Yea, I'll be there in a minute."

Lucky hung up, went to his closet again, retrieved another package, and exited his apartment. He took a shortcut that instantly brought him to the corner store. This time, he got into a waiting Nissan Pathfinder to meet a blonde-haired German nurse. She was still wearing her nursing uniform. Without a word, she gave him a one hundred-dollar bill, and he handed her an eight ball, then got out of the car. Business was booming.

He hurried back to his apartment and as soon as he entered, the phone started ringing once more. Already knowing he was going to need the extra boost, he yelled, "Peaches, make me another cup of coffee."

"Okay, Daddy," she shouted.

He answered the phone. "Hey, yeah. Meet me at the same spot." Lucky went upstairs, retrieved more dope, and made his way back to the same corner store. He climbed in a Chevy Tahoe, took $750 from a stocky construction worker, and gave him an ounce.

"I appreciate it," the man said.

Lucky looked over at him, gave him some dap, and exited his truck. He made his way back home. Peaches had fixed him a plate of chicken wings, fries, and coffee, and was following him, carrying everything. As soon as he reached upstairs, the phone started ringing again. He grabbed a piece of chicken, placed it in his mouth, then quickly snatched it out because it was still so hot.

"Hey, yeah, man, pull over there, in the same place. I'll be there in ten minutes." He hung up.

"Daddy, relax and eat. I'll bring it," Peaches offered.

Yeah, right, Lucky thought, sarcastically. *What do I look like trusting a junkie with my dope?*

Even with misgivings, he got up, went over to his closet, fixed a package, and gave Peaches a quarter ounce of cocaine. He instructed her to go over to the Regal Apartment next door and meet a Vietnamese girl named Lu. "She's going to give you $300, and you give her the dope."

Peaches gazed up at Lucky with glossy eyes. She couldn't believe he still had faith in her. She put on her Liz Claiborne high heel sandals and went to take care of business for her man.

Lucky lay back in bed against the headboard with his plate on his lap and made a phone call. "Hey, Lu a short-haired woman in a red halter top is coming to meet you. Make sure she sees you."

He hung up and started eating. He was just about finished when he heard the door open. "Peaches, is that you?" he yelled.

"Yes, Daddy," she replied. She came upstairs and gave Lucky his money. He counted it and placed it in his pocket, then he finished eating and drank the remainder of his coffee. Satisfied, he lay back with two pillows under his head. Peaches took his plate and cup and headed to the kitchen. Lucky closely scrutinized her face as she reached for the plate. He saw no sign of deceit. He was amazed at how resilient she was. The phone rang again. "Hey," he answered.

"I know you miss me and all that, but I just can't have you over right now." He hung up. Peaches stood on the side of the bed observing him.

"Daddy, you can have your company over if you want. I love what you like," she said while lifting her shirt over her head. She then slid out of her miniskirt.

Damn, she's fine, Lucky thought to himself. Even with the red bruises all over her body, Peaches still looked luscious and good enough to eat. She was a fine exotic dancer. She walked over to the TV and stood with her back facing Lucky. Then she did a little exotic dance routine and jiggled her rear end, making her buttocks clap with intensity. Slowly turning around, she spread her slim legs wide apart, exposing the plump pink lips of her vagina as she used both hands to squeeze and massage her huge soft breasts, pushing them forward.

She glanced at Lucky, who was admiring her, his eyes locked on her delicious body. Teasingly, she released a playful laugh, then walked over and crawled on the bed to Lucky's side. She climbed in his outstretched arms, and he hugged her as she lay on his chest and used the remote to start the DVD movie all over again.

Once again, the telephone rang. This time, Lucky just picked it up, turned off the ringer, and hung up. He had some immediate needs that needed attending.

17 *Marvin*

Chyna arrived in front of her condominium in a new black Bentley GT she picked up from an exotic rental company. The Bentley was riding on 948R 22 x 9 inches front and 22 x 10 in the rear with a full polished finish that made the car look immaculate. The Firepower was parked in front of her condominium to make space in her two-car garage for the Bentley GT. She pulled in the garage and parked. The sound of the engine gave off a constant slight roar, as if the engine was being slightly accelerated. However, it was just the powerful V8 fuel-injected engine.

She turned the car off and climbed out carrying a black travel bag in her hand. She was dressed in a two-piece black Prada business suit with a white Prada dress shirt under her blazer. Emanating an air of sophistication and with her stunning figure, every step she took added to the seductive spell she cast. She went to meet a man in the billboard room. He was cleaning and selecting their new line of arsenal. Spraggs was standing over the pool table with a chrome miniature Gatling in his hand, keenly observing the weapon.

He was dressed in an all-black, fitted Versace short sleeve shirt and slacks. His V-shaped Versace diamond-clustered belt sparkled. New, rimless, Cartier glasses and Versace Italian loafers complimented his immaculate attire. Spraggs was armed with two Desert Eagle chrome 45's on both sides in a leather shoulder strap.

Marvin relaxed on the leather Armani couch with a Portage cigar in his mouth. With his Gucci-framed black glasses, thick beard, and bald head, he looked like Isaac Hayes. He wore a pair of Van

Hansen slacks and a dress shirt with the cuffs rolled up, exposing his arms and a Corum classical Peacock watch from the prestigious Swiss collection. He had on black Wallabee leather Clarks.

Chyna entered the room. Her Desire Blue perfume wafted throughout the room announcing her presence.

"Good afternoon, gentlemen," she said as she placed her traveling bag on the center of the pool table. "Hello, sweetheart," she said to Spraggs as she walked over and gave him a gentle kiss on his cheeks. She marched to the diagonal end of the table where both men could see her. Then she began her brief.

"Well, gentlemen, our shipment has arrived. Twenty keys of pure Middle Eastern heroin."

She unzipped the bag, took out two separate keys, and tossed them on the table as a display. She continued, "We have exactly thirty days to accumulate a million dollars to send back to our contact. Once we establish a distributor that can handle this responsibility, our supplier will send us a shipment periodically. Now, gentlemen, I understand that you have an arrangement in North Carolina. I'll be handling some of our business. In the meanwhile, I pray you both be safe and come back in one piece."

Chyna left the bag and the Bentley keys on the pool table and headed upstairs.

Marvin observed the product and put it back in the traveling bag. "Well, I guess we're ready," he said. He grabbed the bag and the car keys and went to the Bentley GT, opened the trunk with the keyless entry, and placed the bag in it. Entering the car, he removed his .357 automatic pistols, placed them under his seat, shut the door, started the vehicle, and opened the garage door with the genie.

Spraggs appeared two minutes later wearing a black blazer and entered the car with his usual stone-cold military demeanor. Marvin shot him a quick sideways glance out of the side of his eyes, then reversed out of the garage. They drove slowly out of the private community and on to Defoors Drive. Soon, they got on Interstate 75 South, traveled to Interstate 85 North, and continued straight. In three-and-a-half hours, they made it to Charlotte, North Carolina.

When they arrived, Marvin called their contact and informed them they were in town. They drove and parked in front of an

Embassy Suites hotel. Marvin put his .357 automatic Magnums back in his waistline holster and got out, opened the trunk, and took out the black traveling bag. He then walked towards the elevator, pressed the up button, and waited for the elevator to arrive. Spraggs cautiously stood behind him. The elevator door opened and the two stepped aboard, standing side by side.

The elevator arrived at the third floor and opened. They both got off with Spraggs walking 12 feet behind Marvin. When Marvin stopped, so did Spraggs. Spraggs stood with his back against the wall, surveying his surroundings like a CIA agent. After Marvin knocked, the door opened on well-oiled hinges and he stepped in. The door was just about to close when Spraggs wedged his foot between the door and the doorjamb.

"He's with me," Marvin explained to the occupants of the room.

Spraggs entered the room. Two men confronted him, and one sat on the bed with a remote control in his hand. He was dressed in a black Sean John jean outfit and black Timberland boots. He was clean shaven with a bald head and was wearing a New York Yankees baseball cap. One of his comrades sat in a corner chair wearing a Phat Farm gray baggy sweat suit. His hair was neatly braided in cornrows. He had a serious expression on his face.

The other man was standing in a military at ease position wearing DrunknMunkey jeans and a large white T-shirt. This fellow wore a small Afro and was the biggest of the three. He looked like he should have been a linebacker for a professional football team. "Marvin, peace, god," the bald-headed fellow said while standing up giving Marvin some dap.

The man then walked over to Spraggs and extended his hand in a formal greeting. "Peace, god. I am god supreme Allah," Supreme said.

Spraggs gave him a slight nod of acknowledgement while still surveying everyone in the room. His blazer was opened, and his arms folded across his chest in close reach of his weapons. Supreme dropped his hand and returned to Marvin, giving Spraggs a second look.

"Damn, Steve, you left us here high and dry, god. We been out of supplies for almost a year," Supreme said.

"Everything is back to normal. You know how things are," Marvin replied. "Where's the money?"

Everyone became more attentive.

"U-god, get the cash, B," Supreme instructed his braided comrade on the chair.

U-god stood up immediately, went to the bathroom to retrieve two book bags, and handed them to Supreme. Marvin then tossed the traveling bag on the bed. U-god zipped open the bag and started unpacking the product. "Yeah, this some pure shit, god."

"This is straight mud, B," U-god announced while he cut one of the blocks open and examined the product thoroughly. He then took out a metal digital scale and put block after block on the scale. Supreme handed the bags over to Marvin. "There you go, god. It's $2,225,000," Supreme said, while handing over the two JanSport book bags to Marvin.

Marvin reached down in the bags and pulled out bundles of rubber banded U.S. currency in $100,000 stacks. He ran his fingers over the top of the stack like a deck of brand-new cards, looking between the stacks to see the one hundred-dollar bills. Spraggs could see the money through his pitch-black Gucci sunglasses. Marvin put the money back in the knapsack, calmly took two steps over, and switched off the room light. Then he drew his .357 and fired two shots in Spraggs' direction.

The blast of gunfire brought a lighteninglike flash that showed Spraggs jumping on the bed, drawing his two .45-Desert Eagles simultaneously. The room erupted in gunshots in Spraggs' direction, causing him to move in a fury of gunfire.

Meantime, Marvin opened the room door and fled in a crouching position. He escaped from the room with a gunshot wound to his right shoulder, however, and a slight graze on his arm. He flew down the stairs with the two knapsacks, one over his neck and shoulder and the other in his hand. He held his .357 Magnum at his side.

Spraggs was using the constant flash of gunfire for his visual in the darkness. He swiftly spun his legs wide apart as a break dancer would. This positioned him to a sitting position with his legs bent to his chest and his feet firmly on the bed. Then he pushed himself off with all his might to the floor backwards. At the same time, he released a storm of gunshots from his two .45 Desert Eagles. The impact of his assault sent Supreme crushing against the bedroom wall, riddled with bullets, and U-god stumbling over the couch with the 9mm falling out of his hand.

Two men were wiped out under the barrage of constant gunfire. The bigger man of the three ran to the bathroom to take cover. Spraggs could see him running with his .44 Colt Magnum. Peeping over the bed in a crouching position, Spraggs saw the man was panicking. He pushed his Colt 44 around the corner while hiding his body securely behind the bathroom wall and began shooting erratically in the direction that he thought that Spraggs was in.

Spraggs followed the trail of gunfire, ran over and grabbed the muzzle of the gun. He sidestepped to the opening of the bathroom door with his gun extended in front of him and open fired. Two shots embedded in his assailant's nasal cavity and cheek and sent his head hammering against the bathroom door. He slid down the wall with his medulla oblongata and pieces of his skull plastered on the wall and slowly oozing downward, leaving a gory red trail in its wake.

Spraggs quickly switched on the bathroom light and walked around in a circle, making sure everybody was dead in the body-strewn abattoir. He then ran over to the travel bag and tossed everything back in it and zipped it closed, with his guns still in hand. He tossed the bag over his neck and shoulder and took the car keys from Supreme's pockets, then exited the room. By now, occupants of the hotel were cautiously coming out of their rooms to see what the commotion was about. Once they saw Spraggs busting into a sprint with two automatics in his hand, everyone started screaming and scurrying back to their rooms in a hurry.

"He's got a gun!" someone shouted.

Meanwhile, Marvin reached downstairs, opened the car door, tossed the two bags on the passenger's seat, put the car in reverse, and burned rubber out of the hotel parking lot. He turn the volume up on Christopher Wallace's "Life After Death" CD and was beating "Long Kiss Goodnight."

Spraggs ran into the parking lot, frantically pressing the keyless entry, looking for Supreme's car. Then he noticed a blinking light. He ran over to the car, pressing the keyless entry again. The car lit up again. The gray wagon was Supreme's vehicle. Spraggs opened the door, threw the bag on the backseat, and jumped in. He started the car and reversed. A Jay-Z "Reasonable Doubt" CD came on. Appropriately, "Friend or Foe" was thumping through the sound system. Turning the volume down to a mere whisper, he drove off and went back in the direction that he came from. North Carolina patrol cars raced past him to the scene of the altercation.

Spraggs continued on Denmark Drive until he saw the Highway 85 entrance ramp. He took a right on the ramp and headed southbound, accelerating, and the 550 horsepower E55 burst into speed like a 747 jet. Supreme had super-upped the vehicle, adding many pricey accessories.

Spraggs kept his foot pressed on the accelerator. There was no way he wanted Marvin to reach the condo before he did. He handled the supercharged 5.5 liter V8 engine legendary Benz as he glided through traffic with ease. The E55 would break down to 40 miles per hour in three seconds and back to 160 in half that time.

Spraggs was excellent at maneuvering. He came flying through traffic. He even passed a couple of state troopers who did not attempt to follow in pursuit. Spraggs was hidden behind smoky-gray tint. He was halfway through South Carolina when he noticed a car ahead going about 90 miles per hour. It looked like the rare breed of the Bentley GT he was in earlier. Easing up on the accelerator, he drove up on the passenger-side door.

Marvin was driving with his left hand. His swollen right side was numb with blazing white-hot pain. His only thought was getting back to the condominium to see their call-in doctor.

Marvin was quickly jarred out of his thoughts when he felt something rip into his right shoulder. He looked through the shattered passenger window to see Spraggs firing repeated shots out of his twin .45 Desert Eagles. Marvin floored the accelerator and blasted forward, zooming around the surrounding traffic.

Spraggs used his legs to hold the steering wheel steady while he unleashed his onslaught on Marvin with both hands. Then he dropped the clips out his weapons and reloaded them, one after the other, with his extra clips aligned in his shoulder strap holster. Finally he dropped one gun in his lap and used the left hand for steering the car through the congested traffic while the right hand palmed his weapon.

Spraggs then launched forward with his foot on the accelerator. A car was coming up on him with the speed of light. He actually had to turn five seconds ahead to avoid a collision. The cool air nitro intake with its nitro-installed tank and super chip computer systems sent the Benz closing in on the Bentley, topping 170 mph.

Marvin ducked as he heard the shots burst in through his back window and burst out through his front windshield. He drew his .357 and aimed to the back, firing a couple of rounds, but with his hand going numb and his tremendous fatigue, the gun felt like a 50-pound dumbbell.

Marvin was now surpassing 190 miles per hour and redlined the GT. However, the Benz was still on his tail. Spraggs pulled up along the Bentley GT and fishtailed. The Bentley just hugged the road with compassion and maintained a straightaway acceleration.

Cars were dodging the two speeding vehicles and blowing their horns. Irate drivers could not even get a license plate number because the two cars were traveling almost at the speed of light.

The racing vehicles were in the middle of the expressway, exchanging gunshots while rapidly approaching a tractor-trailer. The two assailants played a game of chicken, firing shots on each other's car. At the last moment, they turned out of the way of the oncoming truck in opposite directions, then came back around it in a split second and continued their exchange of gunshots. The reckless driving caused a Range Rover to lose control. It flipped on its side and rolled over four times. This caused a massive head-on collision that would hold up the dense evening traffic up for hours, blocking off the expressway for miles.

Marvin could no longer hold the gun in his hand. His arm dropped with fatigue. Not only had he lost all feeling in his hand, he was dazed by the continual assault. In fact, he was on the verge of passing out. Not able to outrun his assailant, he decided to just step on his brakes.

From his blurry vision, he watched the Benz shoot past him. Spraggs was caught off guard by Marvin's sudden stop. He accelerated past the "Welcome to Georgia" sign, slowed down, and made a U-turn that sent the Benz tires smoking. He then accelerated back towards oncoming traffic.

Several cars that made it around the blockade swerved out of the way and angrily blew their horns at Marvin for stopping. Marvin looked up through his blurry vision. He was losing consciousness fast. He didn't know if he was hallucinating or not, but he saw a Benz rapidly approaching him. He placed his two hands on his gun and started yelling and firing shots through the windshield, summoning the little will power he had left.

Spraggs aimed his twin Desert Eagles and opened a flaming storm of gunfire to the driver's side of the Bentley GT. Marvin's .357 only fired off one round before he was struck in his upper chest, neck, and mouth. He slumped over to the side of his driver's door. Spraggs braked immediately, sending the tires smoking, and came to a sudden stop, right in front of the GT.

The car bumpers barely touched when Spraggs hopped out with both guns aimed at the driver's side. He approached the car, firing his weapons on the driver's side. Once he realized there was no response from within, he opened the driver's side door with his gun still aimed at the driver. Marvin dropped out of the car to the pavement. Not taking any chances, Spraggs shot him one more time in his forehead, holstered his weapons, reached inside Marvin's car, and grabbed the two JanSport bags. He suddenly recognized Chyna's voice coming from Marvin Jenson's cell phone.

"Hello, Marvin. Is everything all right? Did you take care of Spraggs? Hello, hello, Marvin."

Stunned by this latest development, Spraggs turned off the power and placed the phone in his blazer pocket.

An unsuspecting driver pulled up behind the GT and came out, trying to be a Good Samaritan. The young blond-haired teen approached Spraggs. He wore dingy pants that were torn at the knees, a small AC-DC T-shirt, and an old dingy baseball cap. "Hey, dude, is everything all right?" he asked.

Spraggs looked up at the mint-condition, blue-and-white racing striped Mustang, pulled his weapon, and shot the unsuspecting young man in his face at point-blank range. Shocked, the young man stared in astonishment, then dropped dead on the pavement.

Spraggs jogged over to the Mustang and opened the door. It had been left running, Jimmy Hendrix's greatest hit, "Purple Haze," was sounding out of the car. He looked around, then tossed the JanSport bag in the car, ran back to the Benz, retrieved his traveling bag from the backseat, and jumped into the Mustang GT, burning rubber as he escaped into the night.

18 *Keisha*

Keisha was lying on her white Ralph Lauren settee, like a lady accustomed to the prestigious lifestyle, watching her 42-inch wide screen TV. Like the rest of over a million viewers and anybody with a TV for the past decade, she was enthralled with the last segment of *The Oprah Winfrey Show*. She was admiring the elegant grace and persuasive charismatic charm of Oprah. Anyone who knew of Oprah's history had to respect her evolving success in her career and the many endeavors she poured herself into.

Her Tiffany and Co. diamond stud 2-carat earrings, opera necklace, tennis bracelet, jeweled watch, and elegant 2.5-carat diamond ring sparkled off the reflection of the TV light like blue lasers. She wore her white-laced Victoria's Secret lingerie with grace. Her soft, radiant, ebony skin shone as if she just took a milk bath and had lotioned up in pure, creamy coca butter. The show finished, and Keisha stood up, stretched like a graceful cat, and went to the master bedroom.

Meantime, Mark, acting paranoid, was walking back and forth from the bed to the window, opening the blinds and peeking out. Keisha seriously thought that all the money Mark was making and the cocaine he was using was driving him insane. Finally, he sat on his bed and snorted off of a long-handled miniature gold spoon and a golden-rimmed mirror.

The room was completely silent and relatively dark except for the slender rays of light shining through the window blinds. Keisha desired to pleasure him orally, however, she knew he would not stay still long enough to get an erection and for her to enjoy it. She was irritated by Mark's strange behavior, and she was suffering from extreme boredom.

"Baby, I want to go out. I've been cooped up in this house for months," Keisha complained, getting on the bed from the opposite side, approaching him and rubbing her bodice on him like a lovable kitten.

"Go ahead, and take this to my cousin. While you're at it, tell him I'll get all the money he owes me next week," Mark said. He headed over to his walk-in closet, took out a Louis Vuitton suitcase, and unzipped it. It contained a kilo. Then he zipped it back up and put it away.

Keisha went to the bathroom, undressed and showered. She douched and cleansed herself, patted herself dry with her new, plush, Ralph Lauren towel, and applied some Aveeno oatmeal lotion all over her skin. She had wrapped her freshly permed hair accented with tangerine highlights, and now loosed it so that it freely flowed down her back and shoulders.

Next came the Estée Lauder makeup. Cobalt-blue eye shadow, Maybelline Colossal Volum mascara in Midnight Black, and a little blush-on for her cheeks. Last came a light tangerine lipstick and lip liner, and a fake Marilyn Monroe mole on her front cheek, slightly above her lip and one-fourth inch from her nose.

She slipped on baggy Rocawear sweat pants and a bright tangerine, deep V, sleeveless cotton blouse by Baby Phat. Off the closet shelf she picked up her Louis Vuitton portable traveling case, zipped it open, placed her makeup kit inside, along with a kilo of cocaine. Ready to go, she walked over, kissed Mark who was standing at the window once again, then left.

Mark did not even feel the gentleness of her affection. He was oblivious to everything—Keisha, time, and world.

Keisha went out the back door, across the patio, down a couple of stairs, and walked in the garage. Opening the keyless trunk, she placed the Luis Vuitton traveling case inside her BMW 645c, AC Schnitzer.

Carbon fiber covered much of the interior of her BMW, including the three-spoke steering wheel. However, the pedals and handbrake were finished in aluminum. She started her ignition and reversed her Beemer convertible out of the garage, down her long driveway, and onto the road. Her hot-red Beemer with large, chromed tailpipes and a custom spoiler on 21-inch, 3-star chrome rims was hard to miss.

She drove to Lil' Pee's house, pushing down on the accelerator and instantly sending the 4.4-liter V8 to 45 mph. Lil' Pee's mother had purchased a seven-bedroom, red brick house with a finished basement in Pine Lake on All Good Road. Before reaching the house, Keisha took her cell phone out of the middle console and called Lil' Pee.

When he answered, Keisha said, "Yeah, Lil' Pee, come get your work outta my trunk. Bring a bag."

Lil' Pee jumped up and looked out the door.

She placed the phone on the charger and put it back in her middle console. Lil' Pee came out with his hair half-braided. The other half was a wild Afro. He was only wearing his Snoopy boxers, and carried a book bag in his hand. Keisha popped the trunk. He walked over to her first and handed her a bundle of cash.

"No, hold on to that. Mark said he'll come holla at you himself in two weeks," Keisha said, looking into his eyes. Lil' Pee returned the look with desire and placed his money into the open knapsack. Still gazing at Keisha, he walked to the trunk.

"It's in my suitcase," she told him.

Lil' Pee opened the suitcase, retrieved the cocaine, put it into his bag, and scurried back inside his house. Turning up her CD player to amplify Cash Money Millionaires' Hot Boys, she then drove down Ponce de Leon to Pin-Ups and parked directly in front of the club. She popped open her trunk, took out her portable traveling case, and pulled it by the handle, then walked inside the club.

"Yeah, what's up, stranger? Long time no see," the bouncer said as Keisha gave him a light hug. She continued past him.

"Desirée, you look absolutely fabulous. I'm glad to see you back with us," said the general manager. She was also at the front door, at the clerk position.

"Desirée, are you paying your club fee now or later?" the general manager asked with a reluctant smile.

Keisha took out $150 and handed it to her.

"Great, you have a good one, dear," she said as she took the money and gave Keisha back $25. The manager looked Keisha up and down seductively as she sashayed off.

Keisha strolled over to the bar and ordered a double shot of Grey Goose and Red Bull energy drink. She gulped down her intoxicating beverage and proceeded to the back, where she was surrounded by her colleagues' kisses, hugs, and compliments. She accepted their greetings gracefully with smiles. She elegantly brandished her freshly painted acrylic nails with small artificial diamonds in tangerine on the tips, walked over to the dressing room mirror, and admired herself. She looked stunning. Near her, three young girls were hitting lines on the portable mirror. They offered Keisha some, but she refused.

"Who got some triple stacks?" she announced because everyone else was in and out, moving at a hundred miles per hour.

"I got two," said a thick Brazilian diva.

"Let me get 'em." Keisha gave her $50 and swallowed a pill with a sip of her Red Bull. She then strolled to a private dressing room. She could feel the envious stares on her back as she walked to her private area.

Keisha sat on the elevated counter with her back to the wall and her side to the mirror and relaxed in a zone, feeling the bass vibrating off the wall and through her body. She could not even comprehend why she was there, however, that was all she knew. This was where her mind liked to resort to when she wanted to get high, and wanted to relax.

She was sipping her Red Bull when she started feeling the Ecstasy kick in. Then she began vibing to the music and started feeling anxious to get on stage and do her dance routine.

As time passed, she got more and more into the groove. She could not wait to go have fun. Suddenly she was almost startled out of her pubic hairs when a 6-foot, 195-pound, yellow-vanilla-creamed-skin young lady burst through the door. She had buttocks like a stallion. It was impossible not to see her massive buttocks from the front. Her head started bobbing. She came with a severe attitude.

"Bitch, where you been? You gonna make me kill your stupid ass," she said with her face frowned up and her 36 C cups bouncing vigorously. She placed her hands on her hips, which revealed her muscular shoulders. She had erect pink nipples and her shaven, pumped, lustrous vagina was throbbing.

"Bitch, do you hear me talking to you?" The young lady approached Keisha and stood facing her with a scowl.

Keisha looked up at the colossal woman in front of her and became nervous. Then she composed herself and gave the woman a sarcastic smirk. The lady tightened her enraged fist, moved on Keisha, and suddenly gave her a deep, passionate, tongue-filled kiss. She clutched Keisha's firm breast in her hand and inhaled Keisha's scent of Ralph Lauren Romance deeply with all her love and desire.

The woman inserted her middle finger with a long blue acrylic nail into Keisha's vagina and spread Keisha's legs far apart. Hungrily, she suckled on her breast like a starving newborn babe, and worked her way down south. Her hand rubbed back and forth, in and out of Keisha's vagina intensely until Keisha was extremely hot and began to secrete erotic vaginal juices.

Still holding Keisha's legs wide apart, she dove face-first into Keisha's midsection, where she tickled her clitoris with some fascinating tongue tickles and suction, and inserted her fingertip in the very bottom of Keisha's vagina.

Next, she positioned Keisha's back against the mirror and propped Keisha's lower torso so the entire genital region was in her face. Her rigorous licking and suction sent Keisha's hormones into overdrive. Keisha had to place her hands firmly on the counter for balance, while she pumped her midsection forward. Then she began quaking. "Oh ... ahhhh," Keisha uttered and released a burst of secretion onto the young lady's devouring tongue.

"Damn, Sabrina, a hoe needed that," Keisha said, standing up with her hand fondling Sabrina's soft, luscious breast. Then Keisha started licking around Sabrina's breast, gently licking with her long, pointy tongue. She licked and sucked on Sabrina until her nipples were erect and a bright red. She then raised Sabrina's left leg and placed her glass Chanel high heel sandal strapped pumps firmly on the countertop. Keisha placed her tongue on her upper lip and seductively looked into Sabrina's eyes with pure lust.

"Yeah, bitch, suck Mama's fat juicy pussy," Sabrina demanded. Keisha didn't need to be told twice. She attacked under Sabrina's soft, precious warmth, inserted her stiff snake-length tongue inside of her, and twisted it continually in and out of her body.

"Yeah, bitch, you know how I like it," said Sabrina with her hands grasping Keisha's head. She spread her fingers far apart, constantly running them through Keisha's soft, lustrous hair. Keisha's tongue worked magic around Sabrina's privates. She gently curled her tongue and vigorously tickled the estrogen out of Sabrina. Sabrina opened her eyes wide, then closed them in a slight trance. She felt the tingling burst of energy rush from her loins. After her orgasm, she placed her hand under Keisha's throat, raised her up gently, and kissed her passionately. The two inhaled deeply, then exhaled simultaneously.

"Baby, I miss you," Sabrina said in a soft voice accompanied by intense, seductive eyes. They gave each other a passionate hug. "Now, let's go break all these tricks outta their money."

Sabrina stepped through the door reluctantly, not wanting their moment to end. She flaunted her whale of a tail from side to side. Keisha looked in the mirror and straightened her hair. She put on her Fendi G-string and halter top outfit and walked to the bathroom to rinse her mouth with mouthwash. Every step she took in her Fendi high heel sandal straps spoke volumes of arrogance laced with sex appeal. Finally she exited the dressing room through the retracting doors and looked around the establishment.

She felt enthusiastic about her first day back at work and was contented with her livelihood. She didn't care how much money Cat made. Keisha went over to the bar to order another drink. Before she could reach her destination, she was in demand. A blue-collar worker still in his Gabriel Movers uniform gave her $20 for two table dances. Her adrenaline increased instantly. She took the money as an incentive; however, she was known for enjoying herself and having fun, too.

Slowly, she stepped back and turned around with her buttocks facing her client. She seductively stepped out of her panties, with her legs straight and her back bent over in a position where she could touch her toes. She stood up, started jiggling and shaking her legs and buttocks from side to side, all while standing still. Then she turned around, facing her client. She got livelier and swayed from side to side, making her breasts bounce.

She turned around, pushed out her rear end, then bent over and spread her buttock's cheeks so her client could see her insides. She spread her vagina lips, made her vaginal muscles thump, and swayed her buttocks side to side, then dropped to the ground. She swept the ground side to side while rising up. Her client's two songs were up, and she moved on to the next client requesting her services.

Eight ball and MJG came on with "Bounce that Ass," which made Keisha shake her lower body drastically. The DJ spun five quick songs.

Keisha took her $50 and moved on to the next men, a group of Caucasian males in suits and ties that requested her and Sabrina, along with a third party, for $200 apiece.

Sabrina was officiously working the establishment, accumulating a great sum of money, but the rigorous exercise and erotic performances had her drained of vitality. However, now dancing next to Desirée, Red Passion was revived with a boost of energy. She began dancing flamboyantly as the two ladies cheered and slapped high fives with glee.

All of a sudden, Master P's "No Limit" came on with "Freak Hoe." The ladies propped their buttocks into the air, facing their clients as they shook and bounced their buttocks and legs rigorously while squatting and with one hand on the floor, looked back at their clients and each other simultaneously. Finished, they got their money and walked to an empty table to sit down. After ordering some Red Bulls from the server, they counted their money.

"Desirée, you need to give that money to me. You know that's a little bit petty for a rich bitch like you," Sabrina said, eyeing all of Keisha's cash.

"Passion, you know you need to stop. You know a hoe can never make too much money," Keisha countered with a large smile that made Sabrina annoyed.

"Oh, yeah, anyway, bitch, you know my girlfriend got released from the federal penitentiary."

"Which one?" Keisha asked indifferently.

"Ha, ha, real funny, bitch. You know, Tasha," Sabrina snapped lightly.

"Tasha's home?" Keisha said, surprised.

"Yeah, she's home and she's planning to get right back to the money," said Sabrina, with an emphasis on "money." She continued, "She made some serious connections on the inside, and she's about to make an enormous lick, you know, theft. She told me about it, and the shit is foolproof. She just needs one more real-ass bitch on the lick, you feel me?" Sabrina stared intensely across the table down at Keisha.

"What are you implying, Sabrina?"

"*What am I implying,* bitch? You think you sophisticated now or something?

"Bitch, I need your ass on this scam," Sabrina said with a pitiful puppy dog grimace on her face.

"Well, I don't—"

Sabrina interrupted Keisha's sentence. "Look, Keisha, you my baby. You know I never steer you wrong. Baby, I love you. I swear we gonna have it made after this one. You lose your love for the dough or something?" Sabrina spoke in a sassy, seductive New Jersey accent.

"Okay, whatever. It had better be as gravy as you say, Passion," said Keisha with a serious, almost bitter look on her face as she folded her arms over her topless breasts.

"Good, I knew you'd be down. Relax, baby girl, we're gonna be straight," said Sabrina confidently, as she tapped lightly on Keisha's folded arms. The server came back with two Red Bulls and two double shots of Cognac.

"Your drinks are on the house, complements of the manager," the server said with a hiss on her words like a snake. She placed the drinks on the table and slithered away with her huge breasts hanging down and wearing only a thong.

"Come on, girl. Let's go to the back and smoke. I got some exotic pink rosebud, girl. Wait until you try it."

The ladies picked up their glass of Cognac and Red Bull and strutted seductively to the dressing room. The two comrades regrouped in the private cubicle, where Keisha bit half her Ecstasy pill and gave Sabrina the other half. They chased the pill with their beverage. Then they both poured their Red Bulls in with their Cognac and devoured their energy drink.

Sabrina was now wearing her g-string, tiger-striped bikini suit, and the top had barely enough material to cover her nipples in a tiny triangle. She pulled out a Ziploc bag full of fluffy pink floral budded marijuana.

"Passion, the shit looks too beautiful to smoke," Keisha said, fascinated by the beauty of the exotic drug.

"Bitch, this shit cost too much to be smoking," Sabrina replied, taking out a sweet aromatic bud to let Keisha observe up close.

"Wow, how much it cost?" Keisha asked.

"Two thousand an ounce," Sabrina replied.

"What?" said Keisha astonished.

"Yeah, baby girl, you know I ain't gonna pay two thousand for no weed, not when I got this fire head and pussy going. My dope man keeps me smoking, right, bitch?" Sabrina said, slapping Keisha's hand with a high five.

"Give me a blunt I can bring home to Cat," Keisha said.

The request caused Sabrina to pause in motion and give Keisha a shocking look, and then she sucked her teeth lightly with an attitude.

"Bitch, go ahead," she said. "You lucky you my girl. How is your little nigga anyway?"

"The nigga is definitely doing his thing, but all that snorting is driving him nuts," Keisha said. "He don't even want to give me no dick. I got to steal a taste when he finally goes to sleep."

Keisha observed Passion as she pulled two sheets of Bob Marley hemp paper from its pack and put it together to make the paper thicker and burn slower. She broke down the budded substance into the hemp paper and rolled a long, sleek joint. She lit it and inhaled deeply, then pulled in a little gas of oxygen through the grit of her teeth. She relaxed and smoked one-fourth of her joint, then passed it to her comrade. Keisha took a pull then inhaled deeply.

She tried to hold it in but erupted into a cough as the smoke came bursting out of her mouth.

"Yeah, bitch, be easy," Sabrina said, laughing at her. Sabrina's eyes were almost closed shut; you could barely see her pupils. Her movements were more relaxed. She moved with an enchanting grace. They smoked the blunt halfway and began to laugh and giggle with each other as they sat and stared in the mirror.

Eventually they returned to the bar and music where all the action was taking place. Suddenly the atmosphere grew lively. The alcohol and money kept flowing, and everybody was having a great time.

The DJ introduced Keisha to the stage. They placed the spotlight on her as she strutted on to the elevated platform. Sabrina walked over to a table in the back and greeted her girlfriend. They hugged, kissed, and had a seat side by side.

The DJ played a Jill Scott song, "One Is the Magic Number." Desirée started slowly working her hips around in a hula-hoop manner, then spread her legs wide apart and drop repeatedly to the base line. She slowly rocked and grooved her way over to a 90-degree angle, then slowly removed her panties while going all the way down into a squat, with her buttocks poking out.

Desirée had all eyes focused on her as she pranced up in a 360-degree spin, simultaneously moving out of her bodice. She spread her arms and legs widely apart, then went back into her imaginary hula-hoop, slow, seductive dance, with one hand pressing firmly against her vagina. With her two middle fingers spread widely apart lifting her lovely sexual organ for the audience to see, she took her other hand, squeezed her breast forward to an erect nipple that she placed her long tongue on and licked her nipples hungrily. The audience started cheering and hollering. Customers periodically would walk up and tease her with bills, then toss them on stage.

The DJ played "Comin' Out Hard," by Eight Ball and MJG. Keisha became extremely lively as she turned around and started shaking and gyrating vigorously. She landed down with her legs spread and extended straight, then grabbed the bottom of the go-go pole, where she did a handstand on her arms and elbows, then slowly elevated her body upside down. Next, she opened her legs wide, then split them and shook her legs and buttocks rigorously.

Even the customer receiving a table dance dashed over to observe her performance close up. This was too good to miss. The men continually tossed cash on the stage.

Keisha brought her body down in a full split, then made her buttocks muscles briskly jump. She grabbed the go-go pole and pulled herself up while jiggling her legs. She kept one hand on the pole, then elevated her legs to her chest and over her head in a full split. She leaned against the pole and gravitated towards the ground around the pole in a 360-degree rotation, her arms were spread wide apart with her firm breasts and erect nipples projecting out.

By now, the majority of the club gave her a standing ovation. Desirée smiled brightly, bowed, and showed her gratitude. Then she raked the money off the floor into a bundle and walked over to join her comrades and her companion.

"You still got it, bitch," Sabrina said, slapping Keisha a feminine high five. Keisha went over and hugged Tasha, however, Tasha sat emotionless and observed those watching their buzz session.

Keisha took a seat at the opposite side of the table and just looked over at Tasha, better known as T. She studied her appearance and noticed how T had gained weight. She was once 5-foot-10 and 178 pounds of muscle-built firmness, but was now a 215-pound stocky woman with a muscular build. She wore a small Afro and was dressed causally in Sean John jeans, Timberland boots, and wore a large white T-shirt and a 2.5 carat diamond earring in her right ear. She wore no makeup and had a shiny, smooth, boyish face.

"It is good seeing you, baby girl. You look great," T said with a hard straight face. Her voice was soft with a slight baritone.

"I already know you're in on the score. All I can tell you is this is my last scam. After this one, I'll be set for retirement. I'm glad I'm fucking with some hoes that already know how to work this operation. As soon as everything gets precisely situated, I'm gonna call you at the number Sabrina got for you so keep ..."

T paused and waited for the waitress to put their Bahaman Mamas on the table in snifter glasses with a small umbrella and cherry and slice of orange at the side. T gave the server a twenty-dollar bill and ushered her away from the table with a limp upside-down backhand fanning motion. The server gave T an eerie glance and strutted off.

"Desirée, just keep your phone on and make sure you answer Passion's call," said T persuasively.

Keisha gently responded with a slight nod. Sabrina raised her glass in the air.

"To money," she said, toasting her glass forward.

T and Keisha responded, "To money." The three softly clinked their glasses together and then said in unison, "To money," and cheered. Then they tilted their heads back and sipped while locking eyes in silent agreement.

Chapter 19
Willy Johnson

"**W**illy Johnson, pack it up! Willy Johnson! Willy Johnson, pack it up. ATW!" shouted a female voice over the intercom.

"Hey, Willie, wake up, man, it's time for you to go home," said a skinny man with rotten teeth looking down from his top bunk.

"What, nigga?" a big Neanderthal-looking man snapped.

"Willy Johnson, pack it up," the voice screamed over the loud speaker. The behemoth ran to the door with his 295-pound frame squeezed into government-issued 3X boxers and pushed the call button in the center door panel to notify the correctional officer where he was. The door electronically popped open. He pushed it wide open, then hurried and put on his 6X uniform and tossed a list of numbers and the rest of his paperwork into a brown bag.

"Say, Willie, p-please leave me a couple items. My stomach's touching my back," his roommate said with emphasis on the word "back." He had a pitiful, puppy-dog expression on his face.

"You can have all that bullshit," said Willy in an intimidating, thunderous roar.

His roommate gave a missing-rotten-teeth smile and nodded his head in appreciation as he climbed down off his bunk and helped Willie pack up and get his required items to leave the jail. Willie tossed his small mattress over his back, carried out his net bag with his blanket, sheet, towel, face towel, and razor blade.

His roommate looked at Willy with envy behind his back when he was ushered from the cell. He swiftly replaced his expression with a slight smile as Willie looked back and said, "Make sure you come through and smoke some of this good dope I got when you get out."

His roommate nodded in agreement, then looked at him in disgust when he turned his back. He instantly closed the door and hurried over to the brown grocery bags filled with food from the commissary. Rotten Teeth rumbled through the bag in delight and grabbed a honey bun, swiftly unraveled the plastic wrapper, and sunk his decayed teeth into the gooey bun. With the big chunk of sweet bread sitting on his tongue, stimulating his taste buds, he inhaled deeply with his eyes closed and just savored the taste. Pure heaven.

The officer opened the pod door electronically, and Willie pushed it wide open. He walked through it and down the hall. He stopped and tossed his mattress onto a pile of letters and carried his net bag into a multipurpose room to wait on an officer escort. Officer Luis came, knocked on the room glass, and informed Willie to approach him. He instructed the inmate to turn around, place his hands behind his back, then shackled his big handcuffs on Willie.

"So, you finally are getting out of here, huh?" Officer Luis said with a smile, which was unusual for his normal, mean, stern demeanor. Willie did not answer. He compliantly followed Officer Luis, who escorted him through the quadrant door to the elevator downstairs into the processing room for release. After he was uncuffed, Luis handed Willie his net bag, and Willie tossed it into a cart with another bag in it. Then he walked to the sitting area to make a phone call.

"Hey, Nikki. I'm about to be released," he simply said and hung up the phone.

He sat in the waiting area for two hours before they finished processing his paperwork and ran a nationwide fingerprint on him. Finally, an officer opened her office door and pushed out a brown paper bag containing his clothes. He quickly dressed into his Academics denim jeans shorts and plain white tank top, and then went to the clerk at the front door and signed his signature on several documents. The pretty young correctional officer looked at him, squirmed, and said, "Okay, you're ready to go."

She buzzed the metal electronic door next to him. Willie pushed the door and left so fast that he forgot his brown paper bag with his paperwork. He was so glad to be on the other side of that door he didn't even care. He walked over to the correctional officer working at the front desk cashier and showed her his armband with his name and personal information. She cut off the armband and printed him a check for $738.32. It was the remainder of his balance on his inmate account.

He grabbed his check and strutted through the double retracting doors to see Nikki, his babies' mother, standing with her hands folded, waiting on him. When she saw him come through the doors, she was so happy to see him she was about to burst into tears. But instead, she held them back to a teary-eyed, choked-up expression.

Taking long strides, she quickly reached him and hugged him tightly for a moment, then kissed him. Nikki looked up at him for a second, savoring the moment, before she placed her arms around his and ushered him out like on a prom date. They strolled from the building across the streets to the parking lot.

"You got my cigarettes?" Willie asked as he looked down slightly at his tall, 5-foot-11 companion.

"Yep," Nikki replied and handed him a box of Newports from her Guess pocketbook. He knocked the box upside down in his palm, then unraveled the plastic and took out a cigarette and lit it with his lighter that he'd retrieved from his jailhouse property. He inhaled deeply and coughed, then took smaller pulls. A burgundy Yukon Denali awaited him. He paused and scanned over his truck keenly.

"Nikki, what happen to my rims?" he asked as he approached the vehicle.

"I sold them," Nikki replied, matter-of-factly.

"*What?*" Willie snapped. "You *sold* my 26-inch Sprewells?" he said, puzzled.

"Baby, I had to."

"*What?*" he snapped again, looking at her in aggravation.

"Daddy! Daddy!" yelled his little 7-year-old boy and 4-year-old girl, running out of the backseat of his truck to hug him.

"I'll explain later," Nikki said as she handed him the truck keys and walked over to the passenger side. Malice filled his eyes as he stared at her, but he quickly smiled at his kids, ducked down, and scooped them up into each arm. The 6-foot-2 man was massively built, with a mahogany skin tone, a low skin fade, and a bit of peach fuzz on his face.

He kissed his little daughter. "Yeah, you don't know how much Daddy missed y'all. Y'all know how much Daddy love y'all, right?" he said with a bright movie-star smile on his face.

"We love you, too, Daddy," his daughter said as she extended her hand to his chest and arms, hugging him with her head lying on his chest. His son admired him and resented him at the same time. Now he would no longer be the man of the house and wouldn't be allowed the privileges he had when his father wasn't around.

Willie placed his son, Brian, on the ground and kept his daughter in his arm. He led Brian to the truck with a gentle hand on top of his head, then put Tracy in the backseat, strapped her in, and buckled her seat belt. Next, he picked up Brian and placed him on the seat next to his younger sister.

"Son, buckle up," Willie said. All of a sudden he noticed how much his little boy was growing and resembled his mother. He was backing away to close the door when his daughter grabbed ahold of his huge sausage-sized fingers.

"Daddy, where you going?" she asked with a pout and a frown of her eyebrow.

"Don't worry, precious. Daddy ain't goin' nowhere." He kissed her gently on her forehead for assurance, then climbed into the driver's seat. After starting the ignition, he adjusted his seat for more legroom.

"Why you had to sell my rims?" Willie asked as he drove off.

Nikki took a deep sigh before she answered. "Okay. I had just driven your truck to your mom and dad's house so your father could give it an oil change. I was worried if you were going to call with a bond, so I asked your mom to give the kids and me a ride home. Your mama stayed for a while, giving me emotional support.

I was drained from all the crying and worrying. I convinced her I would be fine. I went to get the kids and me ready for bed. I walked your mom to the door, we hugged briefly, and she assured me everything was going to be all right and left. I went to bed. The kids were worried about you so we all slept together for emotional support. I fell asleep right away from all the stress.

"We were all in bed asleep when I heard some rumbling in the back bedroom. I was already timid because you're locked up. So I went to the crack in the door and peeped through. I saw a large shadow lurking in the hall. So I rushed over to the bed and woke the kids up, motioning for them to be silent. We scurried over to the closet, and I took the shotgun off the top shelf and cocked it, then we hid in the closet."

"What?" Willie bellowed. "Mutherfuckers broke in my house? Who was it?" A puzzled frown soured his face.

"Well, baby, I was scared as hell. I heard a lot of rumbling through our stuff, but I could swear I heard someone call another person by the name of Lil' Pee," Nikki said with a depressed look.

"What? Why you took so long to tell me this?"

"Baby, I know you were already stressing over being locked up, and I didn't want you to go crazy," Nikki said.

"Daddy, I was scared. They made me cry," Tracy announced.

"Mutherfuckers broke into my house, fucked with my family, made my daughter cry when I'm locked up like some coward. Aw hell, naw, I'm killing those mutherfuckers."

"Daddy, stop cursing," Tracy said.

"Please, baby, calm down," Nikki said in a soothing tone.

In a nanosecond, Willie shot from a relaxed state to an attentive demeanor and now was transformed into a raging bull.

"What'd they take?" Willie demanded.

"All our money under the mattress, a few guns, and your stuff," Nikki replied.

"*Shit!*" Willie said, pounding the steering wheel with his fist.

"Don't worry, baby, I used the money I had in the bank to fix the window they broke. I sold your rims because I was scared the kids and me would get carjacked for it. I also went back to work at Dekalb Medical. We have a good amount of money saved up," said Nikki, encouragingly.

Willie leaned to the side, took out another cigarette, and lit it. He reached over to his CD changer and pressed play. Christopher Wallace's "Life After Death" came on. Fast-forwarding the tracks to "Somebody's Got to Die," he lowered the car window and sighed, enjoying his first day of freedom with the animalistic treachery of a capitalistic society and the enjoyment of his poisonous toxic smoke.

Chapter 20 Spraggs

The blue-and-white striped Mustang zoomed past a black Porsche Cayman S with limousine tint and parked across the street behind Chyna's garage. Spraggs turned off the ignition and waited for a moment in the silence of the night. He observed the peaceful desolate subdivision. After he took the key from the ignition, he got out and closed the door quietly.

Spraggs stood erect in a militant-like stance and gritted his teeth until his jawbone muscle throbbed with tension. He felt the eerie chill of the night breeze flowing over his skin as he walked determined around to the front door. When he pressed the doorbell, a ding-dong echoed throughout the house. Since no one answered, he rang the doorbell again. He began to walk off, then did an about-face, took two steps forward, and kicked the door in with tremendous force.

The door flew open, and Spraggs scurried in and immediately shut it behind him. He took out his .45 Desert Eagle from his holster and peeked through the window without moving the curtains to make sure he did not cause enough of a disturbance to attract the neighbors' attention.

The phone started ringing. *R-r-r-ring.* Spraggs crept through the house slowly, taking light, cautious steps. *R-r-r-ring.* He eased downstairs to the entertainment room. *R-r-r-ring.* He made his way to the garage door with his weapon extended in front of him and opened the door swiftly. He turned on the lights and motioned from side to side with his weapon extended.

Both the Chrysler Firepower and the XK Jaguar were in the garage. Spraggs walked over and viewed the inside through the windshields. *R-r-r-ring.* The office door was ajar. He turned on the light, his eyes scanning over the room. He noticed the answer machine was unplugged and turned off, along with the computer. He about-faced, leaving the lights on. *R-r-r-ring.* Next, he walked over to the billiard room and turned on the lights. *R-r-r-ring.*

Keeping his eyes on the entrance, Spraggs went over to the pool table, reached down, and pushed the lever. The center of the table rotated to reveal the arsenal; however, the majority of the weapons were missing. He grabbed one of the three handguns left and tossed the .45 Desert Eagles on the pile of guns, then checked to see if there was any ammunition in the Colt .357 Magnum. After that, he fastened the barrel back into position with a flick of the wrist, cocked the hammer back, and pointed the gun forward.

R-r-r-ring. The phone kept ringing, but Spraggs decided not to answer it.

His arm was bent in a ninety-degree angle with the extended muzzle projected in front of him when he walked back upstairs. *R-r-r-ring.* He walked through the passage into the kitchen and withdrew a Jitsu kitchen knife from the knife holder then twirled the knife through his fingers like a cheerleader's baton, until the blade was positioned upside down and the rubber handle was gripped tightly in his hand. He then continued towards the upstairs, scouring the rooms intensely. He walked with the knife and his gun pointed forward.

R-r-r-ring.

Spraggs stepped an immediate left into the master bedroom and walked in. Intentionally, he left the lights off so he wouldn't be recognized. Seeing the room clear, he walked inside the closet to check his suitcase with his money. The traveling bag with the heroin was gone. His face was filled with fury because he realized his traitorous prey was gone with it.

R-r-r-ring.

He looked down and pressed the speaker button. A soft English voice spoke from the speakerphone. "Hello. Hello, rude boy. I know you're there. Hello."

He did not respond.

Chyna continued. "I'm sorry, sweetheart. I can understand that you are a tad bit mad at me, however, there's no need for resentment. It was devious of me to orchestrate your demise. Rude boy, you have violated the number one rule of the laws of power. You have outshined your master.

"Spraggs, surely you remember Don Brown, a very powerful man. As you know, there is no limit to his ruthlessness. Mr. Brown has my parents' captive, and you got a three million pound ransom on your head. I'm sure I don't need to tell you that that's English currency, and it's quite a bit of money.

"Your extermination will make me an extremely rich woman. However, your life would give me someone to love and cherish. So weighing the pros and cons, keeping you alive would keep me content, but for how long? Eventually, I would just jeopardize my own life. Now if I eliminate you, I will save my mommy and daddy's life and be a filthy-rich woman. Sweetheart, this is a no-brainer. Besides, who needs bloody love when you're in this line of business?"

Spraggs came out his trance and stepped over to the balcony window, overlooking the driveway and roadway.

"Anyway, I'll be able to buy all the pleasure my heart craves for the rest of my life."

He noticed a lady in high heels going to a Porsche wearing a grey business pants suit with a stunning body that only Chyna was blessed with. She was carrying the two book bags and a traveling bag over her shoulders. He stared in a paralyzed state of disbelief as he watched her open the door to the Porsche Cayman S. Then she tossed the bags in the backseat.

"I hope you don't take this personally, sweetheart. Ta-tah, as we say in jolly ole England," Chyna said through her hand-free earpiece. She reached down in her pocket, pulled out a remote control device, and pushed a button. Meanwhile Spraggs was taking aim at Chyna's forehead.

A massive explosion jolted Spraggs from a shockwave. The explosion stemmed from the cars in the garage. Fire engulfed the computer room, rushed through the billiard room, and erupted throughout the entire house. The inferno blasted Spraggs through the windows, shattering and showering glass in a rain of deadly splinters. The flames gushed out of the blasted-out windows of the establishment in an upward fiery funnel, similar to the atomic bomb dropped on Hiroshima and Nagasaki.

Chyna calmly got into her Porsche and swiftly raced off into the night immediately after pushing the remote control detonator.

The force of the conflagration catapulted Spraggs airborne through the first-story window, doing the bugle dance in midair, then he came crashing down on top of the Mustang GT roof like a ton of bricks. As he landed on his stomach, the impact forced all the oxygen out of his lungs.

He lay on the roof of the coupé with his body fully extended, limp and motionless, blood oozing from his mouth onto the cracked windshield.

The gloomy dark of the universe smothered the stars that tried to glare down on him, and the full moon lurked behind a cloud as if in malicious agreement with the darkness in their victory over the once-powerful gladiator in the arena of life. He just lay motionless, toppled from grace, his monarchy plummeted by treason—a treacherous and deceptive woman. The eerie mystic allure of the wind gently hovered over his limp body.

21 *Lisa*

Lisa was feeling an irritable, nauseated kind of pain at the pit of her stomach. She lay down and coped with it until the annoyance was too much to bear. Suddenly, she felt her gag reflex muscle contracting and rushed to the bathroom. Barely in time, she lifted the toilet seat and regurgitated all her food from the night before. Vomiting made her feel better every time.

She got up, rinsed her mouth, brushed her teeth, then trudged wearily and lightheaded back to bed where she snuggly wrapped up under her blanket. She looked over at Ricky, who was sleeping on his back while she was facing him on her side, trying to take the tension off her queasy stomach.

Her illness showed in her face as she twisted one of Ricky's dreadlocks between her fingers and gazed upon his smooth, almond-colored skin and his sleek face. She admired his small goatee and peach fuzz mustache, which was as lustrous black as his long, spaghetti-like hair.

Once again, she felt that chronic irritation in the pit of her stomach. She dashed for the toilet and vomited a second time until she felt a dry, burning hoarseness in her throat. After she finished heaving, she felt a lot better and suddenly, she felt famished.

Obviously, the sound of constant regurgitation and the flushing of the toilet woke Ricky out of his state of nirvana. When Lisa walked back into the room, he looked up at her.

"You all right, baby?" he asked, lying on his side with his head propped up, resting in the center of his palm.

"Yeah, Poppy, I'm all right," she responded. "That Fettuccine Alfredo and shrimp casserole has been doing a number on me."

She slithered her luscious naked body over to the side of the bed where she picked up her Polo bathrobe that was hanging on top of the rail of the metal canopy bed, slipped it on, tied the belt into a knot, and ambled to the kitchen.

Once in the kitchen, she took out the frying pan and a small boiling pot, rinsed them with water, then placed them on the stove burners. Her thoughts were filled with what she was going to cook to satisfy her tremendous craving. She opened the cabinet across from the stove and scoured through the cupboard until she located a little Debbie Snack cake, which she devoured and immediately unraveled another.

While eating on the snack cake, she reached into the fruit bowl on the kitchen counter under the cupboard, picked up a banana, peeled it, and ate it along with the snack cake, threw the empty banana peel into the garbage disposal and turned it on. She turned on the water faucet while the disposal was on and also put some water in her tea kettle. After she cooked Ricky's breakfast, she went back into the room. Ricky had fallen asleep again, which was normal for him at six o'clock in the morning.

"Ricky, wake up, I made you breakfast," Lisa said, shaking him until he was wide-awake, with a serious grimace on his face.

"What?" he said in a grumpy tone.

"Sit up, baby, I want you to eat your breakfast."

Ricky lay there cranky, with his arms folded across his chest, as Lisa motioned towards the kitchen. She came back with a serving tray with a bowl of grits, a separate plate of scrambled eggs, four thick slices of bacon, a stack of fluffy pancakes with melting butter on top, a bottle of Vermont maple syrup on the side, and a cup of hot cappuccino. She walked over to the bedside where Ricky was laying and set the serving tray on the night table beside him, then pulled out the bed table from under the bed.

"Baby, sit up," she said, looking down on him with intense eyes. In annoyance, Ricky sat up and placed his back against the wall. She placed the bed table and tray on top of his lap. Ricky just sat there, with a frown fixed on his face and his arms still folded. He pouted like a toddler deprived of his meaningless wants.

"Baby, you ain't going to eat your breakfast after I slaved over the stove all morning?" Lisa snapped.

"You ain't going to let me get no fucking sleep after I been fucking your pussy like a slave all night!" Ricky erupted as he took the table off his lap and placed it on the nightstand. He turned his back to her, trying to get some sleep. However, Lisa had other ideas. Her raging hormones had her feeling irritated, and she wanted her mate to feel her anguish.

"Nigga, please, don't even flatter yourself. Your stupid ass needs to eat this fucking breakfast before I throw it all over your stupid ass," she barked with a dramatic flare and emphasis on all her insulting words.

"Would you shut the fuck up?" Ricky glared back at her with intense aggravation in his eyes.

"You shut up. You ain't anybody," Lisa retorted. Her vicious verbal attack on Ricky allowed her to vent and release a lot of unwanted emotional tension.

However, Ricky's tolerance was getting extremely low. He pounced out of the bed like a madman in his boxers, dashed menacingly right in front of her, and started yelling in Lisa's face like a baseball manager when he believes the umpire purposely made a bad call to insult him.

"What the fuck is your problem? What the fuck is wrong with you? You're acting like a stupid little bitch. I do not have to take your bullshit. I have plenty of better bitches than you chasing me every day. You need to shut the fuck up and watch what the fuck you say out of your stinking dirty mouth to me."

Lisa watched how hard and furious his face was. How his muscles were bulging and his veins throbbing with fury. She listened how his words had a dramatic impact that irritated her heart and the pit of her stomach. She felt a sharp numbing ache in her neck that reflected the anguish burning in her soul. Lisa did not know whether to slap him or to hug him. She was emotionally ambushed between the lines of breaking down and crying or dropping down and satisfying his dominance over her emotions. However, she did what most would do in a state of confusion. She became aggravated.

The ringing of his cell phone interrupted Ricky's malicious attack. They stared at each other with anger and intensity. Finally, Ricky broke the Mexican stand-off and took heavy, monsterlike steps to answer his cell phone on the night table phone charger.

"Yeah, what's happenin'?" he answered.

"You piece of shit, that's all you good for, chasing that damn cell phone with all your dope fiends calling whose lives you destroy chasing dope," growled a malevolent Lisa.

"Would you shut the fuck up now? You see I'm on the phone?" Ricky yelled in rage, his dreadlocks whipping from side to side.

"Look how you talk to the woman you love in front of strangers. You have no compassion," Lisa said in distress as she climbed in her bed from exhaustion.

"Yeah, that's cool. I'll be there in a minute," Ricky said then put the phone down. He gulped down his coffee and used the pancake to create an egg and bacon sandwich. After that, he went to the closet and put on a pair of black Guess cargo pants and a Gucci belt and pulled out a black T-shirt off the top shelf and put it on. Next came some black Tommy Hilfiger socks from the dresser drawer, slipped on his Babe and Apes multicolor sneakers, tied his hair into a ponytail, and went to brush his teeth and wash his face in the bathroom.

Afterwards, Ricky went back to his bedroom, put on his Yushua leather jacket, walked over to the dresser, and grabbed all his accessories—his Yushua watch, wallet, and keys to the Benz M600. Although he was mad, Ricky did not want to leave the house on a negative vibe so he walked over, looked down on a pitiful Lisa, and kissed her gently on the cheeks, which was his departing ritual. He reached over to the nightstand, grabbed his cell phone, and put it into his jacket pocket.

"Baby, don't go," Lisa said with a weary voice as Ricky headed for the front door. He heard her, paused for a moment, and inhaled and exhaled deeply through his nostrils. He felt his tension awakening again as he gritted his teeth. Without responding, he left. He had business to handle, so he continued with confidence. Even so, he was somewhat puzzled about Lisa's strange behavior. He was bewildered. *Why is Lisa acting like that? I mean, things are going great. The car booking business is thriving, and we have more money than I could have ever imagined.*

Once Lisa heard the door slam, she sat up and growled, tossed a pillow across the room in distress, then slumped back into the bed feeling defeated. Then she grabbed another pillow, cuddled it, and started crying. The more she wept, the guiltier she felt about their argument. But most of all, she felt sorry for herself.

Meanwhile, Ricky walked over to his Benz, pressed the keyless entry to open the door, and climbed in.

Still angry at Lisa, he sat in the seat and stared up at her apartment. She was such a bitch when she wanted to be.

Finally, he closed the car door, put the key in the ignition, and started the car. The audio came on blasting Bone thugs-n-harmony: East 1999 CD "Mo Murders," while his car's five TVs came on showing different satellite depictions from news and sports to rap videos.

He turned the sound down low so he could concentrate, put the car in reverse, and drove off slowly, admiring the luster of the 22-inch chrome wheels' reflection in the glass windows as he passed by.

Low on gas, he pulled up at the gas station, not surprised to see how inflated the gas prices were again. Lately, the price had been getting worse. The prices had spiraled from 97 cents before the Iraqi war started to three dollars, and sometimes five dollars, per gallon now. *I wouldn't be surprised to see the gas price shoot to $10 one day, the way things are going, he thought to himself.*

Thoughts rebounded in his head about the way the Western government was entrapping its people. First the powers that be started a war, interfering with the gas market. Next, the price of gas skyrocketed, with the main beneficiaries being the ones who were responsible for starting the war in the first place. This was similar to how certain people manufacture and control the drug market, then arrest citizens for being involved with it.

It didn't surprise Ricky that the country attacked Afghanistan. After all, it is the main grower of the poppy plant, which produces heroin. Next was Iraq, which could supply the world with almost 50 percent of its oil and contains an extravagant amount of priceless historical artifacts, antiques, and documents of historical value. He believed that next, the U.S. would pursue a secret plan to invade Iran, so it could control and dominate the world's single most-needed resource—oil.

Ricky read the newspaper and believed the editorials which claimed that the U.S. government's true desire is for world domination, and that they were building their confidence to enforce the last stage of aggressively imposing their global bias on the New World Order.

Ricky prided himself on his ability to decipher truth out of any lie. It was refined by years of street knowledge. You know how the ole saying goes: You can fool some people some of the time, but you cannot fool a wise man none of the time.

He finished pumping his gas and continued on his journey. While cruising, he reached in the ashtray, retrieved his rosebud rolled in a fonta leaf, and lit it with the car lighter. Two puffs and he was in a state of euphoria. He put the joint back down and accelerated onto the expressway, reclining his seat slightly and enjoying the ride to the eastside.

The sophistication of the Benz's suspension made it feel like Ricky was floating on a cloud. Finally, he pulled up in Popi's driveway and, as usual, went around to the back, where he knocked on the patio door and waited. Popi opened the door in his robe. *At least, I see somebody getting to enjoy their leisure time, he thought wryly.*

"Hey, partner, come on in," Popi said.

He quickly vanished through the door leading inside his house. When he reappeared, Popi had a black leather traveling bag and placed it on the table in front of Ricky, whose credibility had become so good with Popi that the old Mexican man now gave

Ricky everything on consignment. Ricky unzipped the bag and took out ten blocks of cocaine, then placed them back into the bag.

"How much you owe me now?" Popi asked, staring at Ricky with a serious gaze.

"One hundred thousand."

Nothing more was said. Ricky then carried out the package, used the keyless entry to the trunk, tossed the bag in, got back in the car, reversed, and then continued on his journey.

At one point, he could have sworn he saw some police behind him, but after turning into a subdivision and seeing no cars following him, he knew it was an illusion. This marijuana was making him paranoid as hell.

A few moments later, he cruised into his apartment complex and parked next to Lucky's BMW 745i with the 22-inch rims. He recalled selling Lucky on those babies. Lucky's hustling game seemed to have elevated him into a monster.

He parked, looked around, and took out his .50-caliber automatic handgun from the middle console compartment and tucked it into his waistline. Then he got out and scanned the surroundings. A man couldn't be too careful in a high-crime place like this. He popped the trunk and took out the traveling bag.

Walking into the apartment, he saw Lucky and his companion Peaches watching his 50-inch widescreen Samsung High Definition projection TV. After greeting them, he walked past them, went upstairs to his bedroom, opened the door, and walked in. Carefully, he locked the door behind him and tossed the bag on the bed.

Unzipping it, he took out one key for Lucky, three for Cat, three for Blue, and separated two to break down for his other miscellaneous customers. He Scotch-taped the separate orders together, placed them back into the bag, and zipped it except for two keys. Then he placed the bag on the top closet shelf and locked the closet door.

He opened the bedroom door and yelled, "Lucky."

"What's happenin'?" he asked.

Ricky handed him one of the blocks in his hand. Lucky took it and led Ricky to his bedroom. Lucky had been coming up tremendously. Now he even had a 51-inch integrated High Definition TV right in front of his bed with a Canon mini-digital camcorder on top of it with the lens focused on the bed. A Panasonic cordless digital phone stood on his Rubbermaid two-drawer container that he used as a night table. He had a brand-new Toshiba mobile technology notebook opened next to his telephone. Lucky finally had his own live porno service off the ground.

"Hey, man, I had a serious freak fest in here last night, you dig? Man, you should of seen it. As a matter of fact, I have some footage for you. You can always catch it on www.monstar.biz, know what I mean?"

Lucky looked at me, displaying bright white teeth with an infectious smile. I smiled back as he came out from his closet safe and handed me $15,000. I gave him dap, a pat on his back, and proceeded downstairs. Peaches was on the couch with her hair freshly microbraided. Her tight bicycle shorts and Nike sports bra made her look as sweet and luscious as her name.

"Hey, Ricky," she said with a warm smile.

He threw up the peace sign, nodded his head, and said, "What's up?" as he went to the kitchen and grabbed four pots. He filled them halfway with water and placed them all on the stove's burners, turned the burners on mid-high, opened a cupboard and took out four gigantic coffee mugs. After a quick rinse, he set them in a line on the counter.

Next, he took out the digital scale from the kitchen drawer, along with a 36-ounce bottle of super-B vitamin complex. From the cupboard on the opposite side, he took out a fresh box of economy-size baking soda, closed the cupboard, and opened the other kitchen drawer, where he pulled out a folded black bandanna and tied it around his nose and mouth cowboy fashion.

He knocked the square block a few times on the counter to break it into chunks, then burst the seal with his knife. From habit, Ricky took out about four-and-a-half ounces apiece and placed them into each cup, then weighed about 30 to 40 grams of Super B into the cups, and four ounces of baking soda in each cup. By this time, the water started boiling.

Lucky came in the kitchen, opened the refrigerator, got out two Budweisers, then wandered back into the living room. I placed each coffee cup with the substances into the boiling water, one cup at a time. Once they were safely set in the pot, I used a tablespoon to scoop the boiling water into each mug until the substance began to dissolve and combine together.

Next, I filled the cups with more boiling hot water and left them until the dope dissolved and sank to the bottom. I turned off the burners, took out the cups, and let them cool off. That was my foolproof way of cooking crack cocaine. Once the substance turned back to a solid form, I poured off the water and placed the dope into Ziploc bags.

I put everything back in order, placed the pot and cups into the dishwasher, turned it on, and headed back upstairs. Once in the room, I locked the door and placed the remainder of the Ziploc bags into the traveling bag with the rest of the dope and undressed inside the closet where I could put my clothes away instantly. Still holding my cell phone, I walked over to my bed and slumped into it, dead-tired.

In a few minutes, my cell phone would be ringing like crazy. I turned on the TV to the morning news, put my cell phone on silent, got under the covers, and closed my eyes.

Officers
Parker and Pine

The Dekalb County squad car slowed down as it approached the suspect's location. Officer Parker and John Pine drove in the driveway of 499 Vineyard and parked. They both clambered out of the car in their spotless Dekalb County uniforms. Officer Parker opened the trunk, which was loaded with a large artillery. He placed the strap of a rifle over his shoulders. Then the two men moved cautiously around the side to the back of the suspect's house.

Looking in, Officer Pine saw Pablo Martinez, a.k.a. Popi, sitting on the couch, watching reruns of the *Three Stooges*. Suddenly, Pablo felt the eerie feeling of being watched. He looked up, saw the police officer through the window, and scurried for the front entrance to his house, just as Officer Pine turned the doorknob and burst in. The officers were inside. Officer Parker extended his arm, holding his weapon. Popi was furious and armed. He and the officers faced off.

"This fuckin bitch won't allow me to be in peace. Being free is good, mane, but this house detention shit is killing me, mane," Popi shouted as he threw his brown bag on the table.

"You're lucky you're not where you belong—in a cold cell, freezing your ass off, Martinez," Officer Pine said with a look of disgust on his face.

"Yeah, yeah, you got the stuff or what?" Popi asked.

Officer Parker threw the traveling bag on the card table. "There you go, Martinez," Officer Parker said as he picked up the brown paper bag. Martinez opened the traveling bag and emptied it out on the table as Officer Pine glanced up at him. He gave Martinez a dumfounded look.

"What, Martinez? You don't trust us now?" Pine asked.

"No, no, partner. I just want to make sure all 50 keys of cocaine are here, *chico,*" Popi said with a conniving smile.

"Should I make sure the whole $350,000 is here, *chico*?" Pine asked his partner in a mimicking fashion.

"Go ahead. We're not in a rush, chico," Popi said.

"No, Martinez. No need. You ain't as stupid as you look. You low-life Mexican piece of shit. You fuck up once and it's back to the slammer for the rest of your worthless, pathetic life, you hear me?" Pine shouted with his face flushed red with demonic-like hatred.

"Sí," Popi nodded, pitifully.

"Remember, Martinez, your life belong to me and anytime you get out of line and think you're above working for us, you're exterminated, just like a miserable cockroach under my boot," Officer Pine said as they walked through the door and vanished into the evening mist.

The two men walked back to their squad car. Office Pine got in the driver's seat and Officer Parker got into the passenger's side. Parker took half of the money out of the brown paper bag and tossed his partner stacks of $25,000 into his lap. Inhaling the aroma of the money, Pine smiled, picked up the cash, and ran his thumb over the top of the stack of the drug money bound with a rubber band that was condensed as tightly as a deck of cards. He placed it down his shirt under his bulletproof vest. Officer Parker just placed his money down into his bulletproof vest.

Pine started the engine, then spoke in a soft voice, "Parker, it must be the ultimate utopia to control and manipulate both sides of the fence. You know, on one side, you're the head commanding law enforcement officer, and on the other end, you're the one manipulating the drug war. This increases the county's epidemic of drug-induced crimes that's keeping the county jail full. Isn't that a scream?" Pine stared at Parker with a conspiratorial smile and a lot of respect.

"Well, John, I, too, am amazed by the irony of it all. Hey, maybe one day I could be elected sheriff of Dekalb County," Officer Parker said with an idea as bright as a light bulb over his head. The two chuckled before Officer Pine placed the car in reverse and exited the driveway, looking for lawbreakers so that they could uphold their sworn duty.

Chapter 23 *Spraggs*

The gentle mist of drizzling rain and falling ashes pleasantly gravitated to the ground. The flames and the noisy roar of the fire truck's sirens revived Spraggs' senses to an aggravated state of consciousness. He opened his eyes to the glare of flashing lights and the all-consuming pain that convulsed his brain. He awakened from a concussion, distressed with an excruciating headache. His body felt numb and slightly paralyzed.

"I have to get out of here. I *will* get out of here," he told himself.

Spraggs managed enough energy to roll off the car, away from the blazing flames of the house, and onto the pavement on the opposite side of the car. His maneuver landed him on his hands in a push-up stance—before he collapsed to his stomach under the pressure of his own body weight. His migraine was pounding like the hooves of a whole herd of stampeding horses. It felt like his brain was going to throb out of his forehead. He bore the suffering and maneuvered himself by crawling on his arms and elbows to the opposite side of the roadway.

Somehow, he managed to crawl to the grass and hid himself under some bushes. He rested there and through agonizing and blurred vision, he observed the fire truck pulling up adjacent to the house. Fire fighters scrambled to put out the blazing inferno that used to be a mansion.

Spraggs was so weary and in extreme pain. More sirens sounded and flashing lights approached. Inquisitive neighbors rushed out of their houses for their own safety or just out of curiosity. Still crawling on his belly like a slithering snake, Spraggs forced himself to move through his anguish. He crawled on the grass alongside the metal fence of the pool, camouflaged by a blanket of darkness. He made it past the outdoor pool and to the front door of the recreation center. Slowly, he reached up his hand, turned the knob, and the door opened. Sinking instantly back down to his arms and elbows, he crawled in and shut the door behind him. He continued to crawl past the indoor swimming pool and over to the hot tub in the rear.

Next, he crawled over to the circular black marble stairwell into the boiling spa. The hot stream rose into the air. With each breath that he took, it seemed to soothe his aching body. Using his feet, he knocked off his shoes. In agony, he slowly undressed himself and slid down the stairs, feet first, into the water.

There he sat helplessly with his back against the tub, feeling the vibration, then dipped his head underwater, painfully rinsing his smoke-blackened, slightly burnt face and head. Taking a deep breath, he leaned his neck back to the wall of the tub and left his head lying at a slant on the marble as he drifted back to a state of unconsciousness.

Hours passed and it was now morning. Spraggs was awakening out of his nightmare to the reality of it all by laughter and splashes. He slowly tilted his head so as not to invoke the excruciating migraine headache that he experienced after the blast and the fall. The effect from the tilt did not hurt nearly as much as he thought it would.

Slowly he shook his head from side to side to see how much he could handle. Now the aches and pains from his body movement were manageable for him. Cautiously, he stood up and was relieved that his body was beginning to respond to his mental commands without severe pain or cramping.

He stepped out of the spa onto the marble surface and took calm, calculated steps to the circular staircase. He paused as his head elevated over the stairs, giving him a clear view of the pool. His eyes swept and analyzed his surrounding area.

The place was relatively empty except for two Caucasian young ladies who appeared to be college students. Spraggs proceeded to the top of the steps and stood motionless in his boxers as the hot water evaporated off his body. The ladies stopped their splashing and playing to stare at him.

Spraggs sighed, took off his boxers, wrung them dry, and then used them to dry his body off completely. By now, the ladies were wide-eyed with astonishment as Spraggs walked over to the rubbish bin and tossed his Burberry boxer shorts away. He then walked over to his clothes and put them back on, then stretched from side to side like an aerobic instructor and rolled his neck. He still suffered the aftershock of a concussion, but, in contrast to last night, he felt great. He sighed again and walked arrogantly towards the entrance.

"Hey, mister, you want to join us for a swim?" the redhead with the ponytail yelled. Her silicone-implanted breasts floated on the water. Spraggs ignored the remark and kept walking as they giggled and splashed water in his direction. He exited the building to see the aftermath of the fire.

The entire condominium was burnt down, and the side of the condominium next to it was destroyed by the blaze. Spraggs noticed some of the residents of the community going about their morning routine. He took his cell phone out of his pocket, turned it on, and dialed a number. He placed the phone to his ear to hear the operator's voice come on and inform him that his phone service was disconnected. He tightened his face in anger and tossed the phone into some nearby bushes as he deeply and slowly inhaled with measured breaths, then started walking away slowly, plotting his next move.

He noticed the garage of condominium number three opened. A man in a pink Polo shirt and blue Oxford blazer loped out and got into his car. Spraggs increased his pace towards the man. The car exhaust roared with life as the driver started the ignition. Forgetting something, the driver opened the car door, left the car running, and went back into the house.

Spraggs broke into a sprint. He reached the car and jumped into the FXX Enzo, placed the Ferrari into reverse, and quickly backed out of the garage. Shocked, the owner of the vehicle emerged through the open door and made a dash for his car.

"Hey! Hey! That's my car!" he screamed. However, the 800 HP, 250 miles per hour Ferrari with a white racing stripe zoomed off like a mechanical Flash Gordon. It zigged and zagged with a right and left turn, and then shot ahead like a greased lightning bolt. Once on the roadway, Spraggs relaxed. The last few nights, he'd concluded that his life was meant to be a living hell. The two people he most admired had betrayed him. Had tried to kill him. Now his quest was for revenge. This would become his fuel.

Those that cross me must be annihilated, he thought to himself. *If it's the last thing I do, I WILL get my vengeance.*

Speeding along, Spraggs looked at the gas gauge and saw that the gas tank was almost full. He wanted to drive out of state, but he didn't know the roads. He was furious, but he buried it like the rest of his emotions, deep inside him to the pit of his stomach.

He could feel anger boiling inside of him and his soul burning until it reached up and grasped his Adam's apple. His face was flushed with fury, his eyes intense with pain. He was on the verge of exploding, or imploding, but it was not in his program to self-destruct. His upbringing in "dog-eat-dog, robber-rob-robber, killer-kill-killer," mentality converged to turn him into a vindictive virtuoso.

Spraggs spotted a Jamaican restaurant, pulled in front of it, and got out. He entered the restaurant, went to the counter, and looked into the eyes of the cashier as if to read her psychologically.

"Welcome. How can I help you?" she said with an island accent and a pearl-white smile.

"Hi. Can I get a large fish tea, some ackee and saltfish, boiled yams, potatoes, and dumplings?" He took $700 out of his pocket and gave her a $20. Then he walked over, picked up a roots tonic out of the beverage refrigerator, and walked outside. He noticed the young lady admiring him through his peripheral vision. However, he kept his head straight ahead and strolled to a convenient store in the same shopping center.

Inside the store, he bought a bottle Advil, paid for it, opened the bottle, and took two pills instantly, chasing it down with the roots tonic. He tossed the empty roots bottle into the trash can as he walked back to the restaurant and grabbed his bag off the counter. He sat at a table, removed his food from the plastic bag, and ate all his ackee, saltfish, boiled ground food, and dumplings. Lastly, he got a spoon out of the bag and devoured his hot fish tea soup.

Once he finished his meal, Spraggs felt more vibrant. He got up, placed his trash into the garbage container, then exited the restaurant and got in the Ferrari. He reversed, placed the car in gear, and quickly approached the roadway and turned on to Martin Luther King Boulevard.

Spraggs merged on the expressway and drove in the direction of I-20 East. The power of the Ferrari intrigued him immensely. His foot was barely on the accelerator and yet, the car was easily doing 60 miles per hour. Right now, he just wanted to get out of Atlanta. He planned to find a hotel room on the outskirts of town and regroup his thoughts.

He exited at 285 East at Memorial Drive and drove down the street with his car attracting more attention than usual in this neighborhood. He also noticed a police car driving slowly behind his ride, and the officers glaring at him with envy and animosity. Spotting a decent-looking hotel, he pulled in and parked, then walked inside into the lobby and inquired about a room.

"Sir, I'm so very sorry. I have no more rooms available."

Spraggs strutted to his car, gazed around, and noticed the squad car was nowhere in sight. He hopped in the car and drove down Memorial Drive to another hotel. He was about three lights down when he noticed in his rearview mirror that a squad car was rapidly approaching with flashing blue lights. Spraggs relaxed and drove at two miles per hour under the speed limit. The police car came bumper to bumper behind Spraggs' vehicle and yelled over the loud speaker, "Pull over and stop now!"

Spraggs kept his eyes in the rearview mirror and patted himself down. No gun. *It must have dropped in the house during the explosion,* he thought. He searched frantically through the interior of the car to try to locate a firearm, hoping that the victim might have had one in his vehicle. But no such luck. He downshifted, still watching the bald-headed ebony officer through his rearview mirror. This was the officer who had been glaring at him just a short while earlier. As soon as Spraggs put the car in first gear, he took his feet off the brake.

"Turn off your engine and step out of your car," the police officer barked then waited.

Spraggs sat patiently in his driver's seat. Another squad car zoomed by and parked in front of Spraggs. That officer immediately sprang from his squad car, ran for the driver's side of the Ferrari door with his gun drawn, and positioned himself by the vehicle.

Spraggs observed him with a squint, then rapidly put his foot on the gas pedal and gently eased up off the clutch, while turning the steering wheel to the left. The V12, 6.2-liter engine blasted the Ferrari into the opposite direction. The officer paused, positioned, aimed, and fired two shots at the rear of the vehicle. The Ferrari FXX's superior racing performance had Spraggs turning in and out of the way of oncoming traffic like a shark darting through a school of fish. Without delay, the police were in hot pursuit.

Spraggs crossed over the median and back to the other side of the roadway. He upshifted and shot up Memorial Drive. As he passed the county detention center, he could see all the squad cars racing towards him in pursuit. The Ferrari was doing 170 with ease. He was outrunning the squad cars, but his getaway was uncertain because he did not know the area or the roadway. He reached Candler Road and noticed that the police were setting up a roadblock ahead. He stomped on the brakes to bring the wheels to an immediate stop. The car swayed as the tires sparked in a thick, lingering cloud of smoke.

Putting the car in reverse, Spraggs swiftly turned the steering wheel to the left and did a U-turn, blasted across the median and down the other side. He maneuvered in and out of traffic with a slight left and right motion of the steering wheel. His adrenaline was being pumped as fast as he was speeding. Now he heard a new sound—the roar of a helicopter overhead. He was easily outrunning the police officers, but the 'copter stayed with him.

He was running in circles until he was once again on Memorial Drive. There were fewer cars there so he could put the pedal to the metal and reached 60 miles per hour in seconds, causing the rear tires to burn rubber, creating traction as he continued to upshift rapidly.

Spraggs sank back in his seat like he was a part of the upholstery as the Ferrari launched across the roadway like an F-16 jet. Once he hit 250 miles per hour, he realized there was no car in sight. He came to a halt in the middle of the street then made a dash for the woods. Before he made it, he could hear the helicopter overhead like a pestering mosquito. He lurked under the cover of the trees and bushes in the woods.

He kept looking up, irate at the loud sound of the helicopter's propeller that hovered above him. Then he noticed armed police officers approaching. He made a run for it. Ahead of him was an orange brick apartment past a gated fence. He climbed over the fence and ran between two widely separated buildings. He continued running until he was in the center of a brick, U-shaped complex, but stopped as he saw the approaching squad cars and armed officers storming towards him.

There were about six squad cars in front of him, and the pesky, hovering helicopter above him. Breathing heavily, Spraggs turned around and started to dash back in the direction he was coming from. Unfortunately, about eleven armed police officers met him with their firearms drawn and aimed at him.

"Get down! Get the fuck down!" the legion of officers barked at him.

Spraggs stood there, exhausted, bewildered, and extremely aggravated.

One of the officers tackled him from behind and slammed Spraggs to the ground as the rest ran over and knelt on his neck and back. They tried to afflict as much pain as possible while they restrained Spraggs and shackled him. Spraggs' migraine immediately came back. He closed his eyes and just blocked out the brutality and degradation.

24 Peter Lynch

Peter Lynch woke up early in the morning. He was in a decent mood this morning. He reached over and kissed his wife, Jessica, who was lying beside him in the nude. They had been living together for four years and had recently gotten married.

Peter met Jessica Hunter during her junior year in Emory University. The two started dating and had been in a committed relationship ever since Peter separated from his ex-wife, following a 15-year marriage. Although he went through a stressful, rocky divorce, Peter was happy to have met Jessica, who was 20 years his junior. The young college co-ed made him feel wanted and appreciated. He even felt vibrant and young again, even if he suffered from a lack of self-confidence due to his male impotence problem.

Fortunately, Jessica assured him that she was okay with him only being able to please her orally. They had been up satisfying each other orally all night, and Peter was now laying in a peaceful mood. He lifted up the white sheet and looked at the lovely ivory-toned body that lay under it. Jessica was lying on her stomach with her long brunette hair flowing down her petite body. Her sleek, grapefruit-shaped buttocks stood as proud mounds and aroused Peter's sexual urges all over again.

He parted her legs lightly, then kissed her gently on her neck. He then extended his tongue and ran it slowly but deliciously down her spine, awakening every nerve. He positioned himself over her on all fours, then slid his tongue up and down her spine. He eased over the hump of her buttocks, parted her cheeks and inserted his tongue into her rectum. He then licked around her anus and down to her vagina. He artfully worked his tongue up and down her anus aggressively until he got a lively response.

"Oh, Peter," she said in an enchanting, sultry voice. She giggled a bit, then turned over, exposing her thick red vaginal lips. Her pubic hair enhanced the appearance of her vaginal area. He indulged himself in a feast. Her midsection was suffocating him with her erotic breasts that spread apart to opposite sides.

Peter looked up and admired Mrs. Lynch's impeccable breasts that made him happy to have enticed her to have silicone implants that he gladly paid for. He marinated his tongue into her vagina as he glided his hand over her abdomen, onto her voluptuous breasts and squeezed them with delight. His expert oral tongue bath finally achieved its goal of bringing Jessica to her climax that should have made the front-page headlines.

"Oh, yes, oh, yes, oh, *yes*, Peter, *right there*, Peter," she moaned as her arched back rose higher and higher. She erupted into a rigorous quake, then sighed with a growl and placed her hand on her forehead and slumped flat on her back, spent.

"All right, all right, Peter, *please,*" she begged as she contracted her leg muscles, which caused a slight shake. Peter rose from her heated body with a smile, climbed up towards her face, and motioned her to kiss him on the mouth, however, she turned her head.

"Peter, no, that's nasty," she said in a gentle tone that would allow her to get away with murder. Her remark left him with a slight frown and a shameful expression on his face.

"Peter, don't get the wrong impression. I love you. I'm just hungry—" she began until Peter interrupted her.

"No problem, honey. I'll go fix us some breakfast. I was feeling famished myself."

He crawled from on top of her, grabbed his bathrobe off the upper corner of the door, and slipped it on. He made his way down the stairs of his recently purchased three-bedroom, two-and-a-half-bathroom house, with its two-car garage and outdoor swimming pool. He opened the front door adjacent to the stairs, allowed his eyes to sweep over his secluded neighborhood, and inhaled some fresh air.

Searching for the newspaper, he bent down and picked it up as he strolled back to his kitchen. From the refrigerator, he took out two doughnuts, placed one on a napkin and put it on his kitchen counter, and ate the other. From an overhead cupboard, he took out a coffee mug and poured himself a cup of coffee made earlier by the automatic coffee machine. He poured his usual three tablespoons of sugar into the cup, stirred, and drank his morning fix.

His eyes browsed the headline on his newspaper, and he was intrigued. "Cop Killer Toppled." Reading further, he came upon the name Steve McScott, then dropped the newspaper on the counter. He headed towards the mounted telephone on the kitchen wall and called headquarters.

"Hello, yeah, I just read the morning paper. Okay. I'll be there," he said, then hung up the phone. Quickly, he placed a frying pan on the stove, opened the fridge to take out several eggs, bacon, and butter, then took out some waffles from the freezer, which he popped into the toaster.

Peter finished cooking his bacon, slid them on his plate, and sat on an aluminum bar stool, eating his breakfast. He retrieved the coffee pot once more, refilled his coffee mug, and added three more tablespoons of sugar to his second fix.

After eating, he went back upstairs carrying a serving tray with a plate of waffles, bacon and scrambled eggs, and a glass of orange juice for his wonderful wife. He walked slowly, trying not to have any spillage. Upon entering his bedroom, he placed the breakfast tray right next to his wife on the nightstand surface.

"Honey, here's breakfast. I have to get ready for an urgent assignment," he informed Jessica, while heading towards the bathroom. She got up with a sigh, took a piece of bacon off her plate, and started eating it.

Peter busied himself in the bathroom, turning on the lights, grabbing his razor out of the medicine cabinet, and resting it on the bathroom counter while he placed some Gillette shaving gel in the middle of his palms and rubbed his hands together, creating a rich, bubbling foam. Looking into the mirror and foaming the area around his mouth and cheeks, he gave himself a quick, clean shave, brushed his teeth and gargled, spitting out the Scope down the drain hole.

Disrobing and taking off his boxers, exposing his 6-foot even, heavyweight physique, he turned on the shower, stepped in, and rubbed himself down with a bar of Irish Spring, which he also used to wash his thinning hair.

Then he stepped out of the shower, grabbed a towel off the rack, and dried himself as he entered his walk-in closet. He paused first, though, to admire Jessica's voluptuous breasts and her Betty Boob-like nipples sitting erectly in front of her, poking through her hair that lay on her breasts. She was sitting up with her back against the wooden headboard, truly a sight to please a man's eyes.

"Peter, where're you going?" she asked with the remote control in her hands, surfing the channels until she reached *Good Morning, America*.

"I have to go investigate a deceased degenerate in South Carolina, so I gotta hurry. The agency already booked me an urgent eight o'clock flight," he called out from the closet as he slid on his Kenneth Cole slacks.

"So how long you're going to be away from me, honey?" she inquired.

"Not long, sweetheart. Depending on how things go, I most likely will be back tomorrow night," he said in an amplified voice. He walked out of the closet with ties in each hand, stood in front of her wearing his blue slacks, white shirt, and black Kenneth Cole loafers.

"Which one?" He held up a red and blue polka dot tie in one hand and a blue and black pinstriped one in the other. She shrugged her shoulders and pointed to the blue pinstriped tie. He strutted to the dresser mirror across from where she was sitting. Gazing in the mirror, he admired her cleavage and looped his tie at the same time. Jessica folded her hands across her chest. Even so, her breasts and nipples were poking out.

"So I have to spend my entire day off alone," she pouted like a spoiled brat.

"I'm sorry, but, unfortunately, dear, yes," he said.

He then walked to the bathroom, sprayed some moose into his hand, ran it through his receding thin hair, and combed his hair. Next came the Kenneth Cole blazer from his closet and a splash of Calvin Klein Obsession. Lastly, he retrieved his pen, wallet, cell phone, two-way pager, and set of keys.

Jessica sprang up from bed, pressed her massive breasts against him as she hugged him, and gave him a kiss. She gazed up into his eyes. "Promise you'll be back—all right?" she said.

"Well, this one I can't definitely guarantee will be an open-and-shut case." He smiled and gave her a kiss, then broke free and headed downstairs to his garage. Peter would not know what to do without Jessica. She had been there, supporting him through his divorce. His first wife, whom he'd dedicated his life to, took everything away from him, which included his five-bedroom, elegant home that he had been investing in for 15 years, his cars, and his pride. She'd also gotten complete custody of his two sons, and he paid child support for them.

His ex-wife had left him in such a state of depression he was on the verge of committing suicide. If it were not for Jessica's love, caring, and motivation, he would have given up on living.

He stepped into his garage and used his keyless entry to unlock his white Jeep Commando, hopped in the driver's seat, and looked over at Jessica's black Volkswagen Jetta. He did not understand why she chose that color. He hated that color. Shrugging, he started his SUV, pressed the genie, and reversed out of his garage, backed out of the driveway, at the same time, hitting the genie to close the garage door.

Peter was on his way to Hartsfield Airport, where he parked in the overnight parking area. Inside the center compartment, he took out his Ray-Ban sunglasses, but left his Smith & Wesson .45-caliber automatic handgun in the leather holster. Thanks to the new

Patriot Act, it was a hassle to deal with the procedures, even for a federal agent to carry a gun on board an airplane today. He did not feel any need to do so. So he put on his sunglasses, marched into the airport, went to the clerk at the check-in counter, and showed his federal ID.

The woman smiled. "One moment, please," she said politely, as she pushed in some keys on the computer.

"Okay, Mr. Lynch, your American Airline flight leaves in fifteen minutes, Gate L6."

Peter took the ticket from the flight attendant and made haste towards the gate. While he was running, he was caught in a dilemma. He wanted to run back to his car and grab his portfolio. However, he did not want to miss his flight. Peter went through security and boarded the plane. The flight attendant checked Peter's ticket stub and carry-on, then he took his seat. The flight was uneventful, and Peter reclined his seat and relaxed.

The flight arrived at Greenville, South Carolina, in less than an hour. With a strident step, he made his way through the airport to the front exit, where he was approached by a young, 6-foot-1, blond-haired, 190-pound young man wearing a black suit, white shirt, and black tie. He approached Peter with a sheet of paper in his hand of what appeared to be a colored photograph of Peter Lynch.

"Peter Lynch?" The man looked at Peter and waited for his answer. When Peter did not respond, he extended his hand forward for a formal greeting and tried again.

"Agent Lynch, I'm Agent Benjamin Forester. I was sent here on behalf of the agency to assist you," Benjamin said. Peter responded to his formal greeting and shook his hand.

"Right this way, sir. No other luggage?" he asked.

"No, I really didn't plan on being here too long, and by the looks of the newspaper article, this is pretty much an autopsy observation to see how our suspect died," Lynch responded.

They walked towards a Chevy Suburban and climbed in. When they arrived at the office of the Medical Examiner and Division of Forensic Science Laboratories, Agent Forester parked in the lot and they headed for the mortuary. Once they reached the examining room, they entered and met the assisting pathologist.

"Good morning, Dr. Smith," Peter said, looking at the lady's name badge.

"Good morning, Agents Forester and Lynch. I'm Eleanor and have been expecting your arrival. I'm going to be performing this autopsy review."

Peter looked around the walk-in cooler while Agent Forester spoke with Eleanor. He could hear the sucking sound from the ventilation system, along with a noxious odor issuing out through an exhaust fan. Stainless steel cabinets and double sinks lined the walls of the room. The nonstick gray walls were depressing and made Peter wonder what type of person would work in this profession.

Dr. Smith walked over to the sink and washed her hands before she put on a pair of surgical gloves. The running water hit the hollow steel sink like the light beating of a drum. As if the windowless gray walls and matching floor were not depressing enough, when the doctor unzipped the body bag, a nauseating stench filled the atmosphere.

Agent Lynch looked over, identified the decaying body as the suspect, and was ready to leave, however, the doctor was already starting her briefing. What was left of the victim's face was emaciated, and his lips had started turning black. She noted three gunshot wounds that entered through his facial region, which destroyed his cerebellum, and then exited through his medulla.

A gunshot wound had ruptured his Adam's apple, demolished his esophagus and upper spinal column as it traveled through, and had exited the back of his neck. As she worked her way down, she opened the wounds with a scalpel. The autopsy began. Dr. Smith began at the neck and sliced through the vic's clavicle at the sternum and went south through the navel, concluding at this pubis. She opened him up.

Stepping over to a side table briefly, she retrieved a folder and proceeded with her briefing. His heart, his liver, his lungs, his stomach, large and small intestines, and his kidneys were in good condition. Had he not been blasted to smithereens, he could have had a good, long life.

"His upper right shoulder was lacerated, along with his forearm. His left shoulder also ruptured with a severe gunshot wound that tore through his muscle tissue and grazed his shoulder bone. Apart from a few minor bruises and scratches, that seems to be the entire analytical report of injuries sustained." Before the doctor could say anything else, Peter departed.

"Thank you, Dr. Smith. I'll inform your agency to fax us a copy of the initial report of investigation tomorrow morning."

Before she could respond, Peter was out the door. Even after being a 20-year veteran agent, Lynch never got used to the gruesome assignment of an autopsy review. Agent Forrester was on his heels.

"Wow, that suspect looks like he had been executed by a firing squad. With no leads on his assailant, this one look like another cold case," Forrester said.

"Just one less nuisance, you know what I mean?" Agent Lynch patted Forester on his back as they walked up the corridor, laughing lightly.

"Hey, bud, you mind giving me a ride back to the airport?" Agent Lynch asked.

"Why? You tired of our little state already?" Forrester said in a down-home Southern accent.

"No, not at all. I just got through with this assignment quicker than I thought, and I wouldn't want a whole day go to waste. Besides, I have some important business to take care of at home," Peter informed his counterpart.

"Sure, it's no problem. My orders are to assist you in any way. I don't see any harm. I could always fax you the report. We can call it a day," said Agent Forrester.

An hour later, the two colleagues arrived at the airport. Peter went and informed the flight attendant he would like to reserve an earlier return flight back to Atlanta. The flight attendant input his data into the computer and confirmed that, "There is room for a flight, but it is already boarding at Gate A5."

"I'll take it," he said with enthusiasm.

While registering his information into the computer, the flight attendant immediately picked up her telephone and called the gate attendant to inform her that a law enforcement agent would be arriving shortly. She printed out his ticket. "Here is your ticket, Mr. Lynch. Thank you. Have a good day and please hurry. The plane needs to keep on schedule," she said while he walked off.

Peter saw the worried look on her face, so he broke into a jog. He dashed about 50 yards until he reach the airplane terminal. When he gave the gate attendant his ticket, he felt a sudden sharp pain in his chest and a numbing feeling in his left shoulder. He took several deep inhalations to keep from passing out. Finally he got past security and boarded the plane. Sweaty and exhausted, he slumped in his seat, buckled up, and reclined it, then he immediately fell asleep.

By the time Officer Lynch arrived at Hartsfield Airport, he had recuperated. He got off the plane and trudged inside the airport until he arrived at a pizza vendor. He bought two slices of pepperoni and hamburger meat topping pizza and a large Pepsi, sat and ate, then searched until he found a small boutique, where he purchased a dozen roses for his beloved.

A few moments later, he entered the parking lot, found his SUV, took off his blazer, and hopped in. He intended to surprise his wife with the roses. After a long, deep yawn to try to get rid of the stiffness of being strapped in a seat for so long while flying, his muscles finally began to loosen up. However, the annoying sensation he had experienced at the airport earlier was still there.

Exiting the airport parking terminal, he entered Interstate 85 and followed it until he reached Highway 400. Twenty minutes later, he reached his quiet little abode in Alpharetta. He quickly parked and picked up the crystal vase he had purchased with Jessica's yellow roses.

He assumed Jessica was upstairs watching the 42-inch high-def television, having an intense aerobic workout. He could already see her luscious, voluptuous breasts glistering with sweat, bouncing from impact during her routine.

Smiling, Peter opened his front door quietly, gently closed it behind him, and walked in the direction of his bedroom. He couldn't wait to see the expression on his beloved wife's face as every step brought him closer to her sweetness. He knew she would be speechless and so thrilled with his speedy return home and the lovely bouquet of roses he purchased for her. The closer he got to his bedroom, the more he could smell her sweet perfume aroma filling his mind. The door was slightly ajar. He gently pushed it wider and crept in, a huge smile plastered on his face in anticipation of what he would see.

And he saw it clearly. And the smile evaporated. In fact, he was beyond belief by what he saw. Jessica's naked body was glistening with sweat, alright. From all her exercising, she was breathing intensely and emitting a teeth-gritted growl. Her body vibrated with passion, her beautiful breasts were indeed bouncing with vitality, just as he had visualized.

Peter's beautiful, sweet young wife had rhythm and moved back and forth with explosiveness and pure passion. Jessica put her all into it as she watched a porno flick, with an insanely hungry expression on her face that Peter had never seen before. And to top it off, she had a large ebony man working her out with a donkeylike erection, the size of which he had never seen before. Dazed, Peter stepped back out of the room.

He stumbled over to the wall next to the door, positioned his back against it, and slid down to the floor in agony. His heart hurt. He was broken. He felt his life being sucked down into an antagonizing vortex. Depressed, the tears came. He cried loudly as Jessica's sexual screams and moans grew louder. Darkness covered his mind and stabbed his heart. He reached for his .45 caliber from his shoulder holster, took off the safety, cocked it, and placed it into his sobbing, open mouth. Mucous from his beakish nose oozed down the barrel of his gun like boiled okra slime.

He applied pressure to the trigger, but paused as a sadistic thought came to his head. *Why should I let her and her African monkey live and enjoy my life insurance policy?* His rage flamed into insanity that consumed his face.

Peter stood up, motionless, with his gun extended downward. As he took slow, dragging steps back towards the defiled bedroom, he could feel a throbbing, stabbing pain in his chest region, close to his heart. It intensified with each breath. He pushed the door wide open and extended his hand, which was growing numb by the second. The repugnant sight of the orgy sent his adrenaline into overdrive.

Peter pointed his .45 at the back of the ebony stallion's head and pulled the trigger. Jessica screamed as she turned around and saw her husband collapse onto the wooden floor in convulsions. She untangled herself from the lifeless body of her lover and ran over to Peter. Kneeling down, she held his head, resting it against her breast.

"Peter, Peter, please don't do this to me, Peter. I'm so sorry, Peter," she yelled, but there was no response as she broke down sobbing hysterically.

Chapter **25** *Chyna*

Chyna downshifted her brand-new Aston Martin DB9 to first gear. As she approached her extravagant four-level, deep-water estate, she paused and admired the exterior of her lavish new home. The surrounding ocean on her 10 acres of land was breathtaking. She had the top down on the 6.0 V12, which enhanced the view, bringing her closer to nature.

The rich blend of handcrafted natural matériel in her vehicle made her feel like a part of her surroundings. She then opened her ten-space, climate-controlled collector car garage and zoomed in with the radiant sparkle of her 21-inch chrome rims. Stepping out, she walked through her spacious garage with every step of her shoes making a slight echo off the floors. She took out her cell phone and dialed an international number, walked across the garage to the elevator, and pushed the up button. She placed her hand-free device to her ear and waited for an answer.

No one answered, so she voice-commanded her cell phone to redial, which it did. The see-through, acrylic elevator arrived before any one could answer the phone. She stepped on the elevator's highly polished Bianco Venato marble tile imported from Italy with gold trim that accented the house's interior, then pushed the ivory button in the gold panel to the fourth floor.

At the same time, the phone was answered. "Good morning, this is Ms. Lu. May I speak to Mr. Brown, please?"

Chyna waited. She marveled at her breathtaking waterfront view as she gracefully turned 360 degrees inside the elevator, allowing her eyes to drink in the beauty surrounding her. The manse was embedded with Old-World craftsmanship. Its leaded-glass windows overlooked exotic flowers blooming with incredible colors in terra cotta pots on the portico. The estate grounds were well manicured, sprinkled with exotic trees and colorful flowers constantly in bloom. The tropical estate was a piece of paradise.

"Hello, good morning, Mr. Brown. I would like to thank you for your mercy and generosity. The money transfer was a success; furthermore, your people in New York have already arranged to meet my people halfway in Virginia. There should be no problem with transferring two million dollars back every two weeks. I would like to thank you once again for allowing me the privilege of working with such a knowledgeable and professional man as yourself," she said as she heard him hang up in her face.

She expected that from such a ruthless power-fanatic. Unperturbed, she got off at the top floor. From there, she walked into the oversized bathroom with brown Galilea Travertine marble tiles from Turkey. All the faucets and metal fixtures were made of gold. The three shower stalls were designed from crystal glass with a rain finish and the doors were slightly ajar.

The big shower nozzles that extended from the ceiling simulated a rain shower with the push of a button. Twenty feet away sat the Jacuzzi tub with gold trim around the top cylinder. The Jacuzzi sat next to a window overlooking the tropical landscape and the ocean. It was paradise, and it was hers.

Wandering into the elegant master bedroom and its balcony, Chyna stood in awe, taking in the beauty of the sun-dappled, deep-azure ocean. Three rivers ran through the enclosed estate. A boat dock was built on one of the rivers with a luxury yacht for her use, which also contained three bedrooms, three bathrooms, and all with hot tubs.

Chyna stood there in tranquility, mesmerized by the beauty of her surroundings. As the cool ocean breeze gently blew her light, lustrous hair and white knee-length silk Ralph Lauren dress, she sighed in contentment. *This* is what she was born for. Shameless indulgences at any expense.

Chapter 26 *Popi*

Pablo picked up his plate of enchiladas, went into the family room, and left his nagging wife, Maria, to seek some privacy. He bit into his lunch with delight as he pressed the play button on the remote control and watched his videotape with zeal. Intensely, his eyes analyzed everything—every move, every sound—as he listened carefully to every word. He rewound and played the tape again to make sure he had everything documented.

"I show you stinking *cucaracha* to mess with me," he said in Spanish. He devoured the last of his enchilada, picked up the house phone, and dialed a number.

"Mommy, bring me a cold Corona," he yelled to Maria in Spanish, covering the phone. *"Cerveza, por favor."*

"Hello, can I get the office of Richard A. Marshall?" Pablo requested. The telephone operator who answered informed him that Richard was not in his office. He hung up the phone. As soon as his wife returned with his Corona, he snatched it from her hand and started guzzling down the cold amber liquid.

"See, see, you such a pig," Maria said with a look of disgust. *"Eres un cochino!"*

"You shut up. *Cayate!* Don't come into my relaxation room and messa with me," he barked in an animated fashion.

Maria hurried away from his vicious explosion and rushed back into the kitchen. Before she reached the kitchen, Pablo yelled, "Maria, I need my cell phone, hurry, hurry. *Pronto.*" He felt he was making a drastic mistake calling from his house phone. He was nervous that his oppressors might have tapped his house phone, or more likely, the entire interior of the house. Maria returned with his cell phone.

"You always yell, grunt, and shout. *Cochino!*" Maria spat sarcastically as she handed him his cell phone.

He once again became ferocious. "Maria, what I tell you about insulting me? You call me a pig again, I'll kill you, Maria. *Cayate!*" he barked.

He grabbed his cell phone and stalked outside, where he dialed Richard A. Marshall's cell number and waited for him to respond.

"Hello," Richard said, enthusiastically.

"Hello, Richard," Pablo said. "I got it. I got all the evidence that you told me to get. Now you promise me I'll get immunity if I do this. I don't want to work for no one, no more; I want to live my life in peace. Okay, okay. Now you guarantee this before I send it to your address. Okay, I'll send you the tape—express mail. It'll be there first thing in the morning." Pablo hung up his cell phone.

He went back through his rear patio door and locked the door behind him, went to his VCR, ejected the tape, and put it into the *Three Stooges* box. He placed the tape back on the shelf where it belonged. Then he put in his Stooges' tape, pressed play on the VCR, and walked back to his small velvet-covered couch. Drawing a deep breath, he slouched into the soft, cotton-insulated sofa, picked up the remote laying next to him, and turned up the volume. He instantly broke out into laughter. "Moe, no one messes with a Moe," he said aloud to his favorite character.

"*Sí, sí,* no one will mess with me," he added in a hearty laugh.

Chapter 27 *Ricky*

It was another usual, busy day for me. I'd been packaging and serving all morning. Things had been very hectic. I had broken down and distributed nine-and-three-quarter keys in less than two days. Now I was filling an order for two ounces of crack cocaine, so I'm back in the kitchen dropping a two-way, that is, two-and-one-fourth ounces.

All the aggravation of my business was wearing me down. It was time for a vacation. I really needed one, however, my greed would not allow me to stop, and the vicious attitudes of the people I daily dealt with were making me develop into a monster. My behavior had become atrocious lately. When negative people saw you thriving, or even believed that another criminal was escalating up the financial ladder of success, they tried to sabotage you.

I could not let what people thought about me become me, but in some ways, at least psychologically, it seemed that most of the time, what people in our environment thought of you became you. You know—the crab-in-a-bucket syndrome that plagues the black community like AIDS and violent drug addiction.

Dealing with ignorant people on a constant basis, one had to become a monster because people were always searching for your weakness, looking for a way to bring you down. It was like the proverb said: no one can control a strongman unless he overwhelms him with force. Most predators prey on the weak anyway. When someone is high on drugs, he's mentally subject to do anything.

The main rule of being an overseer is to never show any weaknesses to your clientele.

My cell phone's ring interrupted my musings. The phone had been ringing since six o'clock this morning.

"Yeah, yeah, I'm on my way. Now you want another two-way? OK, give me half an hour, I'll be there."

After I finished cooking, I went upstairs to let the substance sit for a while and become more solid. As I passed by Lucky's closed door, the moans and laughter of female voices came echoing out like a woman's aerobic class having an intense workout going down their final rap.

Anyhow, I stayed focused and went to my room, took out two kemp papers from my extract large Bob Marley rolling paper pack, and placed them together to make it burn slower. The hemp paper also gave the exotic marijuana a pristine taste. I had an ounce of rosebud hydro chronic left in my shoe box, so I retrieved it, took out two grams, crushed it into my hemp paper, and started rolling my long joint. The joint came out rolled into a perfect cylinder.

I lit it and inhaled the soothing smoke that eased my mind all the time. Then my cell phone rang again, attempting to interrupt my mental utopia, but I ignored it as I became more relaxed, more comfortable, more mentally focused, and more at peace. The bed beckoned me, so I lay down on it, taking smooth, deep puffs and savoring the fulfilling smoke that rushed to my lungs and induced euphoria to my brain.

I took my time and enjoyed every second of my smoke break. Eventually, I got up off my bed feeling mentally revitalized. All my stress was relieved. I really felt like staying home and watching some DVD movies or something, but, nevertheless, I had to stay true to the game and go make that money because somewhere down the line, life had become a game, and money was the only way for a player to keep score.

I went downstairs to bag and package my cocaine substance that was now rock-solid and put the five ounces into my black army Cargo pants pocket.

When I snatched my cell phone off the counter and reviewed the five missed calls, I decided to call my client back who I was about to go meet. Afterward, I wanted to rendezvous with Lisa at the Hewitt Building in Marietta and take her to dinner. Secretly, I was hoping to rekindle a flame of romance back into our relationship. Lisa had been there for me through thick and thin. I'm the type of person who believes deeply in showing gratitude to my woman. Besides, I love Lisa immensely.

"Hello, I got tied up for a minute. I'm on my way now, and yeah, I'm serious, man," I told Pans before I hung up. Pans was the type of hustler who had been on the same level for over a decade. He was so filled with hatred he could never elevate himself because he kept himself mentally grounded. His bad attitude kept him from learning different aspects and ideals of the game, not to mention his jealousy. Pans always burnt bridges and never seemed to keep a good connect too long. But, I deal with devious people like him all day long.

Wisely, I just kept it brief, took his money, and proceeded with our transaction. Once I exited my apartment and closed the door behind me, I used the keyless to open a rented Toyota Corolla. Things were getting so hectic that I needed something discrete.

Once I got into the driver's seat and started the car, Mike Jones, "Who is Mike Jones?" came on beating on the sound system. I turned down the volume on the music and proceeded to drive carefully. Finally I arrived at an enormous apartment complex called the Lakes in Stone Mountain Apartment. The place was just like the corridor in *New Jack City*. I mean, it seemed this place went from being some elderly people's peaceful community to a crack-infested drug market overnight.

Hoping no one would see me, I drove into the complex and continued driving to the top of the hill in a secluded area of the complex, then got out of the car, went across the parking lot, and hid my contraband in a drainage hole I spotted in a stone and concrete wall. Glancing around to make sure no one noticed me, I went back to my car, sat, and waited for Pans to call back. Almost on cue, the pest called.

"Yeah, I'm in your complex right now. Come meet me at N building to the rear," I told him before I hung up and got out of the car, strolled into a hallway, and took a seat on the steps. Pans walked right past me.

"Yo," I said. The man turned around. If I didn't know him, I wouldn't have recognized him. He looked terrible. His lips were ashy, his eyes protruded out of the sockets, his once-stocky body was now too skinny. When the man looked at me, I could see the hatred mirrored in his eyes.

"What's up, Ricky? Man, you look good, man. If I had your hands, I'd cut mine off," he said, looking at me with a serious, tight-lipped expression. I could see that he was discouraged about something as he took out $2,000 in crisp clean bills.

I took the bills out of his hands and counted them all. They added up exactly right. Then I pocketed the cash.

"So where's the dope?" he asked with an anxious look on his face.

"Kinfolk, you know there's nothing to worry about with me, man. Just follow me over here," I said as I led him, side by side, across the parking lot.

"It's in there," I told him pointing. He stuck his hand in the hole, withdrew the substance, and raised it into the air as if he wanted to see it more clearly in the sunlight before he put the package into his pocket.

He looked at me with a conniving smirk. "'Ight," he said while he lowered his head and stumbled off. I watched him as he disappeared into the hallway and wanted to laugh at how pitiful he looked, suffering mentally and physically, brought on by his own destructive behavior. However, I did not. I just shook my head and strolled to my car, got in, and drove off immediately.

There was an eerie feeling in the air. The vibes were not right. You have to beware of a person who smiles in your face and hates you at the same time if you want to succeed in life. I drove through the complex, observing the constant flow of drug addicts running amok of what eventually became the bane of their existence—the need to get high on drugs.

A few dope fiends approached my car, looking for some products. Some resembled zombies, some looked good enough to be someone's wife, and some were too young to even be out on the streets without their parents' supervision. The visual was like a living nightmare out there.

As I continued driving through the complex, I turned up the volume on the CD player and vibed to the rhythm of Mike Watts 2000.

Before I made it one square block, I saw a police car lurking at the left, turning. I quickly grabbed my seat belt and buckled it. Before I could finish buckling it, the squad car was in my rearview mirror following me, but I didn't worry. After all, I was clean. I'd just gotten rid of the last bit of illegal substance I had on me. Furthermore, my license and my paperwork were legit.

This particular area was notorious for the injustice of law enforcement and prejudiced white supremacy judges. After all, this was Stone Mountain—the home and foundation of the Ku Klux Klan. I relaxed and made sure I was traveling at the speed limit. Then I saw a police car turn in front of me. At that moment, the squad car behind me turned on his blue lights and siren and indicated for me to pull over. I slowed down and pulled over. The other police car backed up directly in front of my car, barricading me in.

The officer behind me and the officer in front of me jumped out simultaneously and ran to my driver-side window with their guns drawn. "Don't move! Put your hands in the fucking air!"

The Caucasian officer was flushed pink in his face as he barked out his orders. Without delay, I complied. I placed both hands on the roof. The pink-faced officer tried to open the door, even though it was locked. Not to be deterred, he started banging on the window with the back of his gun. *This is a little drastic for a minor traffic violation*, I thought. The officer behind me was at the passenger side of the car with both hands on his pistol. When the angry officer could not break the glass, he started yelling, "Unlock your door, slowly now. Make any sudden moves and I'll blow your fucking head off."

Naturally, I slowly eased the door open. The raging officer leapt on me like a starving tiger and yanked me from my seat. In his hurry, this fool almost dislocated his shoulder because my seat belt was still on. I actually heard the cracking of his joints. He backed up a few steps. His face went from ferocious to delirious when the severe shoulder pain coursed through his nerves and reached his brain.

The other officer took over by yelling commands in a military-like baritone voice. "Slowly unfasten your safety belt. Now step from your vehicle with your hands in the air."

Once again, I complied.

"Slowly get on both knees and place your hands behind your head," the calmer officer instructed me while the other officer regrouped.

Then he bellowed, "Place your hands forward on the ground and lay flat on the ground." He shoved his foot into my upper back. As I lay down, I could see the Caucasian officer now behind me with his gun drawn. He held the gun in both hands, aimed at the back of my head. He looked as if he were really enjoying my degradation.

I lay still for about a minute. Suddenly the calmer officer grabbed one of my hands, twisted it behind my back, knelt on my buttocks, then reached for and twisted my other hand behind my back and handcuffed them together. After my hands were secured, he shackled me, then he yanked me up by my armpit. Everything felt surreal. Where did all this come from?

Meanwhile, two more police cars parked on opposite sides of the one-lane street, blocking off traffic. Spectators from the community gathered outside and looked on, curious for a little entertainment to break up the monotony of their lives. The constant mesmerizing flash of the police lights was frustrating. The fact that I was shackled and being paraded around was embarrassing and humiliating.

Then to make matters worse, they brought me in front of the squad car and dropped a package of four-and-a-half ounces in front of me. I knew they were setting me up. My distress turned to depression. Next, they emptied out my pockets and placed my money, cell phone, wallet, and keys on the hood of the squad car—next to the illegal substance.

I looked on as a K-9 police dog sniffed through my car and the cops eagerly tore and ripped up the interior to see what else they could find. They even had the trunk open, searching it thoroughly, where they discovered and brought over my 9mm automatic handgun, placing it on the hood of the police car for everyone to see.

The cops were sending a message. I became a spectacle, an example for any aspiring drug dealer in the community to take note of. A detective came over, walked me to the back of the police car, and placed me into the backseat.

"Is there anything you'd like to say before we bring you in?" the detective asked.

I stayed silent with my head slumped down. He looked at me with a ridiculous smirk, then slammed the door. I watched as they analyzed the items on the hood and placed everything into separate bags for evidence. I guess this was part of their psychological warfare to instill fear in their captive. I was too mentally and physically drained to emotionally react to what they were trying to do.

The cops just laughed with devilish grins and stared over in my direction. Tired of everybody looking at me, I lay down sideways on the backseat, closed my eyes, hoping I would fall asleep and wake up out of this nightmare. However, there were too many thoughts running through my mind, and this was reality. I had been living my dream and in a split second, a beautiful dream turned into a horrible nightmare.

By now, some of police cars left. Then, finally, the officer driving the car that I was in got in and closed his door. He started typing information into his laptop computer as he looked over some paperwork.

"So the guy on the license in your wallet is you, right?" he asked. I lay silent.

"Why don't you sit up?" he said. I still lay silent. After he finished typing his information into the computer, he drove away. I could feel the car moving. I could see the surroundings from where I lay on the seat.

Once we drove past the area, I sat up to see exactly where the officer was taking me. I cut my eyes in disgust once we drove past the Lake Apartment Complex in Stone Mountain. The officer looked into my eyes through the rearview mirror. I guess he could see the bewildered look of frustration in them.

Furthermore, to make matters worse, he started using this opportunity to lay the guilt trip on me. "So what made you want to sell that stuff to your own people?" he asked nonchalantly.

"So what makes you want to arrest your own people?" I retorted in irritation.

"If you had a job and was out here doing the right thing, I wouldn't have to arrest you—did you think of that?" he asked, in a matter-of-fact tone.

"If the government and the law that you pledged to uphold would stop bringing in the drugs and manufacturing the weaponry used to protect the drug business, I wouldn't be in this predicament I'm in right now. Then you would have no one to arrest," I retorted.

"How old are you?" he asked.

I knew that was coming next. Everyone that heard me speak and knew my age never believed I was as young as I am. I guess the constant thinking grew me up extremely fast.

I arrived at Stone Mountain Precinct and was ushered inside. The police officer took me to a jail cell, took off my handcuffs, and slammed the cell door shut. I walked over to the mirror above the sink to look at my reflection and ponder what I'd gotten into and how I was going to get out of this. Reaching down, I pressed the cold-water button, took a sip of water, then rinsed my face with my hands, trying to revive myself. The cell was gloomy and depressing.

Finally, I walked over and lay down on the bottom of the two-man bunk bed. Exhaustion put me to sleep instantly. It seemed only moments later that I was awakened by a loud, obnoxious banging on the metal cell bars. It was an officer waking me up to ask my personal information. He wrote down my answers on some forms he had in his hands.

Half an hour later, he came back and told me my charges. He said I was being held on violation of the Georgia Controlled Substance

Act, conspiracy of possession with the intent to distribute and traffic, and possession of a handgun in the commission of a crime. These were three new felonies added to my permanent record. There goes my right to vote, my right to obtain a legal handgun, my right to obtain any decent job if I were convicted of these crimes.

"The judge will see you in a few hours to set a bond. Do you think you're going to be able to make bail if you get one?" the officer asked.

I didn't respond. I just rolled over and went back to sleep to try to block out the agony and frustration of being set up by my comrade. And I was in misery because of the freezing cold cell. Several hours later, I was once again awaked by a loud banging on my jail cell.

"Jones, get up and tuck in your shirt. You're going to court."

I got up, went over to the toilet, and urinated. Then I washed my hands and drank a little water and stepped out of the jail cell to the side of the awaiting officer. He closed the jail cell gently. "Put your hands together in front of you so I can handcuff you," he said.

I complied. He handcuffed me and took me right next door to a grey-headed Klan's man in a yellow Polo shirt with a black robe over it.

"Have a seat, Mr. Jones," the officer requested.

I took one of the two wooden chairs, seated directly across the desk in front of the judge.

"Well, Mr. Jones, we, the City of Stone Mountain, are charging you with the offense of UGSA, conspiracy of possession with the intent to distribute, traffic, and possession of a firearm during the commission of a crime. Are you aware of these charges, Mr. Jones?" the judge asked.

I nodded my head yes.

The judge leaned over slightly and stared at me intensely. "Speak up," said the officer, now acting as the bailiff.

"Yes," I said.

"Well, do you want to proceed with your bond hearing, or would you like an attorney present?"

"I would like an attorney," I replied.

"Fine. Your case will be bound over to Dekalb County so heretofore, you're going to have to wait until your first appearance to receive a bond," the judge said as he immediately got up from his seat and walked through the room door.

I sat there, hoping I could have changed my mind and got a bond. The officer took me right back to the cell and slammed the door behind me. Now I was really stressed. I could not bond out. I would have to be in jail for two weeks. I was tired. I went to my bunk bed and fell right back asleep, but as soon as I lay down, the officer came right back.

"Let's go, Jones," he said. He opened the cell door, and I exited. He escorted me by my upper arm outside and into the backseat of the cop's car. Then he slammed the door and entered the driver's side of the squad car. We arrived at Dekalb County Jail, the biggest establishment and monument representing the state with the largest black population in America.

Thoughts ran through my mind. In the eighteenth century, black fugitives used to run down Memorial Drive, mobbed by stone-flinging whites. Now in the twentieth century, the same heinous legacy of white supremacist brutality was still systematically upheld through long-established bureaucracy. White supremacists are still placing themselves in high positions of power.

What consequences did slave owners face when owning slaves made them illegally rich and when the slaves where forcibly emancipated, the slave owners were still rich enough to afford to send their children to law schools, to perpetuate new legal forms of slavery through the same racist savage mentality and culture that their forefathers instilled in them. History repeats itself.

Therefore, every accomplishment a person of color achieved in an Anglo-Saxon-oppressed society is remarkable and worthy of the highest honor.

The squad car pulled into a parking ramp through an electronic gate that closed instantly behind us. The officer took me out of the backseat of his squad car still in shackles. We approached the front of the building and waited for the electronic doors to open. Once the entrance door opened, I was escorted inside. The police officer turned over my paperwork to a correctional officer and immediately exited the building.

A new officer placed against the wall and searched me thoroughly. I was told to take off my belt and sneakers. I was then forced through the door of a small cell that the correctional officer slammed shut behind me. There I lay on the cold, steel bench on my back, folded my arms, and appealed my case to the highest supernatural essence in the universe.

After a few minutes of mind elevation, I felt a sense of divine intervention. I realized everything happened for a reason, and once I stayed focused and remained in a positive mental state, I would see the overall good in my miserable situation.

I had also come to the understanding through my life that if one who had endured atrocities can maintain a positive outlook, one will reap the benefits of a good reward. So I sighed and remembered that people more righteous than I had been through worse situations and had kept good faith, even to the point of death. At that moment, I made up my mind to keep my good faith and take this fall with patience and hope. My meditation was broke with a yell.

"Jones, get outta your cell, step on the square, and take your picture."

The door opened electronically, and I walked over and stepped on the square. A woman behind the transparent glass booth took my photograph and told me I could walk through a metal detector and then go to another cell.

This cell was overcrowded with black males. There were three phones on the wall. As I walked into the cell, a foul stench hit me, a combination of disgusting foot odor, vomit, B.O., the repulsive smell from drunks, and the rank stench of urine and human waste. I almost gagged. Stepping over people on the filthy dirty floors, I ran for the first open phone I saw, grabbed it, and called the only one person who could free my pain and give me a sense of comfort—my Nubian woman.

I called Lisa's home phone and was so delighted when she answered. At the same time, I was very ashamed of the predicament I was in. The phone operator already told her she was getting a call from and a Dekalb County inmate, and I'd already recorded my name on the voice recorder so when she answered the phone hysterically, I was not surprised.

"Baby, what happened?" she shouted.

"Baby, bad news. I was set up today and got arrested and am now confined in Dekalb County Jail," I said. I could hear her start crying over the phone. The noise in the background was making it hard for me to hear her words on the other end of the phone. A few inmates were behaving as if they enjoyed the comfort of this shithole, talking about they couldn't wait to get upstairs and a whole bunch of other institutionalized bullshit.

"Baby, baby, don't even sound like that. I need you to be strong for me, everything is going to be all right," I said soothingly. Here I was, the one in the dreadful situation, yet I was having to comfort Lisa in her emotional distress.

"How much is your bond? I'm coming to get you out of there right now," she declared with a realization of hope. She was no longer crying.

"Baby, I need for you to hire me a lawyer with good credibility. I didn't get a bond yet because I requested a lawyer to be present. So they said I have to wait ten days before I go back in front of the judge and get a bond," I said, shaking my head in disbelief.

"But, baby, that's too long," she protested with a whine in her voice.

"I know, I know, but there's nothing we can do but wait, baby."

One of the correctional officers opened the door and shouted out three names and I was one of them.

"Jones, Jones, step right this way," the officer yelled.

"Baby, baby, I gotta go. I'll call you right back." Once I hung up, I felt worse than ever. I walked out into the open area and breathed a deep breath of cleaner jail air.

First, I was fingerprinted by a female officer. It seemed like mostly everybody in law enforcement had a spell cast upon them that caused them to act and look miserable. Then they try their best to make anybody in an inferior predicament feel the misery with their atrocious attitude.

After I was fingerprinted, I was escorted to another jail cell. This one did not reek as bad as the previous one. I stayed there for what seemed like eternity until I was called for a medical examination. A technician took my blood, asked me mental and dietary questions, and injected some kind of germs into my blood. He also gave me a tuberculosis test to see if I had the disease. I was extremely exhausted at this point from emotional fatigue.

When the officer escorted me to the third holding cell, I was already broken into the institutionalized mentality. All I now wanted was a mat, a blanket, and sleep. I was once again placed in a reeking, stinking cell with nothing but black and foreign males packed in like sardines. Men lay all over the filthy floors, sleeping, snoring, and farting. I only had enough room to stand up. My mental suffering was like that of a man in a concentration camp.

Finally, after what seemed to be years later, but was in truth only days later, I was called to the front desk to sign a property sheet and make a free phone call. I felt like such a drag. I could not even bear standing up and speaking. I was told to return to the same holding cell. I was so mentally distorted by this time I went and joined the rest of the inmates on the floor. By now, I had become one of them. I woke up to the shout of my name.

"Jones, Jones," the officer shouted. He looked like he should have been a member of somebody's basketball or football team. However, he was nothing but a failure and decided he was going to take it out on someone else for the remainder of his lousy existence.

I lumbered over to the wall. He motioned for the inmates to stand. Then he shackled eight of us together. He commanded us to move through an electronic metal door, through a long corridor, through another electronically operated door, down a long hallway, through yet another door, and into a transparent pod that resembled the other six pods in our circumference. Once we were commanded to step through the electronically opened door, we were finally in the belly of the beast, where we were unshackled and commanded to strip and change into our bright orange jail uniforms.

I was glad it was not Gwinnett County Jail, where they lined everyone up naked and sprayed the inmates with bug spray. Anyway, I changed and looked like the other prisoners of war.

A lot of us can't help it that we are criminals. We see our families addicted to drugs. We see most of the people we look up to using illegal substances or profiting from it. So it is more or less a social brainwash. Our culture has become infested with drugs and has adapted to criminal activity.

After we were dressed, we were all given an armband that consisted of our name, birthdate, booking number, and cell location, similar to a dog tag that a soldier gets when he goes into combat. We were clueless, fighting a war for our survival to satisfy the high monarchy's selfish lust of power and financial greed. The officer told us to have a seat as he briefed us on some basic rules and guidelines. Then he gave us our new belongings: a sheet of paper, a blanket, two pair of white socks, boxers, and a T-shirt.

We were instructed to put shower shoes on our feet, then again, we were shackled to be transported to our permanent cell locations. Everyone was instructed to grab a thin 6-foot mattress and tote it with us upstairs. Once we were let through the two electronic doors to the elevator in the middle of the corridor, we stopped on the sixth floor.

There, we watched the officer remove our manacles and direct us to our pod location through different electronic doors. Every hall had two sections on opposite sides of the corridor. Inside, I was terrified and didn't know what the future held for me. What was going to happen to me? What was I going to do now?

28 *Ricky*

I was finally on the floor of my "new residence." A cop unshackled me and told to go stand in front of some doors. A door electronically slid open, and I stepped through. A female officer sitting in a transparent booth in the middle of the area spoke over the loud speaker, instructing me to go to the multipurpose room and have a seat. She unlocked the door electronically and allowed me to enter.

I tossed my mat onto the floor and slumped down onto it. I was exhausted. She immediately came back over the intercom and commanded me to approach the intercom and give her my name and location that was listed on my armband.

I complied. "I'm Ricky Jones, and my armband reads 7 SE 313."

"Okay, grab your mat and take it to your room, Mr. Jones."

I was electronically released from the multipurpose room and electronically allowed to enter POD 300. The officer buzzed open my room door. I approached and walked into an impeccably clean jail cell. My roommate was on the top bunk fast asleep with his head under his blanket in the freezing cold room.

I tossed my mat on the bottom bunk, took my sheets and blanket out of my net pack that had been given to me, and lay down on the plastic mattress. Wrapping the sheet and blanket completely around me, I drifted into a troubled sleep. I was awakened by a loud, electronic clicking of my cell door. I looked on as my roommate exited the room and gently closed the door behind him. I could hear the other inmates repeatedly yell, "Trays up."

I was not hungry, and I was not in any rush to eat any jail food. Instead, I pulled the covers back over my head. Shortly, I could hear my roommate enter my cell and close the door behind him. Next, I heard him hop up onto his top bunk, but I fell instantly asleep. Finally, in no time, I was awakened to the obnoxious yelling of a correctional officer at my cell door.

"Get up, get up. All inmates have to come outta their cells in rotation time," he informed me.

"Okay, okay," I replied, staggering out of bed. I rolled up my mat like my roommate and the jail regulation stapled to the wall. I did not know if I was in jail or boot camp. There goes the "you are innocent until proven guilty" factor. It seemed to me one was committed to the state once they placed handcuffs upon your hands.

I went out to the recreation area. The officer slammed shut our doors behind us. We had to sit and wait for all inmates to exit their rooms and for all doors to be closed before the officer in the booth electronically turned on our small 5-channel, 15-inch TV and the 3 collect call telephones inside the dorm.

All the seats by the TV were filling, so I walked down the stairs of the two-level transparent pod and sat on one of the metal chairs directly by the telephone. As soon as they turned on the power in the pod, I picked up the telephone and called Lisa. I was surprised when she answered.

"Hello, baby," she said in a weary voice.

"Yeah, what's up? You was still asleep or something?" I asked.

"Baby, I had to take off work today. I've been having morning sickness, baby. I'm pregnant," she informed me.

There was a moment of silence. I was shocked. I couldn't believe my ears. "You for real?" I asked.

"About 99.9 percent positive," she replied.

"Wow!" At that point, that was the only word I could think of. The silence that followed was deafening. A couple inmates who started begging for a three-way call interrupted me. I had to refuse their offer of a free lunch tray for three dollars every-twenty-minutes phone call. The only thing I could say to Lisa was, "Lisa, I love you, and I am there to support you all the way." It sounded like Lisa was already asleep on the other end of the line. The operator came on with the one-minute warning.

"Baby, I'm sorry. I'm very tired. I have to get some sleep. I'm sorry, baby, but I'm so tired," she murmured.

"Yeah, I feel you. I need for you to come down here and deposit some money on my inmate account," I said.

"Sorry, baby, I'll do it as soon as I get up. I love you, baby, see you soon," she said before the phone hung up. I sat there after I hung up and began to ponder. It was ironic because I was irate and happy at the same time. I sat there and analyzed my environment. The Muslims on the second level prostrated and prayed, the inmates in front of the TV cheered the football game, and some inmates played cards, slapping them on the steel table for impact.

One serious inmate stood in the corner, analyzing me and everyone else. It seemed obvious that 95 percent of the inmates were black and 95 percent of the inmates were involved with mind-altering, highly addictive drugs.

I started hating the fact that I was being used by Satan, seducing so many with the highly addictive white powder. At the same time, I wanted to keep my loyalty to the substance that helped me to elevate myself above poverty and experience a better life for myself. Now, I was caught up in a dilemma. If I stopped supplying drugs, someone else was going to take my place and supply it anyway, and if I continued to supply drugs, I may spend the rest of my life in prison.

I sat there until they served lunch. We had to line up on the steps. They gave all the grown men two sandwiches apiece in a plastic bag. Someone tossed me mine because I was by the phone. Once the inmates got their bag, they started trading slices of cheese, baloney, or bread. It was like trading in the stock market, except for the one person in the corner who was still analyzing everything that was going on.

Soon they opened our cell doors and allowed us to go back into our cells. I could not wait to go sleep off some of my anxiety and depression. I went into my room and the quiet, observant person followed right behind me.

At first I thought it was an inmate that was preying on me because I was a rookie, but, fortunately, the guy didn't pay me any attention. He just hopped straight up off the ground and into the top bunk, leaving me in a defense position like an idiot. I went and closed the door behind him. He was lying flat on his back, staring at the ceiling. I went and lay down and did the same exact thing.

The room door opened three hours later. The booth operator announced that all inmates were to make their beds and come out of their cells. My roommate was already through the door by the time I got up and made the bed. I exited the room and sat until everybody's doors were closed, then they turned on the TV. We placed the TV on the 5:00 p.m. news.

From a distance, I stood and watched the news. After the news finished, I went and took a shower, then I slipped on my same uniform without any underwear, returned, and sat at a table by myself. A couple of inmates came to me, asking questions. Wisely, I just answered in brief yes or no replies until they got the hint and left me alone.

My attention was once again drawn back to my roommate standing in the corner, quietly observing everything. A few hours later, workers there brought in the last meal of the day and served us with the same line-up-on-the-stair routine. I lined up all the way on top of the stairs and got my tray. The meal was so gruesome and nasty-looking I gave it away to another inmate. I noticed my roommate did not eat this meal either. That is an odd man who does not eat or talk. Now I found that interesting.

Once they allowed us back into our cells, I had one of my sandwiches and offered my roommate the other, but he gently shook his head no.

The next seven days went by depressingly slow, but peaceful. That is—until one night when it was about time for lockdown. The Muslims were doing their fifth prostration of their daily praying, and the Christians were doing their nightly ritual of praying and singing. The Christians were singing loud, rejoicing and praising Jesus, which made the Islamic cult start amplifying their Arabic tongue in prayer.

The leader of the Muslim prayer group exploded with a furious outburst. "Can you disrespectful motherfuckers shut the fuck up when you see us trying to pay respects to Allah?" a short, light-skinned, bald-headed, full-bearded Muslim barked.

"Fuck you *and* Muhammad!" A tall, slim, younger fellow stood firm in a boxing stance. As soon as the Muslim got within reach, he was struck with a fierce right hook, but a thunderous left uppercut sent the Muslim staggering back. The Muslim, shocked at first by the offensive impact, regrouped. He placed his fist in front of his face and weaved and bobbed forward twice. He charged the Christian in an attempt to give another right hook, but the Christian bobbed under it and threw a vicious combination of body blows.

The Christian then leaned forward from the impact of a powerful right cross to his stomach. The Muslim threw a fierce, upward right elbow to the Christian's face. The Muslim had all the intensity on his face of a raging madman, but the Christian got wide-eyed and swayed out of the way swiftly. Without warning, he unleashed a fury of right and left hooks to the Muslim's face with determination and intense seriousness.

The Muslim felt himself being pummeled by a storm of nonstop punches. As a matter of reflex and desperation, he charged low and forward. He grabbed both of the Christian's legs together, scooped him off the ground in a split second, then slammed him on his neck with such an impact, the floor shook like a thunderous earthquake. Both men were leaking blood.

The Muslim then attempted to stomp on the Christian's head like he was crushing some disgusting over-sized cockroach. But out of nowhere, he was hit from the back with a right hook that crushed his right jaw like the impact from a sledge hammer and knocked him unconscious.

The 260-pound muscular behemoth paused and shook his right hand until the Muslims, who were already downstairs militantly watching their comrade, took out their jail-made cutlery weapons and stormed the big fellow like a swarm of starving locusts on one lonely stalk of corn. The first razor sliced across his face, from his eyes down to his jawbone, spewing blood like a sprinkler.

Meantime, other Muslims stabbed him repeatedly with sharpened, pointy toothbrushes. The big man tried to fight back but to no avail. It just enraged his attackers even more.

Now the other Christians tried to fight off the vicious Muslims with dropkicks and punches. From my observation, one stab was all it took for the Christian opposition to retreat. I was in one corner and my roommate was in the other, watching the chaotic display of anarchy and religious intolerance. The jail swat team finally maneuvered their way in, opening the doors for those inmates who wanted to escape to their cells.

My roommate and I strolled out into our cells and closed the door. He jumped straight up on his bunk and lay down with his hands across his chest, motionless. I was intrigued by the commotion so I stood there, mouth gaped wide open, and watched. The Christians eventually retreated, and the officers started brutally attacking the Muslims until they finally submitted.

I was thinking, now here was another paradox that could have been prevented if people would stop separating themselves through lack of knowledge.

As history shows, it was the original black ancestors who started religion by having the masses prostrate and worship the higher monarchy. These were the pharaohs of ancient Egypt that sat on top of the greatest geometric monuments known to man, monuments built through a supreme knowledge of mathematics. They maintained a peaceful free-will society that is imitated by other civilizations to this day.

I drifted back to my present-day hellhole. I had bigger problems to contend with than what went on in the past. What was I going to do today?

Chapter

29 *Ricky*

I turned around and noticed my roommate still in his zone. He hadn't said one word to me, however, we have somehow become more open to each other by simple body language. We even worked out and did push-ups together on two different occasions. Now his art of mastering his mouth made me curious about what else this person had mastered.

We made commissary last week, so I know he eats. It might be two instant soups a day, but I'm sure he eats. I glanced back at my roommate. "I can't wait to get back out there," I said. My cellmate remained silent. I thought to myself, *At least he's a good listener.*

"Yeah, man, that rumble out there was crazy, huh?" I added.

He nodded his head gently to respond yes to my question. Therefore, I reached down by the head of my bunk and grabbed a few bags of potato chips and offered him one, but he shook his head side to side in refusal. I opened the bag, set it on the small metal table across from the bunk bed, faced him, and started eating. He looked like a distant man, except for the few small fresh scratch marks on his face. I'd never seen him get any visitations so I asked, "You have any family?"

He shook his head no.

I took his hint. He did not want to be bothered, so I lay down on my bunk.

"They were all killed by my comrade," he finally answered.

That's when I slumped down in my bed with an "I'm sorry I asked" motion. He had a slight accent, as if he were from New Orleans or something.

"All your family killed by your comrade—eh?" I said, not trying to hide my sarcasm.

"I have to get out of here," he said with a gentle but stern, almost commanding voice.

"What're you charged with?" I asked.

"Grand larceny, reckless driving, and obstruction of a law enforcement officer."

"Your bond is only $1,500 at the most," I said.

"You could bond me out," he said with a touch of enthusiasm in his voice.

I paused for a second with a sarcastic smirk on my face. "Why you say that?" I said suspiciously.

"You said 'only.' Plus, you not like the others; you think," he said gently. He then hopped down off the bed, picked up his personal information, and handed it to me.

"You will bond me out once you get the chance, and I will always remember your kind deed," he said with a calm, overconfident voice. At the same time, his serious and penetrating eyes felt as if he were hypnotizing me. I reached for the paper. As soon as I grasped it, he hopped back on his bunk and I did not hear another word out his mouth.

Bond him out, yeah, whatever. I looked over his information. Richard Matthews.

I placed the paper with his information in a small brown pack with my jail documents, then I finished eating my bag of chips. *I should have kept my mouth shut,* I thought then fell asleep. The next day, my lawyer Sunny Boi paid me a visit. I ran upstairs to the special lawyer's visitation booth, was buzzed in electronically, and took a seat in front of the transparent glass in front of me.

My chubby Caucasian lawyer, Mr. Boi, came into the visitation booth in his Armani suit and tie. He picked up the phone and rested his elbow on the metal counter so he could hold the phone with his arm up, displaying his Presidential Rolex watch. I picked up the phone.

"Halloo, Mr. Jones, I was employed by a ..." he glanced down at his paperwork for a second, "Lisa McIntosh to represent you on your criminal case. It appears that you were charged with conspiracy. Right now, it appears that you have been set up so more than likely, they are going to bind your case over to Superior Court, where you'll be charged with the offense of violation of Georgia Controlled Substance along with possession of a firearm in commission, too. So our main objective is to get you a bond," Boi said with his double chin constantly jiggling. He continued observing my silence.

"How much could you come up with if you get a bond?" he asked.

"*If?*" I asked.

"Well, the judge doesn't have to give you a bond in your situation, because it might place the main witness in danger. However, with you never having been convicted of a felony in your adult career and being a native of Georgia, more than likely, I could manage to get you a bond," he said, looking at me through lingering eyes that appeared to be as innocent as a newborn's.

"Well, I might be able to scrape up $5,000."

"Okay. Great, so I'll see you tomorrow in court," he said. "Any questions?"

"No," I replied. I watched as he hastily vanished through the door. A sigh escaped me as I hung up the telephone and pressed the button to exit the booth. I went back to my room, shut the cell door, and went to bed.

If there's one thing I learned since I went to jail, it is the system does not mind a black man being undependable, worthless, and lazy. I mean, how can an incarcerated person learn to rehabilitate himself in this environment? All he meets with is animosity, deceitful influences, and more criminal inspiration in this joint.

I was disgusted with all the thinking of a double-standard society, which said being incarcerated was how you paid your debt to society. No wonder the recidivism rate was so high. I finally tried to sleep my frustration away.

The next morning at like 4:00 a.m., someone called my name for court. I was fed a meager breakfast and placed in a cell with about eighty other inmates. It was reeking with musty odors, bacterial germs, sweltering heat, and body odor. Jail was always extremely hot or unbearably cold, never in between. After that, I had to wait three hours before I was shackled and taken to court.

After going through that experience, I could see how the judicial system manipulated the poor inmates who couldn't afford bond into pleading out to charges just because they couldn't bear the frustration and degradation physiologically.

The calmer officer that arrested me on the day of my arrest escorted me to a building across the street in his squad car. He tried to make small talk but saw I was quiet. I guess my roommate's silence must have rubbed off on me, because I was ensconced in silence. He escorted me to the courthouse, where I saw Lisa sitting next to my lawyer. My lawyer then approached me and confidently told me I would be getting a bond today. I guess Lisa influenced him with more money.

The officer escorted me to the front of the pew right in front the judge's chamber. Lisa was happy to see me, however, she looked pitifully sad. I felt ashamed of myself but carried my strut of confidence to disguise my internal turmoil. The officer asked me to turn around so he could cuff my hands in front of me. My lawyer came and sat beside me. My lady sat two rows behind me.

"Well, Mr. Jones, I got this bond situation taken care of, but by the looks of the police report, there's not going to be a defense for your case," said Boi. He held the police report printout in front of me to read.

"The Honorable Judge Winder has entered the courtroom. Everyone please rise," said a sheriff in the back of the courtroom. Everyone stood until they were instructed to be seated. Then the slim blonde DEA stood up and announced her calendar call and the charges of which I was accused.

"The court would like to first call Ricky Jones, charged with OCGA, violation of a Georgia controlled substance, conspiracy, trafficking, and possession of a handgun during the commission of a crime," the district attorney said.

My lawyer led me to a wooden bench and sat right next to me.

"It was said that the defendant, Ricky Jones, was arrested on the night of January 10, 2007, at West Mountain Street for the offense of trafficking when the defendant sold five ounces of crack cocaine to a special informant whose name remains undisclosed for his safety. Officer Parker was the arresting officer on the scene and is here to present evidence that this case should be heard by the grand jury," the blonde district attorney said before she took a seat.

The officer that was sitting at the table next to the DEA started reading directly from his police report. "Approximately 1300 hours, our informant notified us of a large distributor that he could possibly induce to sell him over two ounces of crack cocaine. Therefore, I had a special team of narcotics agents set up a sting and surveillance on one Ricky Jones. Our informant made a narcotics deal with Mr. Jones to transport two ounces of crack cocaine to his location.

"We then gave our informant $2,000 of marked U.S. currency, just enough for the purchase of his transaction. At approximately 1500 hours, the suspect arrived at the Lakes Apartments in Stone Mountain, a known drug-infested area.

"The suspect then instructed our informant to meet him at the N building, where he committed the offense of violation of Georgia controlled substance of possession and distribution of an illegal substance, crack cocaine. The defendant then exited the complex onto W. Mount Street, where he was stopped and detained by Officer Thompson and myself.

"Once the suspect was arrested and we conducted a search of the suspect's person, we retrieved $2,000 of marked U.S. currency in the suspect's right front pocket. Further search of the suspect's vehicle, a Toyota Corolla, we discovered a PS9 Ruger 9mm handgun fully loaded in the middle compartment of his car. The suspect was then detained and transferred to Stone Mountain Precinct," Officer Parker concluded.

"Any questions, Mr. Boi?" asked Judge Winder.

"Officer Parker, did you witness Mr. Jones making this alleged drug transaction?" Boi asked.

"No, however—" Officer Parker said before he was suddenly cut off.

"Therefore, you did not eyewitness this drug transaction. However, you're sure Mr. Jones was armed and dangerous, distributing crack cocaine on the credibility of a convicted felon," Boi said.

"Yes sir," said Officer Parker.

Before the discombobulated officer could think over his answer, Boi lashed out again. "Where was the crack cocaine found?" asked Boi.

"The substance was given to us by our informant," Officer Parker replied.

"So it was not found on Mr. Jones' person, and Mr. Jones was not arrested immediately after this alleged illegal transaction, is that correct?" Boi asked.

"Yes sir," Officer Parker responded.

"Where was the gun found?"

Officer Parker looked over his police report to make sure he didn't perjure himself in the courtroom.

"We discovered the weapon in the middle compartment of the suspect's vehicle, sir," responded Officer Parker.

"So the handgun was never identified on the defendant's person?" Boi asked.

"No sir," said Officer Parker.

"I have no further questions, Your Honor."

"Any further evidence, Ms. Downier?" the judge asked the DEA, staring at her through rimless reading glasses with silver frames matching his silver hair.

"No, Your Honor," she replied.

"Okay, then I do see enough evidence to accuse the defendant of violation of Georgia Controlled Substance because evidence exists that the defendant may have had possession with the intent to distribute crack cocaine over 28 grams. However, I'm going to dismiss the conspiracy and the possession of a handgun during the intent of a crime because the handgun was not identified on the defendant. Therefore, this case will be bound over to the grand jury for indictment. In addition, I will set a bond of $50,000 on trafficking. Any question?"

The district attorney sprung from her seat. "Your Honor, I don't think it's in the court's interest to give the defendant a bond because it may place our informant's life in jeopardy," Ms. Downier snapped, then regained composure and sat back down.

Attorney Boi stood up from his seat calmly and said, "Your Honor, my client has never been in trouble with the law and is a native of the state of Georgia. He has established and operates a legitimate business in this state, as well as he owns numerous assets. He is also accused of a nonviolent charge. So I see your judgment to be wise and have no reason to disagree with it," stated Mr. Boi.

"Okay, the bond will stay at $50,000 with the defendant restrained from any contact with the witness. My decision is final," the judge stated.

My lawyer gave me a handshake and began to escort me out of the courtroom. The police officer quickly intervened and grabbed me by my back upper arm to escort me, with force, out of the courtroom. Lisa was grateful for the judge's decision. She looked at me, nodded, and then vanished. I already figured she was going to get me out of here as soon as possible.

My lawyer said, "Don't worry, Mr. Jones, we'll have you out ASAP. You can call me or set up an appointment with my secretary to meet me at my office." He handed me his card and vanished out of the building. The officer escorted me to the squad car, then back to the correctional facility.

"Don't think you're independent and free, Jones. I know who you are," the police officer said with icy eyes before he took the cuffs off my hands and locked me in the holding tank.

I went and lay across the steel bench in the now almost-empty cold holding cell. My hands were crossed against my chest like an Egyptian Pharaoh until an officer came and announced he was transporting everyone back to the southeast side. Three inmates hurriedly ran to the door. I got up and joined them. We were handcuffed on opposite hands, two men side by side. I went into my cell and waited for my name to be called for release.

My roommate, the poor fellow, just lay there staring into space. It was taking too long for them to call my name, so I covered up under my blanket and tried to go to sleep. Almost two hours later, a voice yelled, "Ricky Jones, pack it up," from the loud speaker.

I pushed my call button. The officer electronically opened my cell door. I pushed it open even wider and made an enthusiastic motion with my hands that I was there, and I impatiently stood in the cell doorway. My roommate lay there, still motionless, while I packed my things, grabbed my mattress, and slung it over my shoulder. I attempted to give my roommate some dap, however, he did not respond. I didn't take it personally. It just added more definition to his character.

I left feeling great. I was being released, however, it was ironically unjust that I was since I really was guilty and so many innocent people were convicted and incarcerated simply because they could not afford their freedom. But, c'est va vie. By the time I made it downstairs, I had nothing in my hands except for my small brown paper bag. I sat in the phone waiting area and called Lisa, but she was not at home.

I figured she was on the outside, waiting for me. In the next two hours, I was dressed back into my own clothes and sneakers. I signed a couple more documents and placed the copies in my paper bag. The metal exit door electronically unlocked, and I walked through with a right stiff arm in front of me.

At the front desk I stopped and gave the clerk a receipt and lifted my arm. The clerk looked at my armband, then cut it off. She registered my information, then asked me to wait one moment. Shortly, a check was printed out for $1,405, which she handed to me. I put the check into my pants pocket and barreled out.

The first thing I saw when I strutted through the retracting doors was Lisa's face. She was standing by the rear wall with her hands folded across her chest. When she recognized me coming out of the door, she jogged over towards me with her breasts swinging side by side in slow motion. Once she was close enough, I grabbed her with an affectionate hug and picked her up off the ground. We kissed passionately before I placed her back down.

She grabbed me by the hand, leading me out. Her walk was captivating. She swayed her hips seductively, even though she wore Rocawear sweat pants. I followed her lead outside the building to the car where the BMW X5 was parked, and we drove off.

"Baby, first we got to make a stop at the bonding company to sign a few papers, then I'm going to take you home, get you out of those filthy clothes, give you a bath, and cook you a decent home-cooked meal," she said, handing me a blunt of marijuana out of the ashtray.

I took it and looked it over. It was one she attempted to roll herself with the rosebud I'd left in the refrigerator. I could tell by the shabby job, but she tried her best. I leaned over from the passenger side and kissed her on the cheek. By the look on her face, I could tell that gave her the tingling good feeling of love and appreciation.

Deftly, I repaired her blunt enough for an enjoyable smoke and then lit it with the car lighter. After taking two drags, I put it out and placed it in back into the ashtray, let the window down, and exhaled, leaving the windows down long enough to air out the interior of the vehicle.

Shortly afterwards, we arrived at the bonding company. I was feeling great. My essence was on a higher level of consciousness. I went into the bond office where the bondsman was waiting for me. We shook hands.

"I'm Derrick," he said leading me over to his desk. "You just need to sign these four papers and don't leave the state without informing us. Be sure you appear at all scheduled court dates regarding your case." He sat at his desk, and I sat opposite him. I filled out the information on the papers and passed them back to him.

"I need your ID for a moment," Derrick said.

"They took my ID in their evidence. I'm going to have to reapply for one. All I have is this court document as identification right now," I informed him.

"Let me see one with all your information, but I still need your photo ID registered on file," he said.

"Okay," I said as I reached down into my brown bag and retrieved some paperwork.

The property receipt had all my information on it, so I handed it to him. A little piece of paper fell like confetti onto his desk. I looked over at the name. *Richard Matthews.*

30 Blue's Brother, John

Doctor Hartworth returned to the private room with the patient's chart in his hand. The doctor was wearing a spotless, unbuttoned white coat. Like a comic book superhero's cape, it lingered to the rear when he strode forward or made turning movements. He sat directly in front of his patient on a moveable stool and spread his legs, which made his slacks rise up, showing his black and yellow-orange socks. He wore black suspenders and his yellow dress shirt was tucked in, with his pants pulled up to his belly button. Adjusting his specs, he glanced down at the chart clipped on a shiny metallic clipboard, looked up at the patient, then back down to the chart.

First, he cleared his throat. "Well, Mr. Flamings ..." He paused. "I'm sorry to inform you that the virus has progressed into the deadly disease. Your body's white blood cells do not have the ability to fight off minor infections any longer, such as the common cold or flu. That's why you have a fever. I'm going to prescribe more Neopogen, as well as antibacterial medicines. I advise you to keep taking your vitamins every day and stay as physically fit as possible to slow down the process.

"I also recommend that you refrain from all unprotected sexual contact and report to the hospital or call an ambulance to transport you to the hospital anytime you begin feeling too sick to function properly. Once again, I'm very sorry. No one should have to die from such a horrific disease as AIDS." The doctor finished.

He looked at his patient who was sitting motionless, his head bent down from the weight of this shattering news.

The doctor sighed deeply and stood up slowly, attempting not to disturb his patient's moment of silence. He hoped there was a way he could perform a miracle with medicine, but there was nothing he was capable of doing to reverse his patient's death sentence.

Dr. Hartworth walked over and placed his hand on the doorknob. He analyzed the young man whose life has been plagued with an atrocious man-made invention. This brought the good doctor to a mental dilemma. Research foundations for AIDS had paid him remarkably well. In the field of medicine, this was one area that was extremely profitable for researchers.

However, how many more millions of people would have to suffer and die before the Centers for Disease Control released the HIV vaccine or the antidote for the catastrophic disease that had been created in the first place? This disease had been designed to ethnically cleanse a selected race of people.

The doctor smiled gently. "Feel free to call me." He continued out the room about his business.

John was left in the room, crying with his face in his hands. In mental anguish, he was tormented by fear and uncertainty as to what his last days would become.

Chapter

31 Keisha, T, and Sabrina

T and Sabrina arrived at Keisha's residence in a black Audi AL W12 and parked directly behind Keisha's BMW. T picked up her cell phone that was connected to the car charger and dialed Keisha's number, and she answered.

"We're outside waiting for you," T said, then hung up. Donnell Jones was being played at a low volume in the background. Sabrina was looking into her portable mirror, making sure her appearance was professional looking. She was wearing glasses and a business pin-striped suit, making her appearance look more sophisticated and presentable. Her keen perm was pulled back into a curly ponytail. She added lip-gloss on her lips, then glanced over at T. "How do I look?" she asked.

"Baby, you know you look good," T said with a hard frown on her face.

"What's taking this bitch so long?" T snapped. She picked up the phone and called Keisha's number again. This time, there was no answer. Finally, Keisha appeared out the back door, holding her cell phone in her hand, which indicated that she identified T's call. She was formally dressed in a blue Prada business pants suit and soft black leather walking shoes. Casually, she strutted towards the car in a cheerful manner. T unlocked the door to the backseat and let her in.

Keisha slammed the door and relaxed in her seat in a reserved manner.

"Damn, baby girl, what took you so long?" T asked as she leaned back, observing Keisha.

Keisha leaned over and placed her hands on Sabrina's shoulder, then positioned herself closer to where she could extend her hand through the driver and passenger region of the car.

"Girl, I'm about to get married," she said with a slight scream of enthusiasm, brandishing a diamond-studded wedding band with princess cut diamonds. It sparkled with icy fire. "This beauty cost $2,783," she said with a smile big enough to fall into. T was mesmerized by the beauty and couldn't take her eyes off of it, while Sabrina could not help being astonished. Sabrina turned away quickly before anyone could see her jealous expression.

T smiled gently. She held her position and placed the car into reverse, then began backing out of the driveway. None of the women put their seat belts on because they rode behind limousine-tinted windows, making it hard for law enforcement to see inside of it.

"So when did he propose?" T asked.

"This morning," she replied with a light smile and her head miles above the clouds.

"Did he get down on his knees?" asked Sabrina in a slightly vindictive tone.

"Yeah, girl, but that was *before* he proposed," Keisha said. They all laughed, which broke the tension.

"Then he handed me a small pink velvet jewelry box. I opened it and never saw a ring more beautiful in my life. Then I handed it back to him," Keisha said before she was interrupted.

"So you telling me you *didn't* want to marry him?" Sabrina inquired.

"No, no, don't get me wrong. You know Mark is my childhood sweetheart, and I love him to death, but I had to explain to him the way he's currently snorting and associating with cocaine, our lives are going to be in jeopardy. And I don't want our marriage anything less than perfect," Keisha said before she was once again interrupted by Sabrina.

"What'd he do then?" Sabrina asked with curiosity.

Keisha took a moment to look at her ring, then tears began welling in her eyes. "He said, 'Baby, my lady, my desire, I've been waiting and praying to God for the moment when I could be financially stable enough to present you with this ring. Without you in my life, I would have no hope to cope. Baby, I love you, and I'll do anything in my power to keep you by my side. Baby, you alone have been there from the beginning. You always showed concern about my best interest.'

"Then he paused a moment with tears in his eyes and said, 'So, baby, I'll quit using cocaine and quit selling cocaine, because I love you with all my will and need nothing more in this world than to spend the rest of my life with you. So give me your hand in marriage. I want you to reign as my beautiful queen as long as we shall live.'" Keisha finished her story, tears streaming down her face.

"Huh, that's so sweet," Sabrina said with sincerity. It was like witnessing a 3-year-old toddling boy help lift up his stumbling 1-year-old sister and cheer her up with a hug and a kiss.

"Okay, congratulations, girlfriend. Now, let's gets down to business. Sabrina, hand Keisha the material," T said in a serious manner.

Sabrina picked up a black Luis Vuitton suitcase off the floor and opened it up. She took out a leather bank pouch with checks in two stacks of 100, which were authentically duplicated. One stack included checks for $5,700 in the name of Corral Bishop, and the other was for $6,300 under the name of Susan Lavet.

"Okay, baby girl, my inside connection in the bank guarantees that we will have no hassle with these multimillion dollar corporate accounts payroll checks. We'll take two days for the job, and you and Sabrina will hit a hundred banks and check cashing distributors in the Georgia region. It sounds like a mission impossible, but it's not. I have everything planned to the T," T said.

Sabrina took out a map and handed it to Keisha. Keisha could see T had definitely done her homework with every planned location circled according to the most convenient and feasible time.

"Now all we got to do is get Georgia State photo ID driver's licenses. I know this plot is going to be tough. That's why I got two of the most cunning and toughest bitches I know. I also have to keep this discreet or many major people are going to suffer. This is the last sting operation I'm masterminding, so I need you to be confident and professional about this, and once we pull off this master plan, we can all go into retirement, living a life of luxury.

"Let me make this clear. From now on, I get 50 percent of all transactions." T finished her briefing. She changed the CD to Foxy Brown's "Ill Na Na."

Finally they arrived at a small, two-bedroom stucco house and parked in the driveway. T got out of the car, strutted to the front doorbell, looked over at her car, and licked her lips. An attractive, petite Asian woman greeted her at the door with straight, raven-black hair cascading down her shoulders. She wore an open robe which displayed her nakedness and black, dense pubic hairs. She gleefully stood on her tiptoes and motioned for T to come in with a hand extended like a formal butler. The lovely young woman attempted to escort T by her forearm, however, T remained stern and in a less-than-amiable mood, and pulled her arm away.

T followed her into a bedroom that was converted into an office with extensive computer materials, many different forms sitting on the desktop, and printing machines. Some recently forged passports and other important government documents sat on top of a table. The lady went to her desk and withdrew four fraudulent drivers' licenses and handed them to T. As soon as T received them, she was impressed at the authenticity of the documents, which were fully equipped with government state holograms.

"These look excellent, Chang Li. I'll have your money as soon as I get back," T said, immediately heading for the exit.

"T, remember what you promise me, baby?" Chang Li said, seductively pulling the robe over her shoulders, exposing erect nipples on perky little breasts and a plump, moist, waiting vagina.

"I'll take care of you once I get back," T promised, turning her attention from the erotic vision as she proceeded out of the house. T let herself out. When she returned to the car, she gave an ID to Sabrina and Keisha with their photos on them. Then she looked at her navigation monitor on the car's dashboard and pressed some buttons on the device, put the car in drive, and briefly looked at the ladies inside the car with a stone-cold serious face and intense eyes.

"Let's do it," she said, and proceeded to drive.

32 Keisha, T, and Sabrina

I arrived at Popi's residence and parked in the garage, turned off the car, and took a brown paper bag filled with money from the glove compartment. I needed to pay Popi. Even though I made my mind up that I was never dealing with cocaine or any other deadly substance again, I still wanted to pay Popi back what I owed him.

While walking to the cabin in the back, I could sense an eerie, creepy quiet lingering in the atmosphere. The hairs on the back of my neck were standing at full alert. With my luck, the FBI would raid Popi's house this very moment and charge me for tax evasion and money laundering U.S. currency.

I sighed and continued walking. When I reached the cabin and knocked on the door, I could see Popi's feet laying flat on the ground through the small beveled plate frosted glass on his door. I couldn't figure out why he would be sleeping on the floor. I knocked harder to wake him up. The door flew open. It was left unlocked.

Cautiously, I stepped in. It appeared Popi was lying in his own regurgitation. However, when I got closer, I could see a donut-size hole in the back of his head. He was laid out stiff with a legal envelope lying next to him. Immediately, I retrieved my .50 caliber from my waistline holster. The envelope was addressed to the Federal Bureau of Investigation, 666 Century Parkway NE, Atlanta, GA 30345.

After closely inspecting the document, I decided to hold on to it. Popi had no use for it now anyway, and I was curious about what relation Popi had with the Feds. The kitchen door was open, and

I could see a trail of blood that ended in a puddle. I slowly walked to see where the trail led. It was Popi's wife, lying on the kitchen floor dead, with the same style gunshot wound in the back of her head. Her mouth was also covered with duct tape and her hands tied were behind her back. As if Popi's murder was not bewildering enough, now I had to deal with this horrendous image of his wife.

As much as I wanted to get the hell out of the house as soon as possible, I noticed every door in the house was open and my curiosity just pulled me to see what was behind each one. I walked upstairs and crept into the master bedroom. It was furnished lavishly. The safe was still locked. I then stepped across to the adjacent bedroom. My adrenaline was already at its pinnacle.

To my shock, I discovered the most grotesque tragedy of all—two little girls lay straight out next to each other, with their hands tied and mouths duct-taped. With my heart racing and my stomach knotted in an iron grip, I approached closer to try to determine the cause of death. Then I saw the slash and rupture on their necks. I staggered backwards in disbelief. They were almost decapitated!

I was sick to my stomach and began gagging. I ran downstairs with the envelope and pistol in my hand. The garage door right next to the stairwell was opened. I peeked in the garage, looking through the transparent windows in the door to make sure law enforcement agents had not surrounded the house by now. However, the morning was still quiet and peaceful outside. Then I noticed the deep freezer door was wide open.

I thought that was odd because the freezer was on. A noticeable noise came from it. I walked over and looked in. As if the tragic events hadn't been mind-boggling enough, to my surprise, the freezer was filled with blocks of cocaine. I shook my head no and walked backwards, trying to resist temptation. Finally I mustered up enough strength to turn around and began walking out of the garage.

But something stopped me. There they were. On the floor were two economy-sized packs of Hefty garbage bags. *What the fuck?* I thought. I dropped the money and envelope on the floor and quickly grabbed two trash bags and made sure not to touch anything extra. I strengthened the durability of the bags by opening them up and placing one inside the another, then rushed over to the freezer and made haste, loading all the keys into the bag with my gun still in hand, paranoid like I was schizoid.

After finishing loading up the bag, I walked over and tossed the bag of money and envelope inside, lifted the bag over my shoulder, and walked out the same way I entered. I made it to the back door, reholstered my gun, and opened the door, using the back of my hand to avoid leaving prints. I quickly made my way back to my Benz and tossed the bag into the backseat, immediately got in the driver's side and drove off, making sure no one was paying any attention.

Once out of the subdivision, I took a deep breath that released a lot of the distress and tension. I then drove to a local hotel to regroup. Once I got a room at the Economy Lounge, I took the bag out of the car and walked to the room, emptied out the bag on the bed, and counted out 43 keys of cocaine.

I called Lisa, explained that something came up and I needed her to come and meet me at the hotel, where I intended to give her the bag of money and envelope to take to her residence. I then called Lucky, and he was overanxious to help me get rid of the package. I tossed two keys in one of the bags and tied it up, then I placed twenty-three in another bag, tied it up, leaving it on the bed. I left Lucky's shipment on the floor.

When I looked out the hotel room window, an idea struck me, so I dialed the storage number on the billboard right across the street. The huge sign gave me the idea that it would be a good place to keep the goods. In addition, it was located within walking distance.

"Hello, yes, I was inquiring if you have any storage room available," I said. The clerk informed me that there was a storage spot still available, and all I needed was a driver's license and $29.99. I asked him to reserve it for me today.

Lucky arrived first. I told him I wanted $12,500 off every block, and there was more where that came from if he could handle it. He was extremely enthusiastic about the opportunity and with gratitude, he confidently assured me that he would manage my business as if he were me.

I also informed him that I would no longer be dealing with anybody directly, and associates like Blue and Mark would now have to deal with him at his prices. He took his promotion like an honorable general and left.

Shortly after, Lisa arrived and came to the room. She was concerned and worried, however, I assured her everything would be okay and something drastic just came up. She was skeptic, but she had faith in me. We took everything out of the room and got in her car. I convinced her to lease the storage. She came back with the lease agreement and a lock and key. I took it, dialed the push button code to open the gate, and then drove in. Once I reached the storage number on the lease, I parked in front of it, opened it, and walked back to the BMW, where I grabbed the bag, returned, and put it in the storage room. Then I put the lock on the door and left.

33 *Lucky and Blue*

L ucky and Blue's syndicate had been going exceptionally well. Between their business ventures and their womanizing love affairs, the two decided to meet at Lucky's new penthouse establishment to socialize and keep the viewers on the World Wide Web suitably entertained. A mahogany-skinned, petite, topless Asian woman with succulent size C cup breasts was preparing a laptop and video equipment for recording a live, online Internet session.

Peaches was sitting on the couch, enjoying a glass of Richard Hennessy on the rocks. She calmly placed her cigarette to her lips, inhaled, then exhaled in a smooth, sexy manner. She observed Christina arranging and making sure the cameras were recording with a precise digital visual. Peaches was wearing her lace Victoria's Secret panties and push-up bra that made her body look absolutely magnificent.

Along with her freshly styled blonde hair and manicured and pedicured nails, Peaches' buoyant beauty radiated like never before. She slowly glided the tip of her tongue out of her mouth, licking her upper lip. Staring at Christina seductively, she spread her legs and placed the sweating glass between them, cooling her genitals. Christina noticed her with a quick glance. She could not hold back a faint smile through her blushing. Then came a knock at the door.

Shirtless, Lucky appeared in the room with his cell phone in his hands. He wore black Calvin Klein boxer drawers, black pants, and matching socks. He even wore a black .44mm fully automatic Desert Eagle. He was sipping a small glass of Hennessy.

"Peaches, get the door. It's Blue," Lucky said.

Peaches got up and strutted to the door with an elegance that caused Lucky and Christina to admire her immense, sexually appealing buttocks. She opened the door.

There stood Blue, smiling and showing off his new platinum, diamond teeth. He extended his arms with two champagne bottles of Cristal in one hand and his cell phone in the other. Peaches immediately recalled who he was and was surprised to see him in such appealing splendor.

Although Blue marveled at Peaches' appearance, he did not recognize who she was anymore, she had changed so much. He paused, his eyes full of lust, while Peaches stepped aside to let everybody in.

Katrina, Shawn, Stacey, and Kim scurried in behind Blue, ready to start the festivities. They were all wearing exquisite lingerie and exotic robes, like they were all going to a carnal, no-holds-barred slumber party. The women made their way to the large V-shaped indigo linen-and-velvet upholstered sofa.

Three plasma TVs sat directly across from the incredibly spacious sitting area. The TV was mounted on a matching indigo rack with the 60-inch wide screen in the center and two 42-inch wide screens directly on top of it. The ladies could see themselves from different angles in the sitting area on the TVs. Blue watched the activities, but kept his eye on Peaches the entire time. He was intrigued by her sensuality.

His eyes lifted up to the second-story balcony where he noticed Lucky observing him from the master bedroom. He handed Peaches the champagne bottles and went to the foyer where he had a seat at the ebony marble table. There, he had a splendid view of the city of Alpharetta through the floor-to-ceiling glass that merged the illuminated city nightlife with the interior of the suite.

Blue reached into his pocket and withdrew two ounces of Hawaiian skunk marijuana out of his Yushua pants and two boxes of Garcia Vegas cigars. He noticed the glittering of his lavish blue diamond opera necklace reflected in the window. It bore a clustered globe of the world that was intricately designed with the blue half carat representing the ocean and the green emerald representing the earth.

By the time Blue finished rolling his cigar and lit his blunt, Peaches approached him with a champagne glass filled with bubbly Cristal. She put the ice bucket on the table. He turned to observe her as she strutted away. She quickly glanced back at him and smiled. This intrigued Blue, who now fantasized of a rigorous intensive sexual encounter with this ripe peach.

The ladies were now more comfortable, taking off their robes and grooming themselves for the camera. They were excited about exploring their sexual talents in a porn movie. The idea of becoming porn stars made them giddy. They knew they had the right stuff, and none of them were camera shy.

The women were passing around a bag holding almost an ounce of cocaine that they happily sniffed. Even Christina was indulging in the powdery substance.

Peaches looked on with a cavernous appetite for the substance, but her respect for Lucky had her put in a dilemma. She noticed that Katrina did not take part in the consumption of the sinister drug either. Instead, she separated herself away from the others and strutted her sumptuous buttocks over to the foyer table, where she began rolling blunts.

Peaches regained her will power and once again renewed her resolve. She loved who she had become since she left that mess alone and did not want to relapse. She put the metallic champagne bucket on the floor with five champagne glasses in it, took the other gold-rimmed champagne glasses to the foyer, and poured herself and Lucky a glass.

Lucky turned on a DJ Yush mix CD and made his way down the stairs, completely naked except for a Glycine Swiss Airman 7 diamond case watch. He definitely managed to grab everyone's attention as he walked down the carved hardwood steps with his poise and grace and his outstanding hardware. The ladies looked on in marvel and excitement before they decided to give him a standing ovation for his extraordinary Egyptian godlike physique.

Peaches walked over to meet him at the center of the living room with his champagne glass. He stood directly behind the couch where the ladies had sat. With a beatific smile, he extended his hand and opened it. The ladies looked on in delight at the cluster of triple stack ecstasy pills in his palm. They all grabbed two apiece. Katrina also made her way over and took one. Peaches' sexual desire was constantly at its pinnacle, so she was content knowing she was not permitted to indulge.

Blue, who was looking on, was encouraged by Lucky's charm with the ladies and his behavior, so, craving attention, he walked to the center of the living room, whipped out his penis, and started to swing it around like a lasso, gripping it with one hand at its base. This definitely got the ladies' attention. They got even more excited and began dancing to the groove of the music as they seductively undressed. Christina immediately ran to the laptop and pushed enter for the viewers to tune in and record the footage.

Lucky, who was the host, began the inauguration show. "Welcome. As you know, I'm Lucky, and this is my loyal assistant, Peaches," he said. He gradually motioned his extended open hand around the room for everyone to introduce themselves. Each woman from the group did so with an inviting smile.

"I'm Kim."

"I'm Katrina."

"I'm Shawn."

"I'm Stacey."

Christina took Blue by the hand and led him to the sofa area where they could get better footage. "I'm Christina, and this is Blue," she said into the camera.

All the ladies cheered in unison.

Blue let out a cheerful outburst of enthusiasm, either out of admiration or just to satisfy his enormous ego.

Lucky continued, "Let's have some fun," he said as he hopped over the couch and grabbed Kim and Katrina playfully. It was the beginning of a très extraordinaire orgy. Let the games begin.

Lucky held the two women at his side by their waists and pulled them to the sofa. He told Katrina to take off her panties while he positioned Kim on her back and indulged his tongue inside of her.

Katrina lay on her back, extended her legs straight up and wiggled out of her panties, slowly and seductively for the cameras.

Blue wasted no time. He motioned for Peaches to approach him with his index finger. Peaches walked around the couch, grabbed Christina by the hand, and sat her on the sofa. She stood directly in front of Blue who was mesmerized watching her move in a sensuous and slow motion. He watched lustfully as Peaches stood directly in front of Christina. She kissed her passionately, while placing her thumbs in the waistline of her turquoise panties.

Slowly, Peaches went down on Christina's body with her moist extended tongue gliding down her lovely frame as she simultaneously pulled down Christina's panties, in a wide leg squat position. Blue unbuttoned and took off his shirt. He was face-to-face with the most promiscuous sex goddess of the century.

Peaches placed her hand on Blue's chest and glided her nails on his ebony skin gently as she consumed his privates that immediate became a colossal erection. She inserted his entire forbidden fruit into her mouth, causing Blue's eyes to shoot wide open. She then withdraw his magnificent manhood slowly, then worked her way up from a wide leg squat, holding Blue's erection and looking into his eyes.

Blue still did not recognize her, which made it all the more intriguing to him. Peaches turned around and faced Christina, who was standing by Blue. Her eyes bulged in amazement at the massive size of Blue's manhood. She was even more astonished that it disappeared in Peaches' mouth.

Next, Peaches positioned Christina sitting on the couch and spread her legs wide open with her hands gently at her knees. She then stayed in the same position, placed her own legs together and pulled down her panties over her voluptuous buttocks slowly while staring into Blue's eyes. She then spread her legs and engulfed her face in Christina's femininity.

Blue walked over to Peaches holding his erect love muscle, placed his hand on her buttocks cheek, spread his legs wide, then bent slightly to inserted himself into her. He inhaled deeply though gritted teeth as he felt her resilient, hot, succulent vagina. He easily inserted himself into her all the way and smiled from ear to ear.

He placed his other hand on her other buttocks cheek, holding her lower torso firmly and started dramatically pumping into Peaches' gushing-wet vagina.

Stacey decided to beat Katrina to the punch. She hurried over with her vanilla-brown breasts bouncing and knelt between Lucky's legs and started rigorously sucking and blowing on his organ until it was extremely erect and stood out in a salute. This forced Lucky to sit straight up and enjoy his blow job.

In turn, Lucky motioned with his finger for Katrina to come over and put her pussy on his lips. She got excited and hurried over, stepping over Stacey and spreading her legs apart. Lucky grabbed her by her huge round buttocks and pulled her hips towards him, causing her knees to rest on the upper sofa. He indulged in her sensuous sexual warmth, rigorously licking and flicking her clitoris with his expert tongue.

Kim looked over at Shawn. She lay on her side with her slender athletic legs spread completely apart on the sofa with her fingers parting her vagina while she masturbated for the Internet viewers.

Kim did a slow cat crawl over to the center of the couch where Shawn was. Blue and Lucky were on opposite sides of the sofa. Shawn looked up when Kim suddenly inserted her two fingers into Shawn's vagina and started hungrily licking her clitoris and her vaginal lips. Kim's enormous, well-sculptured buttocks were lusciously projected out as she kneeled performing oral pleasure.

She was about to go in-depth when Shawn asked her to position her body in the opposite direction and place her womanhood on Shawn's lips. Meanwhile, Blue performed rigorously until Peaches' legs became tired. Next, they positioned themselves in a kneeling position on the floor. Peaches accomplished her mission when Christina began to quake and climax with a profound outburst of energy. Peaches then suggested to Blue a change of position. She positioned herself and Christina in opposite directions, with Christina lying on bottom.

Blue knelt with one knee on the couch and starting pumping slow, calculated strokes in and out of Peaches. Blue had never felt such delight from a woman's body before as he felt from indulging in Peaches' splendor.

Meanwhile, Lucky told Stacey to stand up, turn around, and sit on his erection. She complied and started pumping with intense vigor. She started moaning aloud and dramatically. Within this context, everyone was now more comfortable and totally engrossed in their enhanced sexual performance.

Blue was exhausted, but rather than surrender to Peaches' resilience, he withdrew his manhood and kissed Peaches on her buttocks. He did so gently. In admiration, he glided his hand over her buttocks like a car fanatic does a newly restored beloved automobile. He looked at himself in the monitor and smiled extensively. He then stood completely naked and walked over to Shawn and Kim.

Blue inserted his erection in Kim; she immediately looked back at him. Squinting her eyes, clenching her teeth together, she started to gallop like a champion racehorse, pounding her sexuality on his erection.

Meantime, Stacey exploded with a tremendous quiver that sent her secretions flowing down Lucky's erection. She then finished by wiggling and gyrating her vagina on Lucky's manhood, then got off and went to smoke a blunt.

Katrina immediately took the opportunity to slowly squat her dripping, moist pussy on Lucky's love muscle, then she rode his erection up and down in smooth, graceful, patient strokes—but not for long. He increased his velocity with upward thrusts that transcended Katrina's mind. She matched his rigorous performance, punctuating those now wildly erotic thrusts with screams and moans.

Kim orgasmed two times before she decided she was too exhausted and needed time to recuperate. She sprang off Blue's erection and strutted her spectacular figure across to the foyer to join in a timeout of indulging in cocaine, alcohol, and marijuana. The women watched the performance on the monitors totally engrossed, and it was almost as fascinating as being the performing co-stars.

Blue changed position to where he was sitting on the couch and Shawn was sitting on top of him, inserting all his pleasure into her with every stroke. This position also provided a better constant visual of the erection going in and out of Shawn's extravagant vagina. The monitor showed as Shawn's juices flowed sensuously down Blue's love muscle.

Peaches led Christina by the hand over to where Blue was. She instructed Christina that she wanted her to lie on her back on the floor and suckle on her genitals.

Christina was ever enthusiastic, however, she didn't know when to position the camcorders on the right side of the sofa for a lower-level viewing of all the action on the sofa from the ground up, in a centered position. Peaches was already on her knees with her legs spread wide open, sucking and licking on Blue's sacs. Christina lay down on her back and positioned her face under Peaches' privates.

"Give it to me, baby," Peaches said as she kneeled, her legs wide open and waiting. At the same time, Christina massaged her own clitoris with her open fingertips. Her shaven pubic area enhanced the small genital jewels immensely. Blue and Lucky both were admiring themselves on the monitors until their attention gravitated to Christina. She looked succulent, precious, luscious. Katrina and Shawn were now facing each other with a look of pure ecstasy on their faces.

They then increased their pumps into a rigorous gallop to see who could orgasm the fastest. Peaches moved vigorously, in upward and downward motions, shaking and clapping her buttocks cheeks for the entertainment of the surly-by-now-spellbound viewers. Blue lay back, enjoying Peaches' craft of excellence while keeping his hands on Shawn's hips and maintaining focus.

Meantime, Lucky grabbed Katrina by her buttocks with both hands and fiercely stroked upward into her luscious, throbbing cushion. Katrina grabbed the back of his head with both hands, squeezing her soft cleavage into his face and climaxed vigorously, her moans filled with intensity and animal passion. Joining in the fashion of the rest of the ladies, she kissed Lucky passionately, then strutted over to join the festivities with the other ladies.

Shawn had already orgasmed a few times and started getting a leg cramp, so she withdrew the pleasure muscle out of her, got on the floor, and stretched.

Lucky went over on his side, positioning his lower torso under Christina's genitals. He glanced at the monitor to see that the camera was in perfect position for his perfect performance. He slowly thrust his incredible erection into Christina's pleasurably tight vagina. Christina stopped consuming Peaches' juices and lay out flat like a virgin under the pressure of Lucky's powerful thrusts. She closed her eyes and almost pierced her nails into the floor, trying to endure his passion.

Peaches gazed up at Blue and moved slightly towards Christina's direction—that said everything. She quickly grabbed Shawn's hand and hauled her off the scene. She purposely left Christina with the wolves and stood back and observed her performance. Blue understood Peaches' hint, reached down, and grabbed Christina by the hand. Christina looked relieved, feeling like she was being rescued.

However, when she stood up and came to her senses, she realized she was the only subject left to face a sexual massacre. She was dreadfully terrified, facing two colossal-sized penises in front of her. She was about to surrender, however, Peaches saw the indecision she was going through and vindictively started to cheer her on with what seemed like loveable enthusiasm.

"Go, Christina Han Lu, you're the star," Peaches said, clapping. She smiled almost to the point of erupting in laughter. The other ladies joined in as her supportive cast. Christina was forced to perform her noble duties and represent her sex's gender.

She reluctantly took Blue's hand and positioned herself over him and inserted his monstrous erection inside her. She moaned and groaned in agony as she felt his strokes literally spreading her hips apart. Lucky sat right next to Blue. Christina kept her performance tasteful for the viewing audience that was constantly logging on, setting a Web site record.

Meantime, Lucky grabbed Christina by her hair and lowered her head down to his hips and inserted his erection into her mouth. To his surprise, she removed his hand from the base of his penis and replaced it with hers. She started performing oral sex on him exceptionally well. She even increased her vigor in pumping her vagina full of sumptuous flesh.

The fulfilling mass caused her mind to generate a constant reflex of orgasms and secretions that helped her vagina endure the constant pummeling. The more rigorous Blue thrust his love muscle into Christina, the more vigorous she sucked Lucky deep into her throat. One action took her mind off the tension of the other. She breathed intensely through her nose like a raging bull. She was caught in a paradoxical dilemma of excruciating pain. At the same time, it was also invigoratingly pleasurable.

Lucky and Blue were passionately grasping her buttocks and her breasts. They were delighted with Christina's remarkable performance. What made it so much more interesting was how impeccable Christina's performance was on the monitor. Even though they were trying to take advantage of her, she managed to look radiantly beautiful and seductive.

Christina held her commanding dominance and kept her poised demeanor. It was the birth of a soon-to-be porn superstar. She felt every bit of their masculinity throbbing in her. She wanted to enter the event, so she got on her knees between them, and motioned with her hands, beckoning them to come on for more.

Lucky knew what to do. He turned his side where the cameras could get a clear shot from all angles, and began to masturbate. Blue got the hint and did the same. Lucky exploded with a groan. His juices erupted into Christina's eyes and mouth. Tears streamed down her face along with the erotic secretion. Blue also positioned himself so he could allow his juices of pleasure to erupt into Christina's mouth. He brandished his sex organ like a fire hose and squirted all over Christina's face.

Their sexual secretions and her tears oozed slowly down her face, setting the mood for their outlandish encounter. She got up, composed her strut, even more confident than ever as all the promiscuous ladies had to gaze at her in sheer admiration. She represented her promiscuous femininity to the fullest, yet kept her poise. A star was born.

A few moments later, she appeared back in the foyer with a towel, wiping her face off. The ladies immediately congregated around Christina, being supportive with hugs and kisses.

"Baby, I knew you could do it. You were fabulous," Peaches said as she handed Christina a glass of champagne.

Lucky went off and looked at the rating on his laptop. "Hey, y'all. Superstar set my Web site record with 153,000 hits," he said enthusiastically. He hurried and disappeared into the kitchen, then came back to the foyer with two bottles of Krug. Using a corkscrew, he popped it open and poured everyone a glass. Peaches brought Blue a glass, who was still sitting on the couch and was contented, viewing himself in all his glory on the monitor. He contemplated his outrageous performance in front of over 150,000 fans.

Lucky walked over to the sofa and stood behind Blue. "Come on, y'all," Lucky said. He motioned for all the ladies to appear on camera. Once everyone was in the footage, Lucky began. "I'd like to thank everyone that viewed this, as well as the entire cast of stars in the film for making this happen.

"For any DVDs or fan mail to any of the stars, please e-mail me at my e-mail address. Cheers to everyone that made this possible, or better yet, this cheer is to SEX." He hoisted his glass, then tapped it against Blue's glass. With a gulp, he polished off the golden amber liquid.

All the ladies cheered and toasted to SEX.

34 *Ricky*

I sat in my bedroom and after weeks, I was still intrigued by the videotape I'd found at Popi's house. I was dumfounded by the fact that Popi was an informant and was involved with a major drug transaction with the Dekalb County Law Enforcement Department. The tape stopped rewinding, and I pushed play again. The conspiracy fascinated me, but I wanted to analyze my Hispanic accomplice that had deceived me for years.

"Baby, here's your cell phone," Lisa said.

"Lisa, the phone is on silent for a reason," I replied, as she tossed the cell phone on the bed and went back to watching a soap opera in the other bedroom. I did not want to be bothered, but I knew better than not to trust a woman's intuition.

I answered the phone. "Yeah."

I was greeted with a mellow accent on the other end. There was no sense of emotional response in Richard's voice. He just asked me what time I could meet him.

"Give me a couple hours. I'll be there," I said, finishing inputting the address into my I-phone.

He hung up before I did. He was not that talkative, however, when he was, it was pleasant and charismatic. My intuition made me really want to see this comrade, partly because we both were captives in the belly of the beast at the bottom of hell, incarcerated in a Babylonian jail cell—at least, that's how I felt.

I quickly showered and dried off with a Polo beach towel. Standing naked in front of the mirror, I tied my long locks in the back in a knot to keep them out of my face. Then I grabbed my Turbo jet clippers and trimmed all the facial hair off my face, except for two thin narrow sideburns. Next came a quick spray of deodorant, hair moisturizer, and a little Aveeno oatmeal treatment for my skin.

Walking into the master bedroom, I pulled out a pair of Blackberry underwear and black DKNY socks and tank top. From the closet came a pair of black Yushua slacks and a black Yushua dress shirt with the two top buttons unbuttoned, then I slipped into my Yushua shoes.

The final touch came from my AIR cologne, then I put on my all-black metallic Versace platinum watch with bezel-set round diamonds, which was complemented by my diamond pinky ring on my left hand and my other platinum diamond ring on the middle finger.

Not be be forgotten, I grabbed my .50-caliber automatic that was in its holster and clipped it in my waistline, and then put on my Yushua belt. All set, I walked into the other bedroom to give my lady a gentle kiss on her sweet lips and walked outside the door where I leisurely made my way to my Mercedes-Benz.

When I hopped in and started the car, Goodie Mob's "Cell Therapy" came on. Turning the music down moderately, I proceeded on my journey. Soon I exited Roswell Road and followed the navigation system directions to my destination. When I arrived at the location, I was surprised to see that Richard stayed in such a prominent neighborhood. I drove up and parked on the mosaics wrapped around three Silver Saw Palmetto palm trees in the driveway. I parked directly in front of the Georgian-style establishment. The garage and front doors were made of carved Teakwood imported from Thailand.

As I approached the front door and rang the doorbell, I noticed the surveillance camera and the motion censors focused on me. The door was opened by a beautiful butler with pecan-brown skin. She was a native Brazilian, a young woman who was flawless in appearance. She invited me in. I stepped in and was immediately impressed with the elegance of the interior decorations.

The interior was modern contemporary with a lot of oak wood finish. The three master bedroom suites were luxurious. What stood out the most to me was the hot tub in the exact center of the living room with a circle of colorful mosaics and an Old World complete oak wood bar, five yards directly in front of it. The rooms were designed with a tropical flavor, and it had cathedral ceilings and an enormous Jamaican flag on the wall, directly across from the foyer. I followed behind my gorgeous hostess whose magnificent, well-defined rear was revealed through her black Yushua dress.

I passed by two vicious-looking young men, possibly in their teens. They sat at opposite ends of the sofa with an icy demeanor, stone-cold faces, and cruel eyes, watching a Jamaican broadcast network by satellite. They were smoking their own separate Bob Marley hemp paper-rolled joints that replaced the aroma of Lancôme Paris Teson fragrance with a redolent of a vibrant fruity marijuana scent.

First, I walked past the one with dreadlocks and then the other fellow with the braids. They were stern and did not budge. The sexy diva led me through a hallway with pictures of Bob Marley, Peter Tosh, Marcus Garvey, Malcolm X, and Nelson Mandela.

Finally, we entered a room that looked like a media room with a large 63-inch plasma TV displaying three channels at the same time. One channel broadcasted a Jamaican satellite transmitted station, one channel had world news, and the History Channel was on the bigger screen.

Once I stepped in, I noticed a reserved Richard with his Gucci wide frame sunglasses on. He was also dressed in all black, except he was in Armani exchange pajamas and Gucci slippers. I could see he was not an enthusiastic person or good at formal greetings by the way he just sat there and did not budge when I approached.

"Spraggs, your company is here," the beautiful butler said and walked out.

I went and had a seat on the black suede sofa that curved around the entire back wall. Spraggs, a.k.a. Richard, was doing great since the last time I saw him. I was beginning to relax and watch the news that periodically switched to the surveillance cameras around the house.

"You like jewelry?" he said. I nodded, not looking at him but watching the news footage. He tossed a jewelry box into my lap.

Curiously, I opened it to see what was inside. It was magnificent. It was an Audemars Piguet Jules Audemars Tourbillon Chronograph watch, a true masterpiece of haute horlogerie.

"Thank you," I said as I immediately slipped it in my pocket.

I remember watching the news once about a recent jewelry heist in Buckhead for over 5 million dollars in exquisite watches and jewelry. I wondered, then I thought, *Nah, not this guy.*

My eyes looked back at the TV, and I viewed my immaculate Benz glimmering on its 22-inch rims on the monitor. After the History Channel went off, Spraggs got up and exited the room. I watched his movements out of the corner of my eye. He moved with grace and elegance. His manner exuded supreme confidence. He returned in some soft leather Yushua slippers and a Yushua leather gun holster. I could see the muzzle and handle of his two side-by-sides black and gold-plated .357 automatic Magnums. He picked up an elegant black, gold, and white Versace robe.

"You ready?" he asked. I nodded my head in agreement and followed his lead. We walked in the opposite direction from where I came in and exited through a decorative wooden door that matched the Teakwood front door of his house. It immediately brought us to a four-car garage.

The garage was organized impeccably with twenty-gauge, steel modular cabinets and accessories. The floors were black and gray tiles. Bright lighting automatically lit up once we walked in, where some expensive wheels were parked. Two motorcycles, GSX-R Hayabusa Hybrid, Gixxer Fame were parked, along with a black Porsche Cheyenne SUV and a Rolls Royce. Spraggs went to the trunk of the Rolls Royce and took out a bottle of Cristal.

While approaching me, he popped the cork and drank a sip directly from the bottle, then he passed it to me. I gladly obliged and drank to the fact that the supreme spirits had blessed us. After all, I did meet this guy in hell, and now we had both elevated to a heavenly state. I began to see my attraction to him. He had a genuine spirit, and his demeanor must be from the trauma that happened in his life. Like a gangster of supreme eminence, he strolled to the driver's side of his Royce with his long robe open in a poised fashion. I got in after him. I couldn't help watching his radiant charismatic demeanor.

The interior of the car was extravagantly designed of wood veneer with an indigo red monogram color scheme. He opened the glove compartment and inside was a smaller red leather cigar compartment. I opened it to see a Yushua cigar and a glass cigar container with a green and white resin all around it. The tub was filled with what looked like a cluster of green and white cotton balls, what they called "Hydro Entertain Ganja," the most extraordinary marijuana in the world.

"This for me?" I asked with enthusiasm.

Spraggs gently nodded his head, "Yes."

I eagerly grabbed the tube and opened it, inhaled the divine aroma, and poured two cottonlike balls of marijuana into my hand. I marveled in astonishment. The beauty of the enchanted substance almost brought tears to my eyes. It looked too beautiful to be smoked, however, somebody got to do it.

I grabbed the cigar and a platinum cigar cutter with the conveniently engineered little scissors at the end. It made me wonder why I didn't have one. It made me wonder why I didn't have a lot of things. Anyway, I rolled the cigar nice and sleek.

Afterwards, I raised the champagne bottle to my mouth, drank another mouthful, and passed the bottle to Spraggs, who was driving with his left hand on the steering wheel, reclined in his seat, leaning to the side where he could pay attention to the passenger and the road visuals at the same time. He took the bottle back, sipped, and placed the bottle between his legs, still holding the top.

Then I lit my blunt and took my first puff. I relished the taste before I exhaled. Next, I slightly reclined my seat, observed Spraggs, who was observing me through his dark sunglasses, through my limousine-tinted passenger-side window. After the second puff, I was forced to put out the blunt. The potency was too high.

My mind had already transcended to a higher realm of concentration. The luxurious, rare automobile rode so smoothly that if I were blind, I wouldn't have known if we were moving or sitting still. Finally, we arrived at an industrial warehouse. Spraggs pushed a button on a remote control device and electronically opened the security gate.

We parked in front of a midsized, 40 feet high and 12,000-square foot warehouse. Then we exited the car. I guess no one worked on Sunday because the industrial complex was empty. He entered an access code and walked inside, but his back blocked my view the entire time. Then he immediately entered the code into his security system to turn off the alarm.

We walked through an office with two functioning laptops on a half moon-shaped oak desktop. The office had a 42-inch plasma TV mounted on the wall and a fluffy, bright tangerine-cushioned sofa in the center, directly across from the monitor.

The office desk had two comfortable-looking, tangerine-colored leather office chairs in front of the desk, and an upgraded tangerine declinable, massage lumbar leather office chair. The five file cabinets behind the desk had European-style oak veneer that matched the desk. The light automatically lit up once we stepped through the door.

I followed Spraggs through the office, through a side door into the spacious 12,000-square feet warehouse area. Those lights automatically came on too as I walked side by side with Spraggs, who walked with purpose. The champagne was still in his hand as we strutted towards the back.

Two brand-new Mercedes-Benz tractor trailers stood in the warehouse. We stopped when we reached some mattresses leaning against the wall. To my surprise, Spraggs took out an extraordinary fly knife made from ivory, natural pearl, titanium, and platinum. It had diamonds and gemstones embedded down the side of it. This move called for my drastic attention.

He twirled the knife in one hand like a magic wand until the blade magically appeared in the blink of eye. Next, he cut the plastic off the mattress in stern militant fashion. He then pulled down the standing mattress from the standing pile of mattresses to the warehouse floor, where he then inserted the knife on the top edge of the mattress and cut his way around the top until he almost reached its starting incision. He did the same flick of the wrist trick to conceal the blade, and then placed it back into his pocket. With his work completed, he took a sip of the bottle of Cristal.

"You still the monster hustler you said you were?" he asked in an articulate manner as he reached down.

"Yeah, but I—" I suddenly stopped when I saw him pull the cover back, revealing fluffy bags upon bags of beautiful, exotic marijuana. The charming vision made me forget my words.

"Can you handle a shipment of 5,000 pounds a month?" he asked.

"Huh?" I replied stupidly. I was still mesmerized by the sight. I quickly counted about one hundred pounds in that mattress and looked over the hundreds of mattress in the warehouse.

"Yeah, whatever you say," I said. Unconsciously, I contemplated my options.

"Okay. I'll have my driver deliver a shipment to your business location tomorrow," he said.

Did I hear him right? Did he just say he was going to give me 5,000 pounds on consignment?

"Just figure out where you want the shipment delivered and how you're going to come up with my $2,000 for every pound."

Yep, that what he said.

As he stood there speaking like a general officer, I came to realize two things about Spraggs. One was that he bordered that extremely thin line between genius and insanity, and two, he had balls the size of Jupiter.

He finished his proposal and strolled towards the exit. I wanted to reassure him that I was confident I could handle the load. However, I had the impression he would much rather see the results. He was a man of action. I think that's our similarity. We both get the job done. I just clasped my hands together and walked, scarcely able to believe my good fortune. On our way back to his residence, I could not do anything but ponder on the magnificent responsibilities that lay ahead.

I loved the fact that I was going to be spreading a substance that was helpful and beneficial, instead of a substance that induced hate, treachery, deceit, envy, misery, and every other sinister deed known to man.

I relished the fact that I was blessed with the present opportunity to spread love, not war, and with the quality of this product, I was going to be able to capitalize on $2,000–$8,000 on every pound. That translates to millions of dollars of profit on the first shipment. I wanted to laugh and cheer and yell in ecstasy, however, I maintained my composure, just like the resolute general.

Back in the car, Spraggs, who still had his hand on his Cristal bottle resting snugly in his crotch, leaned back, arms fully extended, with his back slightly leaning against the driver's side door. He looked like he was doing a little contemplating himself. We arrived at his residence so quickly, I was somewhat surprised. The ride seemed timeless. It seemed to be over almost before it began. He drove directly in front of my car and stopped.

I realized that he was concluding our meeting. I knew better, but I still reached over to give him a handshake. However, he just gently nodded with a pleasant smile that said it all. That was good enough for me. I got my blunt, opened the door, and stepped out. I looked back at him. He was watching me. I slightly bowed my head graciously, paying homage to the great man, before I stood erect and closed the door. He disappeared behind the limousine tint. I strutted to my car, while he drove around his circle driveway and entered his garage.

I lit my blunt before I drove off. My relaxed mood soon turned into anxiety as I was driving along the expressway. I thought of how I met Spraggs. I reflected over the manner in which everything happened, the Popi incident, and my pregnant lady, my court cases, my dope I entrusted to Lucky, and my intriguing life, in general. Then slight paranoia struck my nerves. My mind began to roam with fears.

Spraggs might be with the Feds trying to set me up. Popi must have informed the Feds on me. Lisa was probably not even pregnant. She might just be faking it, and if she were pregnant, maybe the baby isn't even mine. That degenerate, incompetent piece of scum, Pans, was going to make me have to spend the next 3 to 10 years of my life in prison.

I bet Lucky fucked up on that dope. Even worse, he probably got busted and informed on me. I looked down on the long ash on the tip of the blunt I hadn't puffed since I left Spraggs' establishment. *Damn, this the greatest marijuana that I ever smoked.* It took my mind to the farthest region of the galaxy.

I took another puff and thought it through. I came up with the notion that Spraggs was a miraculous encounter because if he were with the Feds, he wouldn't give a kind-hearted, ebony man a chance to get extremely rich and powerful with a substance that wouldn't destroy his community, and if he were, it was already too late to back out now anyway. Even if Popi did inform the law enforcers who I was, I stumbled on enough evidence to crumble their entire conspiracy.

What was I thinking? Lisa worshipped the ground I walked on. She knew I was genuine, so I respected the fact she always was genuine. Pans was going to get a poisonous restitution for his sins against me, and by time I got to court, I would be so wealthy, if they tried to give me a plea bargain I could not bear, I'd just migrate to a country where they couldn't touch me, like Cuba.

Or better yet, I'd buy my way out of the satanic council of this jurisdictional system, with corrupt lawyers and law enforcement, whose only proposal was to impose their will and manipulate free-minded people for their capital gain. I knew Lucky was going to be exceptional as my under boss, and his loyalty over the years had shown no blemish of treason.

I just needed to relax, to have a peaceful mind and a positive outlook on everything, and everything will eventually be positive. I did not want to return to the house yet, so I decide to exit off at McDaniel Street and drive down until I reach the Greyhound Station. Then I parked across the street at Magic City Parking Lot. I left my new watch in the car's glove compartment along with my gun and strolled to the club's entrance. After the usually frisking and identification presentation, I walked into the club.

Once I made it in, I was assailed by three exotic, voluptuously curved lovely ladies. "Do you want a dance or two or three or from one of us or all three?" they offered. I remained quiet and swaggered to the bar. They scurried from my presence to another client coming through the entrance. I admired the beautiful ladies shaking and doing their seductive dance routine. Their naked bodies aroused me and captured my attention as I took a seat at the bar.

Young Jeezy and Bomb "We getting money over here ... what it do pimpin'?" then Gucci Mane, "Freaky Girl," came on and everyone erupted in enthusiastic excitement. I had not been to the club in about a year, being so busy. I was captivated by these people having such energy. The bartender approached me in a G-string that really should be called a string because it parted her vagina lips and hid nothing, and her big nipples that sat erect on her voluptuous, firm, D cup breasts were totally exposed.

"What you drinking?" she said with a beautiful smile that would land her in King magazine.

"Let me have a bottle of Cristal," I replied.

She slightly nodded her head, while pouting her lips in an alluring style and seductive manner. She came over and popped the bottle for everyone to see, then poured me a glass. I handed her my platinum American Express, snatched the bottle, which caused her to look intensely into my eyes, and said, "You keep the glass and drink to yourself."

She slightly nodded in homage and strutted off, throwing her hips extra seductively. I couldn't help but admire her marvelous, plump, magnificent buttocks.

After a moment, I also put the bottle to my mouth and drank to her remarkable figure. As a matter of fact, I looked around the room and saw that she was just one out of a hundred remarkable ebony bodies decorating the establishment. I took another swig to all the beautiful sensuous bodies in the club and in the world. She returned and handed me my credit card.

I took the receipt, signed it, and left her a five tip and strutted off, enjoying the atmosphere and all those pretty little things that delight the eye. Casually, I strolled towards the VIP room, slowly grooving to the rhythm of the bass, periodically sipping on my bottle of champagne. Ladies constantly approached me, exposing their bodies. I blatantly ignored their erotic antics and continued my strut until I reached the VIP room and entered, where the *real* party was.

All the exotic dancers were performing their best for the superstar entertainers, the drug dealers, and the entrepreneurs. I went and took a seat in a secluded area and slouched down. A beautiful young woman approached me, looking like Beyonce Knowles, and asked me if I wanted a dance. I was so tired of refusing all the sexy women that I decided to please my sexual appetite for a few meager dollars. This babe was stunningly beautiful, and her sinewy body would certainly appeal to me. I graciously nodded a yes response.

"Okay," she yelled in a cheerful outburst. She made haste getting out her Yushua G string outfit and started bouncing her breasts and enormous buttocks rigorously to the record label Cash Money's Hot Boys, "We on Fire."

Another sleek, dark, ebony lady was strutting her radiant body across the room with poise. She had thin athletic-type legs with a colossal round torso. This beauty had a definite six-pack in her abdomen, and her breasts resembled C-cup pears. When she looked over, I motioned for her to come to me with my index finger. She strutted over, completely naked, and the closer she got, the more adorable she became. She approached me, and I motioned with an extended open hand in a constant upward movement for her to dance.

She came within touching distance, turned around, and put one hand on her hip. Then slowly, exquisitely, she bent over and touched the ground with her fingers while her legs stood straight. Getting into her groove, she spread her legs far apart, exposing her thick vaginal lips and widespread buttocks cheeks. She started bouncing her buttocks up and down in a fierce shake and rubbed and grinded her luscious flesh on me as I indulged in my lust.

Another lady joined the party and started a slow grind to the music. The girl's body looked like an exact replica of a young Jennifer Lopez, except her breasts were bigger and she had a darker, tropical skin. She was gracefully seductive and danced in a smooth, rhythmic groove like a belly dancer. They were all beautiful and aroused me, just watching them as they entertained me. I lit up my blunt and vibed to Triple Six Mafia's, "I Gotta Stay Fly."

The ladies were displaying their exotic dancing talents while being social, for the most part, even though they were professional harlots. And the more I smoked, the more intrigued I got. The outstanding beauty of my seductresses, the marijuana, and alcohol had me in a mellow mood. Everything was moving slow and enchanting. UGK's "Let Me See It" came on and the bass started quaking the atmosphere.

The four ladies burst into energetic excitement. Succulent breasts and luscious buttocks were being bounced, shaken, and flaunted with sensuous intensity. The server even brought another bottle of Cristal. I gave her my credit card and told her to charge everything on it. The ladies were spectacular. We were all drinking. I was smoking my blunt. They were using their seductive charms to make me feel like an Egyptian Pharaoh. Their submissive, exotic behavior pleasured my male egotistical lust for dominance. I stared at each one of them and every inch of their bodies with feral intensity.

The sexual stimulation entered my psyche, which invigorated my entire body into a highly aroused state. I was almost in utopia. Suddenly the disk jockey announced, "YMS in the building."

All the ladies immediately stopped and became attentive, looking towards the VIP entrance. Needless to say, I was also captivated by the moment. After all, these were the most blatant, radical, renowned gangsters to hit Atlanta since Terry White.

Their leader, a tall, handsome, charismatic tyrant, stepped to the center. He stood firm with his legs apart and his hands in his pockets. He was wearing all-black Yushua clothing and pitch-black wide frame sunglasses. He absorbed his admirers' energy, then his hands erupted from his pockets high into the air, tossing hundreds of one-hundred dollar bills into the air that drifted down toward the earth's gravitational pull like confetti.

Their entrance that caused everyone to pause and take notice was interrupted by the enthusiastic bum rush of lovely ladies. They flocked to the leader that went by his rightful title "Lord," and he just stood majestically as the elegant nude ladies greeted him and threw themselves at him.

The server brought me my electronic receipt to sign. I took my card and put it back into my pocket, but I stayed sitting, slouched in my seat, observing the ladies' fanatical behavior. I took another sip from my bottle of Cristal and enjoyed the view. Soon, I put the half-empty bottle on the table, placed my blunt in my mouth, stood up, poised, and walked out in a groovy sway induced by the combination of potent marijuana and fine alcohol.

There were gangsters in black everywhere, flaunting money like the 1920s stock market. I stepped outside into a spectacle of extravagant proportion. While walking to my car, I saw a black 1956 Chevrolet Bel Air on 22-inch spinners, a Benz CL65 AMG on 22-inch spinners, and a Ferrari. Even a young gangster was out there, showing off, riding on the driver's side windowsill while operating a black and blue Bugatti Veyron EB 16.4, every tooth in his mouth decorated with diamonds and platinum.

The gangsters' ladies were everywhere, wearing provocative, scandalous garments. They were drinking alcoholic beverages, smoking Hydro, and even snorting cocaine. Lust was reigning in the darkness. People were dancing, masturbating, groping, sucking, and getting sexually penetrated in the parking lot just like at Woodstock decades ago.

I sat in my car and watched a black Mercedes-Benz CLK GTR Roadster convertible with the top down on 20-inch spinners and a black Lamborghini Gallardo SE on 22-inch floaters doing simultaneous donuts in opposite directions that gave the glittering, lustrous chrome rims a hypnotic glare. I was infatuated with seeing real individuals united, becoming successful in a monstrous way.

The rumors I had heard were probably factual. They were supplying the entire major market on the East Coast. Where would they be getting over a million kilos of cocaine? In addition, why were they so blatant and open about the extortions and illegal transactions?

Surely their extravagantly flamboyant lifestyle and blatant money laundering induced the U.S. government to secretly investigate them in order to indict them. There had to be was some kind of conspiracy to topple their criminal organization by now. Yet, they had been thriving for years. This was suspicious, but their extraordinary lavish lifestyle was drawing a mass of prominent entrepreneurs in as bait. Everyone wanted some of the action.

It was time to get as far away as possible from this scene because when this one unfolded, it was going to be a political massacre of intriguing proportions. As I was driving down the parking lot, two headlights approached on Suzuki Hayabusa GSX-R1100 superbikes. The Gixxer frame on the bikes were covered with 24-carat gold, with gold-plated spinner back wheels and spectacular rotating rims which captured the eye.

These bikes left streaks of sparks on the pavement. Other bikes zoomed past my car simultaneously, adding more dramatics for observing spectators. If these comrades were genuinely authentic, they had a beautiful thing going—an extravagantly beautiful thing going.

Chapter 35 Blue

Blue closed the door to his new four-bedroom house, which had two master bedrooms. His estate was located in Snellville, and it was lavishly decorated in a European style and furnished in modern contemporary furniture. The interior of his house was equipped with the latest state-of-the-art technology. Like an aristocrat used to such luxury, he strutted down a long walkway that led to his blue-jay colored chariot with a small black Yushua traveling bag and his car keys in his hand.

His car was a brand-new Cadillac Escalade that was customized on 28-inch floaters that dropped to a lowrider with a Lamborghini front and suicide opening Lamborghini doors. He vanished inside the car camouflaged by blue transparent windows and relaxed in the cush seat.

Dressed in his usual leisure attire, consisting of a black Yushua long johns top and his Babe and Apes sneakers, he placed his left hand on the steering wheel, and couldn't help but admire the light reflecting off his platinum and blue diamond-clustered watch.

He started his car and drove from his secluded 13-acre estate. Breathing deeply, a sigh of admiration escaped his lips as eyes gazed over this property that he co-owned with Stephen.

Steven was his partner. They had established a corporation consisting of a chain of Laundromats, which included 32 cleaners, Blue's catering service, a laundry delivery service, and dry cleaning services. The corporation was thriving.

He put his bag on the passenger seat and picked up his one-hundred-round Calico M960 9mm off the floor from behind his passenger seat. As usual, he rode with his finger on the trigger. As soon as he exited the tranquil subdivision, he turned up the volume on the sound system. Cash Money's B.G., "It's All on U," volume 2, came on booming. His two Infinity 15-inch speakers vibrated dramatically from the trunk throughout the interior of the car, penetrating even deeply into his soul.

Blue's satellite 15-inch, front adjustable TV played a MTV rap video at the same time. Next, he lit his already-rolled purple haze blunt and inhaled deeply. Soon he arrived at the complex where his legacy started. Now, he and his comrade literally lorded over this place.

Pulling in front of the complex, he parked. A massive 285-pound ex-convict escorted him from his car with his bag and fully loaded Calico in his hand. The complex had armed guards posted in locations at both ends of the street, with gangster-enforced security stationed all around the facility. His bodyguard opened the door, and they walked in past a frail-looking, skinny dread head who was only about 13 year old, but who diligently guarded the door, armed with a SK 47 with an extended banana clip.

He met Lil' Pee in the rear of the apartment where he and Jasmine were sitting on the couch, smoking a sleek green Optimo embedded with exotic Indian hash. Blue approached Lil' Pee and handed him the bag, then looked over at the 42-inch plasma television. The big screen was on the Business Channel and the small screen in the bottom corner was on CNN headline news. Lil' Pee was looking on the blue caption readout of the stocks update going across the screen.

"My one million dollars' worth of soybean stocks are doing great," he said with an extremely serious face that came from years of street survival as a hard-working hoodlum. Jasmine gazed at Lil' Pee in pure admiration, leaned over, and kissed him on the cheeks, glowing with sincere infatuation.

Blue leered at Jasmine. His eyebrow rose in intrigue as he unabashedly looked over this sensuous supermodel, taking in every inch of her form. Her Versace two-piece short skirt and halter top complimented her sumptuous curves. Her pecan-brown skin was soft and delicate, her bright radiant face was free of blemishes from a vegetarian diet. Her raven-black hair was lustrous, long, and hung with body down to her shoulders.

Blue's sensuous thoughts were interrupted when Lil' Pee led him into the second bedroom that had been converted into an office. Comfortable leather sofas lined the walls and a Nova sofa bed with chrome legs stood near the window.

An 8-foot wide center table 18 inches off the ground stood near the sofas. The center of it had a gigantic electronic universal digital scale embedded in its cherry oak. Then they closed the metal security enforced doors on their complex.

Safely nestled inside the secured cocoon, Lil' Pee sat on the leather couch, unzipped the bag, and tossed kilo after kilo on the table. Blue walked to the center of the room as if he were the chairperson in a business conference overseeing the transaction. In a sense, he was since this was an illegitimate corporation conducting its affairs.

"Pee, we're about to take this thing to a higher level. I'm about to get 1,000 pounds of exotic hydro-green, which'll change the game, cuz. You know you're my ace man, and I want you to oversee this operation. We're about to purchase a two-story brick building in midtown Atlanta. I'm telling you we're about to sell weed like they do in Holland. As a matter of fact, I'm going to call the building 'Amsterdam.'

"I'm going to have all different types of green and smoke shops, and whatever type of exotic weed cannabis we need. I even got this old secluded hotel on 15 square acres of private property with a 12-foot metal security fence that encloses the property. I say we build a brick fence around the building to conceal our operation and install some high-tech security cameras to observe everything from a satellite. You know what I mean?" Blue said, looking straightforward, keeping everything in his peripheral vision.

After all the cocaine was on the table, he looked over at the digital scale readout, which showed 10,115 grams.

"What about the police?" Lil' Pee asked.

"Man, we do what we usually do—pay them off or pay the man over them to get them off of us. I already have the top superintendent in my pocket, you hear me?" Blue said, turning around to kneel on the couch and look through the window blinds that had galvanized, reinforced steel bars guarding the window. Lil' Pee was still standing loading kilos into the traveling bag, one at a time. Blue observed a red Kawasaki Ninja 650R and a blue Vulcan 900.

The customized bikes had silencers on the mufflers. Blue watched as the red Kawasaki zoomed and parked facing his direction and then the blue Vulcan did the same, zooming quickly into a slanted turn maneuver. In the blink of an eye, the riders sat up with their legs spread wide apart to balance the bike they were sitting on while they clutched two S-M8 Airsoft Spring Sniper Rifles. Blue's eyes opened dramatically as he yelled, "DUCK!" and dropped flat on his stomach. Lil' Pee turned his head and looked at him in an inquisitive manner. It was a bad mistake.

"Wha—" he said before he was riddled with bullets. His head hit the table, then he hit the floor with a thud.

The S-M8s blazed furiously, spitting out a rapid, nonstop bombardment on their establishment. The assailants only stopped when their clips were all empty. The security engaged the assailants in a firefight, however, they managed to ride away from the onslaught.

Blue jumped up after they ceased firing and positioned his weapon through the shattered glass window. He fired a blaze of rapid rounds, with bullets popping out of the release chambers. However, the assailants were too fast, and he was too late. Furious, he spun around and noticed Lil' Pee lay sprawled on his stomach. Blue hurried over to his comrade, picked him up, and hoisted him over his shoulder. Someone pounded on the door.

Blue looked in the mounted security camera monitor on the wall next to the door and saw it was Jasmine in a severe state of panic. He input the security code and the door opened. Jasmine saw Lil' Pee's limp body hanging over Blue's shoulder like a bloody sack of potatoes, his Yushua shirt soaked in blood. She burst into violent sobs, throwing her hands on her head in disbelief.

Ignoring her, Blue swiftly passed her and walked with his wounded comrade over his shoulder and his weapon aimed in front of him. The front door was wide open as his hoodlum security force moved frantically into position to cover them. He tossed his unconscious friend in the car. Meanwhile, Jasmine regained her mental composure and hopped into the backseat. She leaned over and held the head of her beloved gently, caressing him like a newborn infant. She sobbed and spoke encouraging words in his ears. Blue raced to the Dekalb County Hospital yelling with passion, "Mutherfucker, don't you dare die on me." Adrenaline pumped through his veins.

Jasmine stayed on her knees, with her voluptuous buttocks projecting like a rare, exotic hippo. She kept cuddling his head and kissing him continuously the entire way to the hospital.

Blue made a sudden sharp turn, burning rubber, and parked directly in front of the emergency room entrance, then sprang from the car while his Lamborghini doors were still rising. He ran to the passenger seat, grabbed his comrade out of Jasmine's grasp by his Cargo shirt collar, and hoisted him over his shoulder once again. With Lil' Pee secured, he ran through the electronic glass doors, raced to the front counter, and lay his wounded comrade on the counter before astonished eyes.

"I need a doctor now, *now*," he yelled. His outburst got the attention of the entire waiting room.

The clerk got on the phone and called for emergency assistance at her desk. Before she hung up, a medical technician made haste to arrive with a gurney and assisted Blue in transferring Lil' Pee's unconscious body on it. The technician then immediately whisked Lil' Pee into the emergency room, where a doctor and his assistant awaited them.

Moments later, the doctor came out into the waiting room and called for any family member of Lil' Pee. Blue identified himself as he hurried over to the physician. The doctor explained about the seriousness of his patient's condition. Blue grabbed the doctor by the arm, pulled him close, and spoke *sotto* voce in his ear. "He dies, *you* die." Blue was serious, staring at the doctor, who broke free from his grasp, assuming the emotional outburst was caused by emotional distress. However, subconsciously, he intuitively took the statement seriously.

Blue's cell phone rang. It was one of the guards who informed Blue that they had seen Big Mo leading the assailants in his Chevy Denali with the 26-inch gold-plated rims.

Blue hung up immediately when he found out who the culprit was that instigated the onslaught. He was glad to have an opportunity to vent his rage on someone. He immediately turned and hurried to his car. His face was cold and cruel. His teeth were clenched so hard that his jaws ached. Blue was a dangerous man, filled with rage and seeking vengeance.

Jumping into the car, he raced away from the hospital, the Cadillac skidding slightly. His hand reached for his Calico, which he swiftly cocked. It was time to visit Big Mo and his family.

In Blue's thinking and moral view, any act of treason against him and his chiefs required a swift, vindictive action, calling for the elimination of the traitor's entire family. He silenced the radio and opened his moon roof to enjoy and commune with nature as he gathered his thoughts.

Once he reached Big Mo's house, he noticed a for sale sign on the front lawn. He made a sharp right turn into the driveway, did a U-turn in the parking lot, and hopped out. After engaging his weapon, he ran to the side of the house, only to discover the interior of the house was completely empty as he looked through a window. This made him even more furious as he walked back to the car, realizing that Big Mo had planned his scheme far in advance.

Now, all Blue could do was to slouch back in his driver's seat, bitterly disappointed. His semiautomatic sat on his lap, his finger on the trigger. Where could he find Big Mo?

His cell phone broke his concentration. It was the hospital. The medical counselor regrettably informed him that Lil' Pee had passed away due to all the trauma he had received. Blue immediate hung up after hearing those words. He felt like his head was about to explode.

He hoisted the Calico through the moon roof and in grief and impotent anger, he screamed with all his being and his index finger pressed the trigger, releasing a volley of bullets from his weapon for a full minute. The exiting bullets caused the chamber to light up like a blow torch.

Blue hollered and squeezed the trigger until the clip was empty. Tears of despair streamed down his face, wetting his cheeks and dropping like a faucet onto his lap. He took a deep breath. He could not give up hope. He was the only one left to carry on his family name. He took his blunt out of the ashtray and smoked, contemplating how life could be so good in one moment, but how Fate could change everything in a split second.

Blue reclined in his seat, the empty gun still in his hand, and looked up at the sky. He smoked and with every exhale, he went deeper into contemplation of the complex reality of life and its golden rule. This day became a turning point for Blue, and he truly appreciated his life.

36 Mr. Sunny Boi

Three months and three shipments later, I was doing well financially, better than I could ever imagine. Spraggs had upgraded my consignment order to five tons a month. Soon I would need to use this apartment just to store all the money I was rapidly accumulating. I had to get two money counting machines and storage compartments just to hide all my cash.

I called my lawyer, Mr. Sunny Boi, and told him if he could settle my case, just make it disappear, I would give him $100,000 up front and $200,000 after it was over. He told me for that type of money, he could have me walking free, even on a murder charge that might occur inside the courtroom. He arranged for us to meet and made the transaction without jeopardizing either one of us. He explained that he would have me vindicated of all charges, and if he needed any more money to pay off any high officials, he would give me a call.

Furthermore, to bring to the public's attention the police corruption going on, I gave Popi's video to Lucky to run through a slew of Web sites, which created a crackdown on law enforcement corruption of epidemic proportion.

Chapter 37 — *Keisha and Mark*

It was a lovely sunny day on Plantation Club Drive in Maui, the second-largest of the Hawaiian Islands. The romantic, tropical Trade winds gently blew, creating mild temperatures and balmy weather. The couple acquired a seven-acre dream house for this momentous occasion. The ceremony was held on the lawn of the estate facing the view of the azure-tinted Pacific.

The 8,300-square-foot residence contained five lavish bedrooms with five spacious bathrooms, each containing a hot tub. The three massive lanai houses had a gigantic Infinity pool with a spectacular waterfall and ocean-view Jacuzzi right next to it. The plush, opulent home was fit for Queen Liliuokalani herself.

A heart-shaped arch was handcrafted from Koa hardwood with a deep rich luster and patina and was free-standing on the lawn. It was decorated with brilliant red and tender pink flowers and vines which covered it. All the guests were able to view the deep-blue ocean through the heart. As if Mother Nature were rejoicing over this joyful celebration, even whales were frolicking and diving in the sun-sequined water. The sky was cobalt-blue with lazy puffs of cumulus clouds dotting the horizon.

The reverend was dressed in black with his white Roman collar. He held his Bible in his hand as he ministered unto the couple, having them repeat their vows as tears began to stream down Keisha's face. She looked up at her husband, who was standing one step higher to even out his slight deficiency of height.

"I do," she said with a slight tremor in her voice. Her white Versace sheath wedding gown with a floral top complemented her sleek, svelte figure. Cat was dressed in all black. He had unbuttoned the two top buttons on his Yushua shirt and wore an opera-length pink diamond necklace which peeked out from his shirt. He topped it off with an open blazer, which showed off his diamond-studded Y-shaped Yushua belt. Even his Yushua shoes had a Y-shaped diamond embedded in them also.

"Do you, Mark Cooper, take Keisha Grain as your lawful wedded wife?" the reverend asked.

"Yeahh," Mark replied.

Peter, who stood directly behind him, handed Mark the brilliant diamond platinum ring. He was dressed in a black replica of Mark's attire with a matching black shoulder strap, bracing his arm to his stomach.

Jasmine was slightly behind Keisha and directly across from Peter, standing with her usual aplomb on the lawn, wearing a sleeveless, cleavage-exposing, floral drawstring lace Versace gown, which elegantly displayed her voluptuous body. She was grateful to be standing across from her beloved. She smiled at him tenderly. One could see the twinkle of unadulterated love shining in her eyes. Mark placed the ring on Keisha's finger, then took her into his arms and gave her a passionate, romantic kiss.

"You may now kiss the bride," the reverend said with a hint of humor.

The ladies were standing on the bride's side of the lawn, formally dressed in pink and white. Angela was graciously smiling from ear to ear, waving a brilliant pink diamond on her expressive hands with matching earrings and a matching pink-and-white diamond bib-style necklace. Her calf-length pink-and-white Sandra Green evening gown complemented her jewels and gave her skin a delicate tone that enhanced her beauty.

Peaches stood near her, wearing a short floral Versace white linen figure-hugging dress, with a diamond tennis bracelet and a platinum chain with a heart-shaped pendent and three-carat diamond stud earrings. Sabrina was standing to her right in a white Sandra Green V-neck silk gown with pink floral designs on the lace bottom that reached her knees. She was wearing acrylic glass Sandra Green high heel shoes and was bedecked in glittering jewels.

The males stood adjacent to the females next to the bridegroom. Blue was in front of his comrade wearing his trademark blue cargo outfit with an elegant blue diamond ensemble.

Lucky was dressed formally in Armani. He made an impeccable groomsman. He wore a nice fade and was clean shaven. His nails were manicured. But Peter stole the show when he approached Jasmine with a jewelry box and kneeled on one knee in front his beloved.

"Baby, you been by my side since you first met me. You have helped me with your encouragement and honest, loving judgment. You are as loving and passionately caring as my mother. You chose me from the beginning, and I want to choose you until the end. Jasmine Banks, will you marry me?" As he said this, Peter looked up, gazing at his beloved with his honest love expressed for the world to see.

"Hell, fuck, yeah," she said, snatching him up off his knee, hugging him intensely, irritating the bullet wounds in the left side of his body. But he endured the pain and allowed his fiancée to continue her zealous antics. He handed her the pink ring case, which made Angela burst into tears.

In her heart, Angela was thanking the Almighty God for guiding them through their struggles and molding her baby into a responsible, mature man. He had really changed after being shot up and actually dying in the Dekalb hospital. Somehow, the doctors were able to revive him after he suffered a major heart attack in the operating room and being declared brain dead for several minutes. The doctors had declared his case a medical miracle, but Angela knew God had had a hand in it. Since his recovery, Lil' Pee had even forsaken that name and insisted everyone call him by his birth name. He was leaving his old, destructive ways behind him.

Jasmine's face was streaming in tears. Enjoying the happiest day of her life, she accepted the case and opened it to reveal a four-carat, square-shaped pink, yellow, and white diamond ring in an extraordinary design. The spectacular brilliance of the gemstones mesmerized everyone close enough to see it. Mark rested his hand on Peter's shoulder. "Congratulations, cousin," he said and gave him a hug.

Conversation flowed freely, as did the champagne. A generous supply of Louis the XIII, Cristal, and Don Perrion was served. The newlyweds marched down the aisle to a steady flow of pink rose petals showering down upon them like confetti, tossed by the smiling females present. The bride tossed her baby-pink rose bouquet. Peaches caught it and looked over at Lucky.

The constant flash of the photographer's camera captured the moment. Finally, Mark and Keisha made their way though the massive liana into the waiting Rolls Royce limousine. The chauffeur opened the door to their carriage. Once inside, smiling, the newlyweds drank to each other while gazing into the happy eyes of their marriage partner. Every eye was upon them as their chariot rode off into the sunset with its lustrous chrome rims spinning.

Mr. and Mrs. Mark Cooper enjoyed their married life as entrepreneurs of two extravagant and exotic nightclubs on the island of Hawaii.

Blue checked his watch and recalled he had an immediate flight to catch. He approached his comrade Lucky and gave him dap, followed by a hug congratulating him on his new venture. He walked to the black and blue Maybach 57 S. The chauffeur opened the door and let him inside. Once comfortably seated, he reclined his airplanelike seat and let out the footrest.

"Where to, sir?" asked the blue-uniformed, capped young man.

"To the airport, I have a private jet to catch," Blue said. Then he lit his exotic kemp and lifted the bottle of Krug he held in his hand and took a sip before placing the bottle in the side compartment. As he lay back, he enjoyed his euphoria, grooving to the serenade of M. C. Hush.

Blue arrived at the airport, breezed through airport security, and the Maybach drove on the runway. He walked up the jet's steps with the blunt in his mouth and his bottle of champagne in his hand, then he took a seat in the business section and reclined fully in his lime-green leather recliner, placed the bottle between his legs, and turned Scarface on the 40-inch monitor.

Before the movie finished, he landed at the Hartsfield Airport. He watched it to the very ending of the credits, then he exited the plane and made his way through the airport. He went to the overnight parking section and climbed into his Jaguar Super V8 luxury sedan on 22-inch deep dish spinners.

Then he drove to the Oglethorpe Cemetery and bought a bouquet of flowers. After that, he walked through the graveyard until he reached the monument marked John Flamings, the stone marker of Blue's late brother. He just stood there staring down at the earth like it was transparent and he could see through it. His thoughts drifted back to how Steven was always his guardian angel, teaching him how to ride his first bike, how to drive a car at nine years old, how to romance the ladies, and memories of how he carried the torch when their mother died.

John was a great, loving, compassionate, humble man. However, like many millions of unsuspecting, naïve people that fell victim to the modern-day bubonic plague called AIDS, one night of lust led to a lifetime of regret. Blue stood there motionless, crying inside his heart although his face showed no emotion.

He knelt to one knee to pay homage to the man who provided and established his profound success. He swore in his heart he would carry the torch for him and his mother, so that they would not have died in vain. At that moment bordering on an epiphany, facing the grim reality of death and its mysterious essence, Blue came to the realization about how priceless and invaluable his existence really was.

Chapter

38 *Ricky*

Spraggs walked from his bedroom terrace to his spacious sweeping veranda. He looked at the calm, deep-blue ocean and his Palmer Johnson 150 sport yacht designed by Nuvolari & Lenard with its 11,250 hp engine.

He stood firmly on the veranda overlooking his 155 acres of private bliss in a celebrity-studded enclave. His manse was state-of-the-art solar-powered, exquisite, had five bedrooms (including *three* lavish master bedrooms) with five magnificent marble and 24-carat gold-plated bathrooms. It was fit for a king, and he was a king. The countertops throughout his house were made from beautiful emerald-green granite imported from Brazil, and all the floors were made from imported Italian marble tiles. Breathing deeply the salt-scented air, he pressed the speed dial button on his phone. When he heard a reply, he began.

"What's your conclusion?" he said. After he heard the response, he hung up immediately and reentered his extravagantly spacious bedroom. A 63-inch liquid crystal television sat directly across from the super king-sized bed. Two 50-inch plasma monitors were mounted on the walls for his surveillance cameras posted miles away surrounding his region on the island called Clove Cay, in the Bahamas.

Spraggs took off his black Yushua robe, exposing his well-defined masculine nakedness. He then walked over and stepped into his bedroom hot tub where he practiced his morning ritual of soaking while he watched the news and waited for his beautiful Barbadian maids to bring his breakfast.

As he marinated in the tub, soaking up his Aveeno oatmeal bath set out by his maid, he contemplated on how close he was coming to be able to vindicate the revenge he so craved. Vengeance had been his fuel. Now he had enough manpower, artillery, and financial reinforcement to make it happen.

He could create a tribal war in Jamaica, the likes of which had never before been seen. He vowed everyone who had committed treason against him would cry out in repentance before he utterly destroyed them.

I hung up the phone with Spraggs. The man was so persuasive. I did not know if I had already sold my soul to the devil through this alliance. Would I meet him again in the belly of the beast, in the pits of hell, when all this was over? He had convinced, or better yet, *forced* me, to assume the position of head overseer of his corporation. I was overseeing the annual shipment of two hundred tons of exotic marijuana coming in from Arizona and Canada. I had three bank accounts to which I periodically wired his money.

But I was not at all worried. I was now so overwhelmingly rich and powerful. I don't even have to lift a finger. All my orders are carried out precisely. All my connections are well established. They all needed me to maintain their wealth and influential power. My job was to make calls, remembering not to say anything criminally suspicious over the telephone, and never to involve myself with incriminating evidence. My lawyer, Mr. Boi, had "convinced" the judge and district attorney to dismiss my case, so I now had a clean record.

I climbed out of my ultra king-sized bed, leaving Lisa to rest.

"Daddy's coming, sugar bear," I said, putting on my Versace robe and slipping on my black Yushua slippers, then hurrying over to my newborn daughter's ivory crib. I picked her up gently, and she immediately gave me a toothless infant smile. I kissed little Diane Danielle Jones and held her close to my chest, cuddled warmly in my arms. I loved this baby girl immensely, and she felt so good.

It was funny how this little creature could make me feel a complete human being. I wanted to make sure she lived the most provident life. I've been even planning her success by purchasing a slew of property across the globe in her name with her own company, Behr's Industries.

Holding my baby close, I walked over to my bed built from granite, including the gigantic headboard and night table attached, and took her bottle off the night table, removing the cap with one hand while holding her with the other. Gently, I placed the bottle into her tiny, open, waiting mouth and continued walking towards the window, where I opened the floor-to-ceiling acrylic Levolor blinds. The glass walls electronically opened onto the spacious ocean view and the terraces of my private island estate in Florida.

Now *this* was spectacular. The view was absolutely breathtaking. I could see straight across the azure water with foamy whitecaps to the modern building complex. The prestigious private island in the middle of the intercoastal waterway was a tranquil, extravagant, very secluded hideaway.

It had 9,000 square feet, six bedrooms, including two sumptuous master bedrooms, and seven full, immaculate, onyx bathrooms, and two extra half bathrooms. The entire interior was decorated with Old World charm. I had a professional theater and antique elevator installed, and the mansion came with a Renaissance-decorated cathedral dome ceiling. Plasma televisions were installed everywhere, even the bathrooms.

My home was equipped with a sophisticated state-of-the-art, smart home computer. The living room was equipped with a 1,000-gallon saltwater floor-to-ceiling aquarium shaped as a large cylinder. It boasted exotic, colorful tropical fish swimming in multicolored, dancing lights with Moray Eels peeking their heads out of rock caves on the bottom of the aquarium.

The kitchen was designed in imported marble. Outside, I had a dock for my small yacht and an enormous Infinity pool. The gate was guarded by security, 24/7, and my security system was exceptional.

Suddenly I noticed my tiny, precious daughter was maneuvering her chubby hand to shield her eyes from the glare of the sun so I moved over towards the shade of the walls. She, once again, sucked peacefully on her bottle.

I looked over from that side position near the window and saw Dwayne up bright and early, removing the roof on his new wagon with its polychromatic, changing chameleon paint, his customized deep dish 23-inch spinners gleaming immaculately in the sun. His indigo tires matched the roof and interior. I swore the boy had a body like a professional body builder. He finally broke his deep concentration and stopped detailing his ride. That was when he realized that I was watching him.

He looked so content. He couldn't help but smile as he saw me holding his niece and pumped his fist of triumph into the air. I politely nodded, sensing his gratitude and love. He was now living in a different dimension compared to where he had come from.

It reminded me of a book I was reading by Ricardo Sinclair, *WASP 100*, regarding strength from persevering in achieving your goals. I was proud of Dwayne's attitude. He had reinvented himself during his incarceration. He studied hard and received his high-school GED. He enrolled in college and acquired his master's degree in political science. Then I gave him a position in my record label, MONSTAR, INC.

"Well, Diane is back fast asleep." Lisa, as usual, crept up behind me and gently rested her hand on my back, looking at the deep-blue water and enjoying the pleasant ocean breeze that blew her silk Sandra Green nightgown against her still remarkable body, even after childbirth. She stepped beside me to observe what I was looking at. Then she looked over at a peaceful sleeping Diane and glanced back up at me.

"Come on, Papa, let's all go back to bed," Lisa said with a smile.

I kissed her on her lips lightly as she held me by my arm an ushered me back to our bed.

THE SAGA CONTINUES ...

www.ingramcontent.com/pod-product-compliance
Lightning Source LLC
Chambersburg PA
CBHW021335250626
47155CB00002B/706